a baby
on the
doorstep

BOOKS BY RACHEL WESSON

A Home for Unloved Orphans

RACHEL WESSON

a baby on the doorstep

bookouture

Published by Bookouture in 2021

An imprint of Storyfire Ltd.
Carmelite House
50 Victoria Embankment
London EC4Y 0DZ

www.bookouture.com

ISBN: 978-1-83888-981-4
eBook ISBN: 978-1-83888-980-7

This book is dedicated to my father, who instilled my love of reading by first telling me stories and then by taking me to the library every week. He believes his three daughters can do anything they want, no glass ceilings for women in my dad's world.

PROLOGUE

The man crept through the bushes, taking care not to step on any frozen twigs. The slightest noise would alert those still awake in the blackness of the night. He looked up at the sky; there was no moon, and for once he was thankful for the clouds covering the stars. He couldn't afford to be seen.

Moving gingerly, tuning in to the sounds around him, he crossed the path. In the distance he heard an owl screeching as it claimed its meal, and the blood-curdling scream of a vixen in response to her mates triple bark. He could hear smaller creatures rustling through the greenery, snorting and sniffing out their supper. He gripped his rifle tighter, the whites of his knuckles visible in the dark, his poaching sack over his shoulder.

He'd made friends with the dog they called Shadow on an earlier reconnaissance trip. As he'd hoped, Shadow came bounding up to him but didn't bark a warning to the house's occupants. The big black animal almost bowled him over with his greeting, jumping up, and attempting to lick his face.

"There now, settle down, there's a good fella. I brought you a bone. Go on now, take it over to the barn. Go on. Before someone hears you, boy."

The dog seemed to sense he wasn't to make any noise, and he wagged his tail. He took the bone, set it on the ground, sniffed and licked the man's hand before picking up the bone again and trotting off to the side of the barn to gnaw on it in peace.

If only men were as reliable as animals. I wouldn't be here now, breaking my woman's heart. And my own. Shaking the thoughts from his head, he moved carefully toward the front door.

The house was in darkness, not one light shining from any window. He pulled the screen door wide as softly as he could, holding his breath as the hinges creaked in protest. He stilled, waiting, listening, but all he heard was Shadow grunting approval over his prize. He drew the screen door open a little wider before setting his rifle down to one side. Tenderly, he opened his poaching bag and lifted out the small bundle. He moved toward the porch swing and sat down for a moment, the bundle in his arms, holding her tight to his chest, enjoying her breath on his skin.

"This is your new home, Maisie. These people will treat you good and give you plenty to eat. You'll be safe here. Your mama and me, we love you but we ain't got no home. The Government took it, said we was squatters. We ain't got no family to live with. We can't keep you with us. If the government men see a baby living rough, they'll take it away and put it in the county home. Here, the ladies will look after ya. Until we can fetch you back." His voice caught as his feelings choked him.

He kissed the infant on the top of her head before laying her gently on the floor just beside the door. With a last look, he moved off the veranda, gripping the screen door gingerly, pushing it shut quietly. He fell back to the forested section at the border of the massive front garden the youngsters used as a play yard, hiding among the trees. He intended to keep watch, to make sure nothing happened to his baby. That no critter would come and hurt her.

The darkness surrendered to the weak wintery sunrise battling through the thick gray clouds. The rain held off as the chatter of birds increased, the rooster crowing as the light grew brighter. He watched and waited for signs of life inside the house. Upstairs a window opened.

His eyes latched onto the bundle by the front door. He held his breath, wanting to race down and recover his child before it was too late. He took a step, only to hear the squeak of the door as a blonde-haired child he'd seen before, Ruthie, stepped out of the house.

"Miss Lauren, come quick. It's another baby. Can we keep it?" The little girl's excited squeal rang in his ears and the tears fell down his face. He kept staring until the dark-haired lady came out and picked up his Maisie. He didn't even blink; Miss Lauren seemed to stare right at him before she turned back into the house, cradling Maisie in her arms, the younger child following behind.

He retreated into the shadows without a sound, his grip tight on the rifle. He'd fight until he got his home back and put a roof over his family once more.

CHAPTER ONE

Lauren placed the baby carefully on the table, gently examining her for signs of injury or malnutrition. She was a little on the small size but her hand grasped Lauren's fingers tightly and wouldn't let go. That was a good sign. Her large brown eyes flitted around the room as if she were wondering where she was.

Ruthie watched, moving from one foot to another, full of questions. "How old is she, Miss Lauren?"

"About six months, I think."

"Why would someone leave her outside the door? They should have knocked and given her to you, not left her on the ground." Ruthie twirled her hair around her finger, something she did when agitated.

Lauren sought to reassure the five-year-old. "She's been well cared for, darling. I'm sure someone kept watch to make sure nothing happened to her on the porch. Becky's gone to check if they left anything else."

Becky walked into the kitchen, a piece of paper in her hands. "Must have fell out when they put her down, it was under the swing."

Lauren cradled Maisie with one hand, the other searching through the cupboard for a bottle. They always had one on hand just in case. "What's it say?"

"Her name is Maisie and we are to keep her, not let her be adopted. If her parents can come back, they will." Becky blew some wisps of red hair out of her face. "Doesn't give her a surname. Want me to hold her while you make up the bottle?"

Despite her casual tone, Lauren knew Becky was dying to cuddle the baby. She passed Maisie over and she immediately grabbed hold of Becky's long braid.

"She's got a good grip for sure." Becky winced as Maisie pulled tighter.

"I told you, you should go to see Ginny Dobbs and get her to cut your hair short. Your coloring is so striking, it would really suit you, make more of a feature of your green eyes. And the children wouldn't be able to grab hold of it so easy. I think Big Will would be pleasantly surprised." Lauren couldn't resist teasing Becky.

Becky raised her eyebrows. "What has it got to do with Big Will what I do to my hair?"

Ruthie said earnestly, "Miss Becky, you know Big Will would like anything you do. He loves you. He told me."

"Becky knows, Ruthie. She's just a bit slow deciding how she feels about him." Lauren quickly intervened in case Becky snapped at the child. Becky was good-natured and cared deeply for the children but, when it came to Big Will, she could be a little oversensitive.

In an effort to distract the child, Lauren added, "Do you want to help me give Maisie a bath?"

Ruthie nodded, jumping up to get a small metal bucket. Becky added warm water, showing Ruthie how to test the heat of the water by putting her elbow into it. Lauren smiled as Ruthie concentrated, enjoying the undivided attention she was getting. She loved all the children in her care but Ruthie was special. They had a bond nobody could break apart after the trauma they had shared.

Lauren held the baby gently as she bathed her in the bucket on top of the kitchen table. Ruthie helped, using a cup to pour the water over the baby's lower body. Lauren knew that whoever had written the note didn't want to lose their baby. They must be desperate, and she was glad they'd come to her. Hope House had a good reputation, at least with people that mattered. Even Sheriff Dillon openly approved of the orphanage, although when Lauren first took over from Matron Werth, he'd believed all children belonged in the county home or in religious-backed institutions.

Lauren laid Maisie out on the warmed towel lying ready on the table and carefully dried her before putting on a clean diaper and some clothes. Her brown curls fluffed out around her precious little head as they dried.

Ruthie sat at the table, her head resting on her hands as she gazed at the baby. "She's pretty, ain't she? She keeps looking around, do you think she's looking for her ma?"

"I don't know, Ruthie."

"Maybe her ma is in heaven with mine."

Lauren didn't remind her what the letter had said. She didn't want to admit to Ruthie that some families couldn't afford to keep their children.

Becky made up a bottle of watered-down condensed milk. She took Maisie in her arms to feed her. It took a few tries before Maisie accepted the bottle but soon she was drinking, gulping down the milk.

"Best make her some mush, she's starving, poor little one." Becky cuddled the baby over her shoulder as she burped her.

Lauren hugged Ruthie to her side as together they watched Becky with Maisie. The baby again grabbed a handful of Becky's hair, trying to push it into her mouth, causing Becky to squirm and say, "Maybe you have a point about getting my hair cut." She moved Maisie onto her other hip.

Ruthie gushed, "She's like a little doll."

"You won't be sayin' that when she dirties her diaper." But Becky looked just as smitten with the baby as Ruthie. "Are you going into town today, Lauren?"

"Yes. I have to collect our provisions from Hillmans' and alert Sheriff Dillon about Maisie. I wish her parents would come and speak to us. Maybe we could help keep them together."

Becky rolled her eyes, but didn't say anything as Ruthie was there.

Lauren knew what Becky was worried about. They were struggling to feed the children they had so how could they take in more orphans? She pushed back her chair. "No point in me going back to bed now as I will never sleep and it's almost morning. I'll have a wash and go into town early. Ruthie, you should go and try to sleep some more. You've been up long enough."

"I'm not tired," Ruthie mumbled, trying to cover a yawn with her hand. Lauren patted her on the head before sending her protesting back to bed.

*

Lauren enjoyed the quiet trip to Delgany. She loved the spring, when all sorts of new lives began. Despite the lingering cold and the past month of freezing temperatures, the plants were growing just as they did every year; the trees losing their bareness as little green buds covered the branches.

As she turned into Delgany her good mood dampened; her beloved home town was showing the effects of the Depression. There were more "To Let" signs on buildings, and boards stating items were on sale. The bank remained closed as did the car dealership. She drove past Miss Chaney's post office, thinking she'd park outside Hillmans' store, but the spaces were occupied. The Baptist church's white picket fence was showing signs of gray; the weather must have prevented painting. One thing you could rely on was that fence got painted twice a year, once in spring and again in the autumn. She drove around the war memorial and down the other side, parking outside the sheriff's office. Pushing the door open, the empty cell reminded her of the time she had found Cal locked up there. She'd been furious at a nine-year-old boy being locked up like a common criminal but the sheriff had been right, the boy could escape from tighter places than Houdini. Thank goodness he'd given up trying to run away to find his ma.

Smiling, she called out, "Sheriff, you here?"

The man came out from the back, bits of shaving soap on his chin, the towel still around his neck. "Morning Lauren, bit early, aren't you? Is there trouble?"

"No, not really." Lauren addressed the top of his head, feeling uncomfortable at having disturbed him mid-ablutions. He was at least wearing a shirt, rather than just a vest, but his suspenders hung around his hips. "I came to tell you we found another baby on the porch, a little girl about six months old with the name of Maisie. She's been well cared for although she's a bit on the thin side. There was a note asking us not to let her be adopted."

"So you reckon the parents might come back for her?" He gestured for her to take the seat in front of his desk before turning to pour two cups of coffee from the pot on top of the small wood stove.

Lauren sat down. "Yes I do. I just wish they had come to see me first. Maybe we could have helped them to stay together as a family."

The sheriff scratched his chin. Lauren wondered if he was thinking or just embarrassed to have been interrupted shaving.

"Can you take her or do you want me to send her to the county home?" he asked, his tone neutral. They had disagreed on the merits of the county home on several occasions.

Lauren shuddered, hoping she'd never have to send a child to live at that place. The county might have been well meaning but it was overcrowded and under-resourced, and the children were treated like animals. "Never, sheriff."

He eyed her closer. "Things good out at Hope House? I thought you were short of money."

That was nothing new. Money had been scarce since she'd taken over the orphanage. There was no point in being less than honest.

Lauren admitted, "We're always running out of cash and it's challenging to find money for the bills and the mortgage. But I won't ever give a child to the county home willingly, you know that."

He looked a bit confused. She wondered why. It was no secret Hope House was low on funds. "Why are you looking at me like that?"

"Lauren, you said you wanted to help the parents. I thought you had found a benefactor."

If only she had. For the first twenty years of her life, she hadn't thought twice about money or how much things cost. She'd just bought what she wanted, spending hundreds of dollars on one dress. Now she worried about the price of sugar, salt, and other essentials. She shook the thought from her mind.

"No such luck, sheriff. Just wishful thinking. I can't bear the idea of loving parents giving up a child. It's not natural."

He sat back in his chair, his hand resting on his belly. "Given the times we live in and the events of the last couple of years, I would have thought you had grown used to difficult times, Lauren."

"The day I don't feel empathy for parents giving up a child is the day I quit, sheriff. You've still got a heart of gold and you've spent your life surrounded by criminals."

His cheeks turned crimson as he stood up and turned his back to her, moving the coffee pot on the stove. "Speaking of criminals, I have a busy day ahead."

She took the hint. She finished her coffee, stood up, and walked to the door. Just before she left, she turned back. "Don't forget to call up and see us. Cal and Fred keep asking when you are going to take them fishing again."

He swung around to face her. "I never took them young 'uns fishing. I was investigating a case and just happened to come across them at the lake. You know that, Lauren."

"Whatever you say, Sheriff." She walked out the door smiling at the crusty old man. He hated people guessing he had a soft spot for children, especially boys like Cal and Fred. Lots of lawmen would have written off the boys as would-be criminals simply because they were poor and illegitimate.

*

Lauren didn't get a chance to sit down again as the rest of day flew by in a whirlwind of chores and children's activities. After reading bedtime stories to the children, Lauren came downstairs to find Becky sitting at the kitchen table staring at a piece of wood.

"What's that you're looking at?"

Lauren's question caused Becky to jump as she hastily tried to cover the object on the table. Lauren leaned over and recognized the Christmas present Big Will had carved for Becky. The wooden shingle said:

Hope House
Proprietors: Lauren Greenwood and Becky Strauss

"Becky Strauss. You have to admit it has a nice ring to it." Lauren kept her eyes on Becky's face to see her reaction, wondering if her friend was having second thoughts about settling down. What would she do without Becky if she and Big Will Strauss got married? They'd want a home of their own.

"Fred found it earlier and asked me when I was goin' to hang it up. Don't be gettin' ideas, Lauren. I ain't changin' my mind about gettin' married." Becky pushed her shoulders back as she spoke but Lauren saw the muscle clenching in her jaw. Who was she trying to convince, Lauren or herself?

Becky's view of marriage had been clouded by her mama being left alone to raise seven children. Her mama and the youngest child, Donnie, had ended up in the colony for the feeble-minded. Three of her siblings had died and her brothers were missing, presumed dead. The pain of her childhood had put her off getting married.

"Will is a good man, Becky. Look at how hard he works around here helping us all the time. If it weren't for him organizing the Hillmans, John Thatcher, and the other men for the barn raising, we'd still be sharing the kitchen with Snowdrop."

Snowdrop was a walking menace despite her lovely name; the goat was on a see-it-and-eat-it diet. She'd created havoc in her first days at the orphanage until Big Will had secured her in a new pen in the barn.

"He gave us his time for free and only charged us what it cost him for the materials," Lauren added when Becky remained silent.

Despite Lauren's soft tone, Becky glared at her. "I never asked him to do anythin'."

Lauren put her hand on Becky's. "I know that. I love you and I want to see you happy. Don't let what happened to your mother and the others wreck your future happiness."

Becky pulled her hand away. "I don't need a man to make me happy. I have all I need right here." As if on cue, Maisie started to cry. Becky sniffed as she picked up the baby. "She needs feedin' and changin'. I moved her cot into my room as she's a little young to share with the girls."

Lauren wasn't ready to admit defeat. She knew Becky loved Will and the feeling was mutual. "You're a natural mother, Becky. Look how Maisie adores you already."

"Babies be like animals, Lauren. They love whoever feeds them." Despite her words, Becky looked tenderly at the baby now in her arms.

Lauren stood up and moved to give Becky a hug. "You don't have to be the strong one all the time."

Becky didn't respond. Lauren left her in the kitchen and headed up the stairs to bed.

*

Lauren lay in bed but couldn't sleep. Her mind was going around in circles. She was a fine one to lecture Becky on not letting the past ruin the future when her feelings for Edward Belmont confused her. He'd fought against her father and Justin from the start, exposing them in his newspaper, protecting Nanny, Sam, and Old Sally. She loved it when he came to visit and missed him when he wasn't around, and not just because he was kind to the children. But when he'd once tried to kiss her, she'd backed away so fast it was as if he had thrown cold water at her. She closed her eyes, remembering the wounded expression in his. She'd apologized, told him it wasn't him but demons from her past. Had he believed her?

CHAPTER TWO

Lauren plumped the covers of the couch before moving it out of the way to sweep the floors. The wall behind the furniture was so white in comparison to the other walls. The living room really needed to be repainted but it would have to wait. She swept and dusted the room, listening to music on the radio as she worked.

The knock on the door surprised her as she hadn't heard wheels on the drive outside. She opened it to find Nanny, her wrinkled face lit up with a smile, on the porch, Edward standing straight-backed beside her. Lauren's heart beat faster, and she quickly focused on Nanny to avoid seeming flustered.

"Nanny!" Lauren hugged her so hard, she nearly lifted her off her feet. "I've missed you so much."

"Lauren, put me down. It's only been a month for goodness sake." Nanny pushed Lauren back but squeezed her arm affectionately. "I missed you too."

Becky came running from the backyard; she must have heard the car or Nanny's voice. She hugged the old woman and stretched up to give Edward a kiss on the cheek in greeting. "Thank you for visiting us, Nanny Kat. Lauren needs cheering up. Come in, Edward."

Lauren sent Edward an apologetic look; she hadn't even acknowledged him. Why couldn't she act as natural around him as Becky did? He looked good, a little thinner than at Christmas but the loss of the few pounds suited him. His hair was a little long, curling at his collar. Was it as soft as it looked? Nanny's voice intruded on her thoughts.

"Try and keep me away. You look tired, Lauren. You too, Becky. Where's Norma?" she asked, looking for Norma Leroy, who along with her husband Bart and their daughters, were a part of the Hope House family.

"She's gone to bed, she's not feeling well," Lauren explained. "Did you bring Old Sally and Sam with you?"

"Old Sally is very ill, darling, so Sam stayed with his mother. It won't be long before she passes but she insisted on us visiting you, didn't she, Edward?" Nanny looked up at Edward then turned back and stared at Lauren's face, making her feel the old lady was reading her mind. "Sally was very insistent I come to see you. Said you needed me."

"Sally missed her calling. She should have been a general," Edward said. "You look good, Lauren, but Kathryn is right, you're tired. You're working too hard."

Lauren shrugged off their words. She was tired, but who wouldn't be after spending hours awake listening to Norma coughing.

"Come have some coffee. We have some apple stack cake. Want cream with it, Edward?" Becky asked.

"Yes please, Becky. I take it the new cows are working out well."

"Mabel and Sunflower."

At Edward's mystified expression, Becky laughed and then elaborated. "The children gave them names. Ruthie insists they are part of the Hope House family. I just hope we don't have any bull calves. I don't want to be the one to explain to her where the meat on the table comes from."

"Where are all the children? It's very quiet. Is this the new arrival?" Nanny moved toward the baby lying in the cot.

"This is Maisie, isn't she a sweetheart? Terry and Carly took the others down to the lake, they won't be much longer. In fact I think I can hear them now," Lauren said, hearing chatter and the rumble of footsteps on the porch.

The children must have seen Edward's Cadillac as they ran in calling his name. Cal was first, as usual, with Fred on his heels. Shelley was next, closely followed by Clarissa, Sophie, Lottie, and Ruthie. Terry, the eldest boy, and Carly, the eldest girl, followed up the rear with Terry carrying a bucket. Ruthie ran straight to Lauren and hugged her tight. Lauren enjoyed the close cuddle for a few seconds as the other children swarmed round the table. The chatter of the children rose several notches as they each struggled to be heard.

Lauren shushed them, saying, "We don't live in that big a house you have to shout. Shush now, you'll wake the baby."

But Maisie was already awake, her large brown eyes following people around the room, though she didn't cry. Lauren stood for a minute and watched her, frowning; she was far too quiet for a baby.

Lauren gave out some milk and oat cookies to keep the children going. It would be a while before they had dinner.

"Caught us a few scrawny ones. The big ones weren't bitin'," Terry said as he handed over the catch to Becky.

"You didn't use the right bait is all. I could have caught the biggest fish ever," Cal said.

"Cal, stop boasting and go wash your hands," Lauren said, but took the sting out of her words by ruffling his hair. "You look like you were playing in the muck."

"I was diggin' up worms, not playin'. I ain't a baby."

Lauren turned her face away so he wouldn't see her grin.

"If you is Miss Lauren's Nanny how comes you live with Mr. Edward?" Ruthie asked Nanny as she sat at the kitchen table eating cookies.

"That's a great question, Ruthie," Lauren said, her eyes on Nanny's face. She'd love it if Nanny came to live with them, but whenever she'd asked in the past her great-aunt always said they were too full and didn't need an extra mouth to feed.

"Don't you want to come and live with us? I thought you liked us even though we're no-good orphans." Ruthie mimicked Mrs. Flannery's accent to perfection, causing laughter among the adults. Nobody admonished the child as Mr. and Mrs. Flannery, the clothing store owners, had made life difficult too many times for most Delgany residents. Ruthie grinned; she liked making people laugh.

"Ruthie, I have a home with Mr. Edward and Sam and Old Sally. They are my friends."

"Yes, but Miss Lauren be your family. And she's our family, which makes you our Nanny too. You should live with us. Mr. Edward won't mind."

"Mr. Edward won't mind what, young lady?"

At the sound of Edward's voice Ruthie turned scarlet and hid her face in Lauren's shoulder.

Shelley chipped in. "Don't you think Nanny should live with Miss Lauren? Until she gets married."

It was Lauren's turn to blush. She knew Edward wanted more, but for now they were just friends—aside from the times she allowed herself to dream otherwise.

"I think that's an excellent idea, don't you, Kathryn?" Edward's eyes twinkled with amusement as he stared at Lauren. "You should live with Lauren until she gets wed. Then we could review the situation."

Lauren didn't know where to look, conscious of his gaze on her. She looked up to see Nanny smiling as the children chorused, "Please come and live with us."

Fred said, "Miss Lauren tells us stories you told her when she was little. We'd like to hear them from you. You can make them real scary, can't ya?"

"I don't know about that, Fred." Nanny glanced at Lauren. "It would be nice to live with my family again although Edward has been a wonderful host. But where would you put me? I'm a bit old to sleep in the barn."

The children laughed.

"You can sleep in my office. We'll take out the desk and put a bed in there. That way you won't have to manage the stairs." Lauren didn't want to put Nanny under pressure to move but she so wanted her to say yes.

"And what shall you do when you need to interview parents? I don't want to be a burden."

"You could never be that. The office only gathers dust. We never use it, and if we ever have to interview anyone, we can use the kitchen. Please say yes." Lauren knew she was begging but she missed Nanny more than she could say. Her support over the years had been one thing she could count on. Even when her father did his best to separate the two of them by sending Nanny away, threatening to harm Lauren if Nanny contacted her, Nanny had been looking out for her.

"I thought you'd never ask."

"Nanny Kat, Lauren's been asking you to live with us since you came back last Christmas. She would move her old maid, Mary, in too if she could. Don't you go pretending otherwise." Becky hugged the old lady while Lauren looked on with tears in her eyes.

Mary had been more than her maid, she was her dear friend. If only she would come back from California, then they would all be back together again. But Mary had a new family and a good life. Lauren could hear Nanny telling her to smile for her friend's good fortune and count her blessings.

CHAPTER THREE

The next morning, the children and Lauren set to work turning the office into a bedroom. Terry and the boys removed the desk and chair from the room, while Becky made some pretty new drapes from a floral material she'd bought on sale at Hillmans' but had never used. Lauren bought a bed and a new mattress on credit, hoping she could afford to pay fifty cents a week until it was cleared in full. Nanny was too old to lie on a straw pallet and, after everything she'd done, she deserved the best. On top of the bed, Lauren draped the quilt she'd saved from Nanny's room at Rosehall.

They painted the walls white to make the room appear bigger. The younger girls cleaned and polished the floor so the whole room smelled of beeswax and lemon. The window gleamed in the sunlight. Big Will built a seat into the window so Nanny could watch the children playing if she didn't have the energy to come sit on the porch. The fire was lit too, to drive the chill from the room.

One week later, Nanny walked into the orphanage with Edward and Sam following behind with her belongings.

"Mornin', Miss Lauren."

"Sam. I'm so sorry about Old Sally. I wish I had seen her before she died. Put that down and give me a hug."

Sam—the son of a slave, who'd protected Lauren and loved her more than her own father—put the case down, but it was up to Lauren to hug him. A lifetime of conditioning was too difficult to set aside. No matter how often she reminded the old man he was her equal, she always had to make the first physical contact.

Lauren linked arms with him. "You've lost weight. You need a woman to look after you, that's what Sally would want."

"Now, Miss Lauren, don't you be gettin' ideas. I don't have time for no lady friends," Sam protested, but his eyes didn't quite meet hers.

She wanted to know more but Nanny had other ideas.

"Leave Sam be, Lauren. Please show me my new room."

"Yes, Nanny." She led Nanny to what had been her office door. "Close your eyes."

Nanny huffed a bit but did as she was told. Lauren pushed the door open.

"I hope you'll be happy here, Nanny."

Nanny opened her eyes and sighed in surprise.

"Lauren, where did you get the quilt? I thought that had gone with Rosehall." Her voice shook as she moved toward the bed, eyeing the quilt she had made years ago.

"I brought it here after you left. I used it on my bed as it made me feel closer to you."

Nanny fingered the quilt. "You should keep it."

"I don't need the quilt now, I have you. I thought it might make you feel at home." Lauren struggled to keep her voice steady. The children crowded in for a look, making the room feel very small. Lauren walked over to the windows and opened them. "Look here, Nanny. Big Will made you a window seat so you can look out on the young ones playing in the garden."

Nanny's eyes shone with tears. "This is so lovely. Thank you everyone for making me feel so welcome."

Becky ushered the children out of the room. Edward and Sam followed as soon as they had placed the boxes inside, while Lauren stayed with Nanny to help her unpack.

"I'm so glad you've come to live here, Nanny. I've missed your wisdom and guidance."

"You won't be sayin' that in a few days, Lauren, when I've reminded you to smile and count your blessings a thousand times. Why don't we do this later? I fancy a slice of Norma's shortbread with some cream."

Lauren turned her face so Nanny couldn't read her expression. "Norma isn't feeling too well, Nanny. She's in bed. Becky made some cookies, I think."

"What's wrong with Norma?"

"She's fighting a chill, that's all. Let's get some coffee."

"Lauren Greenwood, I've known you since you were in diapers. What is wrong with Norma?"

Lauren turned to meet Nanny's gaze. "I have no idea… but I think it's much worse than a chill."

Nanny pulled her sleeves up. "Seems the right time I came to live here then."

*

Within a few days, it was as if Nanny had been there from the beginning. Norma and Nanny worked well together, which left Lauren and Becky more time to deal with the heavier physical tasks such as the laundry and cleaning out the rooms.

Nanny took to cooking breakfast for everyone as she liked to get up early in the morning. She told Norma she didn't like anyone under her feet at the stove, saying, "No kitchen was ever designed for two cooks."

Norma seemed happy to let Nanny take over, confiding in Lauren it was important the older woman felt useful. Lauren held her tongue and nodded in agreement. She didn't want to worry Norma with the truth; that Nanny had insisted she do more to help as soon as she'd seen the change in Norma's appearance.

In the evenings, Lauren and Becky had time to play rounders and hide and seek with the children, leaving Nanny and Norma chatting and sewing at the kitchen table.

*

"The children are better behaved now we get to spend more time with them, aren't they, Lauren?" Becky said one morning after breakfast, as she and Lauren cleared up. Norma had finished cleaning the stove and was measuring out flour, salt, sugar, and butter for her baking.

"Yes. And Nanny seems to have a way of bringing out the good side of Shelley especially. That child is never cheeky to her." Lauren rubbed a sticky spot on the kitchen table where someone had dropped honey.

"She wouldn't be that brave." Becky washed up the breakfast dishes, the cutlery clinking against the side of the sink. "Nanny Kat has a spring in her step, doesn't she?" she gazed out the kitchen window watching Nanny walk down toward the lake with Cal and Fred.

Lauren carried over the last of the dishes from the table to the sink. "The boys are in for a shock. Nanny told me she used to go off fishing with the Rosehall servants whenever she got the chance to ditch her mother or older sisters. If half her stories are true, we'll be eating a feast tonight."

"You love havin' her live here, don't you?" Becky turned to look her friend in the face.

"Yes, even more than I thought I would. I know we can manage just about everything. But sometimes, it's nice to seek an impartial opinion."

"It is, especially when you are spendin' money we don't have."

Hurt, Lauren snapped, "What? I don't do that any more."

Becky's eyebrows rose.

"I'm not as bad as I was, Becky." Maybe because she had less money to throw around but she wasn't about to admit that. Lauren picked up a bucket, filled it with boiling water and a sliver of soap before returning to the table area. She pushed the benches and table into the center of the room intending to take her frustration out on cleaning the floor.

Becky put a hand out to touch Lauren's arm. "You're still a sucker for a story. What about last week? You gave two dollars to that woman at the church."

Despite knowing her friend was trying to calm her down, Lauren couldn't help defending herself. She threw the washcloth in the bucket, splashing both of them. "She had no shoes on her feet and a family to feed. You should have seen her face, both eyes swollen from the beating she'd taken from her husband. She had two children with her and was pregnant too. I couldn't walk by and not give her anything."

Becky's nostrils flared at Lauren's tone and she moved away from the water, crossing her arms. "A bag of food would have been better. The two dollars probably went to her man to drink."

Lauren knew Becky was right but that didn't stop her from arguing back, "If you are so good at managing money, why don't you take over the bills and the food shopping?"

Before Becky could reply, Norma intervened. "I swear you behave like my two girls at times. Sisters in all but blood you are. Both of you do the best you can do and we all make mistakes. So quit gripin' at one another or I will tell Nanny. Lauren, there's no point in washing the floor until I finish this baking. Why don't you go check on the children?"

Becky stuck her tongue out at Norma's back, making Lauren giggle. Norma whirled around but Becky had assumed the innocent expression of an angel and apologized. "Sorry, Lauren, I didn't mean to make you mad."

Norma turned back to her baking, and Lauren threw her towel at Becky before racing out the door, listening to Becky laughing as she went. Only Becky could rile her temper one minute yet set her giggling the next.

*

Later that evening as the adults sat round the table, Lauren listened to Nanny and Norma teasing Becky about Will.

"That man wears his heart on his sleeve, Becky. He would do anything for you, my girl. Why are you keeping him at arm's length?" Nanny directed her piercing gaze at Becky, who squirmed in her seat, reminding Lauren of Shelley when she'd been caught red-handed making a mess of the beds after Clarissa and Carly had made them.

"Nanny Kat, you know why. You saw what happened to Ma."

"Yes I did. Your parents had a wonderful happy marriage, producing seven children anyone would be proud of." Nanny put her hand on Becky's. "Your parents would want the same for you. A good man to stand by your side through the trials and tribulations ahead."

"Pa died. Ma couldn't cope with seven babies. So I had to step up. I done my share of motherin'." Becky's mouth thinned, she was as stubborn as they came. Lauren would have told Nanny to quit if she thought it would do any good.

"Your pa died in an accident. That wasn't his or your ma's fault." Nanny put her hands together as if praying. "If Hetty was here now, she'd give you a shake for the way you are treating Big Will. If you are dead set on not marrying him, you tell him so and let him find another woman."

Lauren watched the emotions flit over Becky's face. She could see how torn her best friend was. Frustrated she couldn't help Becky, she pushed back from the table to go check on the children.

"And where might you be going?" Nanny pinned her to the seat with a glare. "You're no better. Edward has proved himself countless times. He helped me, Sam, and Old Sally hide from your father. He funded Christmas for these children from his own pocket last year. Goodness me, the man even saved Prince. If Edward hadn't ignored his allergy to horsehair and bought him, the stallion would have been sold alongside your father's other assets. And what does he get in return?"

"Nanny! I haven't said or done anything to encourage Edward. I'm always polite to him when he comes here." Why was Nanny picking on her? She knew what she'd been through in the past with Justin. How could she be expected to trust a man?

"I'm polite to Mrs. Flannery, Lauren. That's just good manners." Nanny pointed at Lauren. "You know I love you, Lauren, and I admire what you are doing here. But at some point, you will want children of your own. Edward would make an excellent father, a supportive husband. He's the right kind of man for you."

Lauren knew she was right; and if she married Edward she could officially adopt Ruthie. But what would happen to the rest of the Hope House orphans?

As if reading her thoughts, Nanny intervened again. "Both Will and Edward are man enough to allow the two of you to continue working at Hope House. Neither of them need their wives at home to fetch their slippers or cook their meals."

"Good job, really, else Mr. Edward would be in for a real shock." Norma rubbed Lauren's arm to show she was teasing.

Lauren gave her a grateful smile. Maybe now Nanny would stop lecturing.

Norma's husband and Hope House's caretaker, Bart, stood up. "I reckon I done heard about enough for one evenin'. I'm going out to check on the cows and the goat. Reckon I'll be more comfortable out there." He went off muttering about stubborn women, leaving those behind him in stitches laughing.

Norma said, "That man of mine be so quiet, we forget he's sittin' here listenin'. Nobody asked my opinion but, for what it's worth, I don't agree with gettin' married for the sake of what people might think. But life is much nicer with the right partner by your side to share the good times as well as the bad." A shadow crossed Norma's face before she too stood up. "It's time I turned in. Goodnight, y'all."

CHAPTER FOUR

Lauren shuddered at the earthworms churning through the wet soil.

Lottie picked one up, staring at it as it slithered across her hand. "Don't you like worms, Miss Lauren?" Lottie placed it in the bucket by her side. "Fred will be happy with me, he wants the best worms so he can beat Cal at fishin'."

"You're a good sister. Where is Fred?" Lauren threw some of the weeds she had pulled into the small pile outside the fence Terry had built to protect the vegetable garden from deer and rabbits. Weeding wasn't her favorite chore but they depended more than ever on the produce from this vegetable garden.

Lottie's face flushed as she bent down to examine the newly turned earth. "He's workin' on somethin'. I'm not allowed tell."

Lauren's heart missed a beat. What was Fred planning? Lottie's next words reassured her. "Terry said to let him be."

If Terry was involved, the children were safe and she could relax. As much as that was possible these days. She thrust the hoe into the soil, taking some of her frustration out on the ground, the sting of her blistered hands reminding her to take it slower. Norma would have had this garden in tip-top shape but she had been spending a lot of time in bed, getting slimmer by the day. Lauren had found Nanny whispering with the sick woman only a few days ago but both had fell silent when she passed by.

The sound of children's laughter broke into her thoughts. She turned to find Becky on the kitchen steps surrounded by the children, a puzzled expression on her face.

Fred ran over, but before Lottie could show him her worms, he called out, "Miss Lauren, come inside. Me and Terry have somethin' to show you." Fred pulled at Lauren's arm. "Hurry up."

Becky shifted Maisie to her other hip. "Fred, let Miss Lauren wash her hands, they be covered in dirt. What's your hurry? I ain't put dinner on the table yet."

Lauren rubbed her hands on her apron as Fred urged her to hurry.

"You can wash your hands after. Come on."

Lottie held Lauren's hand as they both followed Fred to the barn. The children gathered in front of the double doors, their eyes shining with excitement. Lauren glanced at Becky but it was clear she didn't know what was going on either.

"Why is Nanny Kat takin' so long? Terry said he'd get her." Fred kicked the ground with his toe.

"She's comin'," Becky confirmed as the older woman, her hand on Terry's arm, walked down the kitchen steps toward them, with Norma and Bart following behind.

Fred pushed open the door before turning. "All the adults have to close their eyes."

Lauren shut her eyes, laughing as she got caught up in the moment. The scent of sweet-smelling hay tickled her nose. Terry did a wonderful job of keeping the barn clean, having let the cows out into the field.

Fred clapped. "You can open them now."

Lauren opened her eyes and gasped. Nanny, Bart, and Norma clapped while Becky, standing with Maisie on her hip, moved slightly forward, her mouth open in an O shape.

"Look, Maisie, it's a chair for you," Becky said. The baby held out her hand and gurgled, making the children giggle.

Lauren ran a hand over the smooth wood of the chair marveling at its design. It was a replica of their kitchen chairs but with longer legs. She found her voice. "Fred, this is fantastic. How?

Who? I can't even speak." She turned toward Bart. "Were you involved in this?"

"I found them some wood but that's all the input I had. I wasn't allowed to see the finished product. It's a mighty fine design."

"Terry helped me. We saw the design in a newspaper Mr. Edward left behind. We thought we could make somethin' like it. Maisie is too small for it but she will grow fast. She can sit in it when we are eatin'." Fred ran his hand over the chair before picking up the cotton belt. "Carly sewed this for her. It's to stop her from fallin' out."

Tears pricked Lauren's eyes as she gazed at the children. "You all knew about this and didn't tell me?"

Heads nodded before Cal piped up. "Terry told us we'd get a hidin' if we said somethin'."

Carly ruffled Cal's hair. "Don't be tellin' tales." She looked at Lauren. "Terry told them they would have to clean out Mabel and Sunflower's stall and the pigsty if they told."

Lauren's heart expanded in her chest as she absorbed the love these children had for one another. "I don't know what to say."

Nanny interjected, "Thank you, would be a good start, Lauren. Children, you've worked as a family. I am so proud of you, all of you."

Becky put Maisie sitting in the chair, holding her carefully as she placed the wooden top down over her head. Maisie thumped the top with her little fists. "Maisie says thank you, she loves it."

"She isn't that small, she could sit in it today." Fred moved closer to Maisie. "She won't fall out."

Becky retrieved the baby before Fred got too excited. "I think she will be big enough in about four or five weeks, darlin'. She wants to give you a kiss for being so clever."

Maisie held her hands out to Fred but it was his hair she was after.

"Ow, she pulled my hair." Fred jumped back, giving the baby a look. "You need to teach her some manners, Becky."

Everyone laughed as Maisie gurgled again before Becky put her head closer to the baby, pretending to listen intently. "She told me I have to give you all some cookies."

The children clapped as they raced after Becky into the house. Lauren stood staring at the chair.

"You like it, Miss Lauren?" Terry's soft voice alerted her to his presence.

"Like it? I love it. Thank you for including Fred."

Terry shook his head. "It was Fred's idea, Miss Lauren. I know he's young but he's got a way of seein' things just as clear as if it stood right in front of him. I helped him as he's too young to use some of the tools on his own but he did most of the work. Me and Cal, we did a lot of sanding. Young Fred is tough to please."

Lauren couldn't speak, her voice caught by the lump in her throat. What had she been worried about earlier? These children always found a way and so would she.

"Let's go wash up for dinner, Terry."

*

Lauren sat up in her bed, wondering what had woken her. She listened but everything seemed quiet in the house. Outside she could hear the crickets and other animals calling and moving around in the night. She put on her housecoat and went down to the kitchen to get a glass of water.

Norma was sitting hunched over at the table, clutching a handkerchief. She looked up at Lauren as she came into the room and gave a weak smile.

"Norma, what are you doing up? I thought you had a chill? Bart said you were staying in bed."

Norma's cough wracked her whole body. Lauren fetched her a glass of water and when she turned back to the table she saw the rust color on the handkerchief, despite Norma's best efforts to hide it.

"Norma, how long has that been happening? You need to see the doctor."

"We don't have money to spare on the doctor, Lauren."

"I'm going to ask Doc Baines to come over. First thing in the morning, I'll drive to Delgany."

"Lauren, please stop fussin' and sit down. I've got to ask you somethin'."

Lauren didn't want to sit in case her friend saw her fear. It was just two years since Norma had arrived at Hope House after her husband Bart had asked if they would take in their two girls. Bart's farm had been repossessed by the bank and he and Norma were taking to the road. On impulse, Lauren had offered Bart a job and they hadn't looked back since. Bart and Norma had supported them all through good times and bad. Their two daughters, Clarissa and Bean—her real name was Sophie—were blonde-haired, green-eyed little darlings.

Looking at her friend's expression, Lauren did what she was told and sat opposite her at the table.

"Lauren, I want you to take care of my girls. Bart will do his best but…"

"Stop it Norma, you're talking like you are dying."

"Maybe I am. That's in the hands of God."

Lauren didn't comment. Norma had deep religious beliefs and Lauren didn't want to offend her. How could God make someone as caring as Norma so sick? Hadn't the woman been through enough already?

"I need to know Clarissa and Bean will be taken care of. Please promise, Lauren. I love Bart and he's a strong brave man, but he'll take this hard."

Tears in her eyes, Lauren's voice left her. She reached across the table and squeezed Norma's hand, trying to recover her composure.

"I have TB, Lauren. I know the signs. Ma died from it when I was little. I thought first it might be the change, you know with the night sweats and all, even though I was too young. But now this has happened." Norma glanced at the hanky. "I can't hide from the truth. I don't need to see the doctor. I have to go to the hospital. The sanatorium over at Blue Ridge."

"No, Norma. You can't leave. We can look after you."

Norma patted Lauren's hand but shook her head. "You and me both know that ain't going to work. I can't risk spreadin' this to any of the children. I feel guilty enough that I may have infected them already. I've packed a bag and, when Bart gets up in the mornin', he'll drive me there."

"Does he know?"

Norma stared out the window, but Lauren didn't think she was looking at the mountain view as her eyes seemed to stare right past it.

"He knows even if he hasn't admitted it to himself yet. He knew the day was comin' but he refused to discuss it. The blood, it's new, and that's a sign I have to go. Look after my babies, please."

"Of course, we will. They… they are going to miss you so much. We all will."

Norma coughed again and it took a while for her to recover her breath. "Lauren, you just about saved our lives back in '32 when you gave Bart the job and us a home. I'll never forget your kindness."

"It's easy to be kind to wonderful people. You and Bart are as much a part of Hope House as Becky and me. The children adore both of you. They will miss your baking, but don't tell Becky."

At that moment Becky bustled into the kitchen. "Don't tell me what? What are you doin' down here? Norma, that cough is gettin' worse. I'm goin' to brew you up some chicken soup."

"Thank you, Becky, but I'm not hungry."

"You be wastin' away. Bean has more flesh on her bones than you and she's only five." Becky turned to the cooker.

"I'm leaving tomorrow, Becky. I've asked Lauren to look after my girls and Bart."

Becky whirled around. "Where you goin'?"

"To the sanatorium. I've got TB, Becky. Sooner I leave the better."

Becky came to stand beside Norma but stopped short of touching her. "You can't know that. Not unless I missed you trainin' to be a doctor? You is just sickenin' with something. A bad chill on your chest. I'll make you a wrap of onions—"

"Becky, please. I love you, but onions aren't going to help me now."

Becky's eyes watered. She took out her hanky and blew her nose. Lauren stood up and went over to give her a hug. "We have to be brave. Norma is and we must support her. We have to put on our best faces for the children."

"Why?" Becky slammed her fist on the table. "Haven't we had enough bad things happen without this? It's not fair."

Norma said, "Becky, it's not up to us to question what's fair. Now dry your eyes and make us a cup of coffee please. I'm not desperate enough to ask Lauren."

The women exchanged a watery smile at Norma's attempt at a joke. Becky made the coffee while Lauren went to get a quilt for Norma. She was shivering but refused to return to her bed. They sat around the kitchen table talking.

"Do you remember when that poor old goat Grouchy stole Ruthie's red hat?" Norma said. "The one you knit for her, Becky?"

Becky nodded, laughing as Lauren said, "I can still see her coming across the front garden with bits of red wool dangling from her mouth. Ruthie was great about it though—any other child would have had a tantrum."

"Ruthie is a special little girl. She's blossomed in her time here, hasn't she? Thank goodness that stepfather of hers never turned up. I reckon Bart would have given him a hiding if he had."

"He'd deserve it, Norma. Nobody should treat a little girl the way he treated Ruthie. If Fred hadn't found her that day, well I can't bear to think of what would have happened."

"Is this a private party or can anyone join in?" Nanny asked as she walked down the hall from her bedroom.

Becky stood up from the table. "Come sit down, Nanny Kat. Want some coffee?"

"Might as well. How's a body to sleep with you three nattering on like a murder of crows."

Lauren choked on her coffee. Trust Nanny to come out with that expression.

Nanny took the cup. "Thank you, Becky." She turned toward Norma. "So, you told them then?"

"Yes. Just now."

Lauren and Becky turned on Nanny. "You knew and you didn't say anything?"

"I didn't know, not for definite, but I had my suspicions. She did a good job of hiding it, but I've eyes in my head. When you can't move as fast as you used to, you see things others miss."

Lauren's eyes pricked with tears once more, but she bit her lip. She could cry later when she was alone.

CHAPTER FIVE

Morning came too quickly. Dawn broke over the mountain as the sky turned to pink, announcing a sunny day ahead. Lauren wanted there to be dark clouds and rain to reflect what was happening.

The night before, Norma had eventually been persuaded back to bed, but Lauren and Becky had stayed up with Nanny talking about the events of the past two years.

"Girls, I know this is one of the hardest days you will face but you have to be brave." Nanny straightened her back as she spoke. Her wrinkles looked more pronounced because of the sleepless night but her eyes were bright and clear. "You owe it to Norma and to the children. Bart will need our support too. Never saw a man as dedicated to a woman as Bart is to Norma. We'll have plenty of time for our tears later, but this morning, I just want to see smiles. Understood?"

"Yes, Nanny Kat," Becky replied, brushing away her tears with her sleeve.

Lauren moved closer to Nanny, putting her hand on her shoulder. "I'm glad you're here with us, Nanny."

"So am I, child, so am I."

*

Clarissa and Bean clung to their mother until Lauren and Becky had no option but to pull them away. They held on tight to the sobbing children as Bart packed up the truck with Norma's suitcase and a quilt to keep her warm. Despite the clear skies and the warm day, Norma was shivering.

"Mama, don't go. Don't leave us here. We want to be with you and Pa," Clarissa sobbed, holding onto her younger sister's hand. Bean was too distraught to talk.

"Girls, please be good for Becky and Lauren. Your ma loves you, but she needs you to be strong, we both do." Bart swiped his arm across his face and then turned to the truck. He held the door a little too long before climbing into the driving seat. Leaning out the window, he waved them goodbye.

Terry rounded up the younger children and with Carly's help they took them indoors, leaving Clarissa and Bean to stare after the truck until it had long disappeared.

Clarissa held Bean's hand. "Come on, we best go inside too, Bean."

Bean stamped her foot. "That's not my name. Sophie is. Only Ma and Pa call me that." Sophie turned and ran into the house, leaving her tearful sister behind.

Lauren kneeled on the ground to put her arms around Clarissa. "Bean is upset, darling. She didn't mean to hurt you. She's scared and lonely just as you are. Be patient with her."

Clarissa didn't react. Lauren took her by the hand and started leading her toward the house.

"Miss Lauren? Is Ma going away to die?"

Lauren glanced at Becky before answering. "Darling, your mama is very sick. She's going to a hospital to get better. We hope she will return to live with us soon."

"Can we visit her in the hospital?"

"I don't think so, sweetheart." Clarissa's face fell. "But you can write to her and draw her pictures. You can tell her what is going on around here. She'd like that."

Clarissa nodded before pulling her hand away and running into the house. Lauren started after her, but Becky put out her hand. "Let her be, Lauren. She needs to have a cry and let those feelin's out."

Lauren hugged Becky as they both shed a tear.

"I hope you were right, Lauren, and she comes back to us."

"She has to, Becky, the alternative doesn't bear thinking about." She gave Becky's arm a squeeze. "Right now, we have Norma's girls to look after. We feel bad but they are devastated."

*

Bart returned in less than a week. Lauren walked around the house from the vegetable garden to greet him. "Bart, you're back. How is Norma? Is she here too?"

His shoulders were slumped. He looked as if he'd aged ten years; the hair on the sides of his head was grayer, and there were dark circles under his eyes.

"No, Lauren. Norma isn't comin' back." Bart's voice trembled. "At least not for a while. The doctors admitted her to the Blue Ridge Sanatorium. I would have been home sooner but they did some tests to see what she had and how far it was gone."

"And?" Lauren restrained her urge to run away; she didn't want to hear bad news—especially about Norma.

"It is definitely TB and it's in both lungs. They said if she had come to them sooner, then maybe…" Bart glanced up, his eyes swimming with tears. "They say my Norma is fightin' for her life."

"No…" Lauren moved to give him a hug but something in his face stopped her.

"I got to be brave and tell my girls."

"Will they let Clarissa and Bean come see her?"

"No. They said we got to be careful. TB spreads very fast."

"It does, but usually in tenements with poor ventilation and unsanitary facilities. Norma was a stickler for cleanliness, we both know that. How many times did the kids grumble about her asking them to wash their hands? She protected us best as she could.

Nobody has a cough or a fever, nor has anyone lost their appetite. Tell Norma she is to worry about herself and nobody else."

Bart nodded. He seemed unable to speak.

"Come inside and have some coffee and something to eat. The girls will be thrilled to see you. Are you staying?"

He shook his head. "Can't do that, Lauren. I got to pay seven dollars a week for the care. I have enough to cover two weeks but I got to get a job."

Lauren grimaced, biting her lip, her chest tightening with guilt. "If I hadn't lost our money in the bank last year, you'd have much more than that."

Bart patted her on the arm. "You weren't to know the bank was going to close its doors and take our money with it. Nobody had a way to know that."

He and Norma had been so nice about it all; Lauren losing their savings and the money the orphanage had put away for the mortgage and Christmas. There had been no sign the Richmond bank had been experiencing financial difficulties until Becky had found the article in the paper announcing it had closed. It had never reopened, and they weren't the only ones to lose their accounts.

"I wish I could help, Bart, but we haven't any spare funds."

"I know that, Lauren, and when you do they are to go to Terry and his schoolin'. I will get a job, live near my Norma. I'll send home what I can for Clarissa and Bean if you are still up to keepin' them."

"This is their home, Bart. Your home too. We'll be waiting for you and Norma to come home, whenever that is."

He blinked rapidly, his hands tightening into balls as he tried to maintain his composure. "Thanks, Lauren."

Lauren let him walk into the house first and watched as his girls nearly knocked him over. As she followed them into the kitchen her eyes caught Becky's across the room and Lauren shook her head. The girl turned back to her cooking, but not before Lauren saw her wipe her eyes with her sleeve.

*

Later that evening, when Lauren was checking on the children, she found the blonde-haired Leroy girls cuddled together in the same bed. Tear stains marked their cheeks. Lauren was tempted to move Clarissa into her own bed, but decided not to. She sat and watched them sleeping for a little while. How young they were to deal with their mother's illness. She had been a little younger when she lost her mother. She could only remember a shadow rather than her mother's voice or image.

She pulled the covers up over the girls' shoulders as the air was chilly. Moving to the window, she pulled the drapes closed. There wasn't a single star in the black sky outside to lift her mood.

Downstairs she found Bart sitting alone at the table. She took a seat opposite him, wanting to make the despair in his eyes disappear but not knowing what to do.

"Can I do anything, Bart? I feel so helpless."

"No, Lauren, but thank you. The girls are upset. I just told them their ma was ill and that they couldn't see her yet."

"Bart, do you remember that first day we met? You told me Norma pulled your children from illness to recovery. She has the inner strength to fight. You tell her not to worry about the girls or anything else but just to get better."

"But the doctors said…"

"What do they know? They get it wrong as much as they get things right. You were told your girls wouldn't survive that time, weren't you? Now look at them. When you go back to that hospital, tell Norma to forget what that doctor said or else to go out of her way to prove him wrong. She has to fight, not just accept what he said."

Bart nodded. She reached across for his hand, which still bore scars from the barn fire, and put hers over it. "We are your family, Bart, and we will always be here for you."

He raised his head, tears streaking his face. "I don't know if I have the strength to be there for her, Lauren. She's always been the strong one, my Norma."

Lauren squeezed his hand. "You are strong too. You believe in yourself. Now before you go back tomorrow, you are going to pack a basket of food for you and Norma. Becky and Nanny have made some real chicken soup. Nanny went looking for some of her herbal remedies too. It can't hurt her—the Irish swear by mullein weed for curing TB."

"Mullein weed?"

"I think you might know it as cowboy's toilet paper." Lauren blushed, and Bart laughed. "It's nice to see you laugh. Why don't you go up and sleep now? You look exhausted."

He pushed against the table as if needing help to stand up. Once on his feet, he swayed slightly before finding his balance.

"I've forgotten what it's like tryin' to sleep in a town or city. It is so noisy with traffic all times of the day and night." Bart stopped speaking as if to collect his thoughts. His face was a mask of pain, and the desolate expression in his eyes made Lauren want to weep. "The people are so busy as well, always hurryin' from here to there. Nobody seems to have time to talk or even say hello. I miss Delgany and not just because of the girls or this place."

She stood, wanting to give him a hug but knowing that wasn't appropriate.

"Go up to bed, Bart. You'll feel refreshed after a good night's sleep."

CHAPTER SIX

After a sleepless night, Lauren gave up tossing and turning and was first to arrive downstairs. She stoked up the stove, adding some kindling to the hot ashes, waiting for them to light before adding larger pieces of wood.

"Mornin', you're up early," Becky commented as she walked down the stairs into the kitchen, yawning.

"I slept about as well as you seem to have. I've put wood on the stove and the water is on to boil. I thought I'd collect the eggs."

"I'll get started on the best breakfast Bart has tasted in a while. That will help…" Becky broke off, her eyes brimming with tears. Lauren squeezed her arm, unable to find words of comfort. Then she picked up a basket and headed out the door.

Taking a minute to appreciate the view of the sun rising over the mountains, she set off toward the chicken coop. The birds protested at being woken early, pecking at her feet as she searched for the hidden eggs. The rooster sat on top of the hen house glaring at her as if reminding her this was his domain.

Terry's voice interrupted her thoughts. "Miss Lauren, I didn't expect to see you up so early."

"The way people talk, you'd think I slept in every day," Lauren replied.

The boy grinned before limping on past to the barn. She watched him go. His leg must be bothering him this morning as the limp was more pronounced. He'd been doing so many extra chores since Bart had gone—was it too much for him? She should find some help but how would she pay for a worker? How would Bart feel if she engaged someone else? He might think she didn't believe he and Norma would be coming home.

She'd just finished collecting the eggs when she heard the sound of an engine. Who could be calling at this hour? She prayed it wasn't more bad news.

She walked around to the front of the house, putting the basket of eggs on the porch before making her way to Edward's vehicle.

"Edward, what are you doing here so early?" Her voice came out sharper than she'd intended.

He got out of his car and came toward her, his hands up as if to show he came in peace. "That's a lovely welcome. Do you want me to leave?"

The look in his eyes warmed her, though she wished she'd had time to check her hair. Knowing her luck she had chicken feathers stuck in it.

Blushing, she responded, "No of course not. Just surprised, that's all."

"I wanted to catch up with Bart. He was due this weekend, wasn't he? I thought he might like a ride back to Charlottesville. I may have found him a job if he's interested. It's a pity my home is on the wrong side of Charlottesville or he could live there but he'd spend hours traveling back and forth to the hospital."

She heard his intake of breath as she surprised him with a kiss on the cheek. "You are so kind. Come in, Becky is making a big breakfast. John Thatcher dropped by yesterday with some bacon and sausages. We have plenty of eggs too."

Edward took a box from the trunk and followed her up the steps to the porch. She collected the eggs and held the door open for him. He put the box on the table beside the sofa. Cal and Fred ran down the stairs hollering, "Good morning, Mr. Edward."

"Morning, boys." Edward took off his coat and put it on a hanger. He opened the box and handed Cal a load of old newspapers and Fred a new whittling knife. Both boys were ecstatic with their gifts. "Where's Terry?" he asked, looking around for the older boy.

"Out in the barn as usual," Lauren replied. "He's probably done the milking but he's always got chores to do out there."

Edward headed to the barn, a brown package in his hand. Lauren called to Shelley and Ruthie to come downstairs and set the table. Carly was giving Maisie her bottle. Clarissa and Sophie had yet to come downstairs but she left them alone. She guessed they were spending time with their dad.

"Cal, move those newspapers somewhere else. Fred, put your knife away and bring in some wood, please. Shelley, mind those glasses, I don't want any broken glass on the floor." She busied herself giving instructions while Becky cooked at the stove.

"Where's the fire? What's all the shouting about?" Nanny asked as she made her way slowly into the room.

"Nanny, I said I would bring you breakfast in bed. You've been overdoing it this past week."

"I have plenty of time to sleep when I'm dead, Lauren. Stop fussing over me. Was that Edward's voice I heard?"

"Yes, Nanny Kat," Fred said. "And look what he got me." He showed her his knife.

"It's wonderful, Fred, now you will be able to make all sorts of things," Nanny said, taking a seat at the table. "You have a real talent for woodwork."

Fred turned scarlet, making his red hair look even more carroty than ever. Lauren's heart swelled. Fred hadn't been blessed with Cal's academic skills but he'd made Maisie's high chair and carved beautiful figures from wood. She wished his teacher could see the care and attention he gave to his work. But all she cared about were his grades.

The back door opened, intruding on Lauren's thoughts. Edward and Terry came in, the latter carrying a book about animal medicine.

"Look, Miss Lauren, Mr. Edward got this for me." Terry's eyes shone as he held the book almost reverently.

Edward rubbed the back of his neck. "It's not a lot, I saw it in a second-hand bookstore."

"It's fantastic. Thank you, Mr. Edward." Terry turned to Lauren. "Can I put this upstairs before breakfast? I don't want it damaged."

"Go on," Lauren responded. "Thank you, Edward, that was a very thoughtful present. Did you know he wants to go to college and become an animal doctor?"

Whatever Edward was about to say was cut off by Bart's arrival downstairs with Clarissa and Sophie right behind him. "Mornin' all."

"Good morning, Bart," Nanny greeted him.

"Edward came by to offer you a lift back," said Lauren.

"But first Becky has cooked up a feast," said Nanny. "Sit down here beside me. I've missed your sensible presence." Nanny sent a look at Lauren.

Lauren didn't get a chance to retaliate as Shelley had other ideas. "Mr. Edward, did we get gifts or was it only the boys?" Shelley demanded, her hands on her hips.

"Shelley, behave yourself," Becky admonished her.

"No, she's right. It isn't fair for just the boys to get something." Edward smiled, and went into the sitting room, returning with the box he'd brought in from his car. He placed it on the edge of the table. "Paper and crayons for you. You are good at pictures, aren't you, Shelley?"

"Suppose so," Shelley responded sulkily.

"We are, Mr. Edward, aren't we, Lottie?" Ruthie chipped in. "Look, Clarissa, you can draw pictures for your ma. There's loads of paper and look at all these different-colored crayons. You're the best, Mr. Edward." Ruthie climbed onto a chair and reached to kiss Edward on the cheek.

Breakfast was a noisier affair than usual. Clarissa and Sophie sat as close to their dad as possible, neither of them making an effort to eat. Lauren's heart broke for the girls. She would have to watch them closely for the next few months to make sure they ate and slept properly. The last thing Norma and Bart needed were the youngsters getting ill.

After breakfast the adults moved into the lounge while the children, led by Carly and Terry, cleaned up. Terry directed the boys on cutting wood, removing the ashes from the stove, and making sure their rooms were clean. Carly supervised the girls clearing the table, washing, and drying the dishes.

"Why can't we cut wood someday and the boys do the dishes?" Shelley said.

"Doing the dishes is girls' work, Shelley," Cal responded from the kitchen floor where he was kneeling filling the wood basket with one hand while trying to read a newspaper. Lauren took the newspaper, folded it, and placed it on the dresser, and Cal took the hint. Lauren took a seat with the adults, all listening to the chatter filtering in from the kitchen area.

Shelley wasn't finished. "Who says so? You eat off a plate and use cutlery so why can't you wash it?"

"Shelley, you can't cut wood. Girls aren't strong enough."

Lauren held her breath waiting for Shelley to tip the wash bucket over Cal.

"Miss Becky does it. She's strong enough. I think the boys should do the washing and drying one day, don't you, Carly?"

Lauren and Becky exchanged a grin as the familiar conversation filtered in from the kitchen.

"She wants to be Frances Perkins," Nanny whispered.

Lauren felt she should stand up for the girl. Shelley was a tough child but, in this instance, she was right. It wasn't fair that girls were expected to wash dishes and clean houses when boys contributed to the mess too.

"I'd be happy if Shelley ended up in government. She's certainly bossy enough and the first female cabinet minister isn't a bad role model to have. She could be like Cal and be a fan of Dillinger and his gang."

Edward laughed but the smile slid off his face when he saw her raised eyebrows. "He's just being a boy, Lauren. We were the same at one time, weren't we, Bart?"

"Sure. Jesse James was one of my heroes when I was a boy. It's a passin' phase. He'll be fine. All the strong women in this house will set him straight."

*

Two mornings after Bart had returned to Charlottesville, Lauren heard Cal and Fred arguing outside, which was unusual as the boys normally got on well. She opened the door to see them dragging a heavy sack between them.

She pushed opened the screen door to get a better look. "What have you got there, boys?"

The boys stopped arguing long enough to look at her.

Fred answered, "Skins, Miss Lauren. There must be about five animals in this sack."

Lauren's stomach roiled. She looked from the sack to the boys and back again.

"Do you want to see, Miss Lauren?" Fred offered. From the grin on his face, he knew how she'd react.

"No thank you, Fred. Who gave them to you?"

Cal responded, "Nobody, Miss Lauren. They were just sittin' beside the barn. Shadow found them."

Why hadn't the dog barked if a stranger had come onto the property? Not for the first time, Lauren thought they should replace the dog with a real guard dog. "Was there a note?"

Cal looked at Fred before answering, "Didn't see one."

Lauren strode into the house to find Becky. "Can you come outside, please, and see something the boys found. They said they're skins. I can't look." Lauren held onto her stomach, the mere thought of the sack's contents making her feel ill.

Becky rolled her eyes. "You still ain't much of a farmer, are you, Miss Lauren. Who left the skins here?"

"Not sure but they're in a bag so it wasn't an accident." She followed Becky back outside where the boys were fighting over who would hold the sack.

"Give it to me." Becky opened the sack and carefully took out each skin.

Lauren turned away, her nose twitching at the smell. She retreated to the porch.

"Lauren, that's a racoon skin and those ones are possum."

Lauren didn't care what they were. "Why did someone dump them here?"

"It's a donation." At Lauren's puzzled look, Becky continued. "The racoon skin could fetch eight dollars if we're lucky. The possum skins sell for about fifty cents, sometimes more."

Lauren couldn't hide her surprise. "You mean someone trapped these for us?"

"I'm guessin' it was Maisie's family. Mountain folk are good trackers. They'd know their value too. Maybe her pa is tryin' to pay for her keep."

"But why didn't he keep her then? If he can track animals for their skins, he can afford to feed her." Lauren couldn't understand it.

Becky shrugged. "Maybe, maybe not. You don't know how long it took him to fetch up these skins. There may be other reasons he couldn't keep her. Her mother may be dead or ill."

Lauren knew Becky understood the mountain way of life better than she did. Still, she couldn't bear the thought of a father missing out on his daughter's first steps and other important milestones. Maisie was settling in and she was a delight, although still rather quiet.

"I wish he'd come and talk to us."

"Mountain folk have their pride, Lauren. He wouldn't want people knowin' he couldn't look after his own. You're goin' into town today. Why not take these to Mrs. Hillman and see what she offers you?"

"I wish you could take them. You need to learn how to drive."

Becky shook her head, the same reaction as always. "I got two legs to take me where I need to go. I'll pack them up so they don't stink out the truck."

*

When Lauren walked into Hillmans' store, Ellie-Mae must have seen her from an upstairs window as she came running down the stairs into the store and flung herself at Lauren.

"You look wonderful, Ellie-Mae. I love your dress."

The blonde-haired girl had blossomed like a flower with the love she got from the Hillmans and their son Earl. Dalton was a changed young man too.

"Ma made it for me. Isn't it pretty?" Ellie-Mae whirled around.

Speechless from the lump in her throat, Lauren nodded. The child who had worn her hair down covering her facial birth mark had turned into this girl brimming with confidence.

Mrs. Hillman walked down from the apartment upstairs, a bright smile on her face. "Afternoon, Lauren, how are things with you?"

"Fine thanks, Mrs. Hillman. I love Ellie-Mae's dress. You did a fabulous job."

Mrs. Hillman's nose twitched. "Thank you. What is that smell?"

"That might be me. We had a gift at the orphanage this morning. Someone left us some hides—one raccoon and some possum. Becky said to bring them to you."

Mrs. Hillman clapped her hands. "I've had an order for a new coat and the woman wanted a fur collar with a hat to match. How much do I owe you, Lauren?"

"How about you and Mr. Hillman have a look and let me know. I can't bear to look at them. I never could wear fur even when Father bought me a mink coat. He laughed at me but…" Then she felt too choked up to continue. She wondered what was wrong with her; her father had died months before.

"Lauren, you are far too sensitive for your own good. Tell me, how is Norma? Do you have any news of her?"

Lauren glanced in Ellie-Mae's direction. The child had known Norma when she'd lived at the orphanage.

Mrs. Hillman caught her meaning. "Ellie-Mae, can you ask your pa to come in and look at these skins please?"

"Sure, Ma. Nice to see you, Miss Lauren."

When Ellie-Mae was out of earshot, Mrs. Hillman apologized.

"No need to apologize," Lauren said. "We all forget sometimes. Norma isn't doing so well. They are very concerned. They said if she had gone for treatment earlier it would be better. I'm sure she put off getting checked because she was worried about money." Lauren felt a sudden wave of anger and slammed her fist on the counter. Mortified, she tried to apologize but the words wouldn't come. She took a deep breath, counted to three, and opened her mouth again. "I'm so sorry, I shouldn't have lost control like that. But why does it always have to come down to money?"

Mrs. Hillman's features softened as she held Lauren's gaze. "I don't know, Lauren. All we can do is pray for Norma. She's a strong lady and she has every reason to live."

Lauren hoped the woman was right, but the last time she had seen Norma she'd looked as if she'd blow away if someone breathed too hard. She squeezed back tears. She couldn't get all emotional in public. "I best go and check in with the sheriff to see if he has heard from Maisie's parents. I will be back in a while."

Mrs. Hillman leaned in closer. "I'll have your money for you then. Chin up, Lauren. We've faced hard times before and come through them."

CHAPTER SEVEN

As Lauren headed toward the sheriff's office, she heard someone screaming her name. Mrs. Flannery. That was all she needed. The thin, wiry-looking woman had a voice that could cut glass. Lauren clenched her hands into fists, the nails digging into her palms. She couldn't afford to be anything but pleasant. The woman and her husband could start a riot just by appearing on the sidewalk.

"Lauren Greenwood, you're responsible for this thievin' little brat. I knew the sheriff was wrong to let you keep that orphanage of yours going. Delgany was a nice place until you set up home for all sorts of illegitimate illiterate brats."

Lauren hurried toward the entrance to the Newmarket clothing store where Mrs. Flannery was holding a child, a girl of about eleven years old, by the neck, just in front of the store door. With every word the woman shook the girl, who didn't seem able to fight back.

Lauren held her hands by her side. She was tempted to grab the child from the woman's grasp, but was afraid she'd hurt the child. "Leave her be, Mrs. Flannery."

"She won't give me back what she took. See how she's hidin' her arm. I bet she has somethin' under it. Hold onto her while I look."

The girl kicked and hissed as Mrs. Flannery tried to work her way around the child's body. Lauren looked about and spotted the sheriff on the other side of the street. She waved at him to come over. The child was shaking with terror, but she had a determined glint in her eyes.

Lauren crouched down at eye level with the girl and spoke firmly. "I'm Lauren and I'll help you."

"I didn't take anything. She keeps screaming at me and hitting me. I was just looking for something to eat. I didn't mean any harm."

"Course you didn't," Mrs. Flannery sneered. "Then why don't you show us what's under your arm?"

"I haven't taken anything."

"What's going on here?" Sheriff Dillon's voice boomed out, as he waited for the traffic to pass before crossing to their side.

Mrs. Flannery's voice grew shriller. "Sheriff, arrest this girl, she's been thievin' from my store."

"You have proof of that, Mrs. Flannery?" The sheriff's steely look would have defeated most people but not Mrs. Flannery. If anything it seemed to make her more determined to press her case.

"I don't need proof. You just need to look at the state of her. She's dressed in rags, no shoes, and she's hidden somethin' under her arm."

Lauren spotted a couple of faces she recognized as a crowd started to gather, but she saw nobody she would call a friend.

The girl stood up for herself. "I don't. I was hungry and thought she might have thrown something out, but I didn't take anything. I'm not a thief."

Lauren put her arm around the girl's shoulders but removed it when she winced. "What's wrong? You're hurt."

"No, I'm fine. I have to go now."

The girl turned to leave but Mrs. Flannery wasn't having it. She grabbed the girl by the collar. "Come back here. I want my stuff back. Sheriff, make her show you what's under her arm."

The girl looked stricken. Her long brown hair was crawling, and she had bite marks on her bare legs. Lauren wondered whether it was fleas or something else.

The sheriff wore his sternest expression. "Look, child, I'll get you a meal if you tell Mrs. Flannery what you have under your arm."

"I don't want to." The girl spoke through clenched teeth, her eyes focused on the ground.

"You have to or else you'll have to come to the cells and I will have to ask you to strip and neither of us want that."

The girl's eyes darted from face to face. Lauren was sure she'd make a break for it, but instead she took off the shawl she was wearing. Lauren had to swallow back the bile in her throat. The child's shoulder and left arm were covered in burn marks, fairly recent ones.

The sheriff opened his mouth but no words came.

Lauren moved closer. "You poor child, what happened to you?"

"I fell in a fire. I was clumsy. That's what Ma said. She said if I were quicker on my feet, Pa wouldn't have caught me."

"Your parents did this?" Lauren whispered, not wanting to have her fears confirmed.

"Never mind the sob story," Mrs. Flannery hissed. "See what's in her pocket." She made a grab for the girl but Lauren blocked her.

"Leave her alone." Lauren struggled to control the anger in her voice.

"I best check." The sheriff glared at Mrs. Flannery as he reached for the pocket. The girl got there first and produced a rag doll. It was old but Lauren could see it was very precious given how the girl held onto it.

She gripped it to her chest as she said, "Old Ma Williams sewed it for me. She said it was my lucky charm. It hasn't brought me much luck so far but it was pretty. Rosie keeps me company at night when its dark and there are horrible sounds about."

The sheriff scratched his chin before turning his narrowed eyes on Mrs. Flannery. "Go back into your store, Mrs. Flannery, before I forget I was brought up a gentleman," he almost spat out. He glared at her but still the woman opened her mouth to say something. But whatever she wanted to say was lost as he took a step nearer and roared, "Inside."

Lauren could have sworn the woman actually yelped before the door was slammed closed behind her.

The sheriff relaxed his shoulders, his tone soft as he spoke to the girl. "Come on, child, let's get you something to eat. Lauren, can you come with us?"

"I think we should take her direct to Hope House. If we turn up at the hotel, we'll be thrown out again." Lauren caught the sheriff's gaze and looked at the girl's hair.

He caught her meaning and coughed. "We could go to the office. Wouldn't be the first time the cells met with those critters."

The jailhouse was the wrong place to take a child, Lauren thought, especially one who had been through so much already.

"What's your name?" she asked the girl, crouching down again to meet her eyes.

"Katie." The child held her rag doll closer.

"Katie, where are your folks?"

"Gone."

Lauren's heart ached, and she glanced up at the sheriff hoping he'd agree with what she was about to suggest.

"Why don't you come home with me, Katie? We'll get you new clothes and something to eat. Sheriff Dillon can call later today to take some details about you and your family. Would you like that?"

The girl's eyes widened as she stared right at the sheriff. "You're not taking me to jail?"

"You didn't do anything wrong, child. Go with Miss Lauren." Sheriff Dillon had a reputation for being gruff but even he had winced when he saw the burns.

Lauren ushered the child to the truck, not wanting another run-in with Mrs. Flannery. She drove out of town as fast as she dared. Katie was shivering although the sun was high in the sky. Lauren wondered whether her burns were infected. Maybe she should have driven her to the doctor's office. Well it was too late now, she was almost home. She'd have to go back to Hillmans' another day.

*

During the drive out of town, Katie stared at the mountains, her face a mask of longing.

"Was your home up there?" Lauren asked, her eyes focused on the road. The rain was coming down so quickly the wipers couldn't keep her windscreen clear. They really needed to do something about the chuckholes on this road. They'd repaired the ones closer to Hope House but had run out of money before working on these ones. When it rained, they filled up with water, making them more difficult to see. She bit her lip as the tires hit the side of another one. She couldn't afford new tires, not at the moment.

Katie shrugged. She hadn't said a word since they'd left town.

As Lauren drove up the drive, she spotted the Thatchers' truck ahead. She helped Katie out of the truck.

Katie stared at the house, her face pallid, elbows tucked into her sides making her appear younger and smaller than her age. "It's so big. You got other people living here?"

Sensing the girl was terrified but also wouldn't want to be treated like a baby, Lauren replied softly, "Yes, lots of children and some other adults."

Katie dropped her eyes to her lap, as she whispered, "Are they like you or that woman from the shop?"

Lauren's urge to strangle Mrs. Flannery increased. She put her hand on Katie's good arm, seeking to reassure her. "We don't have anyone like Mrs. Flannery here, Katie. Don't fret. Everyone will be kind. You'll see."

Katie shrugged off Lauren's hand. "Nobody is kind. Not any more."

Lauren walked up the steps onto the porch, meeting Alice Thatcher as she was coming out.

"Lauren, sorry, I didn't mean... Who is this young lady?" Alice greeted Katie with a huge smile.

"This is Katie. Katie, Mrs. Thatcher is a regular visitor here. She bakes the best gingerbread."

"Hello, Katie." Alice beamed again at the child.

Katie glanced up but looked away just as fast. Alice gave Lauren a questioning glance as she stood back to let them into the house.

"Were you going already, Alice?" Lauren asked.

"No, Lauren, John has gone to talk to Terry. I left something in the truck. Becky said I could give the children cookies once they had finished their chores. They were complaining about doing them."

"I bet they did them in record time."

Becky came out to see what they were chatting about. "That they did, Lauren. I don't know if it was the cookies or their surprise at the lovely Mrs. Thatcher speakin' so firmly. Alice can come supervise chores any time she wants. Now who is this?"

"This is Katie, she's come to live with us for a while. She needs a bath, some fresh clothes, and something to eat." Lauren put her hand on Katie's shoulder to reassure the child, who looked petrified.

"Katie, I'm Becky. Why don't I show you the bathroom so you can wash up? The soup isn't quite ready yet and the bread is still in the oven."

Katie glanced at Lauren who gave a small nod. Katie's shoulders slouched as she followed Becky. Lauren wanted to gather the child into her arms and hug away all the horrible things that had been done and said to her.

"What a sad child, Lauren."

Alice's words got Lauren's attention. "Alice, I swear I could have killed Mrs. Flannery with my own hands this morning. The woman pushes all my buttons. She accused the poor child of stealing some clothes. She hadn't taken anything but was covering herself up. Her whole arm and shoulder are burned. I better follow Becky and take a look. I might need to fetch the doctor."

Alice stood up. "Let me go. You look like you need a strong coffee. I have some experience. Five boys get themselves into a fair bit of trouble. Do you have some of that salve you used on Bart's hands after the fire?"

"Old Sally's recipe. Yes, but Becky insists on keeping it in the barn as it smells so bad. I'll get it and follow you up. We'll need larkspur too." Lauren went out to the barn to retrieve the salve. When she returned to the kitchen, the welcome scent of freshly made coffee hit her.

"I'll take that." Alice put her hand out for the salve. "You sit down and take a minute for yourself."

Lauren didn't argue, handing over the salve gratefully and sitting down at the table with a large cup of coffee. She wondered where she would put Katie. The girls' room was already crowded with Shelley complaining on a nightly basis that there wasn't room to walk between the beds.

Maybe she should ask Becky to share her own room and turn Becky's into another girls' room. But as soon as the idea came, she dismissed it. They'd both agreed that having a bit of private space was key to coping with the challenges offered by the orphanage. They got on like sisters but, just like real relatives, they fought sometimes too.

Should she build on another extension? The men had done a great job with the kitchen. Could they add to the upper floor? She sketched some pictures on the page in front of her and chewed on the pencil as she thought it all over. She shook her head. No matter what they did, it would cost money, and that was in short supply at the moment.

Nanny walked in through the back door, her egg basket almost empty. "Chickens were slow at laying this morning so I went out to check if we missed any. Lauren, you're going to get permanent wrinkles sitting there with a face all screwed up like a skunk left a calling card."

"I was just trying to come up with more rooms. We have another child come to stay, a young girl called Katie. We're spilling over at the seams."

"You should ask young Earl to have a look, he has a way with buildings. He can see things we miss."

CHAPTER EIGHT

Katie's long brown hair curled as it dried. Becky had found new clothes to fit her better. The blouse had long sleeves but was cotton so hopefully wouldn't be too heavy in the heat. From the smell clinging to her, both larkspur and Sally's remedy had been used in vast amounts.

Lauren set the table as Alice fussed around the new arrival. "Come sit here beside me, Katie," Alice suggested as Becky dished up bowls of vegetable soup.

Starving, Lauren took a bite of freshly baked bread, which was delicious with newly made butter, and the ache in her arms from helping to churn it made Lauren appreciate it all the more.

Despite being hungry, Katie ate delicately, with beautiful table manners. She devoured two bowls of soup and quite a few slices of bread. She was a skinny little thing but in time would fatten up.

Lauren stood to get more coffee and whispered to Becky standing at the sink, "Does she need a doctor, do you think?"

"I think the burns will heal of their own accord, but we need to keep an eye on them." Becky kept her voice low just in case they were overheard.

Lauren nodded, lost for words as she stared at the youngster. Alice's eyes kept straying to Katie as she ate. Lauren wondered if she recognized her from the mountain. She must check with her later. For now, they had to deal with the children and their questions.

"You comin' to live here?" Cal asked, as he munched his bread.

"Manners, Cal. You don't speak with your mouth full," Lauren corrected softly.

"It's not full now. So, are you?"

"Yes, I think so." Katie glanced at Lauren who nodded.

"Where's she goin' to sleep? There's no room," Shelley responded, earning herself a dirty look from Carly.

"Katie can have my bed, I can share with the babies for now." Carly smiled across at Katie.

"You can't sleep in a cot, Carly. You is way too big." Lottie's eyes nearly popped out of her face. She had a habit of taking things literally.

"I can sleep on the floor for now, Lottie. We have to make Katie welcome. You don't remember when you first came here, but you were scared and lonely," said Carly.

"I remember the horrible woman who hit Fred."

Lauren didn't want anyone thinking of the woman who'd run the orphanage before she and Becky had taken over. "Yes, Lottie, but she's gone now. Thank you, Carly, that's a very generous offer."

"Carly can sleep in with me for a while until we find another solution. You mind, Carly?" Becky asked.

Carly shook her head as Fred answered, "Depends on whether you snore, Miss Becky. Terry snores his head off beside me."

Katie spoke up, "I don't want to put anyone out of their bed. I can sleep in the barn."

"The barn is just for animals. You're not a cow or a horse," Lottie protested. She held her hand out. "Come and see where we sleep. I'll show you my bed, it's next to Carly's."

"Go on, Katie." Lauren smiled. "Lottie will take good care of you."

Lottie grinned at the praise as she waited for Katie, who moved slowly. Lauren wondered if she was in pain, but she didn't want to embarrass the child by asking. Katie obviously wanted to keep her burns a secret.

The adults remained chatting over their coffee as the children left the table.

Nanny glanced around as if to check the children wouldn't hear her. "Where did you find that poor child?"

"Outside Mrs. Flannery's store, Nanny. That old witch accused Katie of stealing. She didn't bat an eyelid when she saw her burns. The woman is heartless." Lauren replayed the whole scene in her mind, her temper rising as she did so. "They're bad, aren't they Becky?"

Becky's eyes clouded and she frowned. "Worst I've seen for some time. Did she tell you how she got them? She didn't say a word to me and Alice."

"She said her ma told her it was her fault for letting her father catch her."

Alice put her hands to her mouth as Nanny and Becky stared at her, shock on their faces.

"You mean her parents burned her?" Alice's face had turned white.

Lauren fought the nausea in her stomach. "That's what she implied. Even Sheriff Dillon was shocked and he's seen a lot. He looked fit to give Mrs. Flannery a good shake." It was a pity he hadn't. Lauren would have offered to do it with him.

"Had he any idea where Katie came from?" Nanny asked.

"No, Nanny, but on the way over here she kept staring at the mountains. When I asked her was she from up there, she clammed up. Maybe she'll tell us in her own good time."

Becky shook her head firmly. "I ain't never heard anyone speak like her before. She sounds a bit like you do, Lauren. She didn't grow up in the mountains, at least nowhere around here."

Now Lauren realized what was odd about Katie. Her accent and speech didn't correspond with her clothes.

Alice touched her eyes with a hanky, her hands shaking. "Lauren, I don't know how you and Becky do this all the time.

Katie's story just about breaks my heart and you deal with lots of different children all the time. You are amazing."

Becky pushed back her chair, picking up the coffee pot to refill it. She moved the kettle over onto the center of the stove, waiting for it to boil up again. "Stubborn, strong-willed, and impatient might be better words to describe us, isn't that right, Lauren?"

Everyone smiled at Becky's words. Both women were known for terrorizing anyone who said a bad word about their orphans. Sheriff Dillon had said before, if they were men, he'd deputize them immediately to take on any criminals he came across.

"Lauren, how are you goin' to get your crops put in without Bart's help? Anything we can do?" John asked over the rim of his coffee. The way he cradled his cup, as if it was delicate, reminded her of the dinner party her father had hosted the night of her engagement. Everyone had sat around with elegant Old Country Roses china teacups in their hands. She'd thought that was her life. Now, sitting with people drinking out of mismatched cups around a wooden table in the middle of an orphanage, she was happier in herself.

Becky rapped her knuckles on the table. "You're miles away, Lauren."

"Sorry, I was thinking of something else. Thank you, John, for the offer to help. Earl Hillman and Big Will have been helping us a lot. We'll be gathering in the white peaches the second week in July so might take you up on it then if you're free. The children will pitch in too. We can turn it into a picnic."

"Would you like some help with the canning? I don't have so much to do with only three of us in my house now." Alice leaned forward, eager to do her bit.

"That would be great, Alice, thank you. Nanny and Becky will be glad of some expertise as I am still very much learning."

Becky teased, "You are best left out of the kitchen chores, Lauren."

She protested, not wanting to be seen as totally useless. "I can peel vegetables. I get plenty of practice with this lot of hungry mouths." Lauren's words caused the others to smile. She added, "Bart has left the gardens well stocked with broccoli, cabbage, onions, and some asparagus. Plus, we have beans and other greens growing. We won't starve."

Nanny turned to her friend. "John, could you find us someone to butcher the pig? Lauren can't face that this year."

Lauren's stomach heaved as she relived last year's butchering, the pig's squeals of distress still ringing in her ears. "Definitely not. I can still hear that hog squealing, plus it upset the children too. So, if you do have someone who could do that, we would be obliged."

Becky hastily intervened, "We don't pay cash—they can share the pig."

"Don't worry, ladies. John will see to it, won't you?" Alice phrased the remark as a question but everyone knew she didn't expect an answer.

Lauren added, "Maybe Bart will be back in time for collecting in the Gala apples in August. Or maybe the Golden Delicious in September."

"I'll drink to that." John held his cup up and they all raised theirs to join him.

CHAPTER NINE

It wasn't long before mealtimes became an almost daily battle-ground. Katie and Shelley were like oil and water. The two girls quickly became enemies, and, despite Lauren knowing Shelley was difficult, she couldn't help thinking she wasn't the only one at fault. Katie wasn't making much of an effort to fit in; she did as much—or rather as little—as she could get away with.

Lauren was about to intervene when Becky beat her to it. "Please stop fightin' and set the table, girls. There are thirteen hungry people waitin' to be fed and that doesn't include Maisie. Shelley, you do the plates and you do the cutlery, Katie."

Katie stood at the sink, a mutinous expression on her face. "I want to do the plates. It's quicker."

Lauren let Becky deal with her, she wouldn't stand for any cheek. "Do as you are told please, Katie. I've explained the rules in this house. We all help."

Shelley piped up, "You have to tell her again, she's so stupid she doesn't remember."

Katie's temper flared as she roared back, "I am not stupid, and at least I don't look like you. No wonder nobody wants to adopt you and you been here years. Look at the state of you, covered in freckles with that funny-colored hair."

Lauren felt a little sorry for Shelley—she hadn't been blessed by the best combination of looks—but her pity evaporated at the girl's reply.

"You stop it! At least I don't have horrible scars over my arms."

Becky banged a pot on the counter top. "Enough, girls. I mean it. One more word and you will both go to bed without supper."

The girls muttered but they didn't speak to each other. Lauren put the water glasses on the table. Worries about Norma, the tension of the girls fighting all the time, as well as concerns over money were getting to everyone. She yawned, pushing her hair back from her eyes, trying to secure it behind her ears. She needed a haircut.

Becky put the pot of beans and cornbread on the table. As she started serving, Shelley screwed up her nose. "Why do we have to have beans again? That's all we get to eat these days."

Lauren groaned silently. What did Shelley expect? At twelve years of age, she was old enough to know they didn't have as much money as they needed. They had to make do, and if that meant having beans every day, so be it. Although part of Lauren understood Shelley's pain. Her mouth watered as she remembered the dishes Cook used to serve up back at Rosehall.

She was about to rebuke Shelley but Terry got in first. "You should be grateful we ain't hungry. You remember when we only got one meal a day if we were lucky. Becky and Miss Lauren are doin' their best." Terry took a seat at the table.

Shelley pouted; she didn't like Terry telling her off. She looked up to him. "I was just saying. You don't have to give me a lecture."

"Just eat what you are given and be grateful, Shelley. Now who wants milk and who wants water?" Lauren poured the drinks, her mind on the growing list of supplies they needed to buy. She'd have to go to Hillmans'. Thank goodness she had the credit from the skins. Ten or so dollars would buy a lot.

"Whose turn was it to collect the eggs this morning?" Nanny asked. "I found quite a few when I went back to check. We can't afford to lose any eggs."

"It was Katie's turn," Shelley responded.

Katie leaned over the table, closer to Shelley. "No it wasn't, you're a liar. Take it back."

"Won't. I know it was. Just ask Becky." Shelley glanced at Becky with a triumphant expression.

Becky turned to Katie. "Katie, you will collect the eggs tomorrow mornin'. I can't keep doin' your chores. I got my own work to do."

Fury turned Katie's cheeks scarlet. "I know now why you took me into your home. You just want free labor. I will not stay here to eat beans and work my—"

"That's enough!" Lauren interjected quickly, for fear the girl would use bad language. "Leave the table and go to your room."

"I'm not finished." Katie's voice grew posher the angrier she became.

Shelley retorted, "Thought you didn't want to eat beans?"

"You eat them then." Before they knew it, Shelley was covered in beans. Several of the children laughed but it was too much for Lauren. She stood up and roared at Katie to go to her room before she got out a strap and gave her a whipping. Silence reigned at the table as all the children stared at her, horror mixed with fear on their faces. Lauren hadn't raised a hand to any child since she'd come to Hope House. She'd insisted that regime of fear and beatings left with Matron Werth.

Lauren pushed her chair out of her way and stormed outside.

Inside she could hear Becky and Nanny muttering to the children but she couldn't work out what they were saying. She sat down heavily on the porch swing, guilt gnawing in her stomach. What had made her do that? She'd never lost her temper with the children like that before. That last thing those kids needed was another adult abusing them. As for the strap, she didn't even know if they had one, never mind the fact she would never, ever hit a child with anything more than the back of her hand.

After a while, the porch door squeaked. She held her breath, expecting it to be Nanny coming to take her to task for her behavior. Instead it was Becky with a cup of real coffee—not the chicory they'd been drinking over the last few days.

"I saved it just for moments like this. Lauren, don't look at me like a guilt-ridden dog caught with a chicken in his mouth. Everyone has their breakin' point and you've reached yours. Katie and Shelley alone are a handful, never mind when they get together."

A tear rolled down Lauren's face as she murmured, "I threatened the children, I swore I'd never do that…"

Becky sat on the swing beside her. "Won't do them a bit of harm to see we are in charge, not them. I know you would never use the strap and so does Nanny. If the children believe you will, that might not be such a bad thin'."

Lauren knew she was right. She looked at her friend. "You smell nice, Becky."

She watched the blush start at Becky's neck before it covered all her face. "Will brought it for me that last time he came up. He said it suited me. I wasn't sure."

"It does. That was nice of him. You don't get treated often enough."

It was true. The first time Becky had ever eaten at a restaurant was in January after Edward gifted her two tickets to a movie with dinner afterwards for Christmas. If anyone deserved nice things in life it was Becky. But unless the Depression ended soon, there was unlikely to be many treats for anyone.

CHAPTER TEN

The sun was still high in the sky despite it being after seven in the evening. The children were racing around the garden playing baseball and blind man's bluff. Having eaten indoors, the adults, including Edward, who'd come to visit, took their coffee to sit at the picnic table Earl and Fred had made for the front garden.

Lauren loved listening to Edward talk, marveling at the way he made each orphan feel like the center of the universe when he spoke to them. He had such a nice, softly spoken accent, and the children gravitated toward him. He encouraged Fred's woodwork, Cal's reading, and Terry's ambition to go to college. He was equally good with the girls, and even little Maisie, who settled fast when she was sitting on his lap.

Lauren was miles away when Becky broke into her thoughts.

"So what's your idea about, Edward? Lauren said you wanted to run somethin' past us."

Edward caught Lauren looking at him, causing her heart to beat faster. She glanced away but, realizing he hadn't answered Becky's question, she looked back to find he was still staring at her. She coughed and he seemed to collect his thoughts.

"I do, Becky. I was thinking of ways to help you raise funds to build the extension Lauren wants, and to cover other bills. What about if I was to run a story a week in the paper about each orphan?"

Looking confused, Becky asked, "Our orphans? To say what?"

Lauren held her breath. Edward had mentioned the idea briefly but she wasn't at all sure it was a good idea. What if the newspaper articles attracted bad attention? Or what if some of the parents—say Ruthie's stepfather—saw the articles and came forward?

She examined his face as he spoke; his eyes were wide open, his tone genuine. Everything about him encouraged her to trust him.

"We would paint each child in the best light. For example, how devoted Fred is to his sister Lottie. Maybe someone reading it would be able to offer them a home. If they can't afford that, they may be moved to donate a couple of dollars to the Hope House fund. What do you think?"

Offer the orphans a home? But what if they chose Ruthie? She was blonde and sweet-natured. What was it Bart had said when he came to Hope House that first time? Rich folks wanted blonde-haired, cute little girls.

Becky frowned and Nanny spoke first. "I guess it couldn't hurt. What do you say, Lauren?"

Lauren wanted to scream, *No, don't do it. I don't want the children to leave.* But that was selfish. She held up her hands. "I don't know. I wouldn't want to get the children's hopes up. Also, we can't lie, I don't want to mislead people."

It was Edward's turn to look confused, and he rubbed his chin. "What do you mean?"

Lauren spoke rapidly, as if by talking fast she'd convince them to drop the idea. "Take Cal, for example. He looks like an angel and is much better behaved than he was, but he can be cheeky and is still inclined to run away. Plus he believes his ma will come for him some day, so he would never agree to being adopted."

Edward looked to Becky and Nanny before his gaze returned to rest on Lauren. He seemed to be trying to understand her position but failing. His forehead creased in concentration. "We don't have to include the children with living parents. There's plenty of real orphans in need of a home. Carly, Terry, Lottie and Fred, Shelley, and of course Ruthie."

"NO!" Lauren surprised herself with the force of her denial. "Sorry, but I don't think it's the right time for Ruthie to leave. It isn't that long since Christmas. She needs time to recover from what happened."

Edward gave her a questioning glance but she pretended not to see. She shivered despite it not being cold. "It's a bit cool out here, let's go inside." Lauren didn't wait for anyone to answer but walked into the kitchen leaving the others to follow her.

There she found Cal. Thankful for the distraction and change of topic, Lauren asked, "What has you so enthralled in *The Times*, Cal?" Cal had his finger under the words on the paper, tracing along the sentence just as she had taught him. In the last year he had flourished in so many ways. Even Sheriff Dillon admitted the boy he was now was unrecognizable from the child who had constantly run away from the other orphanage to find his ma.

Cal put his head on one side. "Bonnie's mother won't let her be buried with Clyde. I think that's unfair, don't you? It's what she wanted. She's dead so why not let her be happy?"

Lauren met Becky's gaze over Cal's head. Both were worried about the child's fascination with the serial murderers. It didn't help that the couple appeared so often in newspapers, Becky once joked she'd be rich if she found a penny as often as she'd seen their picture.

Lauren spoke softly, not wanting to contradict him outright and make him idolize the criminals even more. "You know they were bad people. They killed men doing their jobs."

Cal barely looked up. "Women always hate guns."

Edward coughed to alert Cal to his presence before he took the paper from the boy. "Most people hate guns when they are used for the wrong purpose, Cal. What would you do if someone arrived at the orphanage and tried to shoot Lauren or Becky? Or any of the other children?"

"I'd shoot them back." Cal pulled his imaginary gun out of his pocket. "Bang, bang."

Lauren and Becky exchanged glances but it was Edward who answered. "I love your bravery, but you need to think about this, son. People like Bonnie and Clyde shouldn't be adored or celebrated for their deeds. Murderers deserve to be punished. They didn't kill because they were desperate to get money to feed their family or to defend their homes or to protect someone." Edward moved closer to Cal, putting his finger under the boy's chin, forcing him gently to look at him. "They shot innocents because they enjoyed getting into trouble. That's no life for you, Cal. You deserve better."

"Sheriff Dillon shoots people. I saw him do it once." But Cal didn't sound so confident now. He appeared to be listening to Edward. He hadn't moved away. Edward placed his hand on Cal's shoulder.

Lauren saw him squeeze the boy gently, handling the situation perfectly. She felt more than grateful. He was a wonderful man. She caught Nanny glancing at her but pretended not to notice.

Edward spoke again. "As sheriff his job is to protect our community. He wouldn't shoot anyone, even bad people, if he had another choice. This is America, son, we believe in justice. That's why everyone, no matter what crime they commit, is entitled to a fair trial. Only a judge can decide on their punishment. How would you feel if someone shot and killed Sheriff Dillon for doing his job? That's what those people did."

Cal took a few second to reply. "Sheriff Dillon is nice now. I wouldn't like him killed but I think people misunderstand Bonnie and Clyde. It said in the paper he went into jail a schoolboy and come out a rattlesnake. Maybe something bad happened to him."

Lauren held her breath, hoping Edward wouldn't expand on what the newspapers had hinted at. Cal might act older, but he was only nine.

Edward nodded. "Prison isn't a nice place and, being young, he would have had a difficult time—but that's no excuse to go around murdering people."

Edward returned to his seat at the table. Cal leaned in, wanting the last word as usual. Lauren smiled, pleased to see the confidence Cal had gained in the year since he'd arrived at Hope House and grateful for Edward's patience in talking to the boy as you would an adult. Her father would have dismissed Cal's questions long ago.

Cal said, "He cut off two of his toes to try to get out of that place. He must have been really sad. I remember the place I used to live." He stared down at the floor, as the memories of his past appeared to overwhelm him. "I would have tried anythin' to get away from there."

Becky put her hands on Cal's shoulders. "You found us, Cal, and we love you so much. We don't want a life like Clyde had for you."

Cal squirmed a little but his eyes glowed. He went back to reading the paper. The adults took their seats at the table but the conversation wasn't over for Cal.

He spoke up. "You're a lawyer, ain't ya, Mr. Edward?"

Edward rolled his eyes at Lauren with a grin. She was about to tell Cal to leave Edward in peace but he answered, "I was, son. I prefer being a newspaperman." He topped up his coffee cup.

Cal plowed on, "So if everyone is entitled to... what did you call it?"

"Justice?" Edward shrugged his shoulders as if to say to Lauren, just let him ask his questions.

"Yeah. So why didn't Bonnie and Clyde have a trial? They could have sent Bonnie and Clyde to prison. Didn't they murder them when they killed them?"

Lauren was proud of Cal's intelligent mind working through the process. It was a good question and she was curious as to how Edward would answer.

Edward stirred his drink, as if giving the question deep thought. The longer the silence lasted, the more interested Cal seemed in the reply. He was leaning forward ready to listen.

"Both those people had been in prison before. But this time it was too dangerous to try to take them alive." Edward held Cal's gaze. "Rather than me answer your question now, I'll get you all the newspaper articles I can find. You can read up on both of them and then make a decision as to whether they are really the type of people you'd want to meet. Or grow into."

"That's the way an attorney talks! They never give you a straight answer." Cal's response made the adults laugh before Lauren gently rebuked him.

"Cal, don't be rude. Mr. Edward isn't treating you like a child so don't act like one."

Cal turned on his "butter wouldn't melt" expression. "I'm sorry, Mr. Edward. I didn't mean to be rude. Why did you stop being a lawyer? I heard they make lots of money and get rich."

Lauren winced. Edward had confided that his mother and father had disowned him when he became a newspaperman. He'd set up his newspaper with money he'd inherited from his grandparents. His parents didn't give him a penny despite being extremely wealthy. Edward worked hard and deserved to be successful, but he often took on stories that upset the wrong people. He'd written a lot of articles about Lauren's father and her former fiancé, who had made money out of the suffering of others.

Lauren stood up. "Cal, that's enough. Off you go and let Mr. Edward have his coffee."

"Just a minute, Cal. I believe you should work at a job you choose and love. My father wanted a lawyer in the family. I was more interested in the news. I became a newspaper reporter later."

"Did you put people in jail or did you try to keep them out?" Cal asked.

By his silence, Lauren knew Edward was trying to frame his reply in a manner the boy would understand. She sat back down wondering what he'd say. She didn't know what type of attorney he'd been but assumed he prosecuted those charged with breaking the law.

"I was a criminal defense attorney, Cal. That meant it was my job to try to protect my client and prove he was innocent."

Lauren put her hand over her mouth to hide her surprise. Edward had defended criminals. If she'd heard that from someone else she wouldn't have believed it. He was always so outspoken about the harm criminals did.

"Was he, always?" Cal put into words the question Lauren wanted to ask. Surely Edward wouldn't have defended someone he'd known was guilty.

"Cal, you should be a reporter. You sure do ask enough questions. Will you leave Edward alone and let him finish his coffee?" Becky ruffled his hair. "You have other things to be doin', like fetching me some wood. Go on, child."

Cal stood up from the table. "Thanks, Mr. Edward, for talking to me. I think being a reporter is more interestin' than being a lawyer. But maybe I should be a bounty hunter. That way I get to shoot people *and* be on the right side of the law."

Horrified, Lauren was about to challenge him but Edward just laughed. "You'll find the right job, Cal, but for now I'd do what Becky asked. She's more frightening than any gun-toting criminal when her temper is up."

"Yes, sir." Cal ran out the back, the door slamming shut behind him.

Becky poured more coffee before taking a seat at the table. "Edward, you're a born father. You are fantastic with the children, particularly the boys."

Lauren saw Edward look her way but she pretended not to notice. She knew he had deep feelings for her. Becky was right, he'd make a wonderful father. But could she trust him? He had never done anything to suggest she couldn't, but she'd trusted her father and her previous fiancé and look at how that turned out.

Becky changed the subject. "Lauren, I think Edward should do those articles. We need more money. It doesn't look like Norma will get out of hospital anytime soon. We need to think about hirin' help to replace Bart, and that will cost more than just providing meals. What do you say?"

All eyes turned to her. She didn't want to look at Edward, so she sought out Nanny's face. There she saw understanding but also trust. Edward wouldn't hurt them, at least not on purpose. She put her hands on the table. "Let's give it a try, but if anything bad happens, we stop."

"What bad things could happen?" Becky looked mystified, but Lauren thought Edward understood what she wasn't willing to admit. She couldn't let Ruthie go, not even if the best adoptive family came forward.

*

The children loved the idea of seeing their names and pictures in the papers. Edward took the pictures himself, telling Lauren he didn't want anyone new to the children interviewing them. She was grateful for his understanding.

Edward stayed for dinner after the photo shoots. Cal asked so many questions, Becky had sent him and Fred out to collect wood despite the fact the baskets were stacked high.

"I don't have your patience, Edward. Those questions were gettin' on my nerves." Becky rolled her eyes.

"I like Cal. If I'm lucky enough to have a son, I'd like him to be as intelligent as that boy."

Lauren could feel his eyes on her but she stared at the table as if it needed all her concentration to set the places correctly. Her feelings were all jumbled. When he spoke about having children and looked at her, she got a warm feeling inside.

Shelley was being helpful for once, offering assistance without being asked. "Can we tell Mr. Edward the type of family we would like?"

Surprised, as the child hadn't shown any obvious interest in the newspaper articles, unlike Cal, Lauren took a seat and indicated Shelley sit beside her. "What type of family would you ask for?"

"One where the parents didn't have any other children. Then if they lost their jobs or money, they wouldn't choose me to give away." Shelley's monotone voice showed no sign of self-pity. Even though it could be difficult to love this prickly child, at times like these, when she showed just how deeply hurt she'd been by her parents, Lauren ached to put things right. But how could she explain to a twelve-year-old that she was sabotaging any chance of getting adopted with her sullen attitude to life?

"I'm sorry your parents made the choice they did. Perhaps your brother was sickly and they knew you were stronger and more capable of looking after yourself. Maybe that's why they left you behind."

Shelley shrugged. "Don't matter why they did it. Don't change nothin'."

Lauren put her arm out, leaving it up to Shelley if she wanted to move closer.

Predictably, Shelley stood up. "I guess I should ask Mr. Edward if I can ask for a rich family like that."

Lauren let her arm fall. Shelley had developed such a defense barrier she doubted anyone could break through and give the child the happiness she craved.

Later that evening, she asked Edward if Shelley had spoken to him.

"No, she just said she didn't want to be interviewed. Neither did Katie. I didn't push them as I don't want to upset anyone."

"Katie didn't? Did she give a reason?" Lauren wondered at the girl's reaction. Usually she wanted to be the center of attention, but she'd run away from the group photograph and hadn't demanded a picture of her own, even though Edward had promised all the children they would get a copy to keep.

"No. She didn't hang around. Said she wasn't feeling too good and went back upstairs. I assumed she found you or Becky. I should have said something."

Lauren reassured him. "Believe me, if something was really wrong, Katie wouldn't find it hard to tell us. She's quite vocal."

"You're finding it tough at the moment, aren't you?" His question surprised her. He didn't miss much, that was for sure. His tone was rich with understanding and tenderness. "Don't push me out, Lauren. I want to help. Tell me what you need." He hesitated for a second, perhaps waiting for her to speak, but then continued, "Please, Lauren, I know you have reservations about us but you can't take everything on your own shoulders. Talk to me. Tell me what your deepest worries are and let me see if I can help find answers."

She stared at him, torn between pretending everything was fine and letting him know the truth: how she was terrified of her growing feelings for him, worried sick about Norma dying and leaving her family bereft, not to mention the day-to-day worries of running Hope House.

The silence lengthened. He put out his hand, placing it on top of hers. She could hear Becky and Nanny chatting in the sitting room, the children playing outside, as if it was all coming from a distance.

"Lauren, let me be your friend. Yes, I want to be more than that but I will settle for friendship for now. Friends trust one another and they share their problems as well as their achievements. Can't you find it in your heart to trust me? Just a little bit?"

She hated herself but she couldn't get past her fear. She met his gaze, her eyes filled with tears. His were full of hurt—and was it anger or frustration... She couldn't speak.

"I could kill him for what he did to you and to us. He's winning, Lauren, can't you see that? He's stealing your—*our*—future. You can't let him do that."

He raised her hand to his mouth and gently kissed it. Standing, he picked up his camera and notebook. In a gruff voice, he said, "I'll send you the photos and articles to approve before they are printed. I have to go away, to New York, for a while. I will be back in time for Independence Day. Take care of yourself. Say goodnight to the others for me, please."

Before she could react he was gone out the back door. She heard the Cadillac door slam, the engine roar as he took off. Only then did she let the tears fall as she put her head in her arms on the table.

CHAPTER ELEVEN

July 4th, the day the children had been dying for, arrived with a gray sky full of dark clouds. Terry came into the kitchen carrying a bucket of fresh milk. "Looks like we may have rain today."

Shelley looked up. "We can't! We're having a party. The teacher said I could be the lead role in the play." She ran to the window. "It's not that bad, and the sky over the mountain is blue. I think it will be a fine day."

"You can't control the day!" Katie smirked.

Lauren groaned at Katie's remark. Why did she have to goad Shelley? True to form, Shelley retaliated.

"You're just jealous you didn't get picked. The teacher likes me and you hate that."

"Don't be stupid, Shelley, nobody likes you. Teacher just picked you to stop you moaning every day about never having been in the play, despite being at the school the longest." Katie took a breath before adding, "I told her to give you my part."

Shelley advanced toward Katie but Lauren put her hands out, holding the girls apart. "Girls, stop it. I won't have you ruin the day with your fighting. Go upstairs and wash your face, Shelley, and do something with your hair. Katie, clear the rest of the breakfast dishes." Both girls ignored her and fumed at one another. Lauren raised her voice. "Now."

With a look, Shelley ran upstairs but Katie stood her ground. "It's not my turn to do dishes. You do them."

Katie ran outside. Any other day, Lauren would have gone after her, but today was special and she didn't want to ruin the celebrations. She cleared the table herself and washed up the few remaining dishes.

Becky came downstairs carrying Maisie, her eyebrows raised. "Katie?"

Lauren nodded. "I swear she and Shelley would argue about the color of the night sky."

Becky nodded in agreement as the kitchen filled up with children coming in from all directions.

Cal ran in from the garden. "Come on, Miss Lauren, I don't want to miss anythin'. Did you know they are putting on a movie outside? A real one. I hope it's Mickey Mouse or Charlie Chaplin but the girls want *Little Women*." He rolled his eyes. "We can sit on blankets and watch it. What do you think they will show?"

"I don't know, Cal." Lauren didn't have time to think about movies. She had to get everyone ready to go. She noticed Katie walking back in, her face a picture of innocence. She'd deal with the girl's attitude tomorrow. "Ruthie, can you take Lottie to the bathroom again? Just to be sure. Clarissa, please grab Sophie's cardigan in case she gets cold. Carly, would you mind helping Katie to do her hair? She wants braids."

"Yes, Miss Lauren."

Lauren smiled at Carly. She was a lovely young woman with a heart of gold. Despite all the horrible things that had happened to her during her life as an orphan, she hadn't lost her good nature and kindness.

"Miss Lauren, can we go now?" Cal hopped from one foot to the other.

Becky sat Maisie in the high chair, giving her a spoon to play with. Maisie gurgled happily as she banged the spoon on the top of the wooden tray, the noise adding to Lauren's headache.

"Leave Lauren to get her breath. Cal, the movie won't be played until after the parade and that will take a long time. Have some patience. We will all get there if we help each other get ready. Fred, you and Cal fill the wood basket, please. I want to leave a stew on the back of the cooker so we have somethin' hot to eat after a long day. Terry is outside with the animals, can you remind him to come in and wash up?"

"Yes, Becky." The children scattered in various directions.

Lauren glanced out the window as a big truck pulled up. Big Will had promised to help with transportation. She waved as he got out, a smile on his face. The truck he'd brought was much bigger than the Hope House one. He'd covered the back with tarpaulin to provide shelter, as the weather wasn't playing ball. Terry was right, those gray clouds on the horizon threatened rain. As she watched, the Thatchers drove up the lane. She walked outside to greet them.

John got out of his truck, leaving Alice waving to her from her seat.

"Mornin' Will, Lauren," John said as he shook Will's hand. "We're headin' into Delgany and thought we could take a couple of the kids with us. Give you room to breathe."

"I'm goin' inside to see what my woman needs me to do. See you down there, John." Will walked into the house.

"Thank you, John. Katie, Clarissa, Sophie, and Ruthie are ready. Why don't you girls go?" Lauren wasn't going to impose on the Thatchers by giving them Katie *and* Shelley.

The four girls didn't need to be asked twice, clambering up on the truck with Ben Thatcher's help.

"Need me to take anyone else, Lauren?"

"No thank you, John. I just need to find Terry and make sure he's coming. He wanted to stay home to make sure the animals were safe."

"He's a good kid. Did you see the papers? Bet you're glad Terry can't answer the call."

The hairs on the back of Lauren's neck stood up. "What call?"

"The US army is seekin' new recruits. Says it wants to fill its ranks. My Ben can't stop talkin' about it. He's that desperate to join up. His young gal has a different viewpoint. He may decide to choose Uncle Sam over her." His grin told her different. Ben was besotted with his young lady. The whole of Delgany knew their wedding would take place someday soon.

Lauren grinned back at John. Ben was a nice lad and Alice had confided she liked his girl a lot. But her smile faded as she processed what John had said.

Terry's limp. She'd got so used to him limping around the place, she never gave it a second thought. But the army wouldn't take someone with a limp. For the first time, she was thankful it prevented Terry from doing something other boys could do. She didn't want any of her boys going to war.

John climbed back into his truck, calling out as he did so, "Any news on Maisie's parents comin' forward?"

Lauren replied, "No, nothing yet. She's settled in well though and it's no work having her here. We like looking after her."

John smiled. "You do a great job. See you in town!" He tooted his horn as he set off.

CHAPTER TWELVE

Edward's Cadillac must have passed John's truck on Orchards' Pass as Edward arrived to collect Nanny just a few minutes later.

Lauren's face flushed as he got out of his car bearing gifts.

"Will I take this inside?" he said, indicating the large sack of groceries.

"Yes please," she stuttered. What was wrong with her? He was just being friendly. He handed her a small bag of ground coffee. "Most girls prefer flowers but I saw this and thought of you." He was teasing her, his eyes crinkling at the corners. She held his gaze, and for a moment all thoughts of everyone else vanished.

Then Nanny interrupted. "What brings you out here, Edward? We were meeting in town."

"I thought you might prefer to travel in style rather than in that chunky old truck, particularly as Lauren has to hit every chuckhole between here and Delgany." Edward's teasing made the children laugh but she blushed again.

"Will's driving, not me." She hated how short she sounded; he was getting under her skin. He knew it too with the way his eyebrow rose at her tone. She busied herself getting the children ready and helping them into the back of the truck. Becky and baby Maisie would sit up front with Will.

"I'd be delighted, Edward, thank you. See you children later." Nanny waved as she got into the Cadillac. Will followed as they set off for Delgany. It rained a little on the way but that didn't dampen the enthusiasm. The girls had made flags from old rags of blue, white, and red and decorated the truck with their creations. They heard the music playing before sighting the transformed green just outside town. There were people everywhere, some with stalls set up selling everything from lemonade to candy, canned goods to fancy knitted items. The children's eyes were like saucers when they spotted the playground.

"Cal, look, that man over there is breathin' out fire." Fred nudged Cal. "Now he's going to eat a sword."

Lauren hoped they'd find something less dangerous to be excited about. "Be careful, boys, you're to behave and show the townsfolk what good children you are. Remember?"

"Yuck, why would anyone want to eat fire? That's just stupid." Shelley sniffed the air, her hand rubbing her stomach. "Do you smell the popcorn and the sugar-dusted doughnuts?"

"Girls!" Fred and Cal rolled their eyes.

Will parked the truck before coming round to the back to help Lauren and the children down. Mrs. Hillman and Miss Chaney called them over to where they were sitting. Lauren and Becky set themselves up beside them and some of the other ladies, but the children took off in various directions. Everyone had to stay in pairs and not leave the town without an adult. That was the only rule Becky and Lauren had imposed. Each child got one cent to spend. Lauren had tipped Terry an extra ten cents as he did so much work. He'd immediately bought an ice cream for Carly.

Becky leaned over and whispered, for Lauren's ears only, "I can see a romance blossomin' there. They act like an old married couple already."

Lauren shifted on the hay bale, trying to make the seat more comfortable. The straw tickled her bare legs.

"Becky, you see love everywhere. Those two grew up together and are protective of each other. They are like brother and sister." But even as Lauren spoke she caught a look between the young couple and suddenly wasn't so sure.

Mrs. Hillman chipped in, "None of my brothers ever looked at me the way Terry looks at Carly. And vice versa. I reckon Becky is right. They aren't blood kin so nobody would bat an eyelid. It would be nice for each of them to have a partner who understood what they went through before you and Lauren took over that house. When I think of how those children suffered, I just want to cry."

Edward and Nanny joined them just in time to hear Mrs. Hillman's words. Nanny said, "Not today. Today is a day for smiling. You can park your troubles on the way into town and collect them on the way out."

Mrs. Hillman clapped her hands together. "Kathryn, I was hoping you would come. I want you to taste my peach cobbler. I tried that trick you gave me, to add lemon juice as well as cinnamon, and it worked. It tastes much better now."

"I'll go check on the children," Lauren said, as she left the ladies to discuss different recipes. She couldn't cook, and had no interest in learning. "Want me to take Maisie?" she said to Becky.

"No, leave the little darlin' here, we'll mind her, won't we, lovey?" Mrs. Hillman drooled over the baby, who held out her arms.

"Mind your hair, Mrs. Hillman," Lauren said as she stood up.

"I'll come with you." Edward offered her his arm and they strolled around the various amusements. "I see the CCC lads have come out in force. Terry might be in for some competition." He pointed to a group of young men, all wearing uniforms, looking quite dashing. The Civilian Conservation Corps had arrived in Virginia back in April 1933 so people were used to seeing the young men in uniform around the place. They worked hard for a dollar a day, six and a half days a week. Not only did they tackle forest fires when they happened but they also set up fire breaks, cleared stones, and were involved in the building of the national parks.

Lauren saw some of the local girls follow the CCC boys around with their eyes, wearing wide smiles. The local boys frowned in their direction, probably wondering how they could compete with well-dressed men who had money in their pockets.

Edward patted her arm and nodded in the direction of where Carly was standing. "I don't think Terry has anything to worry about. Carly only has eyes for him."

Two CCC lads were speaking to Carly, seemingly asking her to go on the amusements with them, but Carly smiled and took Terry's hand. Lauren saw the startled reaction of the boys as they realized she had picked a local boy, dressed in old clothes and with a limp, over them.

Edward moved closer, his citrus-based scent wafting over her face. "So tell me, would you pick me over them?"

Butterflies danced in her stomach, making her feel giddy. Despite them, she retorted, "Don't be silly, Edward. They are just boys, they wouldn't be interested in me. I'm practically an old maid."

"At twenty-three? I don't think so." He held her gaze until she looked away. Then he changed the conversation. "Wonder if any will ask Becky out?"

"I wouldn't if I was them. She hates the park and anyone associated with it, even those CCC boys. She knows they send home twenty-five dollars a month to their families, and she concedes they didn't make her lose her home, but there is no way she would walk out with one of them."

"So I see." They both laughed as Becky turned down one CCC guy after another. Big Will came back carrying two glasses of lemonade and handed one to Becky. The line of young men hanging around her soon scarpered.

"I wish she would put Big Will out of his misery and marry him." As Edward spoke, his gaze held hers. He wasn't just talking about their friends, was he? Yet he'd never asked Lauren to get married, just dropped hints along the way. Flustered, she steered the conversation onto safer ground.

"Edward, should you go and interview some of them for the paper? I think people would like to read about them."

"Are you trying to get rid of me?" he smiled but his eyes were challenging her. He was so close she could count his eyelashes. They were so long, beautiful. Her heart beat so loudly, he must be able to hear it. Her nerves tingled. What would it be like to kiss him?

Furious with the direction of her thoughts, she snapped, "No, not at all. I just don't want to come between you and your work."

To her chagrin, he seemed to know exactly what was wrong with her. He moved even closer, his nearness setting off a wave of sensations. "Lauren, we are both taking a couple of hours off. Now what do you want to do?"

What did she want to do? If only she could be honest.

"Watch the snake charmer." Where had that thought come from? Edward took a step back, his face twisted with a combination of horror and surprise. She'd forgotten how much he hated snakes. "Didn't you know George Freeman Pollock, the guy behind Skyland, used to entertain his guests by playing with snakes? He had the locals catch rattlers and cottonmouths for him."

Edward shivered visibly. "I'd rather him than me. I never did like snakes but don't you go telling Cal and Fred that. With the mischievous streak in those two, they are likely to put one in my car."

"They probably would but it wouldn't be a dangerous one. A rat snake maybe. You could cuddle up to it."

"Lauren!" The warning in his voice made her laugh again. She loved how he admitted his weaknesses. How many men would tell a woman they were scared of anything?

"So aside from seeing the snakes, is there anything else you want to do?" he asked, staring at her face. Why did she feel he could read her mind? Her skin burned. She glanced around, her gaze focusing on a shooting competition.

"Want me to win you something?" Edward offered, as Mr. Flannery shouted at them to give it a try.

"No, I don't want to give him any of my money." Lauren glared at the tall, well-built man with the protruding belly, who'd walloped Cal when he ran off last year. She despised him as much as she did his wife.

"What's he done to upset you?" Edward turned her to face him, holding her shoulders gently.

His touch made her shiver. She forced herself to concentrate on the Flannerys.

"Not just him, his wife too." She told him the story of Mr. Flannery hitting Cal and his disparaging remarks about Cal's mother. Edward threw a scornful look at the man shouting for people to try his shooting game. When Lauren told him about Katie and Mrs. Flannery, Edward's expression was grim.

"People like them make me ill. If I could tell you everything I know about Foxy Flannery and his battles with the law, we would be here all day." Edward took her arm and walked toward the shooting gallery. "Come on, we are going to take his biggest prize. You can get your own back."

"Good afternoon, folks. Try your best."

Flannery's smarmy manner didn't endear him to them. Edward took the gun he offered, pulled out his handkerchief and wiped down the firearm. Lauren had to turn her face away to hide her smile. Flannery didn't comment but his eyes widened at Edward's insult.

Edward wasn't a bad shot but he didn't hit the bullseye on the moving target.

"Better luck next time." Mr. Flannery smirked. The man couldn't hold back his triumph, not that he tried too hard. He went back to shouting for more punters to try their luck.

Lauren wanted to wipe the smirk off his face. She stepped closer to him, trying not to gag at the combined aroma of cheap cologne and sweat. "Can I try?"

"It's not open to ladies, *Miss* Greenwood."

Lauren wasn't about to walk away. She stood her ground, her gaze challenging him. "Why not? The sign says five cents to enter. I don't see anything that says ladies are prohibited."

"Everyone knows a lady can't shoot properly. But it's your money. Five cents for three attempts. The prize is ten dollars."

Lauren knew she should walk away. She had enough problems with the Flannerys without winding up this man. But ten dollars was a lot of money; she could buy sugar, flour, and other staples, as well as help Terry with his school fund. And she'd have the satisfaction of beating Flannery.

She took the gun and walked back to where Flannery had set the target. She aimed, cocked, and fired. Smiling, she returned the gun to Flannery, who had yet to find his voice.

"You cheated. No way a woman could hit a target like that," Flannery shouted as he ran to the target to check. She'd shot right through the bullseye.

"Remind me never to annoy you, *Miss* Greenwood." Edward repeated Flannery's pronunciation but his eyes were smiling. "Tell me, where did you learn to shoot so well?"

"My father insisted I go hunting with him. I had to learn how to shoot so I could avoid killing anything. He dismissed me as being a useless female." Even though she tried to laugh it off, her father's low opinion of her still stung.

Edward pushed her hair back from her face. "He realized what a gem you were, just in time," he whispered.

She didn't want to speak about her father. It was best those particular memories remained in their box. Her pulse racing, her tears not far from her eyes, she put on her most officious tone. "Mr. Flannery, I believe you owe me ten dollars."

Flannery glared at her, his gaze raking her from head to foot, making her wish she could take a bath. "I'm not payin' ya. You cheated."

Edward stepped in before Lauren could say another word. "Mr. Flannery, unless you want to be exposed as a cheat in the *Charlottesville News*, I suggest you pay up. Although I am tempted to write the article anyway. Local lady out-shoots the infamous Foxy Flannery."

Lauren didn't attempt to hide her smile. She watched as Flannery squirmed, his emotions playing across his face.

Flannery turned various shades of red as Edward teased him. He'd been nicknamed Foxy Flannery during the Prohibition days as everyone knew he had a still in the mountain but he never got caught. He handed over the ten dollars but, even as she pocketed the money, Lauren knew she had made an enemy. A dangerous one.

*

The news traveled fast. Cal ran up to them as they walked away, browsing the other amusements.

"Miss Lauren, is it true you shot through the bullseye? I wish I were there to see it." Cal's lower lip curled down.

"I thought you wanted to see the movie, young man?" Edward replied.

"Yes I do, but wow, everyone is talkin' about Miss Lauren. Can you teach me how to shoot that way?"

Cal looked hopeful but his expression turned sulky as Lauren said no.

"You are already obsessed by guns, they aren't toys. Now go and watch your movie."

Edward handed the boy two nickels. "Buy yourself some candy, share with the others, okay?"

"Thanks, Mr. Edward." Cal was gone.

"You spoil the children, Edward."

"It was only a couple of nickels. It mightn't be a bad idea to train the older boys to shoot like you do, Lauren. Does a lad no harm to have those types of skills."

Lauren shuddered as if someone had walked over her grave. "You're talking about the articles calling young men to join up, aren't you? John Thatcher said his Ben was tempted."

"There is nothing wrong in being prepared. Especially as our government knows the Nazis are breaking the terms of the Versailles treaty. They are building up their armaments. And if anyone paid attention to Hitler, they wouldn't dismiss him so easily as a lunatic. He has massive plans for Europe."

"Let's not talk about Hitler or Mussolini today. It's the fourth of July, a day for families and picnics and all things American. For today, you are just a man not a newshound."

"Does that make you my woman?"

Lauren caught herself. She wanted to say yes. But she couldn't.

CHAPTER THIRTEEN

The next evening, Big Will dropped by with some old pieces of wood for Fred to whittle. Lauren, sitting on the porch swing, shifted Maisie onto her other shoulder. The baby had been fussing all day, only sleeping when someone held her. Nanny thought she might be cutting a tooth.

"Evenin', Miss Lauren." He stood there looking but not speaking.

She smiled in encouragement, sensing he had made the trip out from Delgany for another reason. When he didn't speak, she did.

"Did you enjoy the fair yesterday? The children had so much fun. Thank you for the time and money you spent on them. You spoil them, Will."

"They earned it. It ain't easy growin' up without a family."

His wistful expression as he looked to the house made her realize how little she knew about this man who helped them so much. She felt his eyes shift to her face every few seconds. Sometimes she wanted to shake him to make him move faster but he always took his own time. She waited.

"Could I ask you to help me persuade my woman to come for a walk? I need to talk to her about somethin'."

Lauren could take a guess at what it was and understood his nervousness. He wiped his brow a few times with a hanky as he stood waiting at the door.

"Big Will, you look like you are going into the lion's den. Go on in and ask her. Becky loves taking a walk a little up the mountain, especially on nice evenings like this."

Big Will didn't look convinced. "It is a beautiful day, not a cloud in the sky and the sun still up at this time of night, but my Becky, she ain't going to like what I have to say. It might be better if it were rainin'."

More than a little concerned, Lauren stood up and went into the house to fetch Becky. She found her friend up to her elbows in laundry.

"Do you want me to take Maisie?" Becky asked. Lauren shook her head, Maisie now fast asleep on her shoulder despite her moving off the porch.

"Becky, Big Will is outside. He needs to talk to you."

"Can't you see I'm busy? These ain't goin' to wash themselves."

Nanny's voice came from behind them. "Becky Tennant, you can try to hide as much as you like but it's about time you gave that kind man out there a proper answer. He's been courting you since afore you left your mountain home. How many years do you expect him to hang around waiting for you to see sense?"

Lauren jumped when Nanny began to speak; she hadn't seen the old woman when she walked in. Her tone suggested she was tired and upset again. Nanny could be cranky when tired but she wouldn't admit helping with Hope House was too much for her.

Lauren saw the flush at Becky's ears and, knowing her friend might retaliate just as sharply, she quickly intervened. "Becky, go for a walk. We could all do with some space. I'll finish up these. Carly can help me. Off you go."

Becky opened her mouth but with a look at Nanny closed it again. Water drops flew everywhere as she shook her hands dry before marching over to the coat rack by the door and grabbing a shawl. Without a word, she left.

"Nanny! You haven't done anything to help Will. He needed Becky in a good mood, not all fired up ready to attack."

Nanny moved slowly to the table, took a seat and almost fell into it.

Lauren's chest grew tight as guilt filled her. She carefully put Maisie into her cot by the table, praying the child didn't wake. "Nanny, yesterday was far too tiring for you. You've been great since you moved in but you need to rest more."

"How can I? Norma used to do so much and you and Becky are always so busy."

"Nanny, we can manage, we're young."

"I'm old and cranky, is that it?"

Instead of retaliating, Lauren walked over and put her arms around her Nanny. Nanny rubbed her arm.

"I love you, Nanny. We all do. You are overtired, that's all."

"We need to find help for Hope House. We've waited long enough."

"We will find more help, but you are to promise to look after yourself. I couldn't lose you too."

Nanny seemed to drag every bit of strength from her toes up as she straightened, putting a cheeky grin on her face, her eyes twinkling with mischief. "Maybe Big Will could make an honest woman of Becky at last and come live here."

Lauren looked out the window hoping her friend would see what a gift she had.

*

Lauren watched the sun go down behind the mountain as the sky grew darker. There was no sign of Becky. She put the children to bed, helped Nanny to her room, and sat on the porch reading until it was too dark. She was nearly asleep at the kitchen table when she heard Becky's footsteps. She pushed the hair out of her eyes, sitting up, and hoping beyond hope she would be celebrating.

Becky opened the door carefully but jumped when she saw Lauren. "Why are you still up?" Becky whispered.

"Waiting for you. I got worried when it got really late." Lauren saw the tear stains on Becky's cheeks when she stepped into the light. "Would you like some coffee?"

Becky shook her head. "He's goin' away."

"No! Why? Where? I thought he'd live in Delgany forever."

"He says he can't. Says it's my fault." Becky looked younger than her nineteen years for once. Her puffy eyes and swollen face made Lauren's heart break for her, but she couldn't help sympathizing with Big Will too.

"Do you want to tell me what he said?"

"Not all of it. Gene Hillman told him he couldn't give him as many hours in the sawmill no more. The way Will talked, it seems like the Hillmans are struggling more than they let on. He's tried to get other jobs but there's nothin' for him in Delgany and only odd jobs in Charlottesville. Well, aside from…"

When it was clear she wasn't going to finish her sentence, Lauren prompted, "What? Aside from what?"

Becky didn't look at her. "He's been offered a job by Pollock up at the Skyland resort."

Lauren screwed up her face. "That's good news. Or it should be…"

"Lauren, Pollock is one of the reasons the park is progressing. He encouraged the government. Them people stole my land, my home. They're the reason Ma and Donnie and the rest…" The tears flooded Becky's cheeks.

Lauren moved toward her but Becky took a step back, her shoulders rigid. "I told him if he chose the park, I'd never speak to him again."

"Becky, that's not fair. Will needs a job, he has to live. He loves you, he's shown you often enough."

"We'll see." Becky had a look in her eyes Lauren had only seen a few times. It wasn't worth trying to argue when she was in this mood. Maisie moaned from her cot. Lauren picked up the drowsy baby and handed her to Becky, hoping the child's cuddles would help melt the wall her friend had built around her heart.

"I'm going to bed, Becky. Think about what you are doing. A man like Will deserves better."

CHAPTER FOURTEEN

The atmosphere in Hope House was frosty. The children picked up on the tension between Becky and Lauren. Nanny and Becky were also at odds after Nanny had summoned Becky to her room the morning after her evening with Will.

"Why are you and Becky not friends any more, Miss Lauren?" Ruthie asked as she helped Lauren hang the laundry on the line at the back of the yard. "You never laugh any more and Miss Becky looks angry all the time. She scares me."

Lauren put the shirt back in the basket and kneeled down on the grass to give Ruthie a cuddle. "We are friends, darling, but sometimes we disagree."

"Like Shelley and Katie?"

Lauren smiled. "Not as bad at that. We don't fight. Becky is upset over something and she needs time to work out how she is feeling. She still loves you and all the children here. Once she gets her head straight, she'll be back to normal."

Ruthie seemed satisfied with that and they hung out the rest of the clothes together.

Later, everyone was in the kitchen when Ruthie handed Becky a mirror.

"What's this for?" Becky took the small handheld mirror, a questioning look on her face.

"Miss Lauren said you need to get your head on straight. I thought you'd like to do it now."

Lauren burst out laughing and the children giggled as Becky put her hands on her hips, looking at Lauren. Lauren tried to stop giggling but it was difficult.

Between giggles she squeaked out, "I'm sorry, Becky, I was trying to explain your bad mood to Ruthie."

Becky scowled. "I ain't in a bad mood."

"Yes you are, you're behaving like Grouchy used to," Cal offered. "We made Grouchy feel better by feeding her grass." He stood eyeing Becky, making Lauren giggle again. She wouldn't put it past the boy to offer to go pick Becky some grass.

Carly, Maisie on her hip as usual, took over. "Miss Becky, you look so cross you could turn the butter. Miss Lauren, you laughing isn't helpin'. Why can't you two shake hands and forget about what the quarrel was over. Otherwise I think you should go to bed without any supper."

Terry walked over to stand beside Carly, the children following suit.

Becky threw her hands up. "I think we just got told off, Lauren."

Lauren held her expression steady, while holding out her hand. "I'm sorry for laughing."

Becky took her hand, her face set in a serious mask, but Lauren spotted a twinkle in her eye. She pulled the girl into a hug and the children cheered.

"Good. Now can we eat, I'm starvin'," Cal piped up.

Becky ruffled his hair. "Tell me, you weren't really plannin' on makin' me eat grass, were you?"

"I was thinkin' about it." Cal's reply had everyone giggling again.

Becky hugged Lauren and whispered in her ear, "I'm sorry."

"Me too," Lauren replied. "I just love you, and being older…"

"You can't resist tellin' me what to do," Becky interrupted.

Lauren opened her mouth to protest but shut it again. The children were happy.

*

A week later, Lauren walked into the post office, holding her purse tightly—she couldn't risk losing the mortgage payment. She adjusted her hat, thankful Nanny had reminded her to wear one. The sun seemed to be shining all its rays at her head, the humidity making her back feel like a molten lake. She'd love to be off swimming with the children but she had to get this money into the bank.

"Morning, Lauren, weren't the celebrations fun? I can't remember the last time I laughed so much." Miss Chaney grinned, her eyes twinkling. "The fireworks were fabulous. I love them. Kathryn was in great form, I think living out at your place has given her a new zest for life."

"She says the youngsters keep her young. They certainly keep her on her toes. Sometimes I wonder what I have done. The boys are difficult to handle but at least after a fight, they forget about things and let them go. Girls, on the other hand…!" Lauren rolled her eyes.

Miss Chaney picked up some pieces of post, putting them on the counter for Lauren. "I still remember Andrea Harrison."

"Who was she?" Lauren couldn't remember anyone of that name living in Delgany.

"A girl in first grade. She cut off one of my braids. Said it was an accident. But I know she did it on purpose."

Lauren couldn't believe her ears. Miss Chaney was in her sixties, if not older. "First grade?"

"Yes, all those years ago. I refuse to admit how many. I was just illustrating a point. Us women have long memories."

Lauren sighed. What was she going to do about Shelley and Katie?

"Why don't you take a seat and have a nice glass of cold tea with me? I'm trying out a new recipe so you can be my guinea pig. What do you say?"

"That would be lovely. Thank you, Miss Chaney. But first can I post this to the bank? I'll be tempted to spend it otherwise." She was behind in payments on the mortgage but this should bring her up to date.

Miss Chaney took the letter, put a stamp on it, and put it on the pile of post to go out. Then she poured a drink for both of them. Lauren sipped it cautiously as Miss Chaney had a similar reputation to the one she enjoyed when it came to the kitchen. Her eyes widened as the liquid tingled her taste buds.

"This is delicious."

Miss Chaney grinned. "Don't sound so surprised. I'm not completely useless, my dear." She took another gulp. "Although I have to admit it was my third attempt. Even the flowers didn't want the first two. So tell me, what is on your mind? Which girls? Carly seems like no trouble, Clarissa and Sophie are well brought up, and Ruthie and Lottie are just so precious."

"It's Shelley and Katie, the new girl. They are like chalk and cheese. If one says the night sky is black the other will say it's white. It's relentless—no matter what we threaten to do."

"Why not get them a placement in a house for a few days?"

Lauren didn't understand. "Pardon?"

"Ask some neighbors to take the girls in for a few days. Give them a chance of living with a normal family. See how they like that. It might make them realize they have a nice life at Hope House."

Lauren pondered on the idea. It was a good one, but who would take an older child?

"There are many folk who couldn't commit to giving a child a home but would like to help. I think the reaction to Edward's articles proved that. It was a money generator, wasn't it?"

"Yes, he raised about five dollars over two weeks."

"I'm sure some people would love to take a child for a week or so. People who can't afford to give you cash or to take in a child full-time. Might be something to think about? They can't fight if they aren't under the same roof."

"Miss Chaney, I think you are a genius."

"Why thank you, Lauren, you can come again."

*

Lauren ran the idea past Becky and Nanny who both agreed it was worth a try. But who would she ask?

"I think you should ask the Thatchers about taking Katie," Nanny said. "Alice seems to have taken a shine to her. What about asking Ginny Dobbs to take Shelley? She could teach her a trade while she was at it."

"Alice is easy but I'm not sure about asking Ginny. She works all the time."

"You got a queue of other people you could ask?" Nanny asked.

Lauren shook her head. She needed a haircut so that would give her a chance to speak to Ginny.

"I'll go and ask Alice now." She glanced at Becky. "Want to come?" But even as she asked, she knew the answer would be no. Becky hated going up on the mountain now, ever since her argument with Big Will.

"No thanks, Lauren. I'll stay here in case war breaks out."

CHAPTER FIFTEEN

Lauren drove slowly, enjoying the dusk. The pretty pink sky floated above the mountains and now the sun had moved lower in the sky she could appreciate the gentle heat. A wind blew off the mountain helping to reduce the effect of the humidity. She listened to the sounds of nature, thankful that the drilling and blasting noises from the Skyline project had finished for the evening. She arrived at the Thatcher house after they had finished eating.

"Evening, Miss Lauren. I'm not being rude but I have a prior appointment," Ben Thatcher said as he opened the door to her before leaving the house, his ears turning pink. She guessed he was going courting.

"Lauren, so nice of you to drive up here. Is everything all right?" Alice said as she came to the door.

"Yes Alice, I've come to ask you a favor."

Alice's flowers were in full bloom, roses in every color imaginable decorating the outside of the house. She must ask Alice for clippings. Roses blooming around the door of Hope House would make it more attractive.

"We'd love to help. Come in, Lauren."

In the kitchen Lauren smiled before taking the coffee her host offered, the strong aroma making her mouth water. She took a sip; it was just how she liked it. "You don't know what I want to ask."

"I know but we will do anything to help and I know you wouldn't ask unless it was important. John will be back in a few minutes, he just went up to check the animals. The old goat won't come out of the barn, he worries she's dying. I think she's just stubborn but that man of mine looks after those animals like they were children."

Lauren took another sip before placing the coffee on the lace doily on the table. As always, the Thatcher home was clean, with nothing out of place.

"It's about Katie. I think she's struggling to fit in to Hope House. I was talking to Miss Chaney and she suggested I ask someone to take Katie to stay in their house for a few days. Not on a full-time basis, but just to give her time away from the other orphans. What do you think?"

She watched Alice's face but couldn't read her expression.

"We'd love to do that. In truth, it gets mighty lonely around here at night. Ben is off courting and John always has things to do. I spend a lot of time listening to the radio. Evening fireside chats would be better if I had some company to share them with, even if she didn't have an opinion on our president." Alice clapped her hands together. "I wish we could take a child full-time but with the current state of things on the mountain, you know with the park and everything, it's just too uncertain."

Lauren knew Alice was talking about some of the mountain folk being evicted from their land. But that hadn't affected anyone they knew, not yet at least. She pushed the thought out of her mind; she had more pressing things to worry about.

"I know that, Alice, I'd never impose, but I am getting rather desperate. Katie and Shelley do not get on at all. Their fighting is giving me gray hairs."

Alice nodded. "I think Katie needs a mother's love. Not that I don't think you and Becky love those children, but maybe she needs some one-to-one care. When would you like her to come?"

"Why don't you talk it over with John and then come down to collect her when you are ready?"

Alice smiled in agreement. They chatted about this and that as they drank their coffee. John hadn't arrived back by the time Lauren was leaving but in a way it was a blessing. It would give the couple time to talk things over without her being in their way.

*

The conversation with Ginny Dobbs was a lot harder. Lauren asked her to cut and style her hair, showing her a picture of the look she wanted. Ginny chatted away as she cut Lauren's hair to the point Lauren was a little worried she wasn't paying attention. The door to her shop kept opening as various visitors came and went. She hadn't realized Ginny was so popular or so busy. Seemed women did have money to spend on their hair. Some were customers but some just dropped by to have a quick chat. All the time, Ginny's scissors never stopped.

"Have you thought of getting a permanent, Lauren? I think curls would suit you."

"No thank you, Ginny. I prefer it short and easy to style." Lauren couldn't bear the smell of the permanents. She wasn't big into keeping up with fashion. Who had time for that these days? She glanced at her nails, which once had been manicured and long. Now they were short and often had bits of mud or weeds under them. She curled her fingers into her hands for fear Ginny would think she hadn't washed them.

As the time went on, she became less sure about asking Ginny to take Shelley on a part-time basis. The woman didn't have time for a child let alone one as difficult as Shelley. Also, some of the conversations in the salon were eye-opening, an education she didn't think would benefit the girl.

"There. Done. Do you like it?"

Lauren looked in the mirror and gasped. It was much shorter than she'd intended. But when the surprise wore off, she liked it.

"Thank you, Ginny, it looks wonderful."

"I'm glad you like it, but if you change your mind about the wave, you know where I am. Let me brush that off you."

Lauren stood and paid, adding a small tip.

"Thank you, Lauren. Always a pleasure to have such ladylike customers. You take care now."

Lauren was out on the street before she knew it. She stood there for a few seconds wondering if she should go back in but something prompted her not to. Ginny had been the only person they'd come up with but this wasn't the right place for Shelley. With Katie going to the Thatchers, they could cope with Shelley at Hope House until an alternative solution arrived.

*

The Thatchers arrived on the Saturday after Lauren's conversation with Alice. "We had to pick some things up from Hillmans' and got you a few pieces as well. I know you share my coffee addiction, Lauren." John handed her some ground coffee before taking a box out of the truck and carrying it into the kitchen.

Ben followed with some meat. "Pa slaughtered a pig and Ma made some sausages for you. She said to let the ham sit in the smokehouse for a bit. It will taste nicer."

"Thank you, Ben."

Alice turned to face Lauren. "Have you spoken to Katie?"

"No. We thought you might like to ask her."

Alice's face lit up with a smile. "It's like Christmas. Where is she?"

"I'll call her." Lauren hoped the girl would be polite when she came down. To her amazement, Katie walked down the stairs and greeted the Thatchers sweetly. She looked tidy and her hair was braided neatly, almost as if she'd been expecting company. Lauren exchanged a glance with Becky, who shrugged. She'd seen it too.

Katie jumped for joy when Alice asked her. Then she ran upstairs and came down about five minutes later with a small bag and her rag doll. No matter what Lauren had threatened, they hadn't been able to wash the rag doll. Katie always kept it close.

"We'll have her back to you next Saturday. Does that suit you, Lauren?"

"Yes of course. Katie, behave yourself and help with the chores," Lauren said, putting her arm around Katie's shoulders.

"Of course, Miss Lauren."

Lauren coughed, trying to stop herself from laughing. The girl was a good actress, that was for sure. Shelley, meanwhile, was scowling as she watched Katie leaving with the Thatchers.

"Why does she get to go? Mrs. Thatcher is goin' to spoil her and give her lots of cookies and other things."

"She'll have to do her chores there just as we have ours to do here. Shelley, help Becky with the dishes. The rest of you, go clean your rooms. Then the woodpile needs stacking and Terry needs help in the barn. I'm sure Becky has chores for you too."

The children scattered, leaving Lauren staring after the Thatchers' truck until it disappeared into the distance. She crossed her fingers, wishing her friends luck. Maybe Katie wouldn't act out while she was there.

CHAPTER SIXTEEN

Katie came back from the Thatchers the following Saturday with a glowing report. Alice helped Katie down from their truck and held her hand tightly as the two walked toward where Lauren stood on the porch. They were chatting about something, Alice speaking quickly while Katie looked excited.

John handed Lauren a basket. "My missus insisted we bring over some sausages and bacon. Our girl—" John colored. "I mean Katie—likes her bacon crispy. Alice cooked some gingerbread too."

"If I was a suspicious type, John Thatcher, I would accuse you of trying to bribe us," Lauren said, leaning in to kiss the older man on the cheek in thanks.

He colored even more before Alice, holding her hand on Katie's shoulder, said, "Lauren, can we please have Katie to stay again next weekend? Ben could collect her on Friday and have her back Sunday or he could drop her at the school house Monday morning."

Feeling as if she'd lost ten pounds, Lauren sighed with relief. "I take it the visit went well?"

Katie radiated joy. "Miss Lauren, Miss Alice and Mr. John were ever so nice to me. I love their house, it has pretty red-and-white curtains in the kitchen and everything is so shiny and clean. Miss Alice is teaching me how to cook. I helped too, didn't I?" Katie glanced up at Alice, her eyes shining.

"Yes, darling, you did a great job." Alice held Lauren's gaze. "She was no trouble at all. A pleasure to have around. Kept me company when my menfolk were busy."

"That be true enough," John said. "I had to remind young Katie she'd to share the wife with me and Ben." Although John laughed, Lauren picked up on a slight tension between the couple.

"Katie, why don't you go inside and say hi to the others," Lauren said. "They missed you. Can you carry the basket into the kitchen please? We will follow in a minute."

"Yes, Miss Lauren. See you inside, Miss Alice." Katie moved quickly.

Lauren gestured to Alice and John to sit on the porch swing while she leaned against the rail.

"It went well then?" she prompted.

"Yes, it was wonderful, wasn't it, John?" Alice beamed.

John didn't look as enthused as his wife. Lauren waited, not wanting to rush him, but the silence became uncomfortable.

She gave in. "What did Katie do, John?"

"Ah heck, she didn't do nothin'. She's just a mite jealous if Alice spends time with Ben or me. Seems to be very insecure. I don't know how to deal with it. Makes me uncomfortable." John looked worriedly at his wife.

Alice said, "John, we talked about this. Katie hasn't had an easy life so she clings to people. Don't you think so, Lauren?"

Lauren didn't want to offend either party so she chose her words with care. "Katie can get a mite jealous here too but I have never seen her be unkind with it. She enjoys being the center of attention just like all children do. Only it's not possible given we have so many. We try to spend time with each child but there just isn't enough time."

John said, "We know that, Lauren, we weren't being critical. I just hope that by takin' Katie to our house at weekends, we ain't settin' her up to expect more." He twisted his hat in his hands as he spoke, avoiding looking at his wife.

Alice stood up so quickly, John nearly fell from the swing. "We all had a lovely time. It was the first visit, there are bound to be teething problems. That's all it was. No use fussing over it. Let's get inside before we make the poor child nervous." With that Alice sailed past them and into the house.

Lauren stared after her, seeing a different side to the woman who always seemed to follow in her husband's footsteps. John sat, watching his hat as if it would give him clarity.

"John, thank you for taking Katie. Don't feel you have to take her next weekend. Chat with Alice and let us know."

John surprised her by looking at her with such yearning in his face, it took her breath away. "That child has a way of workin' right into the center of your heart. I felt sorry for her at first, when you told us her story an' all. But now, well it's like she was meant to come along. My Alice is just like a bird with a new egg in her nest. All protective and chirpy. I just hope she ain't going to get her heart broke."

"Why would she?" Lauren sensed there was a story behind John's worries that had nothing to do with Katie.

John stood up, patting his hat back into shape. "Don't mind me, Lauren. Alice says I'm a worrywart. Let's get inside, my throat is as dry as old paper."

*

It became a regular occurrence for Katie to go to the Thatchers. Everyone accepted it, even Shelley. Katie always returned with a basket of goodies, which helped ease the jealousies the kids might have felt.

Lauren and Becky were quick to admit the basket of food helped. Without Norma, they didn't have as many baking goods and jars to sell at Hillmans'. They had little extra in terms of eggs too. If Lauren was being fanciful, she'd swear the hens missed Norma singing to them.

One morning, Earl Hillman arrived, carrying a large box of provisions.

"Morning, Lauren."

"Earl, what are you doing? I didn't order these."

"Big Will paid for it. He said to tell you he's coming back next week but not to tell Becky. He wants it to be a surprise."

Lauren clapped her hands. "That should put a smile on her face." She held the door open to allow Earl to carry the box into the kitchen. "This came at just the right time. I was wondering how we were going to stretch our supplies. How are things at the store?"

"Taking it one day at a time just like you, Lauren. Things have to get better soon. I best get back. Can't afford to miss any customers."

Lauren waved him off. As she turned to go back into the house, Terry walked toward her carrying a basket. "Miss Lauren, we've had another visit. This time they left a note and a basket of fruit and some vegetables." He handed a piece of crumpled paper to Lauren.

Please tell my Maisie I loves her. I will try to bring more skins soon.

Lauren looked up in surprise after reading the note. "Did you see anything, Terry? Maisie's parents must live around here somewhere."

"No, Miss Lauren. When I came out to milk the cows this was already in the barn. Shadow must know him or he'd have barked." Terry glanced at the note. "It's nice to see they didn't just abandon Maisie, isn't it?"

Lauren walked to the window and gazed out into the distance. "Yes, but I wish they would come and talk to us. In person."

Terry cocked his head to one side. "Why? You can't help them, you don't have the money to do that. They probably know that, which is why they keep leaving gifts. They'll be back when they can. We just have to look after their baby until they are ready."

With that he limped off carrying the basket into the house. Lauren swallowed the lump in her throat, thinking how lucky they were to have Terry.

*

Lauren, paint in her hair and all over her clothes, finished the last wall of Bart and Norma's room. They'd left it as long as they dared but they needed the space. The boys were too squashed and Terry could do with a place to study. She'd packed up her friends' things, carefully storing them in the attic for when they came back. She'd given Clarissa and Bean first choice of the room but they preferred to sleep in the girls' room as they had always done.

She came downstairs and was surprised to find Becky in tears at the table. "Becky, what is it? Why are you crying?"

Becky never cried, at least not in public. Lauren glanced through the door leading to the living room to check on the children, not wanting them to see how upset Becky was. But they weren't paying attention. They were engrossed in a ghost story Nanny was telling them to while away the rainy afternoon.

Lauren took a seat to the left of Becky, moving a large bowl of potatoes out of the way.

"I found this and it just made me cry. I'm being silly but she's everywhere in this kitchen." Becky held a jar in her hand. Lauren recognized Norma's writing. She closed her eyes, seeing Norma in full health before she'd been struck down. Norma who'd worked harder than anyone to get Hope House self-sustaining, in so much as that was possible.

"Becky, Norma is in the best place. The Blue Ridge Sanatorium is well established, and their staff are used to treating TB."

"I know she needs to be there. It's not just that I miss her." Becky put the jar on the table and took a letter from her apron. "This is from Bart. He's findin' it hard to earn the seven dollars a week to keep Norma in the hospital. He wrote apologizin' for not being able to send money for Clarissa and Bean. He said to send the girls back to him if we can't afford to keep them."

"Send the girls back where?" Lauren replied. "They can't stay in the sanatorium and Bart works all hours. He can't look after them. This is their home and they are staying. We'll manage somehow. Bart should know better than to think we are going to turn out two children because of money."

"Lauren, he didn't mean no offense. He's worried. He knows how bad things are."

Lauren walked over to the sink where she washed out the paintbrush. The last of the paint could be used on the barn, the animals didn't care if the wall colors didn't match. She scrubbed her hands, removing the paint and some of her skin. Only when she had her frustration under control did she speak.

"Norma and Bart are family and families work together to help each other out. You tell him I don't want to hear another word about the girls till he writes to tell me when he can come see them."

"Yes ma'am." Becky grinned. "Why are the children so quiet? I thought they were upstairs but then realized you were up there paintin'."

"Nanny is telling them a ghost story in the living room. They are enthralled but come bedtime I may regret letting them listen."

"At least it's keeping Nanny Kat off her feet. Did you see how swollen they be? She needs the doctor, not that she'll admit it."

"She needs to stop visiting her friends up on the mountain. She walks more in a day than some do in a week. I wish she would take it easier. She's not a young woman any more."

"What age is she?"

Lauren tried to think. Her grandmother had lived through the War Between the States and Nanny was her younger sister. She never spoke about the war so Lauren wasn't sure if she remembered it in person or through the stories other folk told her. People like

Old Sally, Sam's mother, who had been so kind to Lauren. Old Sally was dead now but she'd lived her last years in relative luxury living with Nanny at Edward's home. Sam said his mam got used to sleeping in a warm feather quilt under a roof that didn't leak. Lauren could still see the brand on Sally's neck, put there by the slave catchers when she'd tried to break free during the war years. Sally had been a slave on the Prendergasts' plantation and told Lauren how evil Justin and his family were. Pity she hadn't seen his true colors earlier.

"I've no idea, Becky. She looked after Mama when Mama was a little girl and then raised me. So she has to be at least eighty if not older. She won't tell me. She's real stubborn."

"Who's stubborn? Would that be my girl?" Big Will walked in from the garden, dripping water all over the floor.

Lauren hid her relief. Since Earl had mentioned Will was coming, she'd been looking out for him.

Becky flushed. "Where do you think you're goin'? You're messin' my clean floor. What you doin' here anyway?"

"Becky, be nice," Lauren hissed at her. "Lovely to see you, Will. We've missed you. Thank you for the things you bought in Hillmans'. Here." Lauren passed him a towel. "Want some hot coffee? I was about to make a fresh pot."

"Thank you, Miss Lauren. It be rainin' cats and dogs out there. I knows the ground needs it but I sure wish it would stop comin' down so hard. I got work to be doin'." Big Will sat at the table opposite Becky, who'd pushed the letter back into her pocket and rubbed her face in her arm. "How's my beauty? Did I stay away long enough for you to miss me?"

Lauren hid a smile. Big Will sure was persistent. Becky had been miserable since their argument, but her friend would never admit it.

"I'm not and never will be your anythin'. I done told you, I ain't ever gettin' married."

"I don't mind skippin' the preacher bit, just as long as I can go home to you every night."

Lauren turned her head so Becky wouldn't see her smile. She hoped her friend would see what a kind and honest man Big Will was before it was too late.

"Big Will, that's enough of that talk. The children might hear you." Nanny walked into the kitchen having finished her ghost story.

Lauren watched her with concern. "Nanny, you're limping again. Will you put that foot up or I'm calling in the doctor."

"Stop fussing, Lauren." Nanny tutted.

Becky pushed a cup over to where Nanny had taken a seat. "Lauren can't help it when it comes to you, Nanny Kat. She owes you for all those years you were at her beck and call over at Rosehall."

Lauren swatted her friend across the back of the hand with a tea towel. "Nanny was never a servant, Becky. You take that back."

"No more squabbling, you two. Lauren, did you collect the post? Was there a letter from Mary?"

"Yes, Nanny. I didn't open it as I knew you'd never forgive me."

"Stop being dramatic and tell us what she says. The last letter we got was ages ago. I don't know why the post from California is so slow."

"She's probably busy, Nanny. Let's see what she has to say." Lauren found the letter and opened it up to start reading.

Dear Lauren, Becky, and Nanny,

How I miss you all. Thank you, Lauren, for your recent letter. I got it just before I got Becky's and it was so nice to hear of home. I miss you all so much.

Coleen is coming up for a year old and I can't believe she has yet to meet my family. We ain't seen anyone since

Jed's mother came out and visited last summer. How are things with you at Hope House? Please tell Bart and Norma I am praying for both of them.

Nanny interrupted. "I wish we could go to California and see the little one. Why did they have to go so far away?"

Lauren ignored Nanny and kept reading.

Things are hard out here, so many folk arrive every day looking for work. The people around here aren't so friendly as back home. There are signs up saying Jobless Men keep going, we can't take care of our own. I wish we could come back to Virginia. We both miss it so much and want Coleen and the next baby to grow up around folk we know.

"She's pregnant again. Way she's goin', she'll end up like Ma with seven mouths to feed."

"Becky! Nothing worse than an only child. Coleen won't think the world revolves around her if she has a brother or sister."

Lauren protested, "Nanny, I was an only child."

"Exactly. Lauren, write back and tell Mary to have two more."

Everyone laughed as Lauren playfully stuck out her tongue at Nanny.

"Wonder if Jed and Mary could come back?" Big Will said, chewing on a cookie. "The park is hirin', he could work up there."

Becky got up from the table, her back stiff, her face flushed. "Over my dead body. You know as well as I do the government is just using the CCC boys to do their dirty work. Takin' farms and land from families and pushin' them off the mountain where they were born and their grandparents' parents are buried. It's not right." She marched off up the stairs, leaving Will staring after her.

"What did I have to mention the park for?" Big Will muttered. "I haven't learned nothin' in the weeks I was away. Miss Lauren, I tried to stay away longer to give her time to miss me but it don't seem to be workin'."

"Where have you been, Will?"

"Just about most places in Virginia, Nanny Kat. I didn't take the job at Pollock's place. I've been doin' odd jobs here and there but I can't find nothin' steady. I thought Becky would understand I tried just about everythin' else. The park would give me a secure job on a decent wage, enough for us to get married and..." Will blushed as he stared at his hands.

Lauren poured him more coffee and sliced a piece of apple pie, putting it on the plate in front of him. "Don't mind Becky. The rumors about the national park buying out more properties is bringing up painful memories of her family."

Big Will shifted in his chair.

Nanny raised an eyebrow. "Have you ants in your pants, Big Will, or do you know something you're not sharing?"

"Only more rumors, Nanny Kat." Will looked uncomfortable.

"What now?" Lauren leaned in closer.

"Not everyone who lived on the mountain is gettin' paid to leave. Some are being treated as squatters as their families never filed deeds to register the land. Some like the Hendersons."

Nanny put her shoulders back, sitting as if she had a rod down her spine. "Bill Henderson has a family plot at the back of his place with ancestors going back to the Revolution. His grandfather was alive when I was little. Larger-than-life character, wouldn't take anyone telling him what to do but the first man to volunteer if a neighbor needed help. He cleared that land, tree by tree. Every spring you can see the irises bloom where he planted them for his wife, over a hundred years ago. How can anyone say the Hendersons don't own that land?"

Big Will shrugged as he sat back in his chair, putting distance between himself and the older woman. "Plants, trees, or burial plots don't mean nothin' to those government men in suits who

Becky used to see with the Bramley brothers. They just care about the court records. Not that the Bramley brothers can read them, they can barely scribe their own name. The men in suits been tellin' folk that the records don't lie."

Lauren couldn't believe what she was hearing. Why was the government employing chicken thieves and men with no honor like the Bramley brothers? Those men broke not only the regular law but also the unwritten mountain rules that you didn't steal from your neighbors, especially those worse off than you. They'd pushed Becky's family to the point of starvation. It wasn't fair. She rubbed her temple. "Can't they do something? Go to court and prove they own the land?"

"Yes, Miss Lauren, but that costs money and the mountain folk are short on cash. Someone says it costs two hundred dollars just to go to the court, not counting the attorney fees. Who has that type of money, would you tell me?"

Lauren fumed. It always came back to money. Every single thing.

Big Will said, "People who are illiterate and own less than two hundred and fifty dollars in assets ain't able to vote in Virginia so they can't group together to protest." He scratched his head. "I don't know what's goin' to happen but some of the men I've been talkin' to are determined not to leave without a fight."

"What does Edward have to say about all this?" Nanny asked, looking at Lauren.

Lauren shrugged. "I don't know. I haven't seen him in ages, not since before you took off, Big Will. He's busy with the paper, I guess."

"I don't know what is wrong with the women in this house. Becky disappears when Big Will comes calling and you barely speak to Edward."

Lauren ignored the remark about Edward. "Nanny, you're embarrassing Will."

"No she ain't. I reckon Nanny Kat is tellin' the truth as she sees it, Miss Lauren. There's never been another girl for me since I first laid eyes on my Becky." He stood up and turned to Lauren. "Mr. Edward is a fine man, not many like him around here. Intelligent and educated just like yourself. Brought up in a rich home like you. You got a lot of things in common. Seems to me you could do worse."

Lauren rolled her eyes in response. Seemed everyone had an opinion on her and Edward these days.

CHAPTER SEVENTEEN

Lauren pulled up weed after weed, enjoying the scent of the fresh mud. They had to remove the weeds and fertilize the soil so it would give up its crop the following spring. Norma and Bart used to look after the kitchen garden but now it was everyone's job. Whoever had a spare moment came out to work. Despite the worms, gardening had grown on Lauren. It kept her hands busy but allowed her mind to wander, seeking solutions to the numerous problems facing her.

Becky's voice calling her interrupted her thoughts. "Lauren, there's a truck just turned into the grounds. You expectin' someone?"

"No, Becky." Lauren rubbed her hands on her apron before taking it off and walking around to the front of the house. The grass needed cutting, they couldn't risk snakes or any other pests taking up residence as that was where the children played. Standing on the porch, she recognized the electric company sign. The unpaid bill had sat in the kitchen drawer for weeks. She crossed her fingers the collector would view them with some sympathy.

The driver parked and got out. He swiped his hat off his head. "Morning, ma'am. Company sent me as your bill is past due. I got orders to cut you off unless you can clear the bill in full."

Lauren pulled herself together to reply. "How much is it?" She knew exactly how much it was but she was trying to see what type of man he was. Would she be able to pull on his heart strings?

"Three dollars and thirty-one cents. I'll need the full amount."

Lauren's heart beat faster—the man's lips had thinned as he spoke. He would be difficult to negotiate with. He seemed set on getting his money.

"Would you like a cup of coffee?" she offered.

"I don't have time, ma'am. If you could get the money?" He stepped closer, not in a threatening manner, but one that suggested he was eager to get the job done and leave.

Lauren tried another tactic. "This is an orphanage, mister. Perhaps if you made your bosses aware of that, they would give us a little time."

"They know, ma'am. They be city types. I have my orders." The man took another step toward the power supply at the back of the house.

The porch door slammed in the wind as Becky came out of the house, carrying a crying Maisie on one hip and the jar they kept their savings in in her other hand.

"We have two dollars and ninety cents, mister. That's every penny we have." Becky thrust the money at the collector. "You take it. I got a hungry baby to look after."

The man paled visibly. "I can't leave the power on unless I get the whole amount." He couldn't look them in the eyes as he wiped the sweat rolling down the side of his neck.

Katie came out of the house holding a nickel in her hand. "Here, Miss Lauren, been keeping this for the store. You have it. Miss Alice told me to buy some candy but this is more important, I guess."

"Oh Katie, I can't take your money," Lauren protested.

But Becky took the five cents. She thrust the money at the electric company employee. "Wait here."

Becky thrust Maisie into Lauren's arms before running back into the house, calling the children's names as she went. Lauren stared at the man while he shuffled from one foot to the other.

They heard Becky shouting, asking each child if they had any money hidden.

"But, Miz Becky, I was savin' that for the next time I get to go to the store." Cal's voice soared above the rest.

Lauren heard Becky reply, "I know, Cal, but this is an emergency. I will pay you back, I promise."

Terry spoke up. "Cal, give it to Miss Becky, she needs it more than you do. Here, I have three cents. Do you have enough now?"

"Almost, Terry, two cents more is all I need."

"Take mine, Miss Becky."

Becky came back out, a triumphant look on her face. She counted out pennies until the man had the full amount.

"You tell your boss he took those pennies right out of the hands of babes. He should be ashamed of himself," Becky said as she turned over the last penny.

"I'm sorry, missus, I don't make the rules. It's my job. If I had my way I wouldn't take a penny from a child."

"Go on with ya." Becky took Maisie, turned her back on him, and marched up the steps to the porch door, almost colliding with Nanny outside the front door.

"Wait, please." Nanny hobbled closer to the truck driver, handing him a glass jar. "It's water, not as cool as you'd like but it will quench your thirst. This is a couple of cookies, I'm sure you get hungry on your journey. "

The man ripped the hat off his head and wiped the sweat off his neck once more, his cheeks flushed as he took the drink from Nanny's hand. He gulped it down before returning the glass to her.

"Thank you kindly, ma'am. I wouldn't do this job but for I have six children of my own. They'll end up in a place like this if I don't do what my employer says. There is ten men for every job that's going." He put the cookies through the window of his truck, placing them on the passenger seat. Putting his hat on his head, he took his leave, and walked around to the driver's door.

"We know and we understand. We won't delay you any longer." Nanny stood back and the driver gunned the accelerator and took off.

Becky was the first to speak. "Nanny why were you so nice to that horrible man?"

Nanny, who was watching the truck disappear into the distance, turned toward her to reply. "That man isn't awful, just a father trying to do right by his family. You can't blame him for the Depression. Kindness doesn't cost anything."

CHAPTER EIGHTEEN

Sheriff Dillon met Lauren as she got out of her truck. She sensed he had been watching out for her.

"I'm glad I saw you in town, Lauren, I need to speak to you about something." He didn't look at her when he spoke.

The hairs on Lauren's neck rose. What was it now?

He wiped his brow with a used handkerchief, a flush creeping across his cheeks, shifting from one leg to another. "I've had a complaint. I don't believe a word of it but I have to check it out. Why don't you come into the office and have a seat. Coffee? I need some."

"Sure." Lauren sat, trying to look the picture of calmness when her insides were quaking. She wracked her brain but couldn't think of anything the children had done. He pushed the wooden door open but stood back, allowing her to enter first. It was stifling inside due to the stove piled high with wood. Was he trying to burn away the lingering odor of dried sweat and beer? She tried not to gag, wishing she'd suggested they speak outside.

The sheriff busied himself throwing even more wood on the stove before adding water to the coffee pot. He poured out a cup for both of them, putting hers on his wooden desk. "Don't want to burn you."

He didn't look at her and the silence grew to be uncomfortable. She leaned in to blow on the coffee before taking the cup in her hands, hoping her movement would prompt him to speak. Only when he had drunk half the cup did he speak again; all the while her discomfort was rising.

"A concerned member of the public has suggested you are breaking the child labor rules, Lauren."

Lauren almost spat out her coffee. The idea was laughable. But then she realized he wasn't smiling, his expression serious.

"I found it hard to believe you were sending children to families to do chores."

Lauren put her coffee cup back on his desk. "It's not like that, Sheriff. Some of the children are desperate to find families. As you know, placing the babies is much easier than older children, particularly those that don't look as cute as a button. The children get jealous of Ellie-Mae and Dalton living at the store. One day I was in the post office and Miss Chaney suggested I allow different families to adopt an orphan for a few days."

He focused on her face, his head cocked to one side. "Adopt?"

She clarified. "Not officially of course. But a child like Shelley or Katie could spend time with a family. While they are there, obviously they do chores just as they do at Hope House, but none of the children are working for a living. We're careful who we let have the children and they never go to strangers."

"I guess Miss Chaney thought she was doing something charitable." The sheriff sounded far from convinced.

"I think it's a great idea. Katie in particular…" His eyebrows rose at the mention of the name so she quickly reminded him who Katie was. "Katie—the girl Mrs. Flannery accused of stealing clothes from her shop—she goes to stay with John Thatcher and his wife Alice just about every Friday after school and comes back on Sunday. Their sons are older now and Alice enjoys having a young girl around. She's teaching Katie to bake and do household chores just like any other woman would with a daughter."

"Can she manage? Her burned arm and all…"

"Yes, it's amazing how much she can do given her disability. Katie loves how Alice doesn't treat her any different."

The sheriff seemed to be listening but, when he failed to comment, Lauren continued. "John told me he'd love to adopt Katie properly but he can't make that commitment at the moment. You know the issues with the park people and the mountain folk."

"He has a nice place up there on the mountain. Good man too, never had a problem with him during Prohibition. His wife makes nice meatloaf. You couldn't find better people."

"Exactly! So Katie spending time with them at their invitation is a good thing, isn't it?"

"I suppose." The sheriff scratched his jaw again. "Does John give you any money for Katie's services?"

She retorted, "Sheriff. I'm not selling anything."

"Settle down, Lauren, I'm doing my job."

"Sorry." But Lauren wasn't a bit apologetic. Who had complained? What sort of person would think they would use the children to generate funds?

"John and Alice sent Katie home with a nickel for herself. They sent home cookies for the other children, some coffee for me, and some vegetables from their garden. Alice baked a pie for Nanny. I don't think they did it in return for Katie's labor as they have always been very generous to us." But as she spoke Lauren didn't feel as confident any more; maybe the Thatchers had been more generous than usual as Katie had worked so hard.

"Lauren, stop scowling, it will give you wrinkles. I'm satisfied you are doing nothing wrong. I will close the complaint and that will be the end of the matter."

"Can you tell me who complained?"

"I could but I'm not going to. I've known you from a baby and even when you were little, no more than this high"—he measured a little height off his desk—"you had a temper to give anyone a run for their money. For the sake of peace in our town, forget I said anything."

Lauren didn't say a word.

"Lauren, I'm serious. Don't go borrowing trouble."

"I'll try, Sheriff, but if the person who complained to you mentions anything to me, well I just might…"

Sheriff Dillon looked firm. "Walk away and say nothing. Empty-headed fools don't listen no matter how often you repeat the message."

*

Lauren was going to call on the Hillmans but instead she headed for the truck. She needed to be alone to calm down. When she got this mad, she could start a fight with a paper bag.

All the way home she wondered who might have complained. What if they wrote to the county officials? Ever since Lauren had bought the house and land surrounding it, she'd been threatened with closure. The county liked to keep control over their orphanages. They believed the children would be better in recognized institutions like Saint Joseph's or the Sisters of Mercy or even the county home which was bursting at the seams. Lauren wouldn't let a dog in some of the homes their children had come from. Cal, Ellie-Mae, Dalton, and countless others had suffered abuse at their previous orphanages.

Instead of calming her temper, the drive home only served to stoke it up. Hadn't they been through enough with losing the barn and animals and then her father? She choked back the lump in her throat. The pain was still raw. He'd betrayed her, sold her to another man. But he had, in his own way, loved her.

She arrived back to find Big Will, Earl Hillman, and Bart setting off for an afternoon of fishing. Bart was arguing about the logic of using smaller bait as the fish would be less energetic than they were in the summer. Earl was using something he'd made and Big Will looked as if he'd prefer to stay around the house with Becky.

"Mornin', Lauren, you were out early." Big Will held the truck door open for her as she got out.

"Did you lose your job again?" she teased him, as they hadn't seen him since the day he'd arrived dripping rain all over Becky's floor. He'd written since then to say he was on a job outside Charlottesville. "Thank you again for the food baskets you sent us from Hillmans'."

His ears turned red. "Wasn't much. Didn't gain me any points with my woman, she still tellin' me she ain't settlin' down." Will sighed but Lauren wasn't in the mood to talk about him and Becky. "I'd have been earlier but the sheriff delayed me."

Earl said, "He's a moody cuss that one. Is he why you look like you sucked on a lemon?" He got an elbow in the ribs for his remark.

Bart said, "Careful, son, you never tell a lady she looks anything but her best."

She greeted Bart with a big hug, not having seen him for months. He'd come up to see his two girls and also, she sensed, for some time to clear his head.

Lauren stepped back from Bart, eyeing him closely, watching his reactions. "How is Norma? You look like you're not eating properly."

"Lauren, you sound like Becky. You'd think I was wasting away with the two of you fussin' over me." Bart rubbed his stomach as if to emphasize its size. "Norma is doing a little better. The doctors have her sittin' outside for hours as they said the fresh mountain air is good for her. I gave her them remedies Nanny cooked up and they seem to have helped. I told her about how you said she was to ignore what the doctors said about having months to live. She was tickled pink. She took your advice and now the doctors are scratchin' their heads."

"Bart, that's wonderful." Lauren smiled warmly at this good news.

Bart gave her a look. "Don't be countin' chickens before they hatch, Lauren. She's improvin' but she's still real sick. They did some tests and we are waitin' to hear the results of them. But I'm hopeful she will be home soon."

Lauren decided to concentrate on the positive news and ignore his misgivings. "We are too. We miss the both of you."

"We miss you all too. Ain't many friendly people around that neck of the woods and my landlady, well, she be about as skilled as you are in the kitchen."

All three men laughed at the joke.

"Go on with you or I might just follow and push you in," Lauren retorted, but she was smiling as she walked toward the kitchen entrance, where she found Becky with baby Maisie.

"Where's Nanny?" Lauren asked, moving to take Maisie in her arms. The little girl wrapped her arms round Lauren's neck as if knowing she needed a cuddle.

Becky smiled at the both of them before answering, "She was tired so I sent her back to bed. She's taken on too much with Norma being away." She poured some water into the kettle and placed it on the stove. "Who's upset you? I saw the long face when you got out of the truck before you were joking with Bart and the others."

Lauren kissed the top of Maisie's head before putting her on her blanket on the floor, where Becky had left some toys and spoons, some slightly out of her reach. Maisie crawled over to her favorite, before sitting and chewing on the toy. She then reached for a spoon and it went into her mouth as well.

"Sheriff said he had a complaint about us breaking the child labor laws." Lauren got a drink of water, thankful John Thatcher and the men had plumbed in a proper sink in the kitchen extension.

Becky looked confused. "What? Speak English."

Lauren leaned back against the sink as she took a long sip of water. She stared at Maisie, the picture of innocence playing happily. "Some busybody said we were using the kids to earn money."

"That's a novel idea, maybe we should try it?" Becky's grin slid off her face. "You know I'm jokin'. Why are you lettin' this get to you? You knows we don't treat our children like that. You nearly swatted old Farmer Applejack when Cal and Fred complained he had them sowing seeds for hours. I reckon Applejack hadn't heard a tellin' off like that since his ma put him over her knee and spanked him. Doubt we'll see his face around here for a while."

Lauren grimaced at the memory. Letting Farmer Thompson, known as Applejack because he made quality moonshine, take Fred and Cal to his farm for the day had been a huge mistake. She'd dismissed her gut feeling and allowed the old man who only washed once a year to sway her with stories of what a good time the boys would have. He had horses and she was missing Prince. She'd thought the boys would enjoy the experience. They'd certainly remember it but for all the wrong reasons.

Lauren nodded. "He needed to be told. I don't mind the boys doing chores, that's good for them, but they aren't working for that old cheapskate. He didn't even give them something to eat."

"See!" Becky moved to grab Maisie who'd crawled over to the stairs and was attempting to climb up the steps. "You know we don't use our children to bring in money so why the long face? Sheriff Dillon didn't believe it. He's not a stupid man."

"No, but he wouldn't tell me who was complaining."

"Of course he wouldn't. As I said, he's not stupid, Lauren. He'd know you'd get too het up. Your head doesn't always work proper when the red mist descends. You should have my hair color."

Lauren poked her tongue out at the younger girl. "Becky you need to speak to Will."

A stony expression on her face, Becky went to walk away but Lauren was too quick for her, holding her arms out for Maisie.

"You know he loves you, Becky. He didn't take the Skyland job Mr. Pollock offered him, because of you. Instead he's working all sorts of odd jobs up and down the county."

"That's his choice," Becky muttered.

"Stop it, Becky. You can't keep playing games with that man's feelings. You love him, it's obvious to everyone. He's proved himself to you over and over. Why do you keep pushing him away?"

Becky coughed, tears filling her eyes. "I'm scared. You happy now? I'm terrified."

"Becky, I—"

"You don't understand. I lost everyone I ever cared about because of that park. I couldn't bear to lose him too. Leave me alone. I don't want to talk about this again."

Becky ran away before Lauren could speak. Maisie pulled Lauren's hair, wiggling in her arms, and Lauren noticed that the child had filled her diaper. Lauren had no choice but to see to the little girl. She'd have to find Becky later.

CHAPTER NINETEEN

Was there a full moon or something? Lauren fumed as she marched out of the school house, her hands clenched into fists. How dare the teacher take her to task for the clothes the children wore? They were just as good as many in the class. Sure, the boys wore darned and mended britches, but so did most of the poor families. Hope House children were clean and free of any infestations. But that didn't meet the school teacher's standards.

She stalked down the sidewalk imagining all the things she should have said to the ignorant woman but couldn't. The teacher had caught her off guard coming out of Hillmans' grocery store and she hadn't been in the mood to deal with anyone. The Hillmans were talking about closing their store and going to live nearer their daughter. The trade they were getting wasn't enough to cover their costs. Darn this Depression. No wonder the teacher had got the upper hand.

She heard someone calling her as she walked to her truck. She was tempted not to turn around but that would be rude. Gritting her teeth, she turned to face Mrs. Flannery. Someone had cursed her today, as this was the last person she wanted to meet.

"I've been callin' you, didn't you hear me?" Mrs. Flannery called out.

"No, Mrs. Flannery, I didn't hear you. I have a lot on my mind. Did you want something?"

"I don't like your tone."

Lauren just stood there. She wasn't about to apologize when she was almost one hundred percent sure this woman had been behind the complaint to the sheriff. She knew Mrs. Flannery and the school teacher were close friends.

"I wanted to know what you did with that thief." Mrs. Flannery crossed her arms across her chest.

"What thief?" Lauren chose to deliberately misunderstand. Behind Mrs. Flannery she spotted Ginny Dobbs coming out of her hair salon. She waved a cheery greeting to Lauren but glared at Mrs. Flannery.

"That girl who came to my store." Mrs. Flannery didn't speak, she whined.

Lauren counted to five before answering, determined to hold onto her temper. She was conscious they were standing on the sidewalk and people would see. Her tone cold, she replied, "Katie wasn't guilty of anything but looking for something to eat. Now, if you excuse me…"

Lauren tried to walk past but Mrs. Flannery stepped in front of her.

"You're corruptin' our families letting girls like her go out to different homes. We have good people with clean reputations in Delgany. Just like the schoolchildren, they don't need to be corrupted by children born out of wedlock."

Lauren hesitated. Her head told her to cross the street but her temper won. She snapped back, "That's an old record. It doesn't get any better the more you repeat it. You should settle for what you do best, Mrs. Flannery, and go back to your store." She turned her back and was about to retrace her steps.

"Don't you start talkin' down to me, Lauren Greenwood. We all know where you came from. With your airs and graces, you are no better than the rest of us. Worse, in fact, as your father was a thief and a criminal. He'd be in jail now if your fiancé hadn't killed him. Or was that just a convenient excuse for you murderin' him?"

Lauren pivoted, outrage causing her to battle to keep her composure. Her fingernails dug into her palms as she resisted the urge to slap the woman. Mrs. Flannery stood, hands on hips, ready to continue the battle.

Lauren used her calmest tone, speaking through clenched teeth. "I didn't murder anyone."

"Who says?"

Lauren resisted the urge to slap the smirk off the woman's ugly face. "I do. If you have a problem, go speak to the sheriff. Now excuse me." She turned away but Mrs. Flannery hadn't finished.

"You may have the sheriff in your pocket, but there are some in Delgany who don't act as lapdogs just 'cause you used to be the richest person around these parts. Look at you now. Livin' in a house full of bas—"

A voice called out, "Flossie Flannery, you wash your mouth out with lye soap. How dare you speak to Miss Greenwood like that, and her a lady."

Lauren looked back to see Mrs. Flannery turn on Ginny Dobbs.

"Shut up. You're another of her lapdogs."

Ginny drew herself up to her full five foot two inches, her bosom heaving with indignation, her eyes wild. "I ain't nobody's pet. I knows a lady when I see one and Miss Lauren be it. You aren't fit to lick her boots. You is always complaining about those poor children. If it weren't for Miss Lauren and all those good people out at Hope House those children would be over in the county home or in worse places."

Mrs. Flannery retorted, "They aren't decent. Half of them have no parents. Some haven't any fathers."

The smug look slid off Mrs. Flannery's face as Ginny Dobbs screamed at her, "That's what makes them orphans, you half-wit.

What sort of woman would blame a kid for having no father? That's not their fault, is it? You go on with your day, Miss Lauren, don't pay any attention to that jealous old woman." Ginny Dobbs turned back toward Mrs. Flannery. "You don't come near me again, Flossie Flannery, or I swear I will shave your head and cover you in tar and feathers. That's what they used to do to the women who didn't behave themselves back in Ireland. You are a disgrace. We all know how you earn your extra pay and it ain't by sellin' clothes. You and Applejack have been going at it for years. Now go on with ya."

Mrs. Flannery's veins pulsed visibly in her neck before she gave Lauren a black look and tore down the road. If Lauren hadn't been present she would never have believed the woman could move so quickly.

Ginny moved closer. "Sorry, Miss Lauren, what must you make of me screaming like a hyena in the street. My temper gets the better of me—not that often, but when it does, my old man says everyone near me should run for the hills."

Lauren smiled warmly at the hairdresser. "Ginny, you came to my rescue. I don't care how often you scream at that woman. She has so much hate toward our children. I can't understand why. None of them have done anything to her, least not that I know of."

Ginny looked around before saying quietly, "Flossie's ma was what you'd call a workin' woman. Flossie and me, we went to the same high school. The other kids weren't very nice. In fact some were downright cruel. She didn't help herself. She was a bully and being so much bigger than most the rest of us, she used her fists whenever she felt like it." Ginny looked back at the Flannery store. "Things didn't improve when she got involved with Applejack. Him being wed and all. Rumor has it she got in trouble and had to get hitched fast. Foxy was the only man who'd have her. Then she lost the baby and was never able to have any others. In my more Christian moments, I try to feel sorry for her. But then she opens her mouth and gets nasty about people like you and I forget I am supposed to give the other cheek."

Lauren stared down the road after Mrs. Flannery. Was that the way Shelley would turn out? The child was angry at the world, and used her fists to do her talking. Lauren shuddered. Not if she could help it.

She turned toward her friend. "Thank you, Ginny. It's been a difficult day and I wasn't ready for dealing with that woman."

"Pay her no heed, Lauren. You and Becky, you keep doin' what you do out at that house. No child deserves to pay for the so-called sins of their mother or father."

Ginny rubbed Lauren's arm before turning to walk back to her store.

Lauren watched her retreating back, wondering what Ginny's story was. She knew the woman had an Irish background and was a talented hairdresser, but what had brought her to Virginia? What had caused the look of sadness in her eyes? It had almost felt like her anger about Flossie's view on unwed mothers was personal.

CHAPTER TWENTY

Edward walked in through the door to screams of delight from the children. They hadn't seen him since July. When they had settled down again, thanks to the candy he gave them and children's hour on the radio, Becky and Lauren got their chance to catch up with him.

"Where have you been hidin'?" Becky asked the question Lauren had been dying to ask but couldn't. Her heart had raced when she saw him but his lack of a personal greeting dampened her reaction. *What was I expecting? Him to walk over and lift me into his arms?* Despite telling herself off for being silly, she couldn't help but be disappointed.

"I was up in New Jersey covering a story for the paper."

"Anything interesting?" Lauren asked, her attention partly on Shelley and Katie who were arguing over the candy.

"A fire on a ship that cost a hundred and thirty-seven people their lives, so, yes, I'd say interesting."

Horrified, Lauren took a few seconds to apologize. "Sorry, Edward, the girls distracted me. How could so many die? Were they too far out to be rescued? When did it happen?"

"It's me who should apologize." Edward pushed the hair back from his forehead. He looked like he needed to see a barber and get a good night's sleep. He'd lost a few pounds too, and his skin was rather gray. Lauren wondered was it just the trip up north, or was something else causing him sleepless nights, adding new lines around his eyes…

"I'm still furious," Edward said. "The SS *Morro Castle* was sailing back from Havana to New York. Nobody knows why the fire broke out. Some suspect the ship engines overheated, others blame faulty wiring, some arson and a few papers even said it was a communist attempt to disturb the peace. That later comment was because a crew member rescued a badly burned Cuban writer who has expressed support for some Cuban communist cause. None of it makes sense, the captain didn't even leave the bridge to check the extent of the damage. He also delayed sending an SOS signal…"

"Why?" Becky asked. "I thought the captain had a duty to protect people on his ship?"

Edward sighed. "He does, but this one seemed to forget that duty. Most of those who died were passengers, those in the lifeboats were crew. Some crew did try to help passengers but, by breaking windows to gain access to suites, they inadvertently caused the fire to spread faster by allowing the wind free rein. Those that did get lifebelts didn't know how to use them properly. Consequently, many died when they jumped into the sea by breaking their neck on the life preservers. There were so many mistakes made it's a wonder they weren't all killed. The whole thing is a disaster. They seem to have learned nothing from the *Titanic* or the *General Slocum*."

Lauren had rarely seen Edward this agitated. She could only imagine the sights he had seen. She searched for words of comfort, but nothing came to mind.

Edward stood and walked over to the stove where he poured himself another coffee. "Anyone want a refill? What's the latest news on Norma?"

Lauren wondered how to tell him; after the positive news at Bart's last visit things had taken a turn for the worse. "Bart was here a week or so ago and he had great hopes. It looked like she was turning a corner, but the doctors did more tests. The TB has progressed so she will have to continue treatment." Lauren's voice broke. She couldn't believe Norma—who'd fought so hard to save her little girls and her husband—was now desperately ill. Her husband was doing all he could to save her, but they all knew the odds were stacked against them.

Becky reached out and squeezed Lauren's hand before turning to Edward. "They spoke about an operation, but Bart is against that. He feels she is too weak to survive the surgery. What do you think?"

"I'm a reporter not a doctor. I don't have the expertise to comment." Edward sat back down at the table and sipped his coffee.

"Spoken like a true diplomat, Edward." Nanny leaned on her stick, breathing heavily.

"Kathryn, where did you come from?"

Nanny replied, "I'm old, not sick, despite what Lauren will tell you. I'll sleep when I'm dead. For now, I have a lot of living to do. I'd like to visit Norma, but the girls won't let me."

Lauren ran her fingers through her hair in frustration. Why couldn't Nanny see she was trying to protect her because she loved her?

Edward rose to kiss Nanny on the cheek and helped her into a seat at the top of the table after Lauren fetched a cushion. Nanny had lost weight recently, and Lauren knew that sitting on a wooden chair was uncomfortable for her.

Edward said, "Kathryn, Becky and Lauren are only trying to protect you. You wouldn't be able to fight off TB if you caught it. Norma knows you are thinking of her."

Lauren was grateful for his support. "That's right, Edward, tell her. Nanny won't listen to me, she still thinks I'm a child."

Nanny responded fast. "Not all the time, Lauren dear. Only when you act like one."

Lauren caught the grin on Becky's face before protesting, "Nanny, that's not fair. I haven't got into trouble in ages."

"Weren't you arguing with Mrs. Flannery last week?" said Becky.

Lauren glared at Becky, wanting to throttle her; she'd told her not to mention that incident to Nanny. "It wasn't an argument, just a disagreement."

"That's not what I heard and you can stop glaring at Becky, it wasn't her that told me. She's as bad as you are, keeping me wrapped up in cotton. I may be a bit slower on my feet but there's nothing wrong with my mind."

"So if Becky didn't say anything, how did you know?" Lauren frowned.

"Half the town heard you, Lauren. News travels fast as it's about the only free form of entertainment. Miss Chaney mentioned it when she came up with Mary's letters. She said you put Mrs. Flannery back in her box. She was proud of you."

"Wasn't anything to do with me," Lauren explained. "Ginny Dobbs came to my rescue. The first mention of Farmer Applejack and Mrs. Flannery scurried off so fast you'd think a swarm of bees were after her."

"What was Mrs. Flannery moaning about now?" Edward asked.

"She doesn't agree with us letting the orphans spend time with different families. She suggested our children could corrupt those they came in contact with."

Edward snorted. "That's nonsense."

"I know but she has a big mouth and some listen to her. The school teacher—she's another Mrs. Flannery—told me she's petitioning the school board again. She believes it's time the children had to wear a uniform to school. That way their clothes would be *decent and appropriate*."

"I'll give her decent and appropriate." Becky slammed her coffee cup on the table, spilling some in the process. "She doesn't even have children at the school. We do our best but findin' clothes and food for so many children is hard at the best of times. With Bart gone, we are going to struggle this year."

Nanny spoke softly. "Mrs. Flannery is a very unhappy woman. During Prohibition, that husband of hers had his still up on the mountain so he left her alone. Gave her some peace but now he can drink openly at home, he's always around. She's lashing out because she doesn't know how to handle things."

Lauren, Becky, and Edward stared at Nanny.

"I am not losing my marbles. You can't judge someone else until you spend a moment in their shoes. I think Mrs. Flannery would love to take in a child, give her something to focus on and love."

"She ain't gettin' any of ours. I don't dislike anyone enough to send them to stay with her. Not even Shelley." Becky stood up and raked the ashes in the stove before adding more wood.

"Shelley has her own issues," Lauren whispered. You never knew where the girl was. She eavesdropped regularly. "I know I've said it before but we have to find a way to reach her. She hasn't got over her family choosing to keep her brother not her. She doesn't care they were desperate and couldn't afford to feed both children. In her world, they should have abandoned both of them. That would have been easier to bear. How could any parent decide which of their children should live or die?" Lauren shuddered.

*

Lauren sat on the porch swing, the mending on her lap. She loved sitting out at dusk when the sun disappeared down behind the mountain, leaving a red-and-yellow streaked sky in its wake. Being October, there would be few evenings they would be able to sit out like this. She listened to the sounds of the birds chattering, the crickets singing. If you listened carefully, the owls hooting at each other sounded as if they were having a conversation.

"What are you doing, Miss Lauren?" Katie pushed the door of the kitchen wide enough to let her slim frame through. The eleven-year-old's nightdress blew back and forth in the wind; she looked like she was wearing someone else's. It was hard to get clothes to fit the slight young girl.

"I was waiting to see the first star," Lauren said.

"Were you going to make a wish?"

Lauren smiled as she pushed the mending to one side. "Want to join me? You having trouble sleeping again?"

Katie came forward, climbing onto the swing with her good arm, unconsciously protecting her injured one. She snuggled close to Lauren as she gazed up at the velvet-black sky. She rubbed her burned arm, making Lauren wonder if it hurt.

She pointed up at the night sky. "Look at all the stars, Katie. Have you ever seen anything so beautiful? Do you know there are places in America where people can't see the stars?"

"Why?" Katie's eyes were wide as she looked up at her.

"Those that live in big cities either don't have the room to watch the sky or find it is covered in clouds of smoke and dirt from the factories. We are so lucky here, aren't we? If you see a falling star, you could make a wish."

The girl remained quiet. Something was troubling her but Lauren had learned it was easier to wait for the child to volunteer the reason.

"Think I could wish for a new ma and a pa?"

"Sure, honey." Lauren gave her a squeeze.

"I tried praying for new parents but they aren't interested in girls like me, folks just want babies, don't they?"

"Not all the time, precious. Ellie-Mae and Dalton used to live here and now they live with the Hillmans." The change in Ellie-Mae and Dalton had proved to Lauren that the children, while happy at Hope House, often did better in a home environment. Ellie-Mae didn't use her glorious blonde hair to cover her face any more. The change in Dalton was even more marked. He'd lost the chip on his shoulder and was more likely to be found helping in the sawmill than fighting with the world.

"They're lucky. They get Earl as a big brother."

Earl Hillman had become a regular visitor to the orphanage. He used to help Bart with some of the chores but since the older man had had to move near the sanatorium, Earl had increased the amount of time he spent at the home. Lauren didn't know how they would survive if he and Terry weren't there to help. Mrs. Hillman assured her Earl wasn't slacking on his work at the store. Lauren knew he missed Big Will coming around. She sure did too, but Becky wouldn't even speak his name.

"Aren't you happy here, Katie?"

Katie stared at the sky for a bit. "I guess. It's nicer than the last place I lived. But I want a real family, Miss Lauren. I want to belong to someone."

"You do, darling, you're part of the Hope House family." Lauren cuddled the child, wondering again if she'd made a mistake allowing local families to take the orphans for a spell. Was it cruel to give them a taste of family life only to steal it away again? "Did you have fun staying with the Thatchers?"

"Yes, ma'am. Miss Alice is a great cook. She makes lovely meatloaf, it's nicer than Becky's but don't tell her I said so." Katie licked her lips.

Lauren could tell she was holding something back. "But…" she prompted.

Katie held Lauren's gaze. "I love staying there, but when I have to leave, my heart gets so big and sore, I think it just wants to burst out of my body. I get a lot of water in my eyes too. That doesn't feel so nice."

She snuggled her face into Lauren's side. Lauren stroked the girl's brown hair as she tried to think of how to reassure the child without making any promises.

"Katie, the Thatchers would love to keep you with them but with the Depression, people can't afford to do the things they want to."

Katie pushed away from Lauren. "When will the Depression be over? I'm sick of it."

"We all are, child. Oh look, that was a wishing star. Make a wish."

"Nope, Miss Lauren. Wishes are for babies. They don't come true. Not for kids like me. G'night."

Katie jumped off the swing and slunk back into the house. Lauren let her go, knowing there was nothing she could say to make the girl feel better.

How Katie had come to end up at Mrs. Flannery's store, nobody knew. She hadn't been listed as missing and, when she'd been unable or unwilling to tell where she was from, Sheriff Dillon had suggested Lauren allow her to be properly adopted.

Lauren didn't pick up the mending again but stayed where she was, swinging gently back and forth. How could she help Katie? She knew Alice was desperate to take the child but John worried about the situation on the mountain. The plans for Shenandoah Park included building a park on areas populated by people. At first, Pollock, the owner of Skyline, who was employing lots of the same mountain people, had said nobody would be forced to leave. But now that seemed to have changed. Edward had written a number of newspaper articles on the park's progress. She'd read the paper and knew he tried to see the point of view from both sides.

As she had told Katie, there were families who never got to see a real wild animal or the stars on a clear night. If the park went ahead, these people would have a place to go to see all the things the locals took for granted. But then what of the people who lived on the mountain? The land had been in the families for years. They didn't want to leave, they knew nothing of living down in the valleys. It was a bad situation and would only get worse.

She couldn't do anything for anyone right now. She had to get a good night's sleep. Maybe when morning came she'd have a solution for Katie.

CHAPTER TWENTY-ONE

The next day Lauren drove up the mountain, trying to ignore the noise coming from farther on the ridge. She knew the workers on the Blue Ridge Highway were only doing their jobs but the constant noise echoing over the mountain disturbed the peace. No wonder people were reporting more sightings of bobcats and other animals that usually took refuge higher up. They probably didn't like the dynamite charges used for clearing the roads any more than humans did.

She drove past Becky's old home, or where it used to stand. All that was left was a burned-out ruin. She tried not to look, not wanting to remember Hetty Tennant standing there proud as ever, telling Nanny she didn't need any help. That was Lauren's first introduction to Becky's mother and she'd come to admire the woman for surviving with seven children alone for so long.

She drove on until she reached the Thatchers' home. John opened the door, hailing Lauren with a wave and a shout.

"Mornin' Lauren, you're out early."

"Not too early, I hope." Lauren parked the truck, walking up the path to the door. The white-haired man gave her a hug, which she gladly returned. How many times had this man and his wife come to the aid of Hope House, not just financially but practically as well as emotionally?

"How is Nanny Kat? Is she doin' what you tell her?"

Lauren laughed. "As if! The older she gets the more stubborn she becomes. She's supposed to rest her leg. Doc Baines does his best, but Nanny doesn't pay much attention. She thinks she's a gal in her twenties."

Alice came to the door. "What are you doing standing on the doorstep, Lauren? Come in and sit down. Would you like juice, water, or coffee?"

"Juice would be lovely, thank you, Alice." The rich scent of gingerbread filled the air. "I need to speak to you both, do you have time to sit with me?"

"Always have time for you, Lauren. Let me just tell Ben to get on with the chores." John headed outside as Alice placed a glass of juice on the table and offered Lauren a slice of apple tart. "I know you prefer gingerbread, but it's not baked just yet. It will be ready when you are going home. I'll wrap it up for you."

"Alice, you don't have to give me something every time I come here." But even as she protested, Lauren knew whatever Alice could spare would help them at Hope House. Every penny she had was stretched and triple counted before it could be spent.

"I like baking and there's only so much sweets my two will eat." Alice tried to smile but failed. "It helps me keep busy and keeps my mind off other things."

"Like the park?" Lauren prompted, hoping it wasn't Katie she was worrying about.

"Yes." Alice frowned. "If I met the men who decided it was a good thing to push two thousand people out of their homes for the sake of a park, I might just shoot them myself."

"You haven't been given notice, have you?" Lauren swallowed back the fear in her throat.

"Not yet but many of our friends have. We guess they will get to us eventually."

Lauren's stomach churned. She fought against the nauseous feeling and whispered, "They can't make you go, can they?"

"They say so. John went to see a lawyer, but he said even though John's daddy filed a deed meaning the land is ours, if it comes to it, we have to sell. It's a government order."

"Hasn't come to anything yet so stop borrowin' trouble, Alice." Although John smiled at his wife, Lauren saw the anxiety in his eyes.

Alice gave her husband a shaky smile before turning back to Lauren. "You didn't drive up here just to drink juice, Lauren. What's on your mind?"

Lauren couldn't ask them to take Katie on now. They had enough to think about. She pushed the glass and the blue-and-white china plate to the side. "Thank you for the lovely treat, Alice. I have business farther up on the mountain. I best be going."

"Lauren, I'm the mother of five boys. I knows when someone is lying. Why did you really come here? Is it about Katie?" Alice clutched her hands in front of her heart. "You haven't come to tell us she's found a home, have you?" Before Lauren could answer, Alice continued, "That would be wonderful for Katie and I want her to be happy but…" Tears filled her eyes. "Ignore me, I'm being selfish."

"No, you're not. You love Katie. I did come here for another reason. Sheriff Dillon had a complaint about us using Katie to get money for the orphanage."

Alice frowned. "That's nonsense. Who would make up some lies?"

Feeling awful, Lauren had to tell her. "I don't know… but I thought maybe it would be better for you to stop taking Katie for a while."

"Never." Alice slammed her fist on the table. "I won't live my life on someone else's terms. I love her. Just as much as I love my boys. We want to adopt Katie, Lauren. Even if the worst happens, no matter where we end up, the child is coming with us. Just like she would if she'd been born to me."

John gaped at his wife, his emotions hard to read. "Alice, we spoke about this. It's not fair to put that on the child. We could end up leaving Albemarle County, maybe even Virginia."

Shocked, Lauren stared at him. She couldn't bear to lose these people. Not just because they were so generous to the orphanage, but she valued them as friends. She didn't want them to leave, what could she do to help them stay? She wanted to say something but Alice hadn't finished.

"John, we've been married a long time and I always took your word as law in our home. I don't like to go against you, but this is important. My heart bleeds every time we take Katie back to Hope House. Every time I say goodbye, I leave a little bit more of myself behind. I want to wake up every morning hearing her voice, feeding her, looking after her. Please, John, let her come and live with us. It will help us both. We will have someone to focus our love for this home, this mountain, on." Alice looked around her beautiful home. "We've been lucky, John. We raised five fine boys to adulthood in this place. We ain't buried any of our babes like many folks. They may take our house and our land, but they can't take our memories. Or our family. We can make another home, maybe not as fine as this one but a home all the same. Katie belongs with us and we need her just as much as she needs us."

Lauren wanted to disappear. She didn't know where to look, uncomfortable at being witness to such a private moment. "This is a big decision. I'll go and let you talk."

"No, Lauren, we done enough talking. Katie is coming to live with us and that's final." Alice stood and pushed her chair in under the table, her hands clasping the back, the whites of her knuckles visible.

John Thatcher cleared his throat a couple of times. Then he stood up, and moved toward his wife. He put his arms around her and hugged her, whispering something in her ear. Lauren's face burned but she didn't move for fear of embarrassing them by reminding them of her presence.

John kept his arm around his wife and turned back toward her. "You heard the lady. When do you think Katie would like to move in?"

Lauren gulped, her throat as dry as the frying pan she'd left on the stove too long. She tried again but the words wouldn't come. Taking a quick drink, she stood up. "I think Katie would say yesterday."

They all laughed. Lauren stepped toward Alice and they hugged.

"Can we come and tell her?" Alice asked.

Lauren was tempted to say yes, wanting to see Katie's face, but it wouldn't be fair on the other children. "Let me bring her up to you. It'll make it easier on the other children."

Alice turned this way and that. "I have to get her room ready. She likes my wedding quilt on her bed. She prefers it to the family one I made as she said that caused her sadness." Her face lit up. "I can make a new one with pieces of Katie's old dress, show her she is a member of our family. She'll like that. Maybe we could get her a pup too. She's mad about Shadow, talks about him endlessly."

"Alice, slow down and give the girl a chance to settle in first." John kissed his wife on the cheek. "Now let Lauren go back to Hope House."

Blushing, Alice apologized. "Sorry, Lauren, I get too excited."

Lauren smiled at her friend. "Never be sorry for loving children, Alice, especially our Hope House ones."

She drove down the mountain feeling much lighter than she had done that morning. Katie was getting her dream.

CHAPTER TWENTY-TWO

The children were eating lunch when Lauren returned.

"Carly, Terry, could you mind the children for us while I speak to Katie with Becky please?"

"Sure," Terry replied. "Who's playing baseball?"

The shouts of approval rang out before turning to groans as Becky reminded them they had to clear the table, wash the dishes, and refill the wood box before anyone went playing ball.

Katie, looking white with fear, followed Lauren out to the porch, Becky bringing up the rear.

"Am I in trouble, Miss Lauren?" Katie's voice shook.

"No, sweetheart, far from it. Do you remember a few weeks ago when we spoke on the swing? You said real homes were only for babies."

"Yes." Katie looked down shyly. "I told you I wouldn't wish on the star, but I did anyway."

"I thought you might have. Katie, we don't want you to leave Hope House, we love you so much. But we know you want to be part of the Thatcher family." The child's face lit up with anticipation. "So, I guess the question is, when do you want me to drive you home?"

"You mean it? They are taking me to live with them in their beautiful house?"

"Alice and John Thatcher want you to be their daughter, but they might not be living on the mountain for much longer. I will leave them to explain why. If you say yes, you may have to move away. You might not be able to come and visit us."

"I'd miss you, Miss Lauren, and you, Miss Becky, but I love Miss Alice and Mr. John. I want to be part of a family, a real one. I don't care where we live so long as we are together."

"Then go and get your things, Katie. Lauren will drive you home," Becky said.

Katie ran out of the room, not stopping to hug either of them.

"Out of the mouths of babes," Lauren said to Becky, smiling sadly. "That's all they want, isn't it, to have a real home. They don't like living at Hope House."

"She's overexcited, Lauren. Our children love livin' here because we give them a home where they are loved, encouraged, and safe. But we all need roots, even us grown-ups." Becky walked to the porch rail and stared into the distance. "I miss the mountain and my home every day. I wonder where Mark and Luke are, are they safe? I'd like to see Donnie's and Ma's grave. I can't have the answers. Maybe I will never get them." Becky turned back to face Lauren. "Katie gets her dream come true. She gets her happy ever after. Isn't that what we want for all our children?" She squeezed Lauren's arm before she headed into the house, whispering, "And for ourselves?"

Katie came back out onto the porch with a small bundle in her arms. It was pitiful to see her whole life wrapped up in a clean cloth. Tears were running down her face.

Lauren took a deep breath. She didn't want the child thinking she didn't have a choice. "What's wrong, Katie? You don't have to leave. We aren't pushing you to go away. You always have a place with us."

"No, I want to go but I'm sad too. I'm going to miss everyone, especially you and Shadow."

Lauren held back her smile about being in the same category as the dog. "You can visit us anytime you want. Shadow will miss you too." Katie moved closer to Lauren, who put her arms around her. "I know you will be very happy. Your new parents love you so much, Katie."

"Will they change their mind? When they get to know me, I mean?" Katie's eyes went to her arm.

"No, darling, they want to be your parents forever. They love you and know you are perfect just the way you are." Lauren put her finger under Katie's chin, gently forcing her to look up. "Shall we go say goodbye?"

Katie nodded, looking rather scared.

Lauren took her hand and walked with her to find the others. It shook her that no matter how often you reassured a child they were loved, their past was always there. With time and patience Alice and John would persuade this child how wonderful she was. Just like Gene and Vivian Hillman had done for Dalton and Ellie-Mae.

*

Shelley threw a tantrum when she heard the news.

"They should have picked me. I'm perfect, I have the use of both my arms."

Horrified, Lauren put her arms around Katie, as if to protect her. "Shelley! Go to your room now."

"No. I won't. You made this happen, Miss Lauren. You always hated me from the first day you came here. First you find Ellie-Mae a home and now her. I'm going to have an accident or get a scar on my face and maybe then you will find me parents." Shelley screamed and screamed until Carly gave her a swift slap.

Carly yelled at her, "If you were as kind as Katie or as sweet as Ellie-Mae someone might want you."

Shelley pushed Carly to the ground. The boys cheered as the two girls started pulling at each other's hair. Lauren was about to pull them apart when she saw Becky reach for a bucket. The girls were so engrossed in fighting, they didn't see the cold water until it hit them.

Becky stood, eyes flaming, with the dripping bucket in her hands. "Behave yourselves. Carly, you should know better. Shelley, go upstairs. I will deal with you later. The rest of you say goodbye to Katie. She's lucky to be gettin' away from here. I wish the Thatchers would adopt me too."

Shelley ran but Carly came over to apologize. "I'm sorry for fighting. Katie, don't forget to come and visit."

"Thanks for always sticking up for me, Carly. I'm sure you will get new parents too," Katie said.

"I don't want a family. I got exactly what I want just here. I best get dried off. See ya."

Carly ran off, leaving the rest of the children to say goodbye.

*

When Lauren returned from the Thatchers, she found Ruthie sitting on the porch.

"Are you all right, Ruthie?"

"I was waitin' for you to come back."

"I like that. Do you want to sit on the swing for a bit?"

Ruthie shook her head. "Becky says your dinner is waitin'. I just wanted to know if you were lookin' for a home for me." She stared at the ground the whole time she spoke.

"Is that what you want?" Lauren said, trying to hide the tremor in her voice. She couldn't bring herself to think about Ruthie leaving. She loved her just like a daughter. They had a connection.

"No, Miss Lauren. I never want to leave you."

"Come here, Ruthie." Lauren sat next to Ruthie and put her arms around the girl, and despite her being six years old, she picked her up and put her on her knee. "I don't want you to leave me either. I love you."

Ruthie wrapped her arms around Lauren's neck and squeezed. Then she scrambled off. "Becky said she needs to talk to you about Shelley. They be arguin' a lot. Carly took us to the lake, but we could still hear Shelley screamin'. She's very sad, Miss Lauren. I don't think she likes living here no more."

Lauren held the child's hand as they walked into yet another storm.

CHAPTER TWENTY-THREE

Lauren looked up from the ironing as she heard the sound of wheels outside. She unplugged the iron and went to open the front door. Was it Big Will? He'd sent a note to say he would call for dinner. Becky hadn't commented but had taken most of the children to the lake. It being Saturday they didn't have school today. They were going fishing for dinner; at least, the older boys were fishing. The younger ones and the girls were going swimming. It was just about warm enough. Shelley had been very difficult for the past two days and had stayed back. For now she was upstairs and it was a relief to Lauren to have some quiet time to herself.

"Sheriff Dillon, how are you?" Lauren greeted the man but wondered what brought him here. If the boys had been in trouble in town, she'd have heard about it already. "Come in please."

She held the door open, but he stood near his car. "Got a visitor for you, Lauren. Can you come and get him from the car? He doesn't like me much. Maybe a woman would be better."

Intrigued, Lauren headed down the steps and toward the car. She saw a toddler sitting in the back seat, scowling out the window.

"A boy. What's his name?"

Sheriff Dillon shrugged. "I don't know. I can't get him to speak."

"Where did you find him?"

"I went out to do my rounds and found him digging through the trash behind my office. Guess he was looking for something to eat. The person who dropped him off must have been invisible.

There was no sign of anyone around and nobody saw anything, yet he doesn't look like a kid living on the streets for long. He's starving but his clothes are clean, well they were before he fell in the trash."

Lauren knew someone in Delgany must know about this boy, but for whatever reason they weren't talking. The sheriff's office was on the main street and nobody could do anything without it being reported on and discussed at length. It was one of the drawbacks of living in a country town.

She approached the car window. "Hi there, I'm Lauren. What's your name?"

"Home." The boy's green eyes, large in his gaunt face, stared at her. Lauren opened the door and held out her hand. The child moved closer to the edge of the seat but didn't get out of the vehicle.

"You want to go home? I might be able to help with that if you tell me who you are and where you live…" Lauren smiled at the boy.

"I live up there." The child pointed to the mountain.

Lauren didn't take her eyes off the boy but spoke to the sheriff. "Maybe Nanny will recognize him, or Becky? If not Big Will is due for dinner, he knows a lot of people up on the mountain."

"Dinner, you say?" the sheriff said, looking hopeful.

Lauren turned to him and smiled. "You're welcome to come but there might be fireworks. Big Will hasn't been here for a while. We'll have fried fish if the children do well down at the lake."

The sheriff's face lit up, although he ignored the comment about Big Will. "They gone fishing? Perhaps I should wander down there and check they are safe."

Lauren laughed. "Off you go, Sheriff."

The sheriff hesitated, looking from the boy to the lake and back.

"Go on, Sheriff, take some time to yourself and if you catch a fish, Becky will cook it for you. I'll take our visitor into the house.' She turned back to the child. 'Would you like something to eat? Are you hungry?" The boy nodded. "Come along then."

Lauren's breath froze as she looked at his legs. One was all crooked and misshapen, but he managed to walk up to the front door. He swung his leg out in an odd manner but the strange motion got him up the steps.

She held the door open as he walked inside, looking around him. "Big."

"Yes it is, but when all the children come back, you won't think that. Come into the kitchen and let's get you something to eat. Would you like an egg?" Becky had boiled eggs that morning to make sandwiches so she didn't have to cook anything.

The boy sat up at the table and Lauren took that as a yes. She took the shell off the egg and cut it into smaller pieces. She sliced up a piece of bread into strips and gave the plate to the child. He almost swallowed the plate in his haste to eat every bit. Hadn't the sheriff tried to feed him?

She heard Shelley come down the stairs. "What you doin', Miss Lauren? Who is that?" Shelley hadn't wanted to go fishing. She was supposed to help Lauren with the chores but she'd stayed in her bedroom up till now and Lauren hadn't pushed her.

"A new boy."

"What's his name and what's wrong with his leg?" Shelley said.

"Shelley. He's right here. Why don't you ask him?"

The boy didn't answer when Shelley spoke to him.

"I'm going to call you Pip like the boy in *Great Expectations*. Becky is reading the story. It's about a boy in England, that's across the sea from Virginia. Where did you live?"

"Mountain."

"So are you going to stay here, Pip?" Shelley asked, her hands on her hips.

"Not Pip. Joey," the boy said, frowning.

Shelley flashed a satisfied look at Lauren before asking Joey how old he was.

"I is three. I want out now. Got to pee-pee."

"Shelley, can you show Joey where the bathroom is, please?" Lauren said.

To her amazement the girl agreed and walked the boy upstairs with a smile.

*

Becky returned without the children but holding a brace of fresh fish.

"Sheriff said to tell you he caught the biggest one. He said you promised I'd fry it for him. He also said he brought us a boy."

"I could fry it but I thought you'd prefer we don't risk that." Lauren smiled. "Wait till I tell you. Shelley is smitten by our new arrival. She found out his name is Joey and he comes from somewhere on the mountain and he's three years old. She's been playing in the living room with him since he got here."

"Shelley?" Becky was wide-eyed.

"Yes. She's clucking around him like an old mother hen." Lauren nodded toward the living room.

"This I got to see." Becky moved silently to the door of the living area and looked inside. Lauren got on with peeling potatoes for dinner. There were a lot to peel given Sheriff was staying and Big Will was due too.

"Lauren, she's like another person. She's tellin' him the story of Pip and Estella. *Great Expectations*. And here was me thinkin' she didn't even listen when I told them stories."

Becky gutted and fried the fish while Lauren peeled yet more vegetables. In time the boys and girls returned from the lake. Lauren told the sheriff what they'd found out.

"Maybe I should employ young Shelley as my deputy. That's more information than I could get out of him."

Nanny put a bowl of mashed potatoes on the table. "Children trust other children, don't be hard on yourself, Sheriff."

Joey insisted on sitting beside Shelley. She helped him with his meal, making sure there were no bones in his fish. She gave him a bath and put him to bed, reading him a story. She stayed by his bedside until he was sound asleep, despite her favorite program being on the radio.

"Miss Lauren, he's asleep now but he was cryin' just before. I asked was his leg hurtin' him but he wanted his papa. Said he'd gone away and left him. Then he asked was I his mama now. I is only twelve, how could I be his mama?"

"I think you looked after him so well, Shelley. You did a really good job. I'm proud of you," Lauren said.

"You are?" Shelley gave Lauren the brightest smile before turning to Fred, a serious expression on her face. "You are to call me if he cries during the night, you hear? He's little so don't you dare make fun of him or let any of the others do it or I'll box your ears."

Lauren couldn't look at Becky for fear of laughing. It hadn't taken Shelley long to revert to her old self but at least she had a reason this time. They heard the gravel on the driveway crunch as a truck approached.

Becky stood up. "I'll go."

Lauren exchanged a glance with Nanny but stayed silent. They both listened as the truck door slammed.

Becky's voice trembled. "What are you doin' here drivin' that thing?"

"I work for the park. It comes with the job."

"I don't care what your job comes with. You've no reason to be here. Go away."

"Becky, I tried gettin' another job but there's a Depression on. We should be grateful—"

"Don't you Becky me. You made your choice." Becky walked through the front door, slamming it behind her. She didn't even look at them as she stormed up the stairs, the sound of her bedroom door closing enough to wake the soundest sleeper. On cue, Maisie started crying. Lauren jumped up, as did Carly.

"I'll go to Maisie, Miss Lauren. You might want to check on Big Will."

Lauren took the girl's advice and walked out onto the porch where Will was standing staring at the house.

"Will, I'm sorry about Becky. Come in and have some dinner."

"I don't think that's wise, Miss Lauren."

"I insist. You've had a long journey from Charlottesville and, besides, we need your help."

He eyed her suspiciously.

"I'm serious. Sheriff Dillon found another child and we were wondering if you recognized him. Please come in. Joey is about three and has a wasted leg from polio. At least we suspect that is the cause."

Will took his hat off and walked in the door. He nodded to Nanny and the rest of the children before walking into the kitchen. Sheriff Dillon joined Will at the table as Lauren heated up dinner for him.

"Do you know of any family missing a child of Joey's age?"

"No, Sheriff. Polio is something a lot of mountain families keep quiet about but I ain't heard of any missing children. I'll keep my ear out though."

Lauren dished up the plate of food but Will just stared at it.

"Will, eat up. We can't afford to waste food."

Will took a couple of mouthfuls but pushed his plate away. "I'm sorry, Miss Lauren, it was wrong of me to come and surprise you like this. I best be on my way."

"Stay here and I'll try to persuade Becky to come down." Lauren ran up the stairs, not giving him a chance to decline.

She strode into Becky's room. Her friend lay in the bed pretending to be asleep.

"Becky Tennant, you get downstairs and talk to that poor man. After everything he's done for all of us, you can't treat him this way."

"He made his choice, Lauren. I ain't playin' second fiddle to the park." Becky turned over on her side but not before Lauren saw the stubborn set to her chin. It would be easier to move the mountain than to get Becky to change her mind. She wanted to shake some sense into her friend but that would only make things worse.

She walked slowly down the stairs, her heart breaking as the hopeful look on Will's face dimmed. He stood up, playing with his hat, his eyes on the floor. "I best get goin'. I thought if I took the job, she might see reason. That was stupid."

"I'll come with you." Sheriff Dillon stood up and pushed his hat on his head. "Thank you kindly for a lovely meal. Please pass on my respects to the others. Come on, Will. I got a bottle of Scotch back in the office with your name on it."

"Thanks, Sheriff, but it looks like I should be lookin' for a new job. I can't give up that hot-headed, stubborn woman, so help me."

"The Scotch will help tonight. You can handle the job tomorrow."

Will didn't reply but walked, his shoulders slouching, out the door. The sheriff followed. "I'll be in touch if I hear anything more about Joey."

CHAPTER TWENTY-FOUR

The next morning, there was no sign of Becky. When they checked her room, her bed was made. Lauren reckoned her friend needed some space to think about Will. She was glad Becky was gone—she was so mad at her for hurting Will. Again!

To Lauren's surprise, Shelley continued to spend every minute with Joey, who seemed content to be around her. She let him come with her while she did her chores, explaining what she was doing. Lauren watched, amazed, as Shelley allowed her gentle caring side to shine through. If someone had told her a year, or even six months ago, Shelley would remind her of Carly at times, she would have said they were lying.

"Where do you think Joey came from, Miss Lauren? He says the mountain but where?" Shelley asked as she sat on the couch, Joey asleep beside her. The other children were playing outside but Shelley wouldn't leave the young lad. "The Thatchers don't know him. Big Will doesn't know him either. Does the doctor know what happened to his leg?"

"He thinks Joey had polio." Lauren didn't have to explain what that meant. At twelve years of age, Shelley had heard about it before.

Shelley nodded vigorously. "Like the president. That's good, isn't it?"

Lauren stared at the girl, trying to understand her thinking. She sensed for once the child wasn't trying to be nasty. "Shelley, how could having polio be a good thing?"

"Well it didn't stop the president getting the best job in America so Joey can do what he wants when he grows up. If anyone tries to stop him, they'll have to deal with me."

Smiling at the idea of Shelley fighting off anyone who bullied Joey, Lauren ruffled the girl's hair.

Shelley inched closer to Lauren. "Miss Lauren, can I ask you somethin'?"

Surprised at the child looking for physical contact when she usually stayed miles away from adults, Lauren drew her closer. "Sure, Shelley."

Shelley looked up at her a couple of times before glancing at Joey. "Do you think God sent Joey to me 'cause my parents took my baby brother away? Is Joey like a replacement?"

Lauren had to think how to answer without hurting the child. "Shelley, I love how you adore Joey and you are very good at looking after him, but he isn't yours. His parents may come back for him just like yours might."

Shelley moved, putting distance between them, shaking her head. "Mine? They don't want me. They wouldn't have left me behind if they did. If they was going to come back, they would have done it already. It's been three years, five months since they left."

Disbelief made Lauren ask, "You keep count?"

"I used to." Shelley held her gaze, showing she wasn't lying or seeking attention. "I stopped when Joey came. Up till that time, I marked off the days on a tree over there. I told myself they would come back when I was older. I'm twelve now, I know that was stupid."

Nanny's stern voice came from behind them. "Shelley, you are not stupid. Don't put yourself down, child, there's enough people in the world that will do that for you."

Lauren whirled around; she hadn't seen or heard Nanny walk down the hall toward them. She gave Shelley a quick hug, whispering, "Joey is lucky to have you, Shelley," before asking, "Nanny, are you feeling better?"

"Yes, thank you, Lauren. I heard a car outside. Who's come visiting?" Nanny said.

Lauren shrugged. "No idea. I didn't hear anything. Want to check for me please, Shelley?"

Shelley, still smiling from the compliment, went to the door as Lauren walked into the kitchen to put a large cushion on the chair Nanny was going to use.

"Am I in time for supper?" Edward's voice as he came into the room sent nice quivers up Lauren's spine. She was finding it harder to ignore her attraction to him.

"Of course you are." She called out, "Children, go and wash your hands."

Edward helped put the dishes on the table. There was fried okra, some sort of fish Lauren didn't recognize, Irish potatoes, the last of the greens they had salvaged from the garden, and some beans.

"Help yourself, Edward, we've got plenty."

Becky walked in just as the food was served. She washed her hands and took her seat in silence. Terry and Carly exchanged a look but said nothing. Nanny led the grace as if nothing had happened.

Becky didn't add a word to the dinner conversation and if Edward noticed the atmosphere he didn't comment. It was only when everyone was finished that Lauren got a chance to speak to Becky.

"Where have you been?" she hissed as they took the larger pots over to the sink.

"Walkin' and thinkin'."

"I hope you realize how badly you hurt Will last night. I never saw a man so crushed before."

Becky's face flushed—was it with guilt?—before she turned on Lauren. "Don't you lecture me about men. You have Edward dangling on a string. At least I told Will he never stood a chance."

Lauren opened her mouth to retaliate but closed it again, realizing this wasn't the time or place.

"Can we leave the table please, Miss Lauren?" Cal asked.

She nodded. The children ran outside after supper, leaving the dishes on the table behind them. Nanny claimed she needed help in getting to bed and demanded Becky come with her. Lauren blushed at the obvious attempt to leave her and Edward alone. She picked up the plates, stacking them in the sink. She cleared everything but the coffee pot and Edward's cup.

"You're quiet this evening. That's not like you," Lauren said as she tidied. When Edward didn't answer, she turned to look at him. "What's wrong?"

"I got a letter from my aunt. She's asked me to come and visit."

Lauren topped up his cup as she waited for him to continue. When Edward didn't speak, she asked, "Do you not like her?"

He jerked his head back. "Why do you say that?"

"You look like you've been invited to your own hanging." When his face screwed up, Lauren hastened to add, "I didn't mean to cause offense."

Edward took her hand and rubbed it, but he was distracted, a troubled expression on his face.

"You know my father emigrated to live in America. He came here to live with an uncle. My mother was an only child but my father came from a large Jewish family. He had a number of sisters. They are scattered across different countries. One, Rae, lives in Berlin."

"Germany?" Then she felt foolish. Of course it was Germany, how many Berlins were there? She didn't want him to say yes.

"Yes, she wants me to come visit to see how everyone is. She told me my Aunt Edith is dying."

Immediately feeling guilty, Lauren whispered, "I'm so sorry, Edward, and here was me teasing you. When do you leave?"

"Lauren, Edith died back in the twenties. Here in Virginia. She and her husband died in an automobile accident. I remember going to the funeral."

Confused, Lauren waited for him to explain..

"It's a code. I think Rae needs my help and is trying to tell me to come over in person. She's my father's youngest sister. Closer in age to me than to Father. We were close when we were younger, she supported my choice to become a newspaperman. She spent a lot of time here in the USA but went back to live in Berlin when she got married. Her husband has a high-profile job as a lawyer. At least he did have."

"What do you mean, did have? Is he dead too?" she whispered, dread making the hairs on the back of her neck stand to attention.

"No, or at least not that I know of."

His bald statement shocked her. She gasped.

He didn't wince, just stated the facts. "You read the papers, Lauren. People are disappearing in Germany. Rae didn't mention her husband in her letter."

Lauren knew things in Germany were difficult if you were Jewish. She hoped the stories she read in the papers were exaggerated. She couldn't imagine being imprisoned for practicing the wrong religion or being a member of a certain race.

She wanted to clap her hands over her ears or disappear in a puff of smoke rather than have this conversation. She knew Edward and could anticipate what he was going to do. She didn't want to be right.

"You're going over, aren't you? Is it dangerous for you?" she asked.

"Because I'm Jewish? I think my American passport would protect me."

But what if it didn't? She'd read articles about people disappearing in Germany into places called camps. Not just Jewish men, although they seemed to be at higher risk than the average German, but also those who had opposed Hitler, including priests, scientists, lawyers and social democrats. She shuddered, caring too much about Edward for him to be at risk of being injured or worse. She moved closer, placing her hand on his arm. Could she stop him going? If she asked him not to?

"Can't you just ring her and ask her what's wrong?" But even as she asked, she knew he wouldn't rest until he saw for himself his aunt was all right. Edward was like that, he cared about other people.

Edward took her hands in his, rubbing them in a distracted fashion. "She said Aunt Edith's phone is out of order. I think that means she's worried about someone listening. It's all very mysterious, making me more anxious. Rae isn't a drama queen, she's about as practical and level-headed as a body can be. She's very active in her community, spends a lot of time helping others. Becky reminds me a little of her." He stayed silent for a few seconds before speaking again. "They went through a horrendous depression over there, although things seem to be picking up. Hitler is credited with improving things for the average German."

Lauren tried to concentrate on what he was saying, but she couldn't push aside the stab of jealousy his words induced. She admired Becky too, so why wouldn't Edward?

"What are you two whispering about?" Becky asked as she walked back into the kitchen. Lauren pulled her hands away and Edward gave her a funny look before answering Becky.

"Nothing. I was just telling Lauren I have to go away for a while. I have a story calling me."

"You and your newspaper. That won't keep you warm at night." Becky poured herself a cup of coffee, taking a seat while grinning at Edward. They got on very well, and up until tonight Lauren would have thought they had a brother–sister type relationship. But what if Becky was interested in Edward romantically?

"And this from the lady who swears off marriage," Edward retorted, but his smile took the sting out of the words.

Becky didn't bat an eyelid. "For me only. I was thinking of Lauren."

Mortified, Lauren couldn't look at Edward. She pushed back her chair. "I best make a start on the dishes. They aren't going to wash themselves."

But Becky wasn't about to let her escape. "I'll do them." Lauren thought back to the night she had pushed Becky out to speak to Will. Becky was doing the same now. "You sit with Edward for a while. He looks miserable."

"Thanks, Becky," Edward drawled.

"Well you do. Why don't you two go out on the porch? Then I can listen to the radio while I work. Go on with you."

Edward walked out. Lauren hesitated but Becky mouthed, 'Go!'

She took a seat but he stood at the rail staring into the distance. He spoke with his back to her.

"Lauren, I'll leave you a letter. Just in case."

"In case of what?" She shivered despite the warm evening.

"I'm just being practical. We both know accidents can happen and I want my affairs left in order."

Her skin crawled as a chill crept down her spine. "You're scaring me now, Edward. Can't you just write to her?"

He turned to look at her, his gaze holding hers. "No. Would you turn your back on someone who asked for help?"

Lauren couldn't answer that. They both knew she wouldn't.

"When do you leave?" she whispered, not wanting to admit even to herself she couldn't bear to see him go. She wanted to beg him to stay but that wouldn't be fair.

"On Monday. I expect to be gone about six weeks." He sat down beside her, taking her hand. "Lauren, you know my feelings for you. I haven't kept them a secret. I know things were difficult between you and Justin but I hoped in time you would come to see I'm not like him."

"Edward…"

"No, don't say it. I just want you to know I love you. I think I have from the first moment I laid eyes on you at that New York Ball. You looked like a fawn gazing down the gun sights of a hunter. I wanted to protect you. I still do. But I have to do this."

She tried being flippant. "We'll be fine. Hope House isn't going anywhere."

"I'll leave instructions with my deputy Tom Egan to give you anything you need."

"Edward, please stop sounding like you aren't coming back. In six weeks' time you'll feel a little stupid for talking like this."

That dark look in his eyes returned. "I hope you're right." He leaned in and kissed her cheek.

She tried not to stiffen but she couldn't help her instinctive response. Ever since Justin had attacked her, she couldn't trust anyone, no matter how much she wanted to.

"Edward, I'm sorry. It's not you."

"Don't explain. I have to go. Look after yourself, Lauren. Say goodbye to the others for me."

She watched him as he walked around the side of the house. She stayed out on the swing long after his wheels had sent the dry mud flying as he drove off. She touched the place on her cheek where he'd kissed her. She knew Edward was totally different to Justin. He loved her, respected her, and wouldn't in a million years hurt any woman. But knowing it in her heart was one thing, her head was the problem.

CHAPTER TWENTY-FIVE

Six weeks passed yet there was no sign of Edward. Lauren found herself looking out the window checking for his Cadillac numerous times a day. Six weeks turned into seven and then two months had passed.

It was silly, as she wouldn't usually see him every day, yet she still missed him. She listened to the news every night but it didn't help. She kept dreaming that something had gone wrong and he'd never come back. It was Thanksgiving next week—would he make it home in time? Her mood deteriorated each day until Becky sent her out of the house.

"Don't come back until you find your good humor. We won't stand for you bitin' our noses off no more. You're behavin' like a wounded bobcat, although he'd probably be more tolerant."

Lauren drove over to Edward's place where she found Sam in the stables with Prince. The horse neighed in recognition.

"He misses you, Miss Lauren," Sam said, coming to greet her.

"I miss him too, Sam, and you. When are you coming over for dinner? Nanny would love to see you."

"How is Nanny Kat? She feelin' better?"

"She's fine." Lauren rubbed the horse, burying her face in his neck before focusing back on Sam. "Have you heard from Edward yet?"

Sam turned his back as he pretended to be busy with some saddles.

"Sam?"

Sam turned partially toward her but his eyes didn't focus on her face. His hands kept rubbing the saddle as he mumbled, "I haven't heard a word, Miss Lauren." He poured a little more oil on the leather before vigorously rubbing it in, saying in a stronger voice, "Mr. Edward will be back when he comes back. He is always like this when he's workin' on a story."

She put her hand on his arm to stop him moving. "We both know he isn't working. He told me, you don't have to try to protect me."

Sam turned to face her fully. "I'm sorry, Miss Lauren, but that's a habit of mine I will never grow out of. I watched you grow up in Rosehall, saw the fine lady you grew into. I'll always be careful of you. You is my family."

Lauren blinked back the tears. This old man, the son of an ex-slave, was her family too. He'd loved her more than her real father.

"Sam, I'm worried. I've been having bad dreams. What if the Nazis don't let him come back to America?"

She caught the glimpse of fear in his eyes before he blinked to clear it. "They have to. Mr. Edward is a careful man. He has friends in all sorts of high places. He won't do anythin' dangerous."

"Won't he?" Lauren knew Edward wasn't careless but if someone needed his help he wouldn't consider his own safety.

Sam turned back to polish the saddle. "We got to trust he knows what he is doin'. That's all we can do. Do you want to go for a ride, Miss Lauren?"

His change of the subject showed how worried he was. He couldn't lie to her, so instead he would stay silent. She accepted his loyalty and tried to lighten her tone. "I'd love to, Sam, but I didn't bring a change of clothes and I don't think Virginia is ready to see me riding in this dress." She glanced down at the straight-cut skirt she was wearing.

Sam grinned. "That might just cause some talk."

She moved closer, leaning in to kiss his cheek, whispering, "Sam, please tell Edward to let me know he is back as soon as you see him."

He nodded. "I will, Miss Lauren, but you is likely to see him first. We both know how he feels about you."

Lauren walked reluctantly back to her truck. She knew he was right, and she was beginning to realize she couldn't deny she felt the same. Why had it taken the risk of him being injured or worse for her to acknowledge her real feelings?

*

Maisie chortled as she threw her knitted bunny from her high chair for Carly to pick it up. As soon as Carly handed bunny back, Maisie threw the toy on the floor again.

"She's having the time of her life, isn't she?" Lauren said.

The children barely looked up, their mouths all set in sullen lines. Despite Lauren and Becky's best efforts, they were miserable.

"Why didn't Big Will come today for Thanksgiving? He always makes me laugh," Lottie complained despite a nudge from Carly who glanced at Becky before telling Lottie to be quiet. "I won't. I like Big Will, he is part of our family and should be here for Thanksgiving." Lottie thrust out her lower lip.

Clarissa moved to put her arm around the younger girl. "Lottie, we're all missing people today."

Lauren blinked back tears. Norma, Bart, Big Will, Edward, all missing from their usual seats. Even Nanny was absent from the gathering, having stayed in bed on doctor's orders. He'd diagnosed overwork and tiredness, reminding Lauren, with a stern look and voice to match, that the older woman was over eighty.

Fred frowned and asked, "Why didn't the Hillmans come this year? They have every other year. I miss Dalton and Ellie-Mae."

Lauren replied, "I know you do, Fred, we do too, but the Hillmans wanted to take the children to see their daughter Annie and her new baby. Earl is watching the store so he couldn't come out either."

"What about the Thatchers? Last year they brought us food. Do you remember?" Cal asked.

"Eat your dinner, Cal, you too, Fred. We are lucky to have this food. Thanksgiving is about families and we're family," Lauren said firmly.

"That's right, Cal, we are one big family. Ain't we, Joey?" Shelley asked the young boy who, as usual, was sitting by her side.

"You is my family, Helley," Joey repeated with a big smile on his face. He couldn't pronounce S so always called Shelley, Helley. She didn't seem to mind.

After dinner they tried to get the children to perform their Thanksgiving play but nobody wanted to take part. Eventually they gave in and let the children listen to the radio while they cleared up the dishes. Becky popped some corn which seemed to cheer the children up somewhat. Maisie stood up and tried to walk but kept falling back down on her backside. This made the other children laugh a little.

"Don't think I ever had such a miserable Thanksgiving, have you?" Lauren asked Becky as they sat on the porch. She looked at Becky when she didn't get a reply and saw that she was watching lights coming up the road.

"Bit late for visitors, isn't it?" Lauren said.

"Maybe they are passin' on," Becky replied, craning to see who it was.

But they both knew that the road only led to the orphanage. Lauren stood up. She kept her gun on top of her wardrobe but Bart had one in the new barn. Only Terry and the adults knew where it was hidden. Should she get it?

Becky said, "That's Mr. Edward's car!"

"It is?" Lauren's heart beat faster. He was home and safe. Thank God. She moved to the side of the porch as the car approached, finally coming to a stop in front of the house. She ran down the steps and threw herself at him as he got out.

"If I'd known this was the welcome I'd get I'd have gone away sooner," he said laughing as he hugged her to him.

She slapped him on the arm. "I was worried about you. You said it would take six weeks and you've been gone more than two months." She tried to lead him to the door but he hesitated.

"Lauren, I have a favor to ask you." He glanced into the car and she spotted two small forms asleep on the back seat.

"I brought Rae's children back with me. It's not safe for them in Germany."

The children began waking up, probably because the car had stopped. Both looked at Lauren, terrified expressions on their faces, their eyes darting back to Edward and back to Lauren.

He muttered something to them before telling them to get out of the car. They moved quickly to his side, holding hands.

"Hi, I'm Lauren," Lauren said.

"This is Rachel and her brother, Hans," Edward said. "Children, this is my friend, the lady I spoke to you about. And this is her home."

He led them by the hand up to the porch where Becky was sitting.

She stood up and greeted the children as if it was the most normal thing in the world for them to arrive in the dark. "You look hungry and tired, Edward. Can I make you a sandwich and coffee?" she said.

"Yes please, Becky, if it's not too much trouble. We did stop but, well, it was a mistake."

Lauren looked at him confused.

"They heard the children's accents and the welcome wasn't very southern," he said, looking pained.

Lauren's heart went out to the children. Strangers in a new country with nobody they knew. They must be scared.

Once in the kitchen, Lauren said to the children, "Hans, you can sit here, and Rachel can sit beside you if you wish. Would you like vegetable soup and an egg sandwich?"

"It is good, thank you," Hans replied, in halting English. Rachel didn't speak but stared at the table.

Edward said something to them in German before asking Lauren to step outside.

"Rachel hasn't spoken a word since we left Germany. Well, even before then. She saw some horrible things and they have left their mark."

"Your aunt?"

"Rae is fine, for now. She refused to come with us. I couldn't get her a visa, but I was prepared to smuggle her out. But she insisted on staying near her husband." He looked broken and Lauren instinctively put her arms around him. She held him tight as he shuddered. What on earth had he endured over there?

After holding him for a little while, thankful he had come back safely, his scent and touch made her realize just how much she'd missed him, and she wanted to lift her lips to his and kiss him. But now wasn't the time. He was exhausted, physically and mentally. She hated to break the intimate moment but she had to before she lost control and gave in to her instinct.

She pushed him a little bit away from her. "Why don't you and the children stay here tonight? We've split Norma and Bart's room into two, one for the girls and one for Terry. Terry won't mind you using his. You can go home tomorrow if you wish."

"But people may talk?" His eyes twinkled as if he was teasing her, his arms loose on her shoulders.

She appreciated him lightening the mood and teased him back, "What else is new? Anyway, it's not like I live here alone. Becky and Nanny, never mind thirteen children, are more than adequate chaperones."

He gazed at her, his expression suggesting he wished they were alone. So did she but it wasn't ladylike to admit that, even if only to herself. She tore her eyes away from his and tried to put more distance between them. He didn't let go completely.

"Thank you, Lauren, I don't think I could drive another mile. Your place was closer than mine. At least, that's my excuse. The reality is I couldn't face an empty house. Not tonight."

She kissed his cheek before moving away, heading for the kitchen.

"Come back inside. You can tell me later what happened over there but for now you will eat and drink some coffee. You've lost weight and it doesn't do anything for you."

He laughed as she teased him, but she saw the wounded expression in his eyes still remained. A look that reminded her of a hunted animal.

CHAPTER TWENTY-SIX

Once Hans and Rachel understood Edward was staying with them, they relaxed slowly. Becky made them plenty of sandwiches to go with the soup, as well as some hot milk. Edward put them to bed then came back down to sit in the kitchen. Nanny joined them; she had got up when she heard Edward's voice. Lauren suspected the old woman had been more concerned about his absence than she had let on.

"I can't tell you how grateful I am for your hospitality," Edward said. "Thank you, Terry, for giving up your room."

"My pleasure, Mr. Edward."

"Don't you think you could call me Edward now, son? You're almost seventeen—only slightly younger than Becky."

"Yes sir." Terry beamed with pleasure. He liked nothing more than being included as an adult.

Nanny spoke up. "Edward, you look years older than you did before you left. We can only imagine what you saw and experienced, but don't feel the need to tell us. Not now, not tomorrow. Only if you want to share."

Edward gave her a grateful, sad smile and replied, "Thanks, Kathryn, but it's best I explain. My Aunt Rae lives in Berlin. She married a well-respected—well, he used to be—lawyer. When Hitler first came to the attention of the law, Rae's husband Rudolf spoke some home truths. He'd read *Mein Kampf* and knew what Hitler planned. Not just the takeover of Germany but other things too, including Hitler's wish for war. When the Nazis came to power, Rudolf was warned to leave. He had some friends and admirers who, while not in the Nazi party, were involved with them. One of them was a man called Diels. He came to see Rudolf at his home and warned him his name was near the top of Hitler's most-hated list."

"Why didn't he leave?" Terry blurted, asking the question they all wanted to ask.

Edward shrugged. "Rae has asked that over and over. I guess he felt he was safe, he was in a position of power and had a formidable reputation. He believed in law and justice. He felt a duty to protect those less fortunate than he was. He knew the law and at the start the Nazis were too afraid to take action against him as he was so well connected." Edward took a breath, his expression darkening. "He took too long to realize the Nazis don't believe in anything but their own preachings. They will impose them on the world if their plans succeed. They remove every trace of resistance to their ideals. Not just from Jewish people, but those who have the intelligence to question everything for themselves."

The silence lingered as they all contemplated what Edward had said. Lauren couldn't believe this could happen in a country as advanced as Germany.

Edward continued speaking, almost to himself this time. "They came for Rudolf two months before I arrived in Berlin. Prior to that time, he had been harassed and threatened but never physically harmed. That changed the week before Rae wrote to me. They came in the middle of the night, broke into their home, destroyed it, and beat Rudolf when he protested. Rachel witnessed everything from where her father had hidden her in a cupboard. She saw him dragged away, blood pouring from his wounds. She didn't scream or shout but stayed quiet just as she'd been told. Rae was struck too, in the face. But they didn't take her. We aren't sure why."

"Oh, my goodness, those poor children and your aunt." Lauren squeezed her eyes tight, trying to stop tears falling. She wanted to run upstairs and hug Rachel close, to get rid of her memories. But for the moment, Edward needed her. She inched her chair closer to him.

Edward smiled gratefully. "That's why she wrote to me. But she knew she was being watched and her phone was probably compromised. She has powerful friends in Berlin, but she is hesitant to involve them for fear of putting them at risk. Some volunteered and they are still helping her today."

Lauren was losing her battle with her emotions.

"Where was Rudolf taken?" Nanny asked.

"Nobody knows. Rae felt sure the storm troopers would come back. She knew her husband would be tortured and felt the children would be his weakness."

Lauren put a hand over her mouth. The children were six and ten. How could anyone torture a child?

Becky's voice trembled as she asked, "So, you brought them to America?"

"That sounds so simple. Many in Berlin are already trying to leave. The queues at all the embassies have lengthened but particularly for the US and Britain. I found a man called Geist in the US Foreign Service who helped me. I persuaded my father to act as guarantor for the children. I don't have sufficient funds and am not married. Geist was able to secure two visas exceptionally quickly, due in part to him believing the children were at risk given Rudolf's high profile. I couldn't dare contact anyone to say anything for fear of what could happen."

Nanny commented softly, "Edward, how horrible for you, the children, and your aunt."

The stricken look on Edward's face made Lauren want to run away. She sensed something even more horrible had happened. She glanced at Nanny and Becky but both were staring at Edward, horror dawning on their faces.

"It gets worse. A letter was waiting for me when we docked at New York. Rae got it out of Germany via someone traveling to the USA who arrived before I did. A German officer who knew Rudolf called to see her. He confirmed Rudolf was dead. He apologized with tears in his eyes. I've told Hans but I was worried about Rachel."

Would the news of her father make her worse?

Stunned, all of them stared at Edward who stirred his coffee, unable to look up.

Nanny's expression was horrified. She seemed to collect herself before she spoke. "Edward, you must write about this. People need to know what's going on in Germany. We can't stand back and let Hitler just do as he pleases. This is not the Middle Ages. Countries need law and order. What about the people over there? Surely they don't believe this is right."

Edward suppressed a yawn, his tired expression highlighting the dark circles around his eyes. "Kathryn, you'd be surprised. Hitler and his friends are very good at propaganda. People need to blame someone and the Nazis have picked the Jews. Hitler has done a lot of good in Germany. The people were starving during the Depression and he gave them jobs working on new roads, buildings, and armaments."

Becky shook her head. "We got people starvin' over here, but we don't grab men from their homes and murder them. They be crazy. There has to be some good people who don't believe in Hitler."

"There are, Becky, but a lot of them have been persecuted just as badly, thrown into prison camps without trial."

Edward looked right into Lauren's eyes, making her feel as if it were just the two of them in the room. He looked so haunted, she wanted to throw her arms around him and diminish the hurt and fear in his eyes.

"What of your aunt, Rae? Can you get her out? She'd be safer here and the children need her."

Edward sighed. "I keep trying, but Rae is stubborn. She wants to stay in Berlin and help those she can. Rudolf was prepared for something to happen. He transferred a lot of his money to Switzerland before he was taken. His parents are still alive but are old. They were refusing to leave. His father thinks the people will realize what Hitler is doing."

Nanny spoke, her voice trembling, but with fear or anger it was hard to tell. "I can understand the older folk not wanting to leave the country of their birth. When you get to a certain age, change is frightening. Perhaps he's right. Maybe people will come to their senses, Edward."

Lauren watched Edward as Nanny spoke, seeing from his expression he didn't believe things would change, at least not for the positive. Still he smiled at Nanny. "I hope you're right, Kathryn. Would you mind if I went up? I'm so tired, I could sleep on the table."

"I'll go up with you." Terry hopped up and escorted Edward up the stairs, leaving the women behind.

Nanny got to her feet, slowly. Lauren moved to help her but got waved away. "I can manage, Lauren, but thank you."

After Nanny shuffled off to her room, Becky and Lauren sat in silence, both deep in their thoughts.

Lauren was the first to break the silence. "I wish I could do something. I mean, to really help. Can you imagine how many frightened people there are, desperate to escape?"

"I was thinkin' of our children. What if Maisie was Jewish, or Terry, or any of them? Imagine if they were livin' over there? How would we get them to safety?"

CHAPTER TWENTY-SEVEN

Edward was up, sitting at the breakfast table, when Lauren came down the next morning. He was nursing a cup of coffee, but it wasn't as strong as he usually took. She would have smelled it up in her room if it had been. She guessed he was trying to be careful with their supplies.

"Nice to see you making yourself at home," she said, nodding toward his cup.

"I thought it was safer to make it than to wait for you."

She smiled, glad he was teasing her, but the shadows under his eyes spoke of a night of turmoil.

"That's not nice," she joked. "I'm learning. I can light the stove now, make coffee, and even flapjacks. I'm improving."

They both laughed, knowing that when Lauren had arrived at the orphanage, she'd burned water. She had been brought up to be a lady, which meant her domestic skills had been worse than useless. She knew how to manage a large household but couldn't clear out a room properly without instructions.

Edward's laughter fell away as he stirred his coffee. She made some more, stronger this time, ignoring their small supply. She'd drink chicory for the rest of the week. He needed it more than she did.

The rich scent of strong black coffee brewing seemed to revive him slightly. She took his cup, tipped the contents down the sink, and filled it with the new coffee. Their fingers touched as she handed it back to him, sending a current through her. He must have felt something too as his eyes widened. He looked at her and she couldn't stop herself from staring into his eyes. A loud bang and shout from upstairs broke the moment.

"The boys get up early around here. How did the children sleep?" Lauren asked, wondering if they were up yet.

"Better than they did in the car, thank you." Edward was back to being polite. She wanted to touch him again, to put hope back in his eyes.

"How will your father react to having children around?"

Edward shrugged. "He'll probably ignore them just like he did us. Mother is looking forward to having them though. She said it would help fill her time until her children gave her grandchildren. Hans is a clever boy, was at the top of his school until he got thrown out for being Jewish. Rachel is quiet but Rae says she is clever too."

"I hope Rachel finds her voice again and they both flourish." Lauren sat waiting for him to speak but, watching as he gazed into the distance, she believed he was back in Berlin. "Edward, tell me what I can do to help. Please," she whispered, reaching out to put her hand over his. His fingers entwined with hers and, when he looked up, his eyes were swimming with unshed tears.

"I'm going to write to the Jewish organizations. They must act to save the Jewish people. People are dismissing Hitler and the Nazis but you only have to go to Berlin to see them in action. The atmosphere is one of fear and for good reason. People are being picked up and taken away just for being Jewish. But those brave enough to speak out against the new regime also disappear or suffer a fatal accident. Anyone who listens to any of the top Nazis should be in no doubt. They are sworn to achieve two things: free Germany of the Jewish race and take back what lands they consider theirs."

"You mean they are heading to war?"

"Yes." Edward stared into his cup. "People will dismiss me as a warmonger if I print the truth. I don't want war, the war memorial is example enough of what people around here lost in the last war. But I can't stand by and see innocent people suffer. Especially children like Rachel and Hans. We need money, but more than that we need sponsors willing to take responsibility for immigrants. Geist predicts the situation is going to deteriorate further. And he should know."

"I wish there was something we could do, Edward, but it is taking every penny I can raise and more to keep this place going. I don't know how we are going to keep all our children fed and clothed. You know I'd help if I could."

"I know, Lauren, I wasn't hinting." Edward put his coffee cup on the table and held out his hands for hers. "Lauren, I have to go back to Berlin. I have to persuade Rae to leave with or without her in-laws. I couldn't sleep last night worrying about her."

Lauren wiped her clammy hands on her clothing, before taking his. "Edward, it's not safe over there."

"Lots of American journalists are working over there. The 1936 Olympics are due to be held in Berlin, so they shouldn't want a diplomatic incident with America before then. With the amount of press over there, I would be right at home."

Her chest grew painful as her heart raced. "You mean you want to go permanently?"

"Not forever no, but for a while. I can't sit here and do nothing. I need to help my people."

"No you don't. You explained the Jewish race passed through the mother…" Even as she said the words, she knew she was wrong. Whether Edward had ever considered himself Jewish before Hitler came into power didn't matter now. After what he'd seen, his origins meant more to him.

"Lauren, I have to do this. I'll promote Tim Egan so he can take over the *Charlottesville News*. He's a good man and looking for his next promotion. This way I can secure his services."

"I see. You have been thinking about this for a while." She pulled her hands back.

"Yes. Ever since I landed in Berlin. I don't want to leave you, Lauren, but I have to do this. I couldn't live with myself if I didn't try to help." He looked desperate.

She folded her arms. She refused to beg him to stay. "You have to do what you think best. It's not like I have any hold over you."

He stared at her and looked as if he was about to speak, but whatever he was going to say was interrupted by footsteps on the stairs. Rachel and Hans stood there, eyes wide, holding onto each other as they stared around. The rest of the children came racing down the stairs wondering loudly who the strangers were.

Lauren clapped her hands to get everyone's attention as Rachel and Hans ran to Edward's side. "Children, this is Rachel and her brother Hans. They are Edward's cousins from Germany."

"What are they doing here?" Cal said, his tone suspicious.

"Cal, they are our guests, please watch your tone. Who wants flapjacks?"

"Me, but can Carly or Becky make them?" Fred asked, his cheeks flushing.

"Don't be mean, Fred. Miss Lauren is getting much better. She tries her best to get all the lumps out," Ruthie protested, protective of Lauren as ever.

Fred's comment didn't help Lauren's mood.

"Carly, would you mind? Ruthie, you and Lottie set the table. Clarissa, Sophie, could you try to make our guests feel more at home? Fred, you and Cal need to chop and bring in some wood. Terry's gone to do the milking already. He's bound to have other chores for you to do."

Lauren walked toward the staircase as she dished out instructions. She couldn't bear to look at Edward. The last months with him being away had been horrible. He obviously didn't feel the same. He couldn't wait to leave again.

CHAPTER TWENTY-EIGHT

Lauren stood with the rest of the Hope House occupants as they waved goodbye to Edward and the children. She had managed to avoid being near him since their conversation and didn't shake his hand as he left, never mind hug him. As soon as he drove off, she went inside. She blamed the rain but the reality was she couldn't bear to watch him drive out of her life.

She began washing the breakfast dishes but Becky came over and took the plates out of her hand. "We can't afford new dishes. Go take your frustration out on something less fragile."

Lauren clenched and unclenched her hands. "How could he do it, Becky? It's dangerous over there. He might not come back. You heard what they did to his uncle."

Becky's eyes were warm with sympathy. "Edward is a man of principle. His aunt needs him. Children need him. He has to go back. That's the type of man he is."

She knew her friend was right. All those qualities were exactly what she loved about him, but still her anger won out.

"He has responsibilities here. Christmas for instance. He said he'd help us at Christmas but he's just run off." Lauren knew she was acting like a brat.

"Lauren Greenwood, stop feelin' sorry for yourself. That poor man has been in love with you for years by all accounts and now you discover you share his feelin's, you decide he is being selfish."

Lauren folded her arms over her chest. "I'm not in love with Edward."

"Aren't you? Then you are acting like a spoiled princess. What does one Christmas matter when there are people's lives at stake? Face it, Lauren, if those were English-speakin' children, say over in Washington, you would be the first to go rescue them." Becky glared at her. "Go for a walk."

"It's raining."

Becky lost all patience with her. "I don't care if there's a hurricane comin'. Go outside and shed that self-pity before I shake you out of it. Go on, get."

Wow, Becky was angrier than Lauren had seen her in a long time. She took her coat from the back of the door and headed out into the rain.

She walked to the barn, pushing the door open and taking a second to let the scents wash over her. The pigs didn't smell as bad as usual. Terry was busy cleaning out their sty. Each stall was freshly turned out. Terry was doing a great job looking after the animals. Mabel, their milk cow, was with calf. She was due in early spring.

Terry turned and saw her in the doorway. "Bit wet for goin' for a walk, Miss Lauren."

"Terry, call me Lauren, please."

"Sure. Do you want to, you know, talk about somethin'?" Terry kept mucking out the stall as he spoke. Lauren's heart swelled with love for this boy whose gentle heart had never changed despite the rough hand life had dealt him.

"Terry, have you ever had a doctor look at your leg?"

Surprised, he glanced down at his bad leg. "No. Never saw the point."

"Even when it was first broken?" Lauren asked.

"Matron fixed it up, said she could do as good a job as any doctor."

Lauren's hackles rose at the mention of that woman. She sat on a small stool and indicated Terry sit on the other one.

"How did it happen?"

Terry focused on the ground, his foot tapping. She let the silence linger, giving him time to answer.

"Lauren, that be a long time ago. No point rakin' up those stories now."

"I'd like to know if you can tell me," Lauren said.

He hesitated then stepped forward and sat down on the stool. "Matron was in a real temper, she'd been drinkin'. Her mountain men hadn't arrived and I guess she'd run out. She needed to drink every day although we didn't know that at the time. Carly, she let a bowl drop and it splintered. Matron was real mad."

Lauren gasped. "Over one bowl?"

Terry looked straight at her. "It was full of milk and eggs. Carly was tryin' to make a cake. She shouldn't have been as she wasn't more than nine or so." He focused on something over Lauren's head. "Matron got the strap out and was going to hit her. I grabbed the strap out of Matron's hand and she went mad. She reached out to grab it back, I turned to run but slipped on the mess on the floor and went down. She grabbed something and hit me hard across the leg. She hit me a few times but I didn't feel anythin' after the first one. It hurt so bad, I must have blanked out. I couldn't stand up so she grabbed me by the arms and threw me down the cellar. I landed badly on my leg so I guess that's what broke it." He kept staring at the point on the wall, his knees pressed together, his hands clenched.

Tears ran down Lauren's face as Terry spoke. She ached to say something but what? He clearly didn't want her pity.

"She was real sorry when she sobered up two days later."

"You were down there for two days?" Lauren felt physically sick.

Terry shifted in his seat, pulling at his collar. "Carly sneaked down with some water and whatever food she could. I couldn't eat as the pain was too bad but without that water, I don't know what I'd have done. It was a very hot summer and the sweat was drippin' off me even in the cellar. When Matron came down, she looked shocked at my leg. She kept apologizin' and helped me up to the kitchen, all the time promisin' to never drink again. She splinted my leg and wrapped it up."

He seemed to think Matron had tried to make it right. Lauren stood up and paced. Was it too late to have that woman punished for what she did? She couldn't contain her anger, her tone bitter. "She didn't get a doctor because she was terrified they would report her."

Terry shook his head, holding up his palms. "I don't know, Lauren. Maybe she didn't have any money for the doctor. It wasn't the first time she'd hit us or been mean but it was the first she did lastin' damage. She didn't drink for a while after that. She was nice again. But it didn't last. I guess the hard times became too much for her to bear. She was alone, you have Becky. I know it gets difficult to find the money for everythin' but at least you and Becky can laugh and cry together. Matron was alone. She was a very sad woman."

Lauren stared at the young man in front of her before taking a seat once again. "You are an exceptional young man, Terry."

He shrugged. "I'm just me. There ain't anythin' special about me."

Oh yes there was, but she sensed now wasn't the time he'd believe her.

"Terry, do you know what happened to your parents?" she asked, leaning forwards.

"Matron said they died from Spanish flu but I don't know if she was tellin' the truth or not. I reckon she might have been. Many died around here. Guess I was lucky I survived. Carly, she knows her ma died havin' her. Her pa, he wasn't nice. He didn't love her the way he should. You know?" Terry's blushes told her more than his words.

Her stomach roiled. Carly was such a sweet girl.

"What age was Carly when she came here?"

"She was about eight. Her pa got into trouble with some lawmen over somethin'. There was a shootout and he was kilt. He'd shot a deputy dead so I guess he saw no reason not to stop shooting. But Carly was in that house. She told me she hid under the bed. When the lawmen stormed the house, they found her and brought her here. Guess they saved her life when they kilt her pa."

Lauren loved to see Terry's eyes shining as he spoke about Carly.

"You love her, don't you, Terry?"

He held her gaze, his head straight. "Yes, ma'am. I love her and she loves me. We just waitin' till she's old enough to get married. Then we will have our own place and when we have babies, they are going to be the best loved babies in the world."

Lauren swallowed hard. "I'm sure they will be."

They sat in silence for a minute or so, both deep in thought.

"Lauren, why did you ask about my leg? Do you think they could do somethin' about it?" Terry rubbed his leg.

"I don't know but I think we should ask the doctor. Maybe he'd know someone."

Terry didn't even hesitate. "We don't have money for that, Lauren. I get along just fine and it doesn't hurt so much any more." He stood up, dismissing the subject. His tone changed to a slightly teasing one. "Now, unless you want to get covered in muck, you might want to find somewhere else to hide from Becky."

"How did you know I was hiding?" Lauren frowned.

"I could hear you gals from across here. Neither of you speak softly when you are angry."

Lauren's face burned as she looked away. How much had he heard?

He looked up shyly. "I think Mr.—I mean Edward—is a great man."

She just stared as he limped off whistling.

CHAPTER TWENTY-NINE

Later that afternoon, Lauren saw Edward drive back up the road toward the house. She stood at the door wondering why he'd returned so quickly. Her heart beat faster; she could apologize now. He got out and opened the back door, letting Rachel and Hans out of the car. Puzzled, Lauren called to Becky before walking down the steps.

Edward addressed the children in German and they walked hand in hand past her and into the house. They looked more uncomfortable than they had this morning.

Lauren approached, her stomach contracting. What had happened to these poor children now? "What's wrong?"

Edward fisted his hands, his voice strained with anger. "My dear father. We got to the house and found it empty. Father and Mother left for France earlier in the week to spend Christmas with some friends in Nice."

Lauren's mouth fell open. "But weren't they expecting you?"

Edward kicked at the grass. "They should have had my letter, they definitely got my telegram." At her questioning glance he continued, "My father works on a set timetable and when we didn't arrive he went anyway. Mother planned to bring the children with them but she always accedes to Father."

Lauren wanted to find his parents and shake them. These children had lost their father in a violent way, been torn from their mother's side and brought to a new country and Edward's parents were thinking about their vacation.

"What did they think you were going to do with Rachel and Hans?"

Edward gave her a bleak look. She moved closer to him, resting her hand on his arm. He put his hand over hers. "Stay with me, I suppose. But I can't look after them and work too. I have to get back to Berlin but before I can do that I have to sort out some things at the office. Egan has done a great job in my absence but he has some things he needs me to look at."

"So the children? You want them to stay here?"

He threw his hands up in the air. "I don't know what to do, Lauren. You don't speak German and their command of English isn't good. But there is nobody else. All the German-speaking people I know live in Washington or elsewhere. There are some Jewish organizations here in Virginia but I don't want to just abandon them."

Lauren took his hand in hers, gripping it firmly. She'd spotted the children at the window looking out at them. The last thing they needed was to sense more friction.

"We'll manage. Those children need a familiar face. You can drive over from work a few times a week until you return to Berlin, can't you? Perhaps even postpone your trip until after Christmas? It's only three weeks away after all."

For a second, she thought she glimpsed a hurt child in the look he gave her. His parents hadn't cared much for him, she'd picked that up in the things he had said over the past year. He was hurting for himself too. She massaged his hands in hers. "Trust me," she whispered. "Stay for Christmas."

"I don't think I can wait that long." He put his hand up to her face, his finger caressing the side of her cheek, his expression begging for understanding.

Becky's voice interrupted the moment. "Edward, you came back. Did you miss my cookin'?" She came out from behind the barn, walking toward them.

Lauren jumped away from Edward. "He's brought Rachel and Hans to stay for a while. He still plans on going to Berlin."

Edward glanced at Lauren but she walked into the house. Becky could handle him while she saw to the children. They had moved away from the window, Rachel was now sitting at the kitchen table with Hans standing by her side. They looked terrified and confused.

She gave Hans a smile and spoke softly so as not to frighten him. "Hans, I think you speak a little English?"

"Ja, I mean, yes. Papa... he told us to teach English."

"*Learn* English," she corrected automatically as she tried to figure out where these two would sleep.

Terry came in the back door. "Hello again."

Hans moved closer to Rachel, placing his hand on her shoulder before addressing Terry. "Hello."

"Terry, the children are staying for a while, probably until after Christmas. Could you share with Hans? I can put Rachel in with Carly and Lottie."

Hans' grip on his sister tightened. "We stay together."

"Yes, Hans, in the same house, but I don't have a room for you to stay together in."

"They can have mine, Lauren. I can sleep in the barn," Terry suggested cheerfully.

"Thank you but no, Terry. It's too cold and the weather forecast is for more freezing temperatures." Lauren sat on the bench beside Rachel. She touched the girl's arm to get her to look at her.

"Rachel, I know you speak a little English too. You and Hans are welcome here and you are safe. Nobody will hurt you here. I promise."

Hans spoke German to his sister and Rachel searched Lauren's face as if wondering if she could trust her. She gave her a slight smile but remained silent.

"Come on, children, let me show you where Rachel will sleep." She held out her hand to Rachel but the girl hung back, clutching her teddy. Hans took her hand and together they walked up to the girls' room. Carly was inside making up the beds.

"Carly, Rachel is going to share with you for a few weeks. She understands a little English but we are not sure how much. I know you will be kind to her, but can you also watch out for the others? I don't want anyone making her feel uncomfortable."

"Will do, Miss Lauren. Hello, Rachel. Would you like this bed by the window? Or this one by the door?"

Hans translated and Rachel clung to him even harder. He spoke again, this time using a stronger tone, and she let his hand drop. She sat on the bed near the door. Lauren sighed with relief, although she knew Carly would have given up her bed by the window if Rachel had chosen that one.

They walked out of the girls' room and into Terry's. "Hans, you will share with Terry. Rachel will be just next door."

Thank goodness they had listened to Earl Hillman and transformed Bart and Norma's large room into two smaller ones. By expanding a little under the eaves of the house, the two rooms were a good size and could fit four beds apiece. It didn't leave much room for walking around but the children spent most of their time downstairs.

"Hans, we are eating in about an hour. I'll be down in the kitchen. You and Rachel are free to go wherever you want in this house. The only room off limits is Nanny Kat's room on the ground floor. I will show you that later."

He smiled gratefully. "Danke… I mean, thank you."

Downstairs, Lauren spotted Edward coming out of Nanny's room. He looked like a guilty schoolboy with his hand in the candy jar.

"What are you up to?" she asked him. "Nanny's in the sitting room looking after Maisie…"

"Nothing."

She waited.

"Why are you so suspicious?"

"With twenty-odd children passing through these doors over the last few years, what do you expect me to be? I know you are up to something."

"Shush, you'll ruin the surprise." He pushed open the door and pulled her in, shutting it behind them. They were alone but for the mountain of presents on the floor.

"Edward... what...? When did you have time to do this?" She stared around, amazed.

"I didn't. I left a list with Mother. She's more reliable than Father. There's one for everyone except Hans and Rachel. I'll do some more shopping and drop them over."

She stared at the pile of gifts. "Thank you."

He moved closer to her, pushing a strand of her hair behind her ear. "I love you, Lauren. I know you are angry about me going back to Berlin but it's something I have to do. I am not looking for a story."

She raised her eyebrow, causing him to smile.

"All right, I won't say no to a story but my main aim is to get Rae out of there. I can't turn my back on her."

"Or the children and people she's helping."

"Yes, them too." He moved closer, their bodies almost touching. "I'd like your understanding. I don't want to leave on bad terms."

She looked him in the eyes before her gaze shifted to his mouth. Standing on tiptoes, she reached up and kissed him on the lips. He caught her to him, kissing her, but she could tell he was holding back, waiting for her to deepen the kiss. Her whole body tingled as his hands went to her face, caressing her cheeks, then her hair.

Someone walked down the hall outside the door, causing them to break apart, breathing harder. He looked at her anxiously but she smiled. A real smile. She'd enjoyed his kiss and no horrible memories had clouded it. She leaned in and kissed him again.

"I don't want you to get hurt or worse, but I won't stop you going." She held her head up, seeking eye contact. "I love you too, Edward."

He lifted her up and would have swung her around but for the fact the furniture in the room didn't allow for much freedom of movement. She giggled.

"I was trying to be romantic."

"I know." She put her hands up to his face as he put her down again. "Can you keep this to yourself for now? I need to move slowly. I wish I didn't feel scared…" She could have cut her own tongue out at his wounded expression. "Edward, I am not afraid of you. It's my memories that terrify me. So have patience."

"What do you call waiting for you to realize how fabulous I am for the last four years, if you don't call it being patient?"

She smiled, her mind flitting back to their first meeting at the Woolworth Ball, December 1930. She'd been besotted by someone else then. Someone…

"Don't, Lauren. Forget those times. Look forward to the future. Our future."

"Kiss me again."

He brought his lips down to hers and their kiss was even more intense than before.

CHAPTER THIRTY

"Onkel Edward, wo bist du? Rachel ist verårgert. Sie will nach Hause gehen."

Hearing the voice in the hallway, Edward hugged Lauren. "I have to go, Hans says Rachel wants to go home."

"The poor child. I don't blame her. She's missing her mother, and after what she saw…"

He kissed her lightly before walking out the door, shutting Lauren in behind him. She guessed he was thinking of her reputation and thanked him for it. Not that Becky or Nanny would say anything but she didn't need the children teasing them. Plus, she liked keeping it a secret; she was enjoying these feelings and wanted them to herself for now.

She moved the gifts back against the wall, draping a sheet over them just in case the children got curious. She was tempted to find her gift but resisted. People would wonder where she was. She looked in the mirror, patted down her hair, and walked to the door. She could do this. Act normal.

As soon as she walked into the kitchen, Becky's look told her she knew something had happened. The girl was grinning at her, her eyes dancing with laughter. To her credit she didn't say a word but sang as she was cooking.

Shelley frowned. "Becky, do you have to warble like that? You make my ears hurt."

"Shelley, that's not kind," said Lauren.

"It's not kind to sing like that. She could damage our hearin'," Shelley insisted as she cut up some ham into smaller pieces for Joey.

Becky took the knife out of Shelley's hands and danced her around the kitchen singing at the top of her voice, much to the amusement of the other children. They were all laughing when Edward and his cousins came in. Everyone fell silent and stared at the children.

Lauren moved to their sides. "Hans, would you like to sit beside Terry and Rachel can sit on your other side. Oh." She turned to Edward. "We have ham today. Do they eat that?"

"My family have never kept kosher but I have no idea. Let me ask."

Edward fired off a question to Hans as he took his seat at the table, but the boy's reply needed no translation. Hans screwed up his face as if they had asked him to skin a possum.

"I can cook up some eggs for them," Lauren offered, but Becky insisted on doing it.

Hans said something else and Edward replied in German.

"Can't you speak English? You could be spies for all we know," Cal admonished. "Or baby-killers."

Becky gasped and Hans' eyes widened—although how much he had understood, Lauren didn't know.

"Cal, that's not nice. Apologize at once. I don't know where you get your ideas from." Lauren frowned at Cal. But he wasn't done.

"Hauptmann killed the Lindbergh baby. They said he's going to die in the electric chair. That's what they do to baby-killers and he's a German. He was an army machine-gunner in the last war, for the Germans." Cal glared at Hans.

Lauren spoke firmly, putting her finger under Cal's chin and forcing him to look at her. "Cal, we've spoken about this before. Mr. Hauptmann is a German and he fought in the last war. But that doesn't mean he is guilty of killing the Lindbergh baby. People in America get a trial." She took her hand away. "He will have to be convicted by a jury of his peers, not by the newspapers." Lauren smiled across at Edward. "No offense meant."

"I agree. The coverage of the arrest and Mr. Hauptmann's case has been prejudicial but it's up to his lawyers to argue that." Edward looked at Cal. "My father's family fought for the Germans in that war too. Does that make me a killer?"

Cal didn't look at Edward. "Don't be silly, Mr. Edward. You're American just like us. You were born here." His voice lacked conviction.

"Yes, Cal, but my father was born in Germany. It doesn't make him a killer, just like Hans and Rachel have nothing to do with the Lindbergh baby. Where you come from is not important, it's what is in your heart that matters. Haven't Lauren and Becky been teaching you that?"

Cal looked slightly embarrassed but his inquisitive nature took over. "Yes, but he was speaking German and we can't understand him so…"

"He is right. I apologize. I was rude." Hans spoke up. "I asked my uncle how to say no need to cook new food for us. We can try American food."

Lauren intervened, not wanting an argument to break out. "Thank you, Hans, you can eat what's on the table but leave the ham. Becky will have eggs ready in no time."

"How do you know they aren't spies?" Cal demanded.

"Cal!" Lauren was horrified that Cal wouldn't let the subject drop. She blamed the comics he's been reading for his fascination with spies.

"Me, spy?" Hans asked Cal.

"Yes. Why not, you're German, aren't you?" Cal's hands formed into fists on the table.

Hans didn't shrink back but spoke confidently. "Yes, but Jewish first."

That got Cal's attention. Lauren hid a smile. Hans could have hit Cal for what he said but instead he'd appealed to his intellect and curiosity.

Cal couldn't hide his surprise. "What does that matter?"

"Here maybe not matter. But in Germany, Hitler not like Jewish. He call them bad names. He not want us to live there. He take… people away."

Lauren groaned silently as she saw the inquisitiveness on Cal's face. Now he'd never leave it be. "Cal, I will explain to you later. For now, please just eat your dinner, thank you."

Cal went to ask another question but shut his mouth at the look she gave him.

"It's Christmas soon. Do you have that where you come from?" Ruthie asked.

Lauren winced, waiting for Hans to reply. To her astonishment he smiled.

"Yes, we have what you call Father Christmas too. But to us, he comes on the Eve of Christmas. I think that is a bit different."

Lauren must have looked shocked as Hans continued, "Being Jewish, we shouldn't celebrate Christmas but Papa, he liked the tradition. Every year we went to the Köningsplatz, the King's Square. Mama bought special food such as oranges and chocolate for the poorer families and left them with this lady who collected them."

Ruthie complimented him. "Your parents sound kind, Hans."

Hans' expression clouded. "Yes. But it didn't matter, did it? It didn't save Papa." His voice wavered as he spoke these words. Rachel moved closer to him and grabbed his hand. He whispered something in German and she seemed a little better.

"Christmas here is wonderful. Last year we got sacks of toys, most of us got two presents. We had so much food to eat and nobody got cranky if we ate candy." Shelley looked pointedly at Becky. "This year probably won't be the same if Thanksgiving is anything to go by."

"Christmas will be good for those who deserve it, child," Nanny reprimanded the girl softly before handing Becky a sleeping Maisie to put in her cot.

Shelley blushed but thankfully didn't reply with a smart remark.

Terry said, "Do you want to come with us when we pick out the tree? We go up on the mountain with Bart..." Then he looked like he wanted to swallow his tongue. "Clarissa, Sophie, I'm sorry. I didn't mean..."

"It's okay, Terry. We were thinking of Ma and Pa too," Clarissa answered bravely.

"Your papa is dead like ours?" Hans leaned forward.

"No. Pa works away from here. Near our ma. She's in the hospital."

He nodded. "Ah, I see. She will get better, no?"

Becky stepped in. "We don't know, Hans. Who wants dessert? Apple and berry pie with whipped cream."

Cal grinned. "Mr. Edward, can you come to dinner every day? We always get nice desserts when you come." He got a light tap on the head from Becky for his remark.

"I would be here every day if I could be, Cal," Edward responded, though he wasn't looking at Cal but holding Lauren's gaze.

Flustered, she rose to fetch some plates for the dessert.

Becky joined her and whispered, "If I needed to heat some food, you'd come in mighty handy right now. You're glowing."

"Stop teasing, Becky. It's bad enough with all the children looking at me."

"They haven't noticed, they're too busy eatin'. But I did and I'm glad you took my words to heart. You should listen to me more." Becky gripped her arm in support before turning back to taking the pies from the cooling oven.

*

After dinner the children sat listening to the radio while the adults talked.

"Did you hear about that poor boy in Charlottesville? His ma went out to work and I guess he was freezin'. He built a fire in the middle of his bedroom but the blankets caught fire." Becky shook her head.

Edward said, "It's so cold, much colder than last year. Have you plenty of wood stocked up, Terry?"

"Some, Mr.... I mean Edward..." Terry replied, "but we need more... Don't want to risk being snowed in without the means of cookin' or keeping us warm."

Edward nodded before asking Becky how much she had by the way of provisions.

"I've cans of meat left over from the last pig John Thatcher got slaughtered for us. We canned berries earlier in the year and also some peaches. We've dried apples too and have cans of applesauce and jars of jelly. We have sacks and sacks of beans. We've plenty of flour but our lard is a bit low. So if you happen to be passin' Hillmans', lard and coffee would be handy. And sugar. I want to bake some cookies for the tree and for those who come to visit."

"When are you baking?" Edward asked, rubbing his stomach. For a second, he looked just like Cal. "I want to make sure I call that day or the day Mrs. Thatcher brings down her gingerbread. Nobody can make gingerbread like she does."

Becky's eyes twinkled. "Does that mean you are comin' here for Christmas, Edward?"

Lauren felt Edward's eyes on her. After their kiss, surely he had given up all thought of going back to Germany.

"I hope so, Becky, if I get back in time." Edward coughed.

Lauren curled her fingers into her palms, her nails digging into her soft skin.

"I want to check on Rae, she's my family."

Silence reigned before a cry from Maisie interrupted them. Lauren jumped to her feet. "She's tired and needs changing. I'll put her to bed."

She almost ran up the stairs with the baby in her haste to get away. She changed Maisie, putting her down to sleep before retiring to her own room. She couldn't go back downstairs. She didn't trust herself not to beg Edward to forget about Germany and stay in the USA where he'd be safe.

CHAPTER THIRTY-ONE

Cal and Hans became close friends despite everything. It had a lot to do with Hans describing the Christmas traditions. As they sat in front of the fire the next evening, Cal and Hans spent some time whispering before Cal piped up.

"Miss Lauren, Hans says in Germany Christmas starts on December fifth. That's only a week away. Can we start then too? It would help Rachel and Hans feel at home."

Amused, Lauren exchanged a smile with Carly. "Tell us more, Cal."

"What do you call it again?" Cal asked Hans.

"Sankt Nikolaus Tag," Hans replied in German before translating. "St. Nicholas Day."

Cal nodded and turned back to Lauren. "So the way it works is that us children have to leave our boots outside the door before we go to sleep. Then the next morning, they will be full of candy. You have to do it, Miss Lauren, to make Hans and Rachel feel welcome."

Lauren winked at Carly before adopting a serious expression. "Perhaps I should do it, just for Hans and Rachel's sake of course."

Hans laughed as the other children clapped in delight with calls of "Can we do it, please, Miss Lauren?"

Hans said, "We must clean the boots first. No dirty boots outside the doors. Saint Nicholas not come." He thought for a moment. "He also puts nuts in boots. Nuts is not candy?"

Cal's expression made Lauren and Carly smile. The thought of candy being in the same category as nuts obviously offended him. "Candy is things like chocolate and toffee. You have candy in Germany, don't you?"

Hans either ignored or misunderstood Cal's sarcasm. "Ja. We have lots of these things you call candy. Do you have stollen?"

"What's that?" Cal screwed up his face. "It don't sound nice."

Hans grinned. "You wrong. Stollen is beautiful. It is so tasty. It is like bread but with fruit mixed in. I like it, lots." He rubbed his stomach for emphasis, making them all laugh.

Becky said, "Hans, if you could find a recipe for me, maybe from Edward, I can try to make it for you."

"Thank you, Fräulein Becky."

"So, Fräulein Lauren, will you do Christmas the German way?" Cal copied his friend.

Lauren tried to keep her amusement hidden, adopting a firm tone. "I could do, Cal, but would that involve *all* the German customs including Krampus Nacht?"

Hans burst out laughing as Rachel shook her head.

Cal looked at Hans laughing, and guessed Lauren wasn't talking about presents. A doubtful expression on his face, he queried, "That depends. What is that?"

Hans clarified, "Krampus Nacht is like the devil. He visits children who are bad. I mean, they do not do as they are told. They do not go to school or they steal things. Those children get a visit from Krampus Nacht."

Cal's eyes stuck out on stalks. "You mean they get to see him in person?"

"Ja, in some parts of Germany. Bavaria mainly, but we never saw him, did we Rachel?" Hans repeated his question in German to his sister, who shook her head vigorously.

For a second Lauren worried Cal would find Krampus Nacht intriguing enough to want to meet him.

"I don't think we need that guy here, Miss Lauren. Let's just have Saint Nicholas." Cal turned to Hans. "Why don't you teach us some German words. Like the word for"—he glanced around, the slight blush on his face suggesting the words he wanted translated weren't suitable for his audience and quickly named alternatives—"plate, fork, knife. Those kind of words."

Lauren left Hans listing out each word in German and translating them into English. The children pointed out different things and Hans told them the name in German while they taught him the words he didn't know.

Lauren walked over nearer Becky who was damping down the stove for the night.

"Will you do the Saint Nicholas night for them?" Becky asked.

"Why not? It won't cost a lot and it'll help us get in the Christmas mood."

"It will also get a lot of shoes shined," Nanny said from the kitchen sink. She smiled and turned to them, drying her hands in a dishtowel. "I think it's a wonderful idea. I was reading how Hitler wants to change Christmas. He wants the Germans to put that horrible sign of his on top of their trees."

Lauren was horrified. "A swastika on top of a Christmas tree? The churches won't agree to that, will they?"

"I guess that depends on the church. I'm off to bed, ladies. Becky, thank you for putting the warm stone in my bed."

"I didn't, Nanny Kat. Must have been Lauren."

"Not me." They all looked at Carly, who was holding Maisie and watching the boys.

Nanny commented, "She's such a dear girl, isn't she. Heart of gold."

CHAPTER THIRTY-TWO

The days flew past despite the school being closed due to bad weather blocking the roads. Lauren hated getting out of bed in the mornings and the feel of her feet touching the chilly floor. Looking out at the pristine snow covering the mountains was lovely so long as you didn't get too close to the window. She shivered as she reached for a jumper to wear over her two vests and her blouse. She didn't care that she looked like she'd gained thirty pounds.

She made her way to the kitchen, which was warm thanks to the fact they left the stove on overnight. One thing that was free was wood; it was a good job as they went through so much of it. She filled the pot with water.

Becky followed her down, yawning and wearing as many layers as Lauren was.

"No wonder the children want to sleep down here, the kitchen and living room are the warmest rooms in the house. I keep expectin' to wake up and find snow on my bed like we did in our old house," Becky said.

"Nanny's is cozy too as Terry keeps her fire topped up. She's getting better at staying in bed too, that chill last week gave her a lesson, I think," Lauren replied.

Becky stoked up the stove, adding smaller pieces of wood, waiting for them to catch before using the larger pieces. "What will we do to entertain the children today? There won't be school, not with the snow falling so heavily. Will you be able to get to Delgany?"

Lauren wasn't certain she wanted to drive. The roads were bad enough when there was light snow but with freezing temperatures it was likely they'd be like glass. "I think I might ride in on the mule."

"Bit different to Prince, isn't he?" Becky grinned.

"He sure is. But I wouldn't risk Prince in this weather. If he broke a leg I wouldn't forgive myself."

"Never mind the fact Sam would kill you. Did he confirm whether he is comin' for Christmas or not?"

"He said it depends on the weather," Lauren said, as she took out the cutlery and set the table.

"If I give you a list of things we need at Hillmans', maybe Earl or his pa will drive them out later."

Lauren hesitated before asking, "Is Will coming for Christmas?"

"I don't know. Don't care either," Becky replied firmly.

Lauren stopped what she was doing and looked at her friend, exasperated. "That's not true and we both know it. Becky, why don't you marry Will? You love him, that's obvious."

"I told you before, I don't want to be tied down with a load of kids like Ma was."

Lauren looked pointedly at the table with all the place settings. "Seems to me you already have the children, you're just missing the man. And he's a good one. He thinks the world of you and he's not going to wait around forever. You know you are the only reason he stays in Virginia, working odd jobs in Charlottesville. He'd have gone to California with Jed and Mary if it weren't for you."

"Let him go." Becky turned back to the cooker and started banging pans around. Lauren took the hint and let the conversation go. After a breakfast of bacon, eggs, and grits, she added her slicker on top of her outfit.

"Lauren, take at least one layer off or you will arrive in Delgany in a puddle of sweat. That's not a good look on anyone."

She went up to her room to change. As she took off some of the layers, she heard someone crying in the room above her.

She crept up the stairs to find Rachel alone in the girls' room.

"Rachel, sweetheart, come here and give me a cuddle." Lauren sat on the bed and held out her arms. Rachel had yet to open up to any of them and the only person she showed affection to was Hans, unless Edward turned up. But he had been in Washington this past week trying to secure a visa for Rae and her in-laws.

Rachel moved toward her, hesitating at the last minute. Lauren pretended she hadn't noticed and moved slightly to envelop the girl in a hug. Rachel put her head on her shoulder and Lauren could feel her tears wetting the collar of her shirt.

"There now, darling. What can I do?"

"I miss Papa."

Rachel had talked. Lauren didn't want to do anything to stop her so kept rubbing her back.

"Every night, the dream it comes. Papa is hurt. The bad man take him. He never comes back. Mama is gone too. When will it stop, this dream? Is Papa ever coming back? How he find us? We not with Mama."

The girl shuddered as the tears flowed. Lauren held her until her tears were spent. Then she pushed her back a little and looked her in the eyes.

"Rachel, you are such a brave young girl. Your papa is so proud of you. He loves you so much. Your mama too."

"But when will they come?" Her expression was desperate.

"Edward… he is going to try to bring your mama to you. As soon as he can."

"To this house?"

"I'm not sure if she will come here or to Edward's father's home. Edward will travel as soon as the weather permits. You have to be patient for a bit longer." She wasn't at all sure how much Rachel understood.

"Papa. He come with Mama?"

She couldn't lie to the child. Nothing good would come of it.

"No, Rachel. Your papa won't come. He is…"

"*Tot.* Dead!"

"Yes, darling, he is dead. Your mama didn't know until you had left for America. You should be proud of your papa. He was a brave man." Lauren felt rather silly as she gathered the child didn't understand.

She walked to the bedroom door and shouted for Hans to come up from where he and Cal were chatting about something in the boys' room.

"What's wrong? Did I do something?"

"No, Hans. I need you to talk to Rachel. She spoke to me…"

"She spoke?" Hans came running. He rushed to his sister's side and cuddled her. Rachel's knuckles turned white as she held onto her brother, sobbing her heart out on his shoulder. Lauren sat beside them on the bed.

"I said she should be very proud of your father, that he was a very brave man. I'm sorry, she asked me if he was coming to America and I had to tell her the truth." Lauren slowed down her words so he could follow her.

"You did right. She should know." He fired off a rapid speech in German and, whatever he said, it made Rachel look a bit less upset.

She lifted her head and looked at Lauren, trying to smile. Lauren smiled back, wanting to wrap the child in layers of protection against the horrible experiences she'd faced—and those ahead of her. If America did end up at war how many people would look past Rachel's German origins to see she was a victim too?

Lauren patted Rachel's back before standing up to leave the children alone. "I'm going downstairs. You take as long as you need, Hans. Ask Rachel if there is anything she would like to do for Christmas. Anything special. Or if you have a Jewish celebration you would like us to honor…"

He looked thoughtful. "We have Hanukkah. I think in America you call it the Festival of Lights. It is very special time for Jews."

"Can we do it with you? Or is that forbidden?"

Hans shrugged his shoulders. "I do not know."

"I'll find out." Lauren gave a reassuring smile and went out of the bedroom, pulling the door part-shut to give the children some privacy. She had to find a way of welcoming them to America and helping them make it their home.

CHAPTER THIRTY-THREE

"Miss Chaney, do you know any Jewish people?" Lauren asked the old postmistress. She'd come into the post office to buy some stamps and other bits and pieces. "Living near here, I mean?"

"Jewish?" Miss Chaney held her head to one side as she always did when thinking. "There's quite a large synagogue over in Charlottesville on Jefferson."

"I was hoping I wouldn't have to drive that far."

"Lauren, are you converting?" Miss Chaney frowned, confused.

"No, not at all. We have some children staying with us for a bit—Jewish children—and they are missing home." Lauren hesitated to say "Germany" even to Miss Chaney. She didn't know what Edward intended telling people about his new relations. She didn't want to betray any of his confidences.

"Poor children, what a time of year to be away from your loved ones." Miss Chaney counted out Lauren's change.

"Where are you going for Christmas this year, Miss Chaney? You are always welcome with us. I can find you a bed too if you don't mind sharing with some of the girls. They won't mind sleeping on the floor on a mattress. That way you don't have to worry about traveling at night, especially if it snows."

Miss Chaney smiled. "I'd love to come, Lauren. Now let me think. There is an older couple, German they are, they live over the other side of town down near the canning factory. I don't know if they are Jewish but I suspect they are. Never see them at church, although that doesn't mean anything."

Lauren ignored the barb. Miss Chaney was a regular at the local Baptist church and kept suggesting Lauren join too.

"Do you have their address?"

Miss Chaney rooted through her books. "Here it is. Mr. and Mrs. Victor Meyer." She wrote out the address. "Lauren, be careful. I don't think Mrs. Meyer wants people to know she is German."

"Why not?"

"You see the war memorial daily. Just about every family in the surrounding area lost at least one son, maybe two, to the war."

"That was twenty years ago."

"Yes, but memories are long, especially with that Hitler rattling his saber not to mention the anti-German feeling aroused by the Lindberg baby trial. Doesn't take much to get the good folk of Delgany in uproar, as you should know. I'm not suggesting you don't try, but just be subtle."

Lauren took the address and her change. With a reminder to Miss Chaney not to buy presents for everyone, she went back to her truck.

*

She drove on past the canning factory, trying not to breathe in the smell too deeply. She'd hate living in this part of Delgany between the stench from the canning factory and the noise of the trains. The streets narrowed and she slowed as she tried to find the address. She drove past it twice before parking and deciding to find it on foot.

She double-checked the address Miss Chaney had written before knocking on the door. The house looked out of place in its surroundings. It had been recently painted, the windows were clean, and weeds around the front of the property had been removed. The next-door neighbors' houses were strewn with pieces of rubbish, the paint peeling from the doors. But there were more signs of life as children came and went. Despite the chilly temperatures, the children weren't wearing hats and gloves, some didn't even have coats. She shivered as she knocked on the front door.

Initially she thought there was nobody home as it took ages for them to answer the door. But then she heard a noise, so she waited for the door to open, which it did only sufficiently far to allow a woman to poke out her head.

"I don't need anything, thank you, I have no money."

"Mrs. Meyer?" Lauren gave a friendly smile.

The woman looked terrified. Her eyes kept darting to her neighbors' houses and back again.

"My name is Lauren Greenwood, I live at an orphanage outside of Delgany and I need your help. Miss Chaney sent me."

"Miss Chaney?"

"Yes, the postmistress. She said you might be able to help me."

The woman looked her up and down. "Sorry, I can't help you."

"Mrs. Meyer, please listen to what I need. I promise it's not money or anything. I have two children—Jewish children—and I need some help in looking after them."

Mrs. Meyer shook her head. "I'm too old to care for children."

"I don't mean in that way. Please could I come inside for five minutes? I just…" Lauren looked round her. "I don't wish anyone to hear me."

Mrs. Meyer took a second but she opened the door wider, allowing Lauren to slip inside before closing it again. The inside of the house was like the outside, neat and cared for with everything in its place.

"Please sit down. Forgive me but we sometimes have trouble. People are afraid of us."

Mr. Meyer came through from the back. "A visitor. How nice. What brings you to our home, young lady?"

"My name is Lauren and Miss Chaney is a friend of mine. I look after the orphanage, Hope House, out the other side of

Delgany. We have two new arrivals recently. They're Jewish and came from Germany."

She saw Mrs. Meyer clasp her husband's hand. He patted it before looking back at Lauren. "Please continue."

"The children only arrived in the country a week ago. They were supposed to go to a Jewish uncle but he is away. They weren't expected…" Lauren faltered, trying to work out how much to say.

Mr. Meyer looked as though he understood. "You mean they had to leave Germany in a hurry?"

"Yes, Mr. Meyer. I won't lie to you but I wasn't sure how much to tell you. Their father, he was a lawyer and he criticized the Nazi party. He was taken from his house and never returned. My friend thought the children might be in danger so he brought them back to America."

"This is a very sad story, but how do you think we can help you?" Mrs. Meyer spoke without looking at her husband or Lauren. She stared at the unlit fire.

"Miss Chaney… she thought you might be Jewish."

"How could she tell? Why would she say that?" Mrs. Meyer appeared very flustered.

Mr. Meyer attempted to soothe his wife. "Chana, please sit down. Our guest means us no harm. She has tried to be discreet. We will not be victims, not here."

"But if they find us?" Mrs. Meyer was growing agitated.

Lauren put out her hand automatically. "Mrs. Meyer, I will leave, I'm sorry to cause you such distress. Please excuse me."

She stood up to go.

"Please sit down, Miss Lauren. My wife, she has suffered so much, she is still hurting, still living in fear. No matter how often I tell her the people here in America are different. What help do you need?"

Lauren sat down slowly and chose her words carefully. "Rachel and Hans are so young and alone. They do not speak English very well. Hans said they have a celebration called…" Lauren couldn't remember the name. She blushed. "I forget what he called it, I'm sorry. It is something about lights."

"Hanukkah, the Festival of Lights," Mr. Meyer said.

At his words, his wife sobbed and ran out of the room and up the stairs. Lauren faltered but the man was still looking at her, waiting for her to explain.

"Yes, that's it. I thought if someone explained it to me, we could do it at the orphanage with the other children. To make Hans and Rachel feel welcome."

"You are a very kind young woman, Miss Lauren," Mr. Meyer said, his expression warm.

"Lauren, please. I can't bear to think of what these children have been through. Hans had to leave his school and then Rachel, she watched her father being taken away. She hasn't spoken since, not until today. This morning. I'm afraid I got so caught up in helping them I didn't think of any pain I might inflict on others. I'm so sorry."

"You must forgive my wife. We moved to America many years ago. We had a good life until the war broke out… People we knew well, we thought them friends, turned against us. Our windows were broken, our house defaced. After the war was over, we returned to live in Germany thinking we would find peace and for a while we did. We took our son Pieter with us, our other children remained here at school and such."

Mr. Meyer walked over to the mantelpiece, picked up a photo of a serious-looking young man and handed it to Lauren.

"This was Pieter. He studied to become a lawyer like your friend. We lived in Munich. One night in 1922, Pieter came across a group of Hitler's SA men beating up a man he knew, who the SA accused of being a communist. The man was Jewish, a law student like Pieter who had never attended a communist meeting. Instead of walking by, Pieter tried to help. He told the

SA members that there were laws and everyone deserved a trial, they were innocent until found guilty. Pieter never came home. We heard later what happened to our boy. Chana, she blames herself as she was the one who really wanted to go back to Germany."

"I am so sorry, Mr. Meyer." Lauren looked up at him, her eyes filling with tears.

"You are not to blame." He walked over to a cabinet from which he took what looked like a candelabra. "You will need this for your celebrations. Hanukkah takes place over eight nights. It is now the fifth day. You must light a candle on each night. You should also cook some special food. We also play games."

"Eight nights? I thought it might be something like Christmas. I can barely make coffee or boil an egg."

He smiled. "Lauren, please sit down and I will make us a drink. Please. Indulge a lonely old man. We never get visitors. Our children, they are scattered around the world."

Lauren looked at her watch. She should really go back and help Becky with lunch but she didn't want to be rude, and something about the man made her stay.

"I will just check on my wife. Please make yourself comfortable." He excused himself from the room.

Lauren sat on the chair looking around the room, trying not to shiver. She pulled her coat closer. It appeared the Meyers were struggling. At their age, they should have a fire lit during this weather.

Mrs. Meyer came down with her husband but disappeared into the kitchen. Soon she came back carrying a tray. Lauren moved to help her.

"I'm sorry, please forgive my bad manners. I get upset."

"I can only imagine what you have been through, Mrs. Meyer. I'm sorry I brought back bad memories. Your husband has been very kind."

"Please sit and have some tea. I haven't been shopping so I don't have anything made."

"Tea is lovely, thank you." Lauren accepted the black tea, enjoying the warmth radiating through her hands.

"We would like to come and meet the children. We can help explain how to make the food, if that is acceptable to you."

Lauren smiled. "That would be fantastic, Mrs Meyer, thank you. I can drive us out to the orphanage and then bring you back home. Nanny, she's my grandmother's sister, being surrounded by children craves the company of adults so she'll be delighted to meet you. Becky, she runs the orphanage with me, is from the mountain and has been the victim of prejudice too."

"Becky? You mean she is Jewish—Rebecca?"

"No, she isn't Jewish. She lived up on the mountain but she lost her home after her mother and younger brother were taken to the colony. Donnie, her brother, had some problems and his mother wouldn't leave him. They took them away."

Mr. Meyer looked grave. "The poor woman. Yes, there are many who suffer and they don't have to be Jewish or German. I tell Chana this every day."

"But, Victor, now they talk about war again."

Lauren spoke up. "Mrs. Meyer, please try to give us a chance. Not everyone is like your previous neighbors. The children may say something silly about Germans but you can teach them that we are all just people at the end of the day."

"We go now, yes?" Mrs. Meyer asked. "We must help the children."

Surprised at the sudden change in Mrs. Meyer, Lauren stood up. "I parked up the street."

The three of them left with Mr. Meyer carrying the candlestick and his wife the candles. They drove back to the orphanage with Lauren outlining how Hope House came about, what they had achieved so far, and the trials facing them.

*

The children must have been watching as they came out to greet Lauren when she arrived.

"Children, this is Mr. and Mrs. Meyer," Lauren said as she helped them out of the truck. "They've come to visit us and teach us some things to help Rachel and Hans feel more at home."

Cal cocked his head to one side, his eyes raking their guests from top to toe. "Do you speak English or are you German too?" he said.

"Cal!" Lauren glared at him, willing him to be quiet and behave.

Mr. Meyer seemed unfazed. "Yes to both your questions, young man. We are German and we speak English."

Lauren said, "Cal, can you find Hans and Rachel and ask them to come to the kitchen. Come inside please, Becky and Nanny are probably in the kitchen already. It's a lot of work to make lunch and dinner for this lot of hungry varmints." Lauren ruffled Ruthie's hair as she joked.

Ruthie looked up at Lauren and said, "Becky was wonderin' what took you so long. She said you must have gone to plant some sugar and were waitin' for it to grow. You didn't do that, did you?"

"No, Ruthie, of course not. I visited with Miss Chaney and then the Meyers. I wasn't that long."

She led the group into the house, introducing the Meyers to Becky and Nanny just before Hans and Rachel came downstairs. Mr. Meyer greeted them in German while Mrs. Meyer went over to them both and kissed them on the cheek. She muttered something to them and they replied.

"They are speaking Yiddish, not German, although it is very similar," Mr. Meyer explained.

Becky wiped her hands on her apron and said, "Mr. Meyer, I made lunch. Some soup and homemade bread. Would you like some?"

"Thank you, Miss Becky. We would, if it isn't too much trouble."

"No trouble, but you may find it rather noisy."

The children had set the table but Lauren soon found two more bowls for their guests. "Why don't you sit right here?" She indicated the two places. "Hans and Rachel, sit here."

The Meyers took a seat as Becky called for the children to join them. The children came running, all chattering at once as they took their places at the table. Lauren helped Becky, dishing out the water for drinks as Becky filled up soup bowls. Carly sat Maisie up in her high chair then cut the bread and placed it on the table with plates of butter. Nanny spoke with Mr. Meyer and they soon found out they knew people in common. Lauren exchanged a smile with Becky as everyone seemed to talk at once.

It was only when the bowls were empty the questions started.

"Hans says he likes something called Stollen. Do you know how to make it?" Cal asked Mrs. Meyer.

Before she could answer, Ruthie said, "Do you know a horrible man comes to visit the children in Germany if they are naughty? He doesn't come here." The girl shivered visibly.

"Do you open your presents on Christmas Eve because you are German or on Christmas Day because you live here?" Shelley asked.

Lauren stood up. "Children, stop pestering our guests with all these questions. You aren't giving them time to answer." She directed her attention to the elderly couple. "Mr. Meyer, if you don't mind moving into the sitting room, you could explain Hanukkah to the children in more comfortable surroundings. Becky and I will clear up in here and follow you in."

Mr. Meyer stood up, offering his hand to help his wife. "We will chat to the children until you are ready, Lauren, but it is important you hear the message too."

Terry topped up the fire with more wood. Carly, Shelley, and the younger girls cleared the plates and glasses. Lauren washed the dishes while Carly dried, and then Shelley swept the floor. Nanny sat with the Meyers.

Becky said, "They seem like lovely people, Lauren. I sense they are lonely."

"Yes, Becky, I think they are. They are so kind to come up here. Hans and Rachel already look happier, don't you think?" Lauren said.

"They do but they ain't the only ones. Look at Nanny Kat. She's enjoyin' the company of people nearer her own age. She misses her regular chats with Old Sally."

"Becky, the Meyers are only in their sixties," Lauren replied, though she knew Becky was right.

"That's still closer in age than us."

CHAPTER THIRTY-FOUR

Once Rachel found her voice, she blossomed. Lauren had taught Terry to drive the previous summer, so some days he drove into Delgany to collect the Meyers and bring them out to the orphanage. Often Hans or Rachel or both would go with him.

Mrs. Meyer showed Becky and some of the children how to make potato pancakes called latkes and jelly-filled doughnuts. The boys, Cal in particular, loved the doughnuts.

"Do Germans all eat like this?" Cal asked, his mouth smeared with jelly.

Mrs. Meyer beamed. "It's a Jewish tradition but yes, many Germans like doughnuts too. They like playing ball and soldiers and make models just like you do, Cal. People from different countries are very much alike in ways."

"But they are bad, those Germans. Not you and Hans but the rest of them." Cal spoke with his mouth full, earning him a reprimand from Carly.

Mr. Meyer overheard his comment. "No, not everyone is bad. There are good Germans too. Where you are from or what God you praise does not make you bad or good. The choices you make"—Mr. Meyer pointed his finger at Cal—"they are what determines if someone is good or bad."

Cal hesitated as if thinking before he asked, "Like Hitler, as he's bad, isn't he?"

"Yes, I'm afraid he is, but maybe some time ago he could have been good if he'd made different decisions." Mr. Meyer sighed heavily. "He is not a happy man and he blames a whole people for that unhappiness. The thing is he can never be happy."

"He thinks he will when he becomes all powerful," Fred added as he worked on his figures. Once the Meyers had seen the figures he made for the crib last Christmas, Mrs. Meyer had shown him the wooden Christmas angels they had brought back from Germany. Fred used one as a model and was now happily making his fifth. The children loved them.

Mr. Meyer looked sad. "Even then he will not be happy. In June this year, he killed a lot of his friends. Those men and Hitler once drank together, chatted together, even laughed. But he had them shot."

"Why would he kill his friends?" Cal asked, his head resting on his hands as he stared at Mr. Meyer.

"Because he thought they were a threat. When people become very powerful, they are forever looking over their shoulder wondering who is going to push them off their perch. Hitler got into power by doing bad things and hurting other people. He knows the people around him could do the same to him."

"So he kills them before they murder him?" Cal asked.

"You are an intelligent boy, young Cal."

"Well that's just stupid. He'll run out of friends and who will he talk to then?" Cal looked baffled.

Lauren waited for Mr. Meyer to answer but apparently he was as stumped as she was.

The sound of wheels on the drive announced the arrival of Edward. Lauren was the first to the door, glad to see him.

"How was Washington?" she called as he came into the hallway.

"Cold, miserable, and lacking the most important people in my life." Edward's response made her blush. She hid her face by taking his coat and hanging it up on the hooks. Hans and Rachel ran to him.

"Rachel speaks now, Onkel Edward," Hans said, looking at his sister with pride.

She spoke to him rapidly in German before switching to English. "Thank you for bringing us to live here. We are very happy. Come and meet Mr. and Mrs. Meyer."

Rachel introduced Edward to the couple. Becky made more coffee while Edward caught up with the happenings at the orphanage.

"So you celebrated the Festival of Lights here?"

Hal said, "Yes, Onkel Edward, and everyone joined in. We are going to join in with the Christmas celebrations. Nobody here cares we are German."

"Because you are good Germans," Cal added.

Lauren frowned at Cal as Mr. Meyer said, "Cal? I thought we spoke about this? You don't hate a person just because of their country or their religion, do you?"

"Me? No, Mr. Meyer, but someday I may have to fight and then I will hate Germans as they will be shooting at me."

Becky and Lauren exchanged a look of horror. Where had the boy got the idea that war was inevitable? The government was working on a neutrality pact. Most Americans did not want another war in Europe. Many believed if one did happen, it was best for America not to get involved.

"So who's been good for Father Christmas?" Edward asked, his voice loud enough to distract the whole room.

The children's voices rang out, shouting, "Me! Me!"

"Are you going to be here again this Christmas like you were last year?" Ruthie asked Edward.

"I hope so, Ruthie, but I have to go away to Washington again for a while first."

"You better not be long. Miss Lauren is bringing us up to the mountain to choose the tree. We are goin' to set it up on the twenty-third as that's the day before Christmas Eve. Will you try to be back in time?"

"I will, little darling. I will."

Lauren's stomach turned warm as she watched him chatting so sweetly with Ruthie.

CHAPTER THIRTY-FIVE

Lauren walked through the streets of Delgany, the Christmas lights only serving to make her more depressed. The Hillmans were leaving town; they had announced that they would shut up the store in the new year. She'd cried along with Mrs. Hillman when she'd told Lauren. They hadn't said anything to Ellie-Mae and Dalton yet as they were worried about how the youngsters would take the news. They loved Delgany as much as the Hillmans did. They would spend Christmas with their daughter Annie and her family. Earl was remaining at home so Lauren insisted he come to the orphanage for dinner.

Her arms hurt from the weight of the provisions in the box. She'd saved fifty cents a week at Hillmans' in order to have money for Christmas. Earl would drive up later with the larger boxes but Becky needed sugar, flour, and salt for baking, as well as coffee to help them get through two more days of children being overexcited.

She greeted those she met with a smile and a "Happy Christmas," hoping they would take her tears for snow hitting her eyes. Not that there were many out on the sidewalk, the snow was coming down hard and sticking. The wheels of the truck were already half covered and she'd only parked an hour ago. She couldn't get near Hillmans' but had parked up beside Ginny's hairdressing salon.

As she approached the truck she heard Ginny's voice. "Lauren, there you are. I've been watching out to try to catch you. Here, let me hold that while you get the back down." Ginny took the box from Lauren. "Gee, this is heavy."

Lauren jumped up on the back of the truck to take the box and put it safely behind some other others so it didn't fall over. She covered it with the canvas Bart had put in. Why did she have to think of Bart and Norma now? They wouldn't be coming back for Christmas either.

"These are for you. It isn't much but I tried to remember all the children. You can tie them to the tree. I've packed two extra just in case. Maybe you could put the names on them." Ginny handed Lauren the bag she was holding on her arm. It was full of men's mismatched socks, each holding a pile of candy.

"Ginny, that's so sweet of you."

Ginny smiled. "I wish I could give you something decent but things are tight again this year. Last year I was happy to be losing a few pounds in weight. This year, I'm starting to lose my boobs and that's a bad thing for us women, isn't it?"

Lauren burst out laughing as Ginny lit up a cigarette.

"What did I say?"

"Ginny, you are what Nanny calls a tonic. I was feeling so down and you made me laugh. Thank you." Impulsively Lauren kissed the woman's cheek. "I hope you have a wonderful Christmas, Ginny. I'm sure 1935 will be a much better year for us all."

"I'll drink to that, Lauren. You kiss those children for me." She took another drag before grinding out the cigarette and putting the unfinished part back in her purse. "I best get back or Mrs. Eaton will look like that poodle of hers. Merry Christmas, Lauren."

Lauren smiled as Ginny ducked between a couple of cars before heading back into her salon.

*

Lauren drove back to Hope House, the windscreen wipers working at full speed but failing to keep the windscreen clear. Maybe she should drive back to Delgany to collect the other provisions. If it kept snowing like this, Earl might not be able to make it out this far. She made her way up the road slowly, avoiding the worst of the chuckholes. Come the new year she was going to get them fixed, even if she had to do it herself. One of these days they could cause a nasty accident.

The children poured out onto the porch to meet her though she could hear Becky yelling at them not to go outside without their coats. Terry came forward to carry the box. Carly followed and took the bag of candy from Ginny Dobbs.

"Carly, can you put that in my bedroom before the little ones see it, please?"

"Sure thing, Miss Lauren." Carly took the bag upstairs, telling Shelley to mind her own business when she asked what was in it. Lauren took off her coat and boots at the door, hitting the boots against the side of the house to dislodge as much snow as possible.

"Will you close that door, you have a blizzard comin' in on top of us," Becky yelled from the kitchen.

"Coming." Lauren hung up her coat on the rack and moved the boots to the back door.

"Sit down there and drink this up quick. You look half frozen to death." Becky handed Lauren a mug.

Lauren gratefully accepted the hot drink, not bothering to ask what it was. It was heat she needed and Becky hadn't had a chance to unpack their provisions yet.

"So what's the news from town? Meet anyone nicer than yourself?"

Lauren took a sip of her drink. "I met Ginny Dobbs, she gave me a sack full of gifts for the children. I asked Carly to take it to my room. Earl said he would try to bring out the rest of the provisions later today. Though maybe I should drive back into town, that snow doesn't show any signs of stopping."

"Earl will be fine, Lauren. You've done enough."

Cal came running in. "Are we goin' to find the tree, Miss Lauren? You promised we'd go today."

Becky frowned. "Cal, leave Miss Lauren be, can't you see she is half frozen?"

The boy's shoulders slumped as he took a seat at the table. "I've been good. Done my bed and my chores and cut enough wood to last till doomsday."

Lauren gave him a smile. "Thank you, Cal. I will go with you today. Just give my feet a chance to defrost, will you please?"

"You should wear your pants. Dresses are stupid in this type of weather," Cal said.

Becky grinned. "You know, Cal, that might be the most intelligent thing you've said this year. We should all wear pants."

"Over my dead body. I never wore them and I'm not about to start now," Nanny exclaimed as she walked into the kitchen. Lauren noted she wasn't limping as much. One thing good about the weather was that Nanny refused to go outside for fear she would fall. She had no option but to rest; talk about every cloud having a silver lining.

"Did you have a chance to go to the post office, Lauren?" Nanny asked, taking her seat at the table.

"Yes, Nanny. Miss Chaney gave me letters from Mary and one from Bart. Some cards too. I've left them on the seat in the truck."

"I'll get them." Cal leaped up.

"What's with the long face, Lauren. Bad news?" Becky asked, taking a bowl of walnuts to the table along with some newspaper.

Lauren set her cup down on the table. "Gene Hillman has decided to close up. There isn't enough business for him to make the store work now he no longer has the sawmill. They are going to talk to Annie about moving near her when they see her for the holidays."

Nanny tutted. "This darn Depression. When will it ever end? I thought Roosevelt was going to fix everything."

Becky looked up from shelling walnuts. "He's tryin', Nanny Kat. We just have to be patient."

"Hard, at my age, to be patient, Becky. I am the wrong age to be losing my friends."

"Now don't you start. I have enough with Lauren bein' down in the dumps. This is Christmas and after the year we've had, those children deserve the best one we can give them. So if you have to paste on smiles, do it. I won't stand for anyone ruinin' Christmas now when we had such a miserable Thanksgivin'."

Lauren raised her eyebrows. "Who are you and what did you do with Sensible Becky who always said Christmas came and went, it was more important to worry about mortgage payments and having a roof over their heads?"

"She was far too sensible. This Becky likes to have fun. So for one thing I am going to look for the best Christmas tree ever. Are you comin'?"

Nanny said, "Go on, Lauren. I can look after Maisie, Joey, and whoever else wants to stay."

Becky gathered up the children, including Hans and Rachel who were very excited about going up the mountain.

"We never picked out a Christmas tree before," Hans explained. His English had come on so well. Rachel's had improved too. It was largely due to the Meyers who visited as often as Lauren could drive over to collect them. Children learned fast. Cal was studying German, astonishing everyone with the speed with which he was picking up the language.

*

The snow was still falling, the children dashing around trying to catch snowflakes on their tongues. They were all dressed for the cold weather with hats and mittens as well as scarves. Everyone came apart from Lottie and Shelley. Lottie had a slight chill and

Shelley wouldn't leave Joey behind. He was too small to climb up the side of the mountain, especially with his bad leg.

They split into two teams and threw snowballs at each other as they went. The children sang Christmas carols, Hans and Rachel singing "Silent Night" in German so beautifully it brought tears to Lauren's eyes.

"This one," Cal shouted as he ran to a tree.

Terry followed him with the ax before shaking his head. "You can't take that one. Look." Cal and the children looked up to find the nest Terry was pointing at. "Some critter is quite cozy in there. So let's find another one."

They'd gone up much farther than Lauren had planned before the children decided they'd found a perfect tree. By this time Cal was teasing Hans and Rachel over the mountain cats they might encounter.

The snow stopped falling for a bit as they moved to a safe distance from the tree. Lauren didn't want anyone suffering any injuries or mishaps. She pulled Rachel back when the girl got a little too close.

Terry hit the tree with an ax followed by Fred. Between the two of them they felled it.

"Now we just have to carry it home," Becky said, as they stared at the tree, which looked even bigger now that it was on the ground.

The sound of bells carried over the wind.

"Someone's comin'. Look there," Becky said.

The children pointed in the distance. By squinting Lauren could make out two sleighs heading in their direction. "It's Big Will, I think."

They watched the men approach and soon Big Will pulled up, closely followed by Earl Hillman on the second sleigh.

"We figured you might need a hand getting the tree down the mountain. Anyone want a lift?'

The children chorused out "Yes." Terry and Earl attached the tree to the back of Earl's sleigh while the children crowded around Big Will.

Lauren said, "Becky, you go with Will, take Cal, Clarissa, and Sophie with you, and I'll travel down with Earl and Terry and the other children. Go on."

She pushed Becky in Will's direction, causing Becky to stumble. Becky would have fallen but for Will holding out his arms and grabbing her. He kissed her, picked her up, and carried her over to his sleigh—all the while she was protesting in his arms. She wasn't fighting him too hard though, Lauren was pleased to see. Maybe his long absence had worked and Becky realized what she was missing.

The children cheered so loudly that the men hushed them, telling them they might cause an avalanche. Of course there was no truth in that but Lauren giggled as she saw the wonder on the children's faces as they stared up the mountain.

The mountainside became alive to the sounds of Christmas carols echoing back as they sang all the way home. Her hands frozen, Lauren shoved them inside her coat. Despite the lack of feeling in her limbs she was thrilled Becky had insisted they all go out.

CHAPTER THIRTY-SIX

Back at the orphanage, Nanny had mulled wine waiting for the adults and hot chocolate for the children. Everyone sat around the table holding the warm cups in their hands, their noses red from the cold.

"That was amazing," Cal said.

"Ja, very amazing," Hans commented, causing much laughter.

Rachel said, "We have to decorate the tree. Can we ask the Meyers to come and watch? I think they get lonely."

Lauren replied, "That's kind of you, Rachel, but I can't drive to Delgany in that snow."

"I can get them on the sleigh," Earl offered.

"You have barely defrosted from the last trip," Lauren said. "The Meyers are coming tomorrow."

"Let me get them, Miss Lauren. It will help put me in the Christmas mood too."

Lauren met Earl's eyes. She knew he didn't want to leave Delgany. She nodded. "If your parents don't need you to do deliveries. Maybe suggest the Meyers bring some clothes for a couple of nights. They might as well stay here than try to get home with this weather."

"Sure." He drained his drink and left. Rachel wanted to go with him but he suggested she stay home as it was so cold.

The children wanted to decorate the tree but Lauren insisted they wait until Earl came back.

"Sure it's Earl you're waitin' for?" Becky teased from where she sat at the table opposite Will.

Lauren didn't reply. Edward had been hoping to be back by Christmas but they hadn't heard from him in days. The processing of Rae's application for a visa was taking longer than he had expected.

*

The Meyers and Earl turned up a few hours later, covered in snow and chilled to the bone despite the numerous layers they were wearing. Terry and Hans moved out of their room and into the boys' bedroom. Carly and Lauren made up the double bed for the Meyers, causing Mrs. Meyer to cry when she saw it ready for them.

"You are so kind. When I think what I said to you the first time you came to see us…"

"That's all in the past now, Mrs. Meyer," Lauren said, giving her arm a pat.

"Chana, please. I baked some foods for you. They are in my other bags. My grandchildren, they like to hang cookies from their tree."

Lauren's confusion must have shown on her face.

"My grandchildren are not Jewish. My daughters, both of them, married Christian men. So their children are baptized and they go to church. They celebrate only Christian traditions. When we visit, we follow my daughters' wishes."

Lauren didn't know what to say. Was Mrs. Meyer happy or sad about her family turning their back on their heritage? It was not her place to ask. She clearly loved and missed her family.

She put her arm around Mrs. Meyer and gave her a squeeze. "We are very glad you are here with us. Please make yourself at home and eat or drink whatever you like. You may need to come up here for some quiet time over the next few days as the children will get very excited."

Mrs. Meyer smiled. "They are excited now, no?"

"Yes they are," Lauren admitted as screeches from downstairs traveled upward. "They are calling for us to decorate the tree. Want to come?"

"In a minute. I will follow you."

Downstairs Lauren saw that Clarissa and Sophie were hanging back a little from the rest of the group.

"You all right, girls?" Lauren asked, sitting on the floor beside them.

"I keep thinking of Ma and Da. Da put the Christmas tree up last year, do you remember?"

"Yes, Clarissa, I remember. Terry is using the cross Bart made for the tree so it stands up straight."

Clarissa looked sad. "I wish he was here. Mama too."

Lauren cuddled the girls. What could she say to make them feel better?

Carly asked the girls to string popcorn for her while Shelley helped Joey paste his Christmas decorations together. Shelley also included Lottie as Joey liked working with Lottie. Terry got the ladder out to hang the Christmas angel on top of the tree before Fred shouted at him to stop.

"I hear bells outside. Do you hear them?" Fred said, his eyes wide.

"It's too early for Father Christmas," Shelley protested.

"It not Father Christmas, silly," Fred replied. "It's someone comin' up the drive. See."

They gathered around the window, trying to make out who was coming. Lauren grabbed her coat, heading to the door. It could only be Edward. She held the porch door open but before she could step into the snow he called out to her to wait.

"It's deep. Just stay put."

Edward and another figure Lauren was thrilled to recognize walked toward her, both holding onto each other with one hand

and ringing a bell with the other. As they reached the house Bart smiled at Lauren, putting his finger to his lips. Lauren hugged him before opening the door behind her to let him in. Screams of "Daddy!" greeted Bart as he moved to hug his girls.

Lauren turned to Edward. "You're a regular Father Christmas, aren't you? First presents, now Bart."

"I'll be whatever you want me to be if it means you smile at me like that. Merry Christmas, Lauren." He held something over her head; just in time she saw it was mistletoe, though she would have welcomed his kiss anyway.

"You're freezing, how did you get here?"

"We drove as far as we could but had to abandon the Cadillac about a mile or so back. We were lucky to make it that far. I guess someone wanted a clear road so they cleared a lot of the snow. Not sure how we will make it out of here though. Not at the rate this is falling."

Lauren willed the snow to fall harder. She didn't want anyone to leave. They had plenty of food and drinks, wood for the fire. What else did they need?

"I picked up these, I hope you don't mind." Edward produced a box before they walked inside.

She took the box from him and looked inside. "Christmas lights. The children will be so pleased." She leaned in for another kiss. She could have stayed in his arms forever but Becky called out, reminding them they risked freezing to death.

"I don't think we do, but I'd rather not explain why," he teased Lauren as he kissed her again quickly before they walked in the door. The children all threw themselves at him while Lauren took in the scene, smiling widely. This was what Christmas was all about.

Ruthie said excitedly, "It's Christmas Eve tomorrow. That's when Rachel and Hans celebrate Christmas so Miss Lauren said we can open one present each."

"Tomorrow *night* you can open a present. A small one," Lauren quickly clarified.

Earl said, "I should try to get back to town. Dad will have locked up the store but tomorrow is a busy day."

"I'll go with you," Big Will offered, but his eyes were on Becky. Lauren willed her friend to give the man some encouragement to stay, but she remained silent.

Lauren took charge. "You are both welcome to stay here and head into town at first light. It might be safer. You can sleep on the floor in front of the fire. We have quilts."

"I can share with Lauren and you can have my room, Bart and Edward," Nanny insisted.

It would be a tight squeeze but nobody minded. Chana helped Becky cook supper while Carly peeled potatoes and other vegetables for the next day. They had two wild turkeys waiting to be dressed, currently hanging in the barn. They also had a ham in the smokehouse. With the provisions Lauren had bought at Hillmans' there was no risk of them running out of food.

"That was the best idea you ever had, Lauren. Saving fifty cents a week for the last three months really helped us, didn't it? Look at all this stuff," Becky said.

"I think the Hillmans may have contributed quite a bit to that box too," Lauren replied, looking up from the churn. They had to have fresh butter for Christmas Day and this was one job she couldn't mess up.

*

On Christmas morning, Lauren lay in bed for a couple of seconds with her eyes shut, reliving her dream. She'd got married to Edward and he was living here at Hope House. She didn't want to open her eyes and face reality.

"Lauren, are you getting up anytime soon?"

Lauren leaped out of bed at the sound of his voice. She'd been dreaming, yet here he was, calling her to get up. Then she remembered he'd stayed overnight again, along with Will, as the roads were shut. She giggled at her reflection in the mirror. How silly could she be yet it gave her a thrill to know he was downstairs. She took extra care dressing, wanting to look nice for him.

Terry whistled when she walked downstairs as Ruthie came running. "You look like a princess in that dress, Miss Lauren. Happy Christmas."

She bent to kiss and hug the child, her eyes meeting Becky's. Her friend gave her a hug at the same time whispering in her ear, "He hasn't a hope, you look sensational."

"Where is he?"

"He and Will went to collect the eggs. Said it was too cold for me to do it. They must think I'm delicate."

They both burst out laughing at that idea and, feeling brave at Becky's obvious good mood, Lauren risked asking, "So you and Will? I saw the kiss he gave you on the sleigh."

Becky's eyes glowed. "That was nothin'." Lauren was about to protest when Becky added, "You should have seen the kiss he gave me last night."

"So is it official?"

Becky shook her head. "We haven't made any plans if that's what you are asking but we are getting on better."

The arrival of the men changed the topic of conversation.

"Happy Christmas, darling," Edward whispered as he picked her up in his arms and whirled her around the room. The children roared laughing, bringing Nanny to the kitchen to find out what was going on.

"Again, Mr. Edward. Do it again," Ruthie pleaded. Edward obliged making Lauren feel more than a little dizzy. Just then the Meyers descended the stairs and she blushed.

"Sorry, we're behaving worse than children."

"Not at all, my dear Lauren. It is a joy to see such happiness isn't it, Kathryn?" Chana asked.

"It's about time that's what it is," Nanny responded but with a gleam in her eye.

They ate a noisy breakfast feast comprising of ham, eggs, sausages, cinnamon rolls, doughnuts made by Chana as well as other German treats that tasted delicious even if Lauren couldn't pronounce the names.

"Can we open our presents now, Miss Lauren?" Shelley asked.

"Let's clean up first and then move into the sitting room."

The children didn't argue but the kitchen was cleared in record speed with everyone, including Shelley, lending a hand.

"Never thought I would see these children move so fast. Norma won't believe it."

"How is she, Bart? Really?" Lauren asked.

His eyes sparkled with hope. "She is doin' really well, Miss Lauren. The doctors, they say she is an amazin' woman. They wish their other patients had such a strength of will to fight. She is goin' to surprise everyone. Next Christmas she is goin' to be sittin' here celebratin' with us all."

Lauren hugged him, not caring whether it was the correct thing to do. "I hope so, Bart, I really do."

CHAPTER THIRTY-SEVEN

Lauren heard the sound of the truck outside. "Becky, looks like we get a break from cleaning. We have visitors."

The children cheered, spring cleaning not being high on their list of fun activities. Shelley ran to the door.

"It's Katie and the Thatchers." Shelley shouted as she ran toward the truck. Lauren, Becky, and Nanny took off their aprons. Becky filled the large kettle and moved it into the center of the stove, while Terry added more firewood to the fire.

"Afternoon all, hope we ain't interruptin'," John called out. Despite his cheerful tone, Lauren exchanged a glance with Nanny. Something was wrong.

Alice handed Katie a parcel. "Take this into the kitchen, darling, and maybe Becky will allow you and the children to have some of it with a glass of milk."

"You brought gingerbread. Oh yeah." Cal rubbed his stomach appreciatively. "I love when you come to visit, Mrs. Thatcher."

Alice's eyes filled up at the boy's comments, causing Lauren's stomach to churn. Something was very wrong.

"Becky come in and sit down with us. Carly, would you mind looking after Maisie and making the coffee?"

Carly took the hint and picked up Maisie, ushering the other children to the kitchen. The adults stared at each other.

"What's wrong? Sit down and tell us," Nanny implored the couple as she took her usual seat by the fire.

Alice sat but John stood beside his wife, his hand on her shoulder. "That snake, Stratton, the government agent, he called by with a big smirk on his face. He handed us our eviction papers. We have to be out by the summer. August fifth to be exact."

"That's only six months away. That stupid park. Why did they have to do this to us?" Becky rubbed at her eyes with her sleeves.

"What did he say?" Lauren asked John. "What will you do?"

"They've offered us the bare minimum. Land values are down due to the Depression but still we're luckier than most. They knows we owned our land, thanks to Pa filing the deeds." He broke off talking as Carly came forward with the coffee and some of Alice's gingerbread.

Once she left, Lauren spoke, "I'm so sorry about what is happening to you. Do you know where you will go?"

"They want us to go to the resettlement houses, as they call them," John replied, his hand shaking as he took a cup of coffee and passed it to his wife.

"I've seen those houses; they all look the same and are about the same small size on a piece of land not much bigger than this house. How do they expect us to provide for our families?" Alice took her coffee. "John and me be lucky, all our children are grown apart from Ben and Katie. Ben's courting and will be married soon enough. His girl isn't wanting to live with us and who could blame her. Only one woman should rule a kitchen. But what of the folk with young 'uns to feed? Where are the women goin' to find berries and fruit to supplement what they can grow in those tiny spaces? And the houses, they look like they'd fall down in a good wind. Why couldn't they give us something decent?"

John spoke up. "They aren't givin' us anything, Alice. We have to buy a house if we want it. That's another issue, Lauren, most mountain folk don't have much use for cash. They barter services and goods for what they need. We don't know many with a mortgage. How are they goin' to meet those payments? You tell me."

Lauren couldn't. She knew first-hand how hard paying the mortgage could be.

Alice sat up straighter. "We want to find us a small farm, not far from Delgany and our friends. We don't want to wrench Katie away from the school and all of you. It doesn't have to be a big place but enough to allow us to grow potatoes, greens, squash, and such. I want to take my roses with me to plant around our new front door. We'll take the cows and the pigs too as they can be reared and slaughtered for meat. John probably won't be able to run a sawmill no more. Transporting the trees down to the foothills will cost too much and the men in suits said we had no right to be cutting down trees. This is our land, why do they think they can tell us what's what?" She grabbed a corner of her apron and patted her eyes.

John sank onto the sofa beside her. "Now, Alice, don't be workin' yourself up again. We'll find a way, you knows we will. So long as we got each other, our darlin' Katie, and enough to live on, that's all we need."

Lauren swallowed hard. What could she say? She wished she had an answer but she didn't. She couldn't offer them a home at Hope House as they didn't have the room. She glanced at Becky and Nanny to find they looked as helpless as she felt.

"It's not right, first the Hillmans leaving to go live with their daughter, Annie." Nanny wiped her eye. "Now you having to move. Whoever will be next?"

Lauren took a sip of her coffee. "I know people need a park where they can go and see birds and trees. When myself and Mary were in New York, we saw areas of that city where you didn't even see a dog. But when they planned the park couldn't they have picked somewhere else? Somewhere people didn't live?"

John said, "That's the question on everyone's mind, Lauren. It's since that book, *The Hollows*, was published. Have you read it?"

Lauren shook her head. She'd never heard of it.

John exhaled sharply. "Some readin' that book could be forgiven for believin' we are a bunch of backward hillbillies who never read a book or wrote a letter in their lives. We wouldn't know the Constitution if it came up and bit us and we think the Confederates won the War Between the States."

"Who on earth wrote that book? You only have to spend time with the families to see that's not true. Becky grew up on the mountain and she's read more books than most. You and Alice are God-fearing Christian folk who brought up their families and schooled them properly. It's just so unfair." Shaking with anger, Lauren crossed her arms against her chest.

John paced for almost a minute before he asked, "If they come looking for your place, have you got any money to fight your corner, Lauren? You're looking at costly fees, maybe up to five hundred dollars or even more."

Lauren blew the hair out of her eyes, uncrossing her arms and tapping her foot against the floor. "It might as well be fifty thousand dollars. I don't have a penny that hasn't been spent twice already." She pushed back against the table and stood up. "If I have to defend this place with my bare hands, I won't let it go. My children have been through enough. They don't need to lose this place on top of everything else." Lauren stopped, covering her mouth. "I'm sorry, that was insensitive. Me talking about battling against the people who are taking your home."

Alice stood up and hugged her. "We know what you meant, but you might want to think of an alternative just in case. Not many go up against the government and win."

Lauren didn't want to think about that. Alice gave them a weak smile and changed the subject. "How is Norma? Bart seemed to think she was recovering, that the Sanatorium was working."

"Norma is doing really well. She wrote a letter to the girls for Christmas and said she was feeling better. The recent tests show the disease hasn't got worse. That's a good sign." Lauren forced herself to sound cheerful. Norma hadn't got any better either but that was a discussion for another day.

"And what of Maisie's parents? I heard a rumor you had news of them."

Lauren grinned. "Delgany doesn't need a postal system or telephones. The rumor network is better."

Becky laughed. "We had a gift of some more skins. Looks like Masie's Pa is good with his hands too as he crafted some wooden toys for her to play with. He also left a freshly slaughtered pig."

Lauren shuddered visibly making the others laugh.

Becky continued, "Will had to carve it up, we gave half of it to Earl Hillman to sell at the store. He's determined to make a go of it and get his parents to return."

John raised his coffee cup. "To his success."

They all cheered, Lauren thinking how typical it was for John to be so thoughtful of others, especially when he had troubles of his own.

CHAPTER THIRTY-EIGHT

A few days later, Lauren was coming out of Hillman's when the sheriff collared her.

"Lauren, wait a minute. You'll save me a trip. I need to talk to you. Come into my office, will you?" The sheriff wouldn't meet her eyes but was looking at a spot above her head.

"What's wrong?" Lauren asked.

He beckoned her in. "Come into the office. We best discuss this in private."

Her stomach felt as if she had eaten lead for breakfast. The sheriff didn't like drama so something bad had happened, but what? Her thoughts flitted around her head like moths around a lightbulb.

"Tell me, please," she asked as she entered the office.

"Lauren. Sit down. You're making me nervous standing there. I got this yesterday. Look like anyone to you?" He handed her a piece of paper.

She took the sketch from the sheriff and stared at it. "Katie... She looks like Katie."

"This girl's name is Cassie. Read the description, Lauren."

Lauren read the text, astonished. They were looking for Katie—the description of the burns and the likeness couldn't be misread.

"Who's looking for her, her parents? 'Cause they should be arrested."

The sheriff leaned back in his chair, the silence turning awkward. "Katie, or Cassie, is in quite a lot of trouble, Lauren. Turns out that story she told us was just that—a story. Her parents didn't cause those burns."

She looked up at him, confused. "But she said they did. They aren't likely to admit it, are they? Nobody is going to say to a lawman, 'I pushed my child into the fire on purpose.'"

The sheriff met her gaze. "They aren't going to say it because they are dead. Katie's parents died when she was five years old. They were driving to see family when the bridge their vehicle was driving over collapsed and the automobile ended up upside down in the river. By all accounts, her father is the reason Katie escaped. He pulled her free and brought her to the shore before going back for her mother and baby sister. He didn't surface again."

"Oh no." Lauren stared again at the drawing in her hands, trying to process what she was hearing.

Sheriff Dillon stood up and went over to the stove to pour out some coffee. He handed a mug to Lauren but her hand was shaking too much to take it. He put it on the desk in front of her.

"The local sheriff knew the family, said they were as happy as could be. Cassandra Hamilton, known as Cassie, was an adored child, indulged by loving parents who were comfortably off. Some would suggest she was downright spoiled."

Lauren raised her eyes from the picture. "What happened to her?"

He stirred his drink absentmindedly as he spoke. "She was sent to live with her grandmother, her father's mother. They were estranged by all accounts. Grandma lived in a big old house and had quite a different way of bringing up children than her son. Seen and not heard was her motto." He took a sip of his coffee before continuing, "Cassie took a long time to adjust, running away on several occasions. They kept finding her on the steps of her old house despite it being some distance away from her grandma. The old lady got tired of her running away and put her in a boarding school for young ladies. The reports from there make for grim reading." He fell silent.

Lauren glanced at the drawing again. What did they expect? The poor child lost her family, her home and then was sent away to school.

"Lauren, the child was a bully and made the lives of those around her miserable. She believed she should be the center of attention and anyone who took that attention away, they suffered."

When he fell silent again, Lauren prompted, "In what way?"

"She's responsible for broken bones and other things. She pushed one girl down the stairs. At least she is believed to have done these things. The school can't find their records—likely they want to maintain silence for fear of damaging their reputation as a nurturing school for rich little darlings."

Lauren stood up and paced. "You mean they believe Cassie, or Katie, is dangerous? She and Shelley fought but she didn't harm any of the children. She was wonderfully patient with Maisie."

"The girl she pushed down the stairs broke her legs—the school told the parents it was an accident."

Lauren leaned against the metal bars of the cell, her foot tapping against the stone floor. She didn't like how the sheriff seemed to have decided Katie was a bad 'un. "It might have been!"

His eyes narrowed at her tone. "If I was investigating it at the time I would have thought so too. But after the fire…"

Lauren, feeling weak and dreading what she was about to hear, sat down. "The fire?" she whispered.

His tone softened. "Cassie was burned in a fire at her grandmother's house just outside Washington. She was the only survivor. Her grandmother and uncle died in the blaze."

Feeling lightheaded, Lauren murmured, "No, poor Katie, she lost all her family."

"Lauren, the sheriff's department in Washington believe she was the one who set the fire!"

Lauren jumped to her feet. "An eleven-year-old girl? How could they think that? She'd have to be some sort of monster. Who would burn themselves? That doesn't make sense." She stared at the image before her, seeing Katie in her mind's eye. No, it couldn't be true. "Sheriff, she's a child." Despite her best efforts, her voice was shaking.

"That doesn't stop her from being dangerous, Lauren."

His sympathetic tone made it worse. He believed the story. But he didn't know Katie, not like she did. John and Alice adored the young girl, they wouldn't love her if she was a cold-blooded killer.

Desperate to find proof the authorities had got it wrong, she asked, "Why would they think it was arson? Fires happen."

The sheriff's monotone voice and slumped shoulders suggested he found it hard to argue with the facts. "The grandmother's bedroom door was locked from the outside. They found her lying on the floor just inside the door."

Lauren sat down on the edge of the chair, leaning over his desk. "The uncle?" She feared his answer.

He held her gaze. "He was what you might call 'slow'. The servants said Cassie made his life a misery. He had a collection of trains, which he played with day after day. He couldn't tell you the day of the week or the time of day but he could tell you every make and model of train ever built. He had lots of train books and magazines."

"So?"

"The grandmother had a couple who lived in a small cottage in the grounds of the house. They were the ones who alerted the fire department and the police. When interviewed they said Katie was forever torturing her uncle, stealing his trains and making him beg to get them back. She burned a few of his magazines and papers too, but always blamed him."

"Could he have caused the fire by accident?" Lauren was grasping at straws.

The sheriff shook his head. "He was found in his bed. Tests on a glass in his room showed signs of laudanum." He pre-empted her next question. "Her grandmother was on laudanum, she had cancer."

Lauren stared at the sheriff. "You believe Katie is guilty, don't you? How did she get burned?"

"That's a bit of a puzzle. There was kerosene spread over the carpets downstairs. Her grandmother had electricity but she also kept kerosene lamps in case of storms knocking out the utilities. My guess is Katie spilled some on herself and it caught fire. The fire department found her quickly, she was near the back entrance. The front of the house was badly damaged. Her bedroom was at the back overlooking the garden."

Lauren shook her head, muttering to herself. It couldn't be. A child couldn't be a murderer. But if she was, Lauren had sent her to live with Alice and John Thatcher. Had she put them in danger?

She looked up at the sheriff. "Why now? I mean, how did Katie end up here and why are they looking for her now?"

"She was in hospital for a while with her burns and suffering smoke inhalation. The doctors believed she was in deep shock as she didn't say a word. She never spoke in the whole time she was in the hospital. Three months is a long time for someone who can speak to play dumb."

"She was probably terrified. Maybe it was an accident but she thought after what happened at the school nobody would believe her."

"Maybe. But it's more likely the visits from the sheriff made her realize the game was up. His report says he asked her a lot of questions. One day he told her the story of how he thought the fire had happened. She became hysterical and the medics had to sedate her. They barred the officer from visiting again so he took the evidence to a judge. The judge issued a warrant for her arrest—reluctantly, I'd imagine, given her age. But when they went back to the hospital she had gone."

"And then she turned up here."

"Yes."

"She's been here months. Why haven't they been looking for her?"

"They were but nobody believed she'd travel this far. She's only eleven. Someone saw the missing person's report I filed and they put two and two together. A couple of detectives are coming down tomorrow to interview her. If she's the same girl, and it looks like she is, they will take her away."

"And put her where?" Did they put children that young in prison?

"Lauren, the child needs help you can't give her. If what they say is true, this child has killed people. Murdered them, Lauren."

Lauren shook her head. "She's a child. How could she be a killer?" she asked herself aloud. "Sheriff, please let me talk to John and Alice Thatcher. Please."

Sheriff Dillon pulled at his collar. "The police will be here tomorrow. I can't ignore this, Lauren."

"I'm not asking you to. Just let me speak to them first. I'm sure John will come and see you himself. I feel responsible… I asked them to take Katie."

CHAPTER THIRTY-NINE

Lauren drove to the Thatchers' not noticing the scenery around her. She was about to break Alice Thatcher's heart. Why had she ever suggested the Thatchers take in Katie when they were already facing heartache over their land? She went over and over how Katie had behaved since the day she met her. Katie was insecure and acted jealously if she thought someone was getting more attention, but that could be because of everything she'd been through; all her family had died and she was only eleven… To have lived through her parents' deaths was enough tragedy, but then her grandmother and uncle as well…

Lauren had never seen Katie being unkind though, and she was super gentle with Maisie and Joey whenever she visited. Yes, she and Shelley fought, but if that was a crime, most of the residents of Hope House would be guilty.

She pulled up outside the Thatchers' house and parked, but she couldn't get out of the truck yet. She dreaded telling her friends what the sheriff had discovered. She waited a while, then she saw John come out the front door, waving at her, probably wondering why she hadn't left the truck.

He walked down to greet her. "Lauren? You feelin' ill? You look rather pale."

She looked around. "Is Ben here?"

His eyebrows rose, a grave expression on his face. "Yes, why?"

Lauren wanted to turn and run before she hurt this wonderful man, but that wasn't an option. "Could he take Katie out for a walk or something? I need to speak to you and Alice, alone."

When John hesitated, she put a hand on his arm. "It's important, John."

He nodded, called for Ben and Katie and asked Ben to take Katie to check some of the animals out in the field. "Come back when I call for you, son."

Although he looked confused, Ben did as he was asked. Katie went along reluctantly only when John promised that Alice would make her hot cocoa before bed.

Lauren followed John into the house. Alice was making coffee and arranging cookies on a plate.

"I saw you pull up, Lauren. You always say yes to cof…" Alice's voice trailed off as she saw her friend's expression.

Lauren looked at the floor. "Please, both of you, sit down. I have some bad news."

They sat and stared at her as she told them what she'd heard from the sheriff.

When she finished speaking Alice jumped to her feet, her face a mask of fury. "Get out of my house. How could you come here and say such horrible things? There is no way my daughter did any of this. She isn't a killer."

John pulled his wife's arm. "Alice, sit down. Our girl is innocent, Lauren. Katie isn't a killer, you should see her with the animals. She's not made like that. There must be another explanation."

Lauren put her hands on the table. She understood their feelings, she didn't want to believe the story either, but it wasn't up to them to make any decisions. "I don't know, John, I hope we're right in what we believe Katie to be, but the evidence is fairly compelling. Sheriff Dillon has to take her into custody after contact from the police in Washington. I asked him to let me come here as I thought hearing it from me might make it a little easier. I was wrong. I'm sorry."

Alice pierced her with a look full of pain, anger, and maybe just a little hate. She pushed her husband's hand away. "I want you gone from my house. You tell your friend the sheriff my girl isn't going anywhere with anyone. You hear?" Alice gave a sob and then ran from the room, her face in her hands.

Lauren stood to go but she hesitated, glancing at John to see if he felt the same as his wife. John sat, his head hanging down in sorrow. He looked up. "Lauren, I'm sorry for what Alice said. I will bring Katie into the sheriff tomorrow."

Lauren pushed her feet into the floor so she wouldn't run. "John, if there was another way…"

"There isn't, but I don't believe a word of this. I want to go and meet those people who think that girl is capable of doing something so horrific."

He was reacting just like she had, but something pushed her to play devil's advocate. "We haven't known Katie that long, John."

John looked up and held her gaze. "She's lived in our home as our daughter for the last six months. Don't you think we would know if she was a killer?"

Lauren pressed gently. "But, John, you complained about her, said she was needy and jealous of you and Ben."

John shook his head, disagreeing vehemently. "She's an insecure, screwed-up child, Lauren. Anyone can see that. But it's a big jump to murder and I don't think she's capable. Do you? Hand on your heart, do you?"

Lauren didn't even stop to consider her answer. "No. I've gone over every minute from the day we met outside Mrs. Flannery's to the day she left to come here and I can't see any reason to believe the worst. But, as Sheriff Dillon pointed out, she did lie about her burns and her parents."

"She did. And there could be several reasons why. I'll stake my reputation she isn't a killer."

"I don't want to believe a child is capable of what Sheriff Dillon said, but for you and Alice's sake you might want to keep an open mind. I wish I had never brought her here and caused you this pain."

John jumped to his feet and looked at her imploringly. "Lauren, never wish that. The last six months have been a blessing for us. Katie gave us hope for the future. No matter what comes ahead, we will always be grateful."

Lauren left without saying goodbye. She couldn't speak, the lump in her throat was too big. She saw Ben and Katie in the field, the older boy pointing out something to the young girl. She looked so innocent standing there among the animals.

CHAPTER FORTY

Sheriff Dillon drove over to the orphanage the next morning to ask Lauren to be present when the Thatchers came in with Katie. He thought it might help.

Lauren shook her head. "I'm the last person Alice Thatcher wants to see."

"Maybe, maybe not. I think she and John will need their friends more than ever now. Don't you?"

Becky surprised them both. "I'll come too. Lauren, you can't deal with this alone. Nanny Kat, Carly, and Terry can mind the orphanage."

Together they traveled to the sheriff's office. There they found Alice in pieces, unable to do much more than hug Katie and cry.

When Sheriff Dillon outlined the story to Katie, she burst into tears. "Please don't make me go back, they'll kill me. Please…" The child held onto both Alice and John, her knuckles turning white. The scars on her burned arm were even more evident today.

"Nobody is going to kill you, Katie, they don't do that to children." Sheriff Dillon seemed to have assumed she was talking about the death penalty but Lauren watched the child closely. She was terrified.

"They will. They tried before," she cried.

"Who, Katie? Who tried before?" Lauren asked.

"Those people who worked for Grandmother. The Dickensons. They wanted her money. I heard them. They said she was going to die and leave everything to Mr. Trust and they would be homeless.

They got very angry. They said they'd had to take orders for years. Grandma could be difficult but only when she was in pain."

"Mr. Trust? Who is he?" demanded Sheriff Dillon.

Lauren looked at Katie closely before turning to the sheriff. "I don't think Katie meant a person. I think she misunderstood what she heard. What if these Dickenson people believed the old woman was going to put her money into trust for Katie—I mean Cassie—to inherit?"

Sheriff Dillon scratched his chin, his expression one of disbelief. "Rather convenient, don't you think? To blame the help?"

"As opposed to accusing a young defenseless child of murder?" Lauren retorted, sharing an outraged glance with Becky.

John said, "What if Lauren is right? These people might be tryin' to pin the murders on Katie, I mean Cassie, so they inherit. There is no other family, is there? You said the uncle died in the fire and Cassie's parents are dead." He turned to Lauren. "There has to be some way to prove this. Otherwise we just have their word against Ka—I mean Cassie."

Lauren turned to the little girl, and said softly, "Katie, what happened at the school? When you pushed the girl down the stairs?"

Katie looked up at her, her face streaked with tears. "I didn't mean to hurt her. I did push her but she fell backward and tripped over a box and then fell down the stairs. She was being really mean. Worse than Shelley. She said it was a pity I hadn't died with my parents and my sister. She wanted my doll but I wouldn't give it to her. It was all I had left of Papa."

"Why did you tell us your ma and pa caused your burns?" Lauren asked.

Katie hung her head and took a few seconds to respond. "I didn't like lying about Papa and Mama but I thought it might make you feel sorry for me and then you might be kind. Nobody's been kind to me. Grandma tried but she was old and had a lot of rules. Robbie, my uncle, he was nice sometimes unless I touched his trains or tried to play, then he hit me. So Grandma wouldn't let me play with him. When I was in the hospital I heard some of the nurses talking about a baby who died after his parents let him fall in a fire. Maybe if people believed that about me, they would give me a home."

"Oh Katie! You made things worse by lying," Alice mumbled as she hugged the young girl.

"Did I?" Katie asked, her voice wobbling. "Would you have taken me in if I told you what they said about me in the hospital? I heard the doctor and the policeman talking. They said I killed my grandma and Robbie. They said I gave Robbie something to drink which made him sleep and then I set the fire. But I didn't do any of those things."

Sheriff Dillon asked, "So what did happen that night?"

"I woke up coughing. The smoke was really thick and I couldn't see. I crawled along my floor and opened my door. I couldn't get to Grandma or Robbie as they were on the other side of the staircase and that was in flames. I tried to call out to them but I couldn't speak, the smoke wouldn't let me. I tried to climb down the stairs but I got my foot caught in my nightie and I fell. I didn't hurt myself really, but I banged my head. The smoke got thicker and thicker, it was so hot, I tried to get out the front door but the flames were too big. I tried to run for the kitchen but then something fell down and it landed on my arm. It made my nightdress go on fire. I pulled it off but not before I got burned. Someone poured water over me. I don't know who that was. The pain, it was so bad and I was so scared, I just closed my eyes. I woke up in the hospital."

The tears were streaming down the child's face. "Why would I kill my grandma? She'd told me she was dying. She had something wrong with her stomach. The doctor used to come a lot. Robbie didn't understand. Grandma said Robbie would have to live somewhere else. When I asked her where I would live, she used to pat my hand and tell me I'd be able to live in the house. Papa grew up in the house and Grandma gave me the same room he had when he was little. I would sit in my room trying to think of him being there."

"But you ran away a lot." Sheriff Dillon tapped the paper. "Says here you didn't like living with your grandma. She was mean to you."

"Mean? No. She wasn't mean. At least I don't think she meant to be. She was different. Papa used to say she lost her heart when Grandpa died in the war. She didn't smile very often but she did laugh sometimes. She said I made her happy. When I first had to live with her, I wanted to go home."

Katie took a deep breath. "I had a dog at home but Grandma wouldn't let me have one in her house. They make her breathe funny. I didn't know what happened to Pepper. Papa called him that as he was different shades of brown. He must have died too as he was never at our old house. The policeman who lived near our house said dogs always made their own way home but Pepper didn't come back. He was in the car too but I remember him swimming. He helped Papa get me to shore. Then Papa went back in the water. I begged him to stay with me, I was so scared."

Katie took another breath, tears glistening in her eyes. Her voice shook. "Every time I went back to my old house, Grandma would drive and collect me. She'd be angry but she was also sad. She kept saying Papa was in heaven and I wouldn't find him at our old house."

Becky leaned in to whisper in Lauren's ear. "Either that child belongs in Hollywood as she is an amazin' actress, or the poor thing is totally innocent."

"Cassie," said the sheriff, "I have to keep you here until the men from Washington come for you."

"Sheriff!" Alice sounded hysterical. "You can't lock a child up in your cell."

"What do you want me to do?" he replied, desperation in his voice.

Becky spoke. "Nobody has to be locked up, looks like the Washington Cavalry has arrived." She pointed out the window at the shiny police vehicle.

Katie clung to Alice and John as the sheriff went outside to speak to the new arrivals. Becky and Lauren watched through the window. After much gesturing, he returned.

"Alice, you can go with Cassie and stay with her," Sheriff Dillon said.

John stood up. "I'll go too."

The sheriff said firmly, "John, you need to hire a lawyer. This isn't going to go away just on Katie's or Cassie's say-so."

Lauren and Becky held back as the family said their goodbyes.

"What am I goin' to do?" John asked the sheriff.

"Honestly, John, accept the offer for your place and use that money to find the best lawyer you can." The sheriff held his hands up. "Don't look at me like that. I actually believe your daughter is innocent, but it's not up to me. The case will go to trial and that will take time. You should be prepared for a long fight."

CHAPTER FORTY-ONE

Leaving John Thatcher with the sheriff, Lauren drove herself and Becky to Edward's newspaper office in Charlottesville instead of returning to Hope House. As they parked, Becky said she had to go to see someone and would meet Lauren back at the truck. She didn't give Lauren a chance to question her as she strode off.

Lauren spotted Edward walking down the street alone. She walked toward him but he seemed lost in thought, not seeing anyone. She called his name and then, picking up her skirt, she ran. She didn't care what people thought. Edward would make this right.

He looked up and smiled when he saw her approaching. "Lauren, what is it?" She threw herself into his arms. "Not that I am complaining at you flinging yourself at me." Although smiling, his expression in his eyes showed his concern.

"Edward, I need to speak to you. I'm sorry I just turned up but I—"

He interrupted, taking her arm. "You never need an excuse, Lauren. Let's go for a coffee. The office is very busy and there would be far too many people wanting an introduction to the beautiful woman on my arm."

She knew he was teasing her in an effort to distract her, for which she was grateful. A lady didn't burst into tears on a city street.

They walked a few blocks in silence. Edward ushered her into a place where the staff greeted him by name and showed him to a table for two. He ordered coffee and some pastries.

"Edward, I'm sorry…" she began.

"Lauren, stop apologizing. Just take a deep breath and then tell me what's wrong."

She did as he suggested, outlining the facts as unemotionally as she could. She didn't look at him for fear of seeing pity in his eyes, knowing that then she would break down. Her voice trembled a little and her hands would have been shaking but for her clasping them under the table.

When she had told him everything he said, "I'm glad you came to me. John needs a criminal defense attorney. A good one. I know quite a few. Don't worry, Lauren. We will get the best there is."

"I don't think John has a lot of money. In fact I know he doesn't. The sheriff suggested he ask the park to give him the money for his land as soon as possible."

Edward put his hand out toward her. As he clasped her fingers in his, a feeling of warmth spread through her. She'd been right to trust him. In all the time she'd known him, this was the first time she'd actually sought him out and asked for his help. They both knew their relationship had taken a step forward.

"I would do anything for you, Lauren, you know that. I know I shouldn't be happy, not given the circumstances, and I wouldn't wish ill-will toward the Thatchers or any of the children, but I can't help being thankful. You trust me. Maybe only a little but it's a start."

They drank their coffee as Lauren told him what else had been happening at Hope House.

"I missed this," Lauren said. "Just being able to talk to you about what's going on. I'm glad you weren't still in Germany."

He held his hands up in mock surrender. "I'm sorry, it took a little longer than I thought."

"A little? You left in January and it's now March!"

He took her hand, his eyes clouding as he described the injustices he had seen.

"You wouldn't believe it, Lauren. Men are simply disappearing. Well-known men. Some say there is a list of all those who ever said anything bad about Hitler or the Nazi policies. It isn't just Jews but people from all backgrounds. The official line is they are being taken into protective custody. Ironic really since the people doing the 'protecting' are the ones causing the danger."

"And what about your aunt Rae?" she asked.

"She is the most frustrating woman in the whole world." He looked into Lauren's eyes. "Maybe the second most difficult one to understand. She won't leave. She refuses to listen to me or her parents-in-law who want her to be with the children. She just keeps saying there are those who need her more. I came close to kidnapping her at one point. I have to go to Washington again for a story but I'm going to speak to some people there to try to highlight what is going on in Germany. Rae has to get out."

She squeezed his hand, understanding his frustration. "I guess she is old enough to make her own choices and you've got to respect that. Have patience, Edward."

He smiled ruefully. "Patience should be my middle name. Speaking of which, what is going on with Becky and Big Will?"

Lauren sighed. "I'm not sure."

"Is she at Hope House now, with the children?" Edward asking, finishing his coffee.

"No, she's in Charlottesville too but I don't know where. We drove in together but she left saying she had something to do. I best get back to the truck in case she is looking for me."

Edward paid the check and then, his arm under hers, escorted her from the coffee house back to her truck where Becky was waiting—and she wasn't alone.

"Big Will! Where did you spring from?"

Big Will grinned. "Afternoon, Miss Lauren. I was workin' but when I heard my woman needed me, I came runnin'. Just like I always do."

Becky opened her mouth to protest but closed it just as quickly. She moved from one foot to the other like a child desperate for the bathroom. "I thought Will might be of help to John. They go back a long way. I thought he might know some people who could help tend his farm while John is busy with…" Becky turned scarlet as Edward and Will exchanged a glance and laughed.

"When this is all over, I reckon we both owe John Thatcher more than a handshake." Big Will clapped Edward on the back. "With your brains and my brawn we got this one covered for our women, don't we?"

Edward looked like he wanted to agree but had decided diplomacy might be the better option. "Lauren, take Becky home now and leave myself and Will to come up with a plan. We will drive out tonight and fill you in on what we can do. Tell John we will meet him at Hope House."

Big Will lifted Becky into the truck while Edward escorted Lauren to the driver's side. He put his hand under her chin and gently turned her face his gaze. "Think positively, Lauren. We'll get Katie, or Cassie, out of this mess. In this country, innocent children don't land in jail."

Lauren wanted to believe him and almost did, but she knew him too well. Despite his words, there was a trace of anxiety in his eyes that he couldn't quite hide.

She reached up to kiss him on the lips. "I know you will do your best. That I believe."

*

John Thatcher was waiting at Hope House when Lauren and Becky returned. They found him talking to Nanny at the kitchen table. For once the rest of the house was completely deserted.

"Terry and Carly took everyone, including Maisie and Joey, to the lake for a picnic. They knew we would need some privacy to catch up," Nanny said.

Lauren nodded as she set down her bag and took a seat at the table. "John, we found Edward and he is going to come here later to talk to you. He will find you an attorney. Big Will is coming too."

Nanny's eyebrows rose. "Will?"

Becky cleared her throat. "Yes, Nanny Kat. I did what you said and got out of my own way. Will has always been there for me and I guess I took him for granted." She flushed, her freckles becoming more obvious on her face. She looked down at her hands as if choosing her words before speaking again. "He had to go away in order for me to realize how I feel. I started seeing sense at Christmas."

Nanny grumbled, "About time too."

Lauren glared at Nanny before turning her attention back to Becky, who continued, "I asked him to come home, where he belongs. He said yes." Becky's eyes lit up with fire and determination as well as love. "He is going to help us all."

Before she could explain how, they heard the distinctive sound of Edward's Cadillac on the drive. Becky ran out to greet them while Lauren put on more water to boil. She loved seeing Becky so happy but her heart broke at the defeated look in John's eyes. With Alice and Katie gone, he seemed to have lost all confidence and belief.

Edward walked in with Becky and Will, hand in hand, following behind.

He said, "John, saw the truck was all packed up. You're heading to Washington?"

"Yup, left Ben in charge of the farm."

Lauren said, "Will, Edward, take a seat and tell John your plans." She gestured toward some chairs as she set cups on the table along with milk and sugar.

"I found an attorney to represent young Katie, John. David Little is one of the finest men I know. He has the nose of a reporter. I've telephoned him and set up a meeting for you and Alice with him tomorrow."

John rubbed his eyes with one hand, but couldn't stop the tears streaming down his cheeks. "Sorry… blubberin' like a woman. Thank you, Edward, but I…" John's face flamed.

Edward anticipated what he was going to say. "Don't worry about costs for now. David will come up with a solution. Put all your energy into your family."

Big Will spoke up. "On that note, you can't be thinking about the farm either. I've quit my job and will move into your farm to help Ben. I've an idea to get your sawmill workin' overtime until that rattlesnake Stratton turns up on August fifth."

John held his hands out as if to physically stop Will. "Sheriff Dillon said to sell them the land straight away to get the money."

Big Will put his hand in his pocket and took out some notes. Edward did the same.

John shoved his chair back, away from the money. "I don't take charity." His gruff voice was barely audible.

Big Will replied, "Who says it's charity? That's my rent for the sawmill. Edward is investin' too. We are goin' into partnership. We aim to take as much lumber as we can to avoid Stratton gettin' his hands on it. But if you's goin' to get uppity, then maybe we should just let him have it."

Lauren twisted her hands. She could see through Will's plan but would John? Even if he did, would he realize he couldn't afford to say no?

Nanny gave him no option. "Well it's about time us Delgany folk showed what we are made of. Will, you and Ben will come here every day for your evening meal. Becky will do your washing. After all, they say true love is washing your man's dirty socks."

Big Will squirmed in his seat like a little schoolboy, but Nanny's focus wasn't on him for long. "John Thatcher, you take that money and count your blessings. You have a wife and daughter that need you. Off you go and drive carefully. We don't want no more trouble around here. You tell Alice to write and keep us updated. I've baked some food to keep you going."

"Yes ma'am," John mumbled, looking grateful.

CHAPTER FORTY-TWO

After a trip to Delgany to post letters to Bart and the Thatchers, Lauren pulled up outside the orphanage, hearing shouting as she drove up the drive, and recognizing Becky's voice. What now? She scrambled out of the truck, almost tripping herself up in her haste.

The noise was coming from the back. She hurried around the side of the house, passed the newly built barn, and came to a sudden stop. Becky was standing with her hands on her hips yelling at two men in a suit. Lauren saw some other men in the distance near the lake. They seemed to be surveying the area but for what?

She spotted two other men standing to one side; they looked like mountain folk and resembled each other.

Terry limped toward the mountain men, a gun in his hand. Before she could utter a word, he shouted, "You heard the lady. Get off our land and stay off or I'll shoot you." As if to show his intention, he fired the rifle into the sky.

The suited men jumped but the mountain men quickly drew their guns and pointed them in Terry's direction.

"Stop it!" Lauren ran forward, putting herself between Terry and their guns.

Becky shouted out, "That's Miss Lauren, the owner of this land. She'll repeat what I've told you. This be private property and you are trespassin'. So, go on, git, and take those rattlesnakes with ya," she ordered. "Lauren, you haven't had the pleasure of meeting the Bramley brothers before, have ya?"

One man, obviously the most senior, if his graying hair and imperious look was anything to go by, took a step closer to Lauren. Terry cocked the gun.

"My name is Raymond Stratton. I work for the government. Kindly tell the boy to put down his gun. Or I shall come back with the sheriff and have him arrested."

Terry stood his ground. "I'm not leaving you alone with these…" He looked Stratton up and down before saying "*gentlemen*."

Mr. Stratton's chest puffed out. All Lauren needed was a battle of egos. "Terry, please go. We will be fine. You can keep watch from the window." She put her hand on his arm and squeezed, dragging his attention away from the men and back to her. "Thank you for protecting us."

The mountain men jeered him. "There's a good boy, limp off right back to where you came from."

A red mist descended. Lauren took the gun from Terry's hands and fired it at the Bramley brothers. The muck flew as her shot went just wide of the taller one's foot. "Say another word and I will shoot it off."

"You can't do that, lady, you nearly had my toes off."

She aimed and fired again. This time a little closer.

Stratton shouted at the men, "Shut your mouths. We don't need trouble." He spoke more softly to Lauren. "Perhaps we could take this inside and discuss it over a cup of coffee, like reasonable adults. I have paperwork allowing me to be here." He took the papers out of his pocket and held them toward Lauren. "You will see we were granted permission to survey all the land in this area. We are just doing our jobs."

Becky started shouting. "Your job involves puttin' women and children out on the street. You stealin' people's land, land that they have in their families for generations, and you say you is actin' on behalf of the government. I don't believe you and neither does Lauren. She's an excellent shot, as you have seen. So, take those rattlesnakes and the men down at the lake and leave. Then maybe the air will smell a little fresher around here."

Stratton's chest nearly burst it was so puffed out, his face turning a motley range of colors from red to purple.

Nanny spoke up from the porch. "Becky, that's enough. Please ask the gentleman to come in and discuss this like reasonable adults. The children are scared, and I won't allow that for any reason, government business or not." She hit the floorboards with her stick to emphasize her point.

Lauren knew she was right. She put the safety catch on the gun.

"Please come inside, Mr. Stratton." Lauren adopted what Becky called her Rosehall voice, using the skills she had learned at finishing school. "Your men at the lake are also welcome but I won't have those two in our home. Please tell them to leave and our discussions will benefit greatly."

"Charlie, Benjy, you heard the lady. Go on, get back to base."

The brothers glared at her, but Lauren didn't even glance at them. She turned to Becky. "Becky, please join us."

"I'd rather go—"

Lauren cut her off. "Becky, please. You are as involved as I am."

"I'll go make the coffee, if we have any." Becky strode off to the kitchen.

Nanny waited on the porch until Mr. Stratton walked up. "You could have handled this much differently, Mr. Stratton. A true gentleman would have asked permission before going traipsing around a home."

Nanny turned on her heel and followed Becky, leaving Mr. Stratton staring after her. Lauren hid a grin at the old woman chastising a man in his fifties as if he was a young child.

"Please excuse me, I want to check on the children. I will be right back."

As she suspected, the children, all huddled together in the sitting room, were on edge. Cal and some of the other boys were excited by the "gunfight in the backyard," as Cal called it. Lauren thought again that he would make a reporter one day with his gift for sensational drama. Carly cuddled the younger girls to her, Lottie beside her. Ruthie held baby Maisie and Shelley held a squirming Joey on her lap. Terry stood toward the back of the room.

"Terry, would you please join us in the kitchen?" Lauren said.

"Me?" Terry's eyes widened.

"Yes, you. You are the man of the house. You should be present. Children, there is nothing to be scared of. These men just came to talk. I want you to sit and listen to the radio. Nobody is to come into the kitchen. When they leave, if you've been good for Carly, we will pop some corn. Would you like that?"

"Yes, Miss Lauren." The children's chorus rang out.

"Cal, come here please."

Cal, looking pale, came over.

Lauren bent down and whispered, "Cal, can you ride the mule to Delgany and fetch Sheriff Dillon please?"

His face lit up.

"Shush, don't tell anyone where you're going. Be careful now and come back straight away."

Wide-eyed, Cal asked, "What if he isn't there?"

"Try to find Earl. Be careful, now. Go out the front door and go quietly."

"Yes, Miss Lauren."

Lauren returned to the kitchen with Terry in tow.

"The boy has no call being here." Stratton spoke with a mouth full of cookie, showering crumbs everywhere.

Lauren retorted, "Terry is a man, not a boy. This is his home."

Terry put his shoulders back as he took a seat, his eyes not leaving Stratton. Lauren pushed the hair back from her eyes. She

sipped her coffee, waiting for Mr. Stratton to speak. She wasn't
going to make it easy for him.

"As I was saying, miss, the law gives me the right to survey all
the land around these parts."

"Since when did the law allow you onto private property
without permission?" Lauren asked.

"You don't seem to understand, young lady, these papers are
all the permission I need."

"My name is Lauren Greenwood, Miss Lauren or Miss
Greenwood, your choice. The title deeds to this land are in my
name so please remember who you are speaking to. I am not a
child, Mr. Stratton."

Mr. Stratton licked his lips as if his mouth was dry. Lauren
glanced at Nanny, who gave her a slight nod.

"Can I please see those papers?"

Lauren extended her hand, but he held them back.

"You don't need to see them. I've told you what they say."

"I'd like to read for myself."

"But…"

"Mr. Stratton, as you have seen, I don't have much patience.
The papers, please."

He handed them over. Lauren read every word, slowly, and
then read them again. The longer she took, the more likely it was
that Sheriff Dillon would arrive. She didn't trust these government
men as far as she could throw them.

Mr. Stratton eased back his chair. "Now you have seen the
papers, we can get on with our job."

"Please sit down. Why are you so interested in Lauren's property?" Nanny asked, her cornflower-blue eyes pinning Stratton
to his seat.

"As I said, I work for the government—" he began.

"Yes, you've said that numerous times. You must be used to
dealing with people who are hard of hearing or impressed by

that line. We are neither. Tell me the truth, Mr. Stratton, why are you really here?"

Stratton pulled at his collar, inserting a finger between his neck and his top button. He took out a handkerchief and wiped the sweat from his brow. He stood up once more.

"I don't have to give you any further explanation. You saw the papers. I have my orders. The sooner I complete the survey the better for all concerned."

"Don't threaten me, young man," Nanny thundered.

Lauren couldn't look at Becky or Terry for fear she would laugh. Nanny was on a roll.

"You can stop your huffing and puffing. I don't care what's written in those papers. This here is private land and we don't want your survey. So, take your men and leave. Now."

Nanny went to stand up. Terry rushed to her assistance. He held out his arm for her, turning to Mr. Stratton.

"You heard the lady. Leave and don't come back."

Stratton pushed back his chair. His anger was palpable, but Lauren guessed he was unsure of how to proceed. His upbringing would have taught him to be mannerly with older women, but he was a man used to getting his own way.

The sound of wheels on the drive caught everyone's attention. Becky rushed to the window. "That's the sheriff's car. Were you expectin' him today, Lauren?"

"I'm glad he came. He will tell you people to allow me to do my job," Stratton barked before picking up his hat.

The porch door rattled as Sheriff Dillon walked into the kitchen.

"Morning, folks. Is that coffee I'm smelling?"

"Strong and black just the way you like it, Sheriff."

"Thank you, Becky." The sheriff took off his hat and took a seat at the table, causing Mr. Stratton to look at him open-mouthed.

"Sheriff, you need to help me," Stratton said.

"I will, Stratton, but after I've had my coffee and said hello to my hosts. Nanny Kat, you are looking mighty fine this morning. Life is treating you kindly?"

"It *was*." Nanny held onto Terry's arm. "Will you please excuse me, Sheriff. I need some air."

Terry escorted Nanny to the porch, returning alone to the kitchen.

Red-faced, Stratton roared, "Sheriff, this woman shot at my men after this young man threatened us with his gun."

The sheriff looked to Terry. "Want to explain, son?"

"I shot into the air, Sheriff, as these men were arguing with Becky. She was telling them to leave and they refused. The Bramley brothers, they said some horrible things. I can't repeat them, or Becky will wash my mouth out with lye soap."

Lauren saw the sheriff struggle to keep a straight face. "I see. Did Lauren shoot at them?"

"Yes, Sheriff, but she only hit the mud beside Charlie's toes. Then when Benji said something, her next shot came closer, but she never hit them."

"Beginner's luck." Stratton glared at Lauren.

The sheriff whistled through his teeth before saying, "Stratton, if I was up against Dillinger and Lauren was a man, I would nominate her as a deputy without hesitation. She may be a real lady, but she is also an excellent shot. If she wanted to do harm, your fancy clothes would be covered in blood."

Lauren couldn't help but smile at the look on Stratton's face.

"Not that I encourage the citizens of Delgany to take up arms. Lauren did warn me that if anyone ever tried to hurt the children or people under her care, they would leave here in a box. Can't argue with that. Are you intending on hurting them?" The sheriff's question sounded casual but the look he gave Stratton was anything but.

"Of course not. We aren't in the business of hurting people."

Terry spoke up. "Some would argue that point, mister."

Becky said, "You government people took my home and burned it to the ground. All those years my ma and pa put into working our land. You pushed my ma and brother into the colony in Virginia, and you made my other two brothers run off. Don't you stand there and say you don't hurt women and children. You be lyin'."

"Nobody was burned out of their homes. Squatters were removed. Anyone who held deeds to their land was adequately compensated. The Shenandoah National Park will be an asset for all to enjoy."

Eyes blazing, hands on hips, Becky almost spat out the words, "So, you paid Ma for her land?"

"What was the name?"

"Hetty Tennant—Henrietta, I mean." Becky's voice faltered. "We lived in Meehan's hollow." Terry came to stand behind her and squeezed her shoulders.

Stratton pulled a list out of his pocket, scanning it quickly. "Tennant. Oh yes. Your family were squatters, Miss Tennant. They had no legal right of residence. We helped your mother to move. Nobody forced her out. The house was burned down later as tramps and hobos kept setting up home there."

Becky took a step toward Stratton, her voice firmer now. "Not our land? How can you say that? My grandpappy died in the War Between the States."

He smirked. "Dying in the Civil War has no bearing on this matter."

"Her pappy lived there before he died in the War Between the States." The sheriff emphasized the name the locals called the Civil War. "Becky can't understand how that doesn't mean her family owned that land. I have a similar issue. Her pappy's father is buried up there and his great-grandfather. They came over on a boat from Ireland and settled on the mountain. They never moved away. So, generations have been buried up there. What proof do you need someone's family owns the land?"

"Burial plots don't prove ownership. Deeds do," Stratton sneered.

Lauren needed some time to recover her composure; she was so angry, she could hit Mr. Stratton, and that wouldn't help anyone. She went toward the door. "I have a deed to this land. I'll just fetch it."

She returned from her bedroom with her legal file and handed the deed to Stratton.

"The deed appears to be in your name, Miss Greenwood, but you have an outstanding mortgage to the bank. I believe you to be behind in those payments."

"How dare you? How did you get information on my account? We will clear the twenty dollars' arrears next month. I have an arrangement with the bank manager." Lauren's face was burning with fury.

"Your arrangements are no concern of ours." He gave her back the deed and then handed her another piece of paper. "You can check with your sheriff. This gives me permission to complete my survey of your land."

Lauren read the paper and handed it to the sheriff. She watched the grim expression on his face harden as he read.

Stratton said, "Now, Sheriff Dillon, perhaps you could persuade your friends to comply or face the consequences."

Feeling the control slipping from her grasp, Lauren snapped, "Go and do what you have to do but I want you gone from my land today. Don't come back tomorrow."

Stratton dipped his hat, but it was a gesture of victory, not manners.

After the door shut behind him, everyone started talking at once.

The sheriff coughed loudly. "Settle down. Shouting isn't going to help. Lauren, you heard from Edward lately?"

"He's away in Washington on a story. Why?"

"He's a lawyer and a newspaperman. I got a bad feeling about all of this. Wouldn't hurt to ask him to come back the next time you speak to him." The sheriff stood up and put his hat on his head. "I have to adhere to the law even when I don't like it. At the moment the law is on Stratton's side and he knows it."

Becky said, outraged, "So, you won't help us?"

"Becky Tennant, I will always try and help you but sometimes my hands are tied. You need someone whose wages aren't paid by the government."

"Sorry, Sheriff. I appreciate you comin' out here." Becky calmed down.

"I didn't have much choice. Cal is rather persuasive. Way he told the story, you had a gunfight out here along the lines of Bonnie and Clyde. Now I got to go and speak to the Bramley brothers and offer them shelter in the jailhouse tonight."

"You're going to arrest them?"

"They don't have reason to be trespassing. At least not a good reason."

Lauren hugged Sheriff Dillon. "Thank you, Sheriff."

"You listen to me, Lauren. Do what you can to get Belmont here soon. He has both the legal knowledge and the circulation with the paper to maybe stop Stratton, whatever his plans are."

"But they couldn't take this land? They wouldn't? What would the children do?"

"Most believe they should be in the county home or the religious homes. Like I once did."

CHAPTER FORTY-THREE

Lauren headed into Delgany to see if Earl Hillman could sell the skins they had found in the barn the other night. Shadow again hadn't given any hint that a stranger had come to Hope House, which made Lauren all the more curious as to who Maisie's parents were. Earl was sure he could sell the skins so she drove back feeling hopeful.

Becky came to find Lauren as she arrived back at the house, her face anxious as she handed her a letter. "Will called by earlier when you were out. Miss Chaney asked him to give you this."

Lauren opened it, scanning the contents. Without a word she gave it to Becky.

Becky read the letter. "Those b—" She caught herself just in time. "I can't believe they are taking my home again. We have to stop them, Lauren. You need to find Edward and tell him what's going on. We have to tell people what the park are doing. Maybe if they see they want to make all these children homeless people will listen to us."

"I don't know but it's worth a try. Can you handle things here?"

Becky nodded, kissed her on the cheek, and watched as Lauren turned the truck around. She could call Edward from Miss Chaney's post office.

*

Big Will drove into the drive of Hope House, followed by Terry in Lauren's truck, and Earl Hillman driving his. The trucks were packed up with the Thatchers' belongings, some of which were being stored in the old, smaller barn.

Lauren stood watching, her hand in Becky's. "Will made the old barn weatherproof but it still seems wrong to store the Thatchers' belongings there."

Becky didn't agree. "Better they are stored here than let Stratton or those Bramley boys get their hands on them. They have a reputation for takin' stuff that don't belong to them."

John had hoped to have his whole house cleared before August 5th but Katie's trial had kept them away. Will and Becky stepped in and between them and Earl the house was now packed up.

"It's good of Earl to take the more valuable items to his place. They will be safe there," Becky added.

These days Becky was seeing the blessings in everything, with Lauren being the opposite. Lauren wondered why she couldn't be more positive. Good things had happened—Big Will and Becky were together. But the enormity of the court case frightened her. All these people depended on her.

Big Will put his arm on Becky's shoulder. "I'd love to see Stratton's face when he and his boys come to close up Thatcher's place. There's nothin' left in the house. The Bramley boys are in for a shock."

Becky kissed Will on the cheek. "They deserve it. Won't see me wasting any sympathy on them. You got everythin' from the sawmill too?"

"I sure did. We dismantled the whole lot and carted it down to Hillmans'. Earl and myself are going to be working together on some new projects. Things are lookin' good."

They celebrated with a picnic. Edward arrived with the Meyers and Miss Chaney. Lauren read out a letter from Bart giving them an update on Norma.

"Doesn't sound as good as he seemed to think things were at Christmas, does it?" Chana Meyer asked as the group fell silent.

Will heaped more firewood on the fire, sending sparks into the air.

"No, but I guess we should be prepared for setbacks. The treatment for TB is never straightforward. I will pray especially hard for her tonight." Nanny crossed herself. "Have you news of the Thatchers and young Katie?"

Edward nodded. "David will look after the Thatchers. He knew of the case already from the newspaper's reports. The fire was suspicious from the very start and he's roped Tim Egan, my guy, to help him investigate. That's a good sign."

Nanny responded to Edward. "Rumor has it you are heading back to Germany."

Shocked, Lauren stared at Edward's face to find the truth written all over it. She turned her focus back on Nanny. "How did you know?" She didn't wait for an answer but confronted Edward furiously. "Why didn't you say anything to me?"

His eyes begged her forgiveness as he said, "I meant to but then we got talking and the time got away from me."

"Don't you baby me. You didn't want to tell me as you know my feelings. Why do you insist on putting yourself in danger?" Lauren said, trying to keep her voice calm.

Edward stood up and held out his hand. "Come for a walk with me. The others have plans to make."

Embarrassed, as she had forgotten the rest of her friends were there, she stood up.

"Why did we have to pick such fiery women?" She heard Edward comment as she left the group and walked toward the lake, but not the response from the others.

She paced up and down the path in the yard deciding to listen to what he had to say—but as soon as he came near her, she exploded. "Why do you have to leave? John needs you here and so does Will. How will he manage at the sawmill?" Lauren knew she was being stupid, it wasn't as if Edward was going to start chopping down trees. But she wasn't about to admit she needed him. Hadn't she done that earlier today? Yet he was still going.

He surprised her by pulling her into a hug, his arms holding hers by her side, his strength stopping her from pacing, his nearness making it hard to think, never mind stay angry. Her fury turned to terror; what would she do if he got hurt or wasn't able to come back?

He held her tight and said, "I love you, Lauren, and I would be by your side if I thought you needed me. The Nuremberg rally starts September tenth and finishes on the sixteenth. It's important as there are people from all over the world going to see what Hitler does. The reception he gets, the mood of the general population. I need to do this. I have to do it."

She wanted to yell at him that she didn't need Earl or Will or anyone else but him.

"Lauren, look at me. You can handle Stratton and anything else that comes your way. You're a survivor, you have proved that over and over. I will be back in time to watch you win. You do not need me."

She shook her head, refusing to hear his words.

"You don't *need* me but I love the fact you want me by your side. One more trip is all I have to do. I finally got a visa for Rae. I am going to try this last time to persuade her to leave Germany; her children need her. When I come back, we will plan our future. I know it will involve Hope House, I'd never ask you to walk away from your dream."

She looked up at him, the expression in his eyes warming her very soul. He believed in her, her ability to stand on her own two feet.

His body trembled as he held her. "Lauren, I have to do this. Please give me your blessing."

She reached up and kissed him. He loosened his arms around her, allowing her to wrap hers around his neck, pulling him into a deepening kiss. It took a few seconds for her to hear the cheers of the children.

"Nanny Kat, Miss Lauren is kissin' Mr. Edward!" Shelley's strident tones broke them apart but Lauren didn't lose her grip on Edward. She held his hand and, looking straight into his eyes, said, "Go to Germany. But don't you dare not come back."

He hugged her so tight he lifted her off her feet, and swung her around so much she got dizzy. Protesting but laughing, she told him to let her go.

"I will come back but it will cost you one more kiss."

She happily gave in.

*

Later that evening, Edward took Hans and Rachel for a walk to tell them of his plans to go to Berlin. The children took the news bravely, but at dinner their facial expressions mirrored those of Clarissa and Sophie. All four children looked worried and burdened. Feeling helpless, Lauren suggested they light a fire outside and pop some corn while telling stories.

Big Will sat with his arm around Becky, while Lauren sat holding Edward's hand. Carly and Terry were also sitting together. Shelley had Joey on her lap while Nanny held baby Maisie. Ben Thatcher and Earl Hillman also joined them.

Lauren rested her head on Edward's shoulder as she looked at the children's faces. She loved them so much and would do anything to make sure nights like this were more frequent in future.

Ruthie pointed to the sky. "A wishing star, Miss Lauren. Make a wish, quick."

Lauren didn't have to think twice. She wished for a perfect Christmas surrounded by all these people, plus the Thatchers and Miss Chaney, all together in their forever home.

"Did you wish for a long white dress?" Becky teased Lauren later.

Lauren gave her a playful slap. "No, I left that to you."

"So, what did you wish for then?" Becky's face lit up with curiosity.

"Can't tell you that, it will ruin the magic. Now Miss Tennant, we got work to do. Nobody is taking our home without a fight, but first we have to organize the harvest and get the apples in. We need cash to fight Stratton and, as you once kindly reminded me, there ain't no money trees growin' round hereabout."

Becky burst out laughing as Lauren mimicked her accent.

"I feel almost sorry for Stratton, Lauren."

Lauren couldn't hide her surprise as she waited for Becky to explain.

"He doesn't know what he's taken on with us two," Becky said.

Lauren grinned. Edward was right, they would fight this battle and win.

CHAPTER FORTY-FOUR

Lauren wiped the sweat from her forehead as she took a drink of water. She never wanted to see another apple again. Not even in her favorite dessert.

"You slacking?" Becky asked cheekily, as she moved past with yet another basket full of apples.

"No, just waiting for you to catch up with me," Lauren teased back. The work was backbreaking but it had to be done. She couldn't think of blisters or sore knees, exhaustion, or thirst. They needed this harvest. The bank didn't care they were fighting for the right to stay on the land, the mortgage had to be paid and the utility bills taken care of. Big Will came to help when he could but he was busy at the sawmill with Earl.

Terry limped past, heading for the trees, an empty basket in his hands.

"Terry, take things slower. You're limping worse than—" Carly's words were cut off by a dagger look from Terry.

"So long as there's fruit on those branches, I'm going to keep working. Stop naggin'," he yelled back.

Becky and Lauren exchanged a look but didn't say anything. Carly could handle herself. It was out of character for Terry to snap at anyone, let alone his girl, but the pressure they were all under was taking its toll on everyone.

Lauren went up to Carly. "Carly, why don't you go back to the house and check on Nanny and the babies. Tell her I've sent you indoors to get out of the heat otherwise she'll know we are checking up on her. Try to get her to go to bed, she's exhausted and too old to mind Maisie and Joey all day. The Meyers will help tomorrow."

Terry said suddenly, "Miss Lauren, there's some folk comin'…"

His words distracted her. She shielded her eyes with her hand but couldn't recognize the figures approaching. The hair on her arms stood up—were they friend or foe? The gun was in the barn, too far away to be any use.

"Recognize them?" she whispered to Terry.

He shook his head, his eyes still on the visitors.

Annoyed with herself for just standing there, Lauren moved forward. This was still her land.

"Afternoon, Miss Lauren. We wondered if you needed extra help. We'll work for a meal and a basket of apples if that is acceptable to you."

Becky appeared beside her, holding one side of her stomach and breathing rapidly. "You're mountain folk. What you be doin' so far down here?" Although Becky's question wasn't too friendly, her tone was curious rather than rude.

"We heard you be in need of some help. We're hungry so we thought you'd do a trade."

One silent man on the outskirts of the group seemed to be looking for something or someone in particular as he scrutinized each child.

"We can't afford to say no. Come right on in, the baskets are over there, you fill them with good apples, the not so good ones you can put in those containers. That's what we'll split after the harvest. Dinner is at seven."

The men put their hats back on, the women moving quickly to the trees.

Lauren whispered, "Do you recognize that man, Becky? Look how Shadow is greeting him, seems to me he knows him."

"Shadow thinks everyone is his friend, Lauren. I reckon Will was behind this. That man of mine just keeps on givin'." Becky wandered off beaming but, despite her friend's confidence, Lauren wasn't convinced about the stranger. She'd keep an eye on him for sure.

The arrival of the new workers seemed to help everyone increase their pace. Carly took Shelley back to the house with her. She could entertain the children while Carly took on the job of cooking for their guests.

"Ruthie, Lottie, girls… come here." Lauren called the younger girls over. "You go on in the house now for a while. I want you to rest. It's too hot out here."

"We want to help, Miss Lauren." Even as Ruthie spoke, a yawn interrupted her sentence.

Lauren said, "You are helping. Lots. Clarissa, take Rachel with you. She's not used to this heat and I don't want her burned to a crisp."

"Fred is burning too, Miss Lauren, it's his hair," Clarissa said.

"I ain't goin' nowhere. I got work to do." Fred's retort was loud and clear.

"Put a hat on your head or you will get sunstroke," Lauren admonished. She'd leave him be for a while before she sent him and Cal fishing. The boys worked hard but they were too young for long working days.

They were missing Bart and Norma. Her good mood dimmed. Norma was losing her fight and the stress was telling on her husband. He hadn't been to visit the girls in some time and his letters had got shorter and scarcer. What would he do when Norma passed? Would he come back to Hope House or move on to start afresh somewhere else?

*

Terry's whistle to signal the end of the day came as a surprise to Lauren. She'd lost all track of time, concentrating on picking. Apple after apple, just one more, as she kept repeating to herself.

Terry came over. "Miss Lauren, we got three times as much in as we did on our best day. Those mountain folk really know how to work."

"Yes, Terry. Thank goodness they turned up when they did. I best get into the house and see how Carly is faring with the meal. We want these people back tomorrow and the next."

"I reckon we'll be finished by Friday if they keep up this pace."

On the high of good news, Lauren made her way back to the house. She didn't hear the man come up behind her until he said her name, causing her to jump in fright.

He looked at her shyly, and said, "Beggin' your pardon, ma'am. I didn't mean to startle you. I just… I wondered… I…"

"Yes?" Lauren didn't like being followed, let alone startled—it reminded her of her past.

"Name's Whitworth, ma'am. Tom Whitworth. I left my young 'un with you last year. I've been leavin—"

"You're Maisie's father?" Lauren interrupted, amazed. "You left us gifts and skins! I'm so pleased to see you!"

The man took a step back, obviously overwhelmed by her enthusiasm.

"Mr. Whitworth, have you come to take Maisie home?" she asked.

The man looked so lost for a moment, Lauren didn't know what to say or do. She waited.

"Nothin' I'd like better, ma'am, but I ain't got no home for my girl. The park people they said I was a squatter. I've never took nothin' that didn't belong to me but they said different. I was goin' to protect my land with my life if I had to but the missus she didn't… she thought different. She got hurt real bad and made me swear to get a job and get our Maisie a safe home, away from the mountain. I promised my Molly I wouldn't do nothin' illegal. I gave her my word, all I had left to give." He paused, looking at Lauren bereft. "She passed with a smile on her face."

Lauren couldn't bear to listen to any more. "Please, Mr. Whitworth, Tom… don't tell me any more. Maisie is in the house, would you like to see her? Hold her? She's such a cute little thing. Bright too. She's always on the move eager to explore the world around her."

His face lit up. "I'd love that, ma'am, but I can't take her just yet. I took a job with the CCC. They'll pay me thirty dollars a month. Twenty-five dollars would be paid to you and I get to live on the mountain. You got to promise you won't let nobody take Maisie. I is comin' back one day to bring her home."

Lauren put her hand on his arm, ignoring the smell of stale sweat and tobacco. "Maisie has a home with us as long as she needs one. You can be sure of that."

The man blinked rapidly. "My missus said she'd look out for us. I think she's doin' that right now. I best get washed up. I don't want my little girl seein' me like this."

Lauren nodded, totally unable to speak due to the large lump in her throat. She watched as he headed toward the lake, Shadow bounding after him.

Twenty-five dollars a month would help them too. She'd put ten dollars away in a savings account for Maisie, but fifteen would go toward her pot for the battle looming ahead.

*

Every muscle in her body ached that night but the thoughts racing around her brain stopped her from sleeping. She took out her writing pad and wrote to Edward, telling him all about Maisie's reaction to her father; how she'd grabbed him by the finger and wouldn't let go. It was as if the child recognized him, something Lauren thought impossible, but Becky was convinced it was nature at work.

She tried not to press Edward on when he was coming home but couldn't help asking him to write.

*I know you're busy but even a one-word telegram would
help. I keep having the same dream where you are just
out of arm's reach. Your hand is reaching for mine, you're
calling my name but you can't hear my reply.*

She bit her pen. Was he in trouble? Is that what her dream
meant? The rally had been incredible by all accounts, regardless
of which side you were on. Mr. Meyer listened to the German
broadcasts, translating them for Lauren, Becky, and Nanny. It
seemed the German people loved Hitler and everything he stood
for. What was to become of the world if horrid people like him
inspired such devotion?

Lauren couldn't write anything about the rally or her feelings about Hitler. The letter wouldn't get past the censors they
suspected were watching the mail. She read her letter back before
screwing it up and starting again. This time she took out all
mention of her dream.

*The children miss you and want reassurance you will be
home by Christmas. Big Will confided he asked you to be
his best man so that's one wedding that can't happen till
you get home. So hurry up and write or better yet just drive
up Orchards' Pass.*

I miss you. I love you.

CHAPTER FORTY-FIVE

"How do I look?" Becky asked as she walked out of her bedroom wearing one of Lauren's Rosehall dresses, as Becky called the clothes Lauren had owned when her father was alive. Miss Chaney and Mrs. Meyer had helped to remodel the dress to suit Becky's figure.

"Beautiful, Becky," Lauren replied.

Carly said approvingly, "You look like one of those movie stars, Becky. Doesn't she, Miss Lauren?"

"Yes, Carly. She certainly does—or she would if she stopped shaking." Lauren grinned.

Becky said, "I'm nervous, getting all dressed up like a cat's dinner."

Nanny chipped in, "Young ladies will get further if they take care to present themselves in the best possible light. You said it yourself once, Becky. Nobody sees a poor person."

"True, Nanny," Lauren said. "Are you sure you don't want to come with us?"

Nanny shook her head. "No, Lauren. If I came I might just have to wipe the smile off Stratton's face with my hand. He riles me up faster than a queen bee when someone is after her honey. I'll stay here with Carly and the other children. We're going to make a Christmas pudding. Mrs. Meyer swears by a recipe given to her by an Irish neighbor when she lived up north. It has to be made eight weeks in advance so all the ingredients can settle."

Christmas. Lauren couldn't even think that far ahead. If they failed in this action, they might well spend Christmas by the roadside.

They drove up to the courthouse, taking care to park the truck some blocks away, deciding it didn't really match their new look. Becky fiddled with the collar of her dress all the way.

"Becky, stop it," Lauren scolded. "You look like you've something to hide. This is our land and nobody is going to take away Hope House. Agreed?"

"Yes, Miss Lauren," Becky chanted like the children, making them both laugh for a second. "Lauren, you ain't goin' to lose your temper in there, are you?"

"Me? Of course not. I will be on my best behavior." Lauren hoped she would, anyway.

Becky rolled her eyes.

There were twenty other families with cases up before the judge. All had similar reasons and arguments for why the evictions shouldn't go ahead. They sat and listened as, one after the other, the judge ruled in favor of the park. Lauren fidgeted as much as Becky. This wasn't looking good.

After a break in proceedings the next case was postponed for a hearing on December sixteenth.

"This is it, it's our turn," Lauren whispered.

Lauren and Becky sat forward to listen to the evidence read out to the judge. Stratton outlined how he had surveyed the property two years previously and given Hope House notice to quit.

Lauren stood up. "That's a lie. You came to see us in June last, not two years ago."

The judge banged his gravel as the courtroom erupted with people talking and shouting over each other. "Miss, you can't interrupt like that. Next time I will throw you out of my courtroom."

"But, Your Honor, with all due respect the man is ly—" Lauren persisted, but at a steely look from the judge she corrected herself quickly. "Mr. Stratton is confused. Both Miss Tennant and I were present when he first arrived on the property. We called out the local sheriff so he can bear witness to the truth. The first visit occurred in June this year. We haven't had enough time to defend our case."

The judge frowned. "You do understand, young lady, that this is a government order, a compulsory purchase."

Lauren drew herself up and said, "No, judge. I don't. Why would any government want to make children homeless, especially in December? These children are the most vulnerable members of our society, they have already lost or been abandoned by their parents. How could anyone be so cruel as to put them out of the only home they've known?"

The judge coughed as the audience chatter grew louder. He looked from Lauren to Stratton and back before banging his gravel. "Court adjourned until December sixteenth, when I trust all parties will be properly prepared. Miss Greenwood, should you wish to speak in court, please add your name to the witness list unless you are a qualified attorney."

"Yes, Your Honor, thank you." Lauren felt her legs go from under her and sat down heavily.

"You won, Lauren!" Becky whispered.

"No, Becky, we just gained a few weeks. You heard him. This is a compulsory order—how can we win against that?"

CHAPTER FORTY-SIX

Lauren steeled herself not to look at Stratton as they left the Charlottesville courthouse. She didn't trust her restraint if he smirked at her. As they left, several reporters came up asking her questions. One was Tim Egan, the man Edward had left in charge of his paper, but he was at the back of the group. The newspapermen started shouting their questions.

"Is it true that you and the children have nowhere to go, Miss Greenwood?" one reporter called out, almost singeing Lauren's hair as he pushed his cigarette in her face.

She turned her head away to be hit with the flash of another camera, a man asking, "Are you the daughter of William Greenwood, the tax dodger? You don't expect us to believe you don't have thousands sitting in some bank account?"

Another shouted, "Why don't you let the children go to the county home? That's what it's there for."

Becky held Lauren's hand tight but it didn't stop Lauren panicking. *I can't breathe, I can't...* She opened her mouth to gulp in more air but there didn't seem to be any, just more and more reporters all multiplying and milling around her. She couldn't make out faces any more yet the questions kept coming.

"Weren't you engaged to the murderer, Justin Prendergast?" a man shouted. "That fella alone is the reason why many around here are living in poverty. While he was buying you sapphire rings, what were you doing to help the people?"

Tim Egan pushed his way through. "Sorry, fellas, the ladies have granted the *Charlottesville News* the first interview."

"Not fair, Egan, this is a matter of public interest," one reporter objected.

"It is, Donovan, but we plan on putting together an impartial response. Nobody cares about Miss Greenwood's past. It's the future that matters."

The men weren't happy and kept up with the questions, their camera bulbs flashing in Lauren and Becky's faces. Lauren clung to Becky who was shielding her with her arm. Lauren could handle questions about the children, could argue to the moon and back about what they needed, but she hadn't expected comments about her father, and that man. Why did Justin Prendergast's shadow follow her?

Tim Egan signaled to another man and together they formed a protective barrier between the girls and the press and escorted Lauren and Becky to a car. "Hop in and I'll drive you back to the office. You can freshen up and have some coffee."

"Thank you, Mr. Egan," Becky said. Lauren was too bewildered to speak.

"I love rescuing pretty damsels in distress, particularly when there is a good story behind it." He winked as he drawled, immediately putting Lauren at ease.

They drove in silence to the offices. Lauren had known they were up against Stratton but she hadn't bargained for the enormity of the battle or how much muck would be raked up. What if they went after Becky? The story of her losing her siblings to illness, her mother and younger brother being taken to live in the colony for the feeble-minded… Could Becky handle that?

She squeezed Becky's hand as they stopped in front of Edward's newspaper's building. Together they walked in, in silence.

She knew they were being stared at, despite the clacking tap-tap from the typewriters, the noise of reporters on telephones, and the

general humdrum of the office. Their stares made the hairs on the
back of her neck stand up. *Walk tall, Lauren, walk tall.* Nanny's
voice rang in Lauren's ears as she put her shoulders back, strolling
through the office as if she didn't have a care in the world. The
effort was immense, the reward a pain in her shoulders, but she
couldn't falter at the first hurdle. She wasn't responsible for what
her father and fiancé had done. This wasn't about the Greenwoods,
it was about Hope House and the innocents living there.

Tim pushed the door to the office open. "Come in, ladies,
please. Martha will show you where you can refresh yourselves.
I will be in my office. Would you like coffee or hot tea?"

"Coffee, please," Becky answered for both of them.

Lauren turned to follow the young woman in her black dress
suit and high heels. Her makeup and hair were immaculate. She
didn't smile but led them to the ladies'.

Once there, Lauren let out a big sigh and turned to her friend.
"Becky, I never thought it would be like this."

"You knew it would be difficult. Men like Stratton don't like
to lose, particularly to a woman."

"Two women," Lauren corrected. "We are in this together.
What if they drag up your ma and Donnie? Are you ready for that?"

"I ain't got nothin' to hide. Ma and Donnie and all the others
who were sent to that place are all victims of the same thing.
People who see dollar signs and discounted the ordinary folk
on the mountain. Let them bring it up. We didn't do nothin'."

Lauren hugged her friend before looking in the mirror,
straightening her hair and makeup. Only then did she feel ready
to deal with what lay ahead.

Martha escorted them back, knocking on the door to Tim's
interior office before retaking her seat where she started typing.

"Ladies, sit down. I ordered some sandwiches too as I assume
you had an early start this morning. I'm sorry I got to the courthouse late, we had a story."

"Please don't apologize. Thank you for getting us out of there," Lauren replied, trying to force a smile.

They ate and drank the coffee, making small talk, until Lauren finally faced the elephant in the room.

"Have you heard from Edward—I mean Mr. Belmont?" she asked.

"The last I heard he was at Nuremberg covering the big Nazi rally. He must be working on another story."

Lauren frowned. "The Nuremberg rally was over on September sixteenth. You mean he hasn't been in touch with you since then?" she asked. Heart hammering against her chest, she couldn't think straight. "I've had a letter since then, he was fine after the rally. He wrote to say it was horrible, described thousands of people all praising Hitler, looking on him with the adoration we would reserve for Shirley Temple." She shuddered. How could anyone adore a tyrant like Hitler? "You had to have heard something. Have you tried contacting the people he knows in Berlin? What was the name of that man?" *I'm talking too fast but he is all right. He has to be.* Lauren glanced at Becky but she stared blankly back.

Tim squirmed a little in his seat, glancing at Becky before looking at Lauren.

Lauren knew something was up. "What is it? Tell me, please."

Tim admitted, "We haven't heard from him in two weeks. He was due back but he didn't turn up at the meeting he'd organized in Switzerland last Monday. We've been waiting for word."

Lauren's eyes grew wide. "He's disappeared? You didn't think to tell me—I mean, us? They must have him."

Becky turned to her. "Lauren, don't do that. You're borrowing trouble. Edward is clever, he may be following another story or he could be helpin' someone. Trust him. I'm sure Mr. Egan is doing all he can."

"Thank you, Miss Tennant," Tim said. "I've been in contact with various people in Berlin both in our own embassy and among my press colleagues. As soon as I get word, I will send you a note." He coughed. "Now we best get to this matter. You need to retain an attorney, Miss Greenwood."

She tried to think straight. "Lauren, please. I've tried but nobody is interested. They said it's a cut and dried case. Nobody has ever beaten a compulsory purchase order before."

"There is always a first time. Bet Amelia Earhart was told she couldn't fly solo but she did it anyway, didn't she?" Tim picked up the phone. "Martha, can you get Ian Stewart in here please?"

Lauren could hear the woman reply, "Yes, Mr. Egan."

Tim replaced the handset and looked at Lauren. "Edward asked me to help you if you ever needed anything. I hope you will trust me as you trust him."

Lauren and Becky exchanged a glance. They didn't really have a choice.

Lauren nodded before saying, "I believe we should also write to the governor, the minister of the interior, and the president, and his wife. If we could generate support from your readers, maybe they could also write to these people."

"Many people support the creation of national parks. How would you handle that?" Tim asked.

"I believe in creating places of nature and letting everyone have access. We met people in New York who had never seen a waterfall or any animals other than those on display in a zoo. But people like Stratton are wrong. They shouldn't force people off their land. Just how big a park does he need? Would it have cost him to allow the elderly people to live in their houses until they died?"

A knock on the door paused their conversation. An elderly gray-haired man walked with the aid of a cane but stood straight as a soldier.

Tim stood to introduce him. "Ladies, this is Ian Stewart, our resident legal eagle. He may be able to help you with your case."

"Miss Greenwood, Miss Tennant, pleased to meet you both." Mr. Stewart spoke with an English accent.

"Thank you for joining us, Ian. The ladies are—"

Mr. Stewart interrupted, "Fighting the government for their land. I was at court today. Quite an impressive show of restraint you put on, Miss Greenwood."

Lauren's cheeks heated, wondering if he was being sarcastic.

"Lauren can't find an attorney to take on the case. They have all advised her it's unwinnable," Tim said.

"Nothing is unwinnable, Tim. But I would say the odds are very heavily stacked against you ladies."

"Will you take on the case, Ian?" Tim asked.

"I haven't practiced law for a long time but I still retain my license. Unlike Edward, I specialized in contract and civil law. I should like to look through your papers, Miss Greenwood. I will also need to interview you both, separately of course. I should also like to visit Hope House and meet some of your residents."

"You aren't going to print their private stories, are you?" Becky asked.

"I am not making you any promises, Miss Tennant, apart from one. I will always act in the best interest of the children."

"Mr. Stewart, we would love your help but... how much do your services cost? We have a limited budget." Lauren blushed but she had to be honest.

"I don't require a fee. There will be some court costs but we can deal with those later."

Hesitant, Lauren studied the man in front of her. He held her gaze, his eyes not wavering. "You have questions, Miss Greenwood? You wonder what is in it for me perhaps?"

"Yes, I suppose I do. Not many people would offer up their time and expertise for free."

He smiled. "I am in a fortunate position. I have a very comfortable life. I have no need to work for my living. Edward was one of my favorite law students and when he started the paper and asked me to join the staff, I did. I like to keep my mind active and, frankly, gardening and the other activities open to a man of my age are dull."

Lauren decided she liked Mr. Stewart. He reminded her of Nanny.

"My other reason for helping is I grew up in an orphanage back in England. Perhaps you have heard of Dr. Barnardo? An Irishman from Dublin who moved to London and set up houses for orphaned boys and later girls. I am one of his success stories. But for Dr. Barnardo and his lady wife, I could have had another life altogether." He stretched out his hand. "Do we have a deal?"

Lauren looked at Becky for her agreement before she shook his hand. "Deal."

"Right then, ladies, our work begins. Tim, could you entertain Miss Greenwood while I interview Miss Tennant. I will need to borrow Martha to take notes."

"Go ahead. She prefers working for a *proper* gentleman." Tim's smile took any sting out of his words. Mr. Stewart escorted Becky out of the room, leaving Lauren with Tim.

"Tim, is there a way I can contact Edward?" Lauren glanced at the carpeted floor. It was one thing admitting to herself how she felt, another admitting it to this man.

"You're worried about him," Tim said, his expression compassionate. "I wish I could tell you not to be. I'm concerned too, I won't lie to you. The transcripts coming in for what happened at the Nuremberg rallies make for grim reading. I certainly wouldn't want to be Jewish in Germany."

"You think it will worsen over there?" Lauren asked.

"It's already started. Hitler's introduced a number of laws, one of the worst of which is the so-called law for the protection of German blood and German honor. That forbade marriage and"—Tim pulled at his collar, his cheeks turning scarlet—"other acts between Jews and so called Aryan nationals. Another law was the Reich Citizenship Law which declared only those of German blood were eligible to be Reich citizens. They issued a supplemental decree last week outlining their definition of who is Jewish. Do you understand what that means?"

"People are being classified as Jewish who don't identify that way?"

"Yes, but more importantly those people have no citizenship rights. They have become stateless overnight and that has its own implications. Not only are they more at risk of being treated harshly by the German regime but their applications to gain entry to other countries are impeded too. Countries are more likely to offer asylum to those who have the right to return to their own lands in time."

"But when you are stateless…"

"You understand the problems that creates."

Lauren's stomach clenched. How would Rae, her family, and friends get out of Germany now? "Is Edward still protected? By his American citizenship, I mean. Surely the Nazis still recognize that?"

"They do and they don't. On paper they do but we've heard it can be different at local levels. There have been reports of American and British journalists being harassed. They believe their hotel rooms are bugged and the journalist conferences they are invited to by Goebbels are heavily regulated. People who express an interest in speaking to the world press have a tendency to disappear. The number of unexplained accidents is increasing."

Lauren inhaled sharply, causing Tim to get up and walk around the desk. He sat on it, opposite her. "I'm sorry, that was tactless of me. Edward is a very clever man with lots of valuable contacts. Please try not to worry too much."

She tried to smile but didn't master it. "I seem to be struggling for good things to take my mind off my problems."

A Baby on the Doorstep

"Your problems aren't as big as they were. Ian Stewart has a marvelous reputation with several more wins to his name than losses. I for one can't wait to see the expression on the face of that pompous buffoon Stratton when he realizes who he is up against."

"Thank you so much, Tim, for your help." Lauren stood to leave.

"Can I please come with Ian when he visits your place?" Tim asked. "I'm intrigued by your story, I won't deny it."

"Daughter of murdered tax evader and fiancé of murderer helps the children. Is that it?'

He shrugged. "I would have come up with a better tagline but you have to see the temptation for a newshound like me."

She laughed at his response.

"My mother always told me honesty is the best policy," he said. "You never argue with an Irish mammy."

She smiled again. "Yes, you can come, but no cameras. At least, not the first time you visit."

His eyes shone with anticipation. "Done."

CHAPTER FORTY-SEVEN

Lauren drove the truck home with Mr. Stewart as a passenger, Becky traveling with Tim Egan. By the time they reached Delgany, Lauren had told Mr. Stewart her life history and how she came to be at Hope House. He was very easy to speak to and she found herself telling him about Patty, the fourteen-year-old Rosehall servant who'd been raped and made pregnant by Lauren's ex-fiancé, only to find herself thrown out by Lauren's father. Patty's baby had died and she'd committed suicide, but Lauren kept the suicide details to herself as they had covered that up. Guilt over what had happened to Patty was partly why Lauren had ended up at Hope House.

As they drove toward the orphanage, the mountains loomed up ahead of them.

Mr. Stewart took a deep breath. "I can see the attraction of the area. This is beautiful country. Imagine waking up every day to this view."

"I don't have to imagine it, my bedroom looks out on all this. Hope House is just around the corner."

She drove on in silence, trying to imagine the large white house with its green shutters from the point of view of someone seeing it for the first time. In her mind it was much improved on the original version she'd first seen back in 1932 but would it look neglected and shabby to this man? He stayed silent so she followed suit. The children heard the truck as they came out onto the porch. Carly and Terry held them back, seeing a second car pull in after Lauren.

Lauren hesitated before getting out of the truck. "Here are the children. For now, I will just tell them you are a friend of Edward's. I don't want to worry them."

He smiled in agreement before getting out. Using his cane he made his way to the front door. Lauren spotted Nanny at her window and waved.

"Children, this is Mr. Stewart. The man with Becky is Mr. Egan. Both are friends of Mr. Edward's. He sent them to check up on us."

Cal said, "Is Mr. Edward comin' back? We miss him, especially as it will be Christmas soon. He always buys us the best presents."

"Cal!" Carly admonished the boy before addressing Mr. Stewart. "Please excuse Cal, he gets a little excited."

The old man grinned at Cal. "I would be the same. What are you hoping for this year, Cal?"

"My own gun. I want to learn to shoot like Miss Lauren."

"Really, tell me more." Mr. Stewart gave her a look but she pretended not to see it.

The Meyers stood just inside the front door, a troubled look on their faces. It tore at Lauren's heart how they mistrusted people almost as much as some of the younger orphans had when they first arrived at Hope House. She pushed open the door to allow the visitors to pass through. "Please come in and make yourself comfortable. This is Mrs. Chana Meyer and her husband, Victor. They are almost part of the furniture here."

Cal slid his hand into Mrs. Meyer's. "Nanny Chana makes delicious cakes. Funny names but they taste great. She makes jelly doughnuts for us too. She taught us all about Hanukkah last year when Hans came here first. They are good Germans."

"Cal, quiet. Please let Mr. Stewart sit down." Lauren glanced at Mr. Stewart's face to gauge his reaction to Cal but he seemed amused, not annoyed.

"Sorry, Miss Lauren."

She ruffled Cal's hair before sending him and the other children out to play.

"It isn't that cold and it will do you good to run off some energy," Becky said in her do-not-argue-with-me voice when they started to whine.

Lauren helped Mrs. Meyer make the coffee. "He is here to help us. Do not be afraid of either of them," she whispered to the older woman as she squeezed her arm.

Hans ran back inside saying he'd forgotten his hat.

"You are Hans?" Mr. Stewart asked.

Hans stopped and stood upright, his expression unreadable. He wasn't used to being singled out. "Yes, sir. From Berlin. Pleased to meet you. You are English, yes? You sound like the BBC reporters."

"I do indeed but I didn't always sound that way. Nice to meet you, Hans. Edward has told me a lot about you. I knew your papa. He was a fine man and one I was honored to call my friend."

Hans' whole body perked up with curiosity as his eyes widened in wonder. "You did? Will you tell me about it? Please?"

"Yes, but later. I have to talk to Miss Greenwood now," the old man said with a kind smile.

"Miss who?" Hans rubbed his neck.

"Lauren, darlin'," Becky answered. "Hans, off you go and don't go near the lake."

The boy got his hat and ran off again.

"The children seem very happy here," Mr. Stewart said before turning to Mr. and Mrs. Meyer and greeting them in German. He then switched back to English when Nanny came into the room. A warm smile lit up his face.

"Miss Johnston, it's been a long time."

Lauren and Becky exchanged a look. Nanny knew this man. Nanny said, "It certainly has." Was she blushing?

Mr. Stewart took her hand and kissed her cheek. "Too long. You look fantastic. The children must keep you young."

Lauren and Becky grinned as Nanny was definitely looking pinker in the face. "Oh, Ian, you always had a smooth tongue. So what has you calling out this way?"

Mr. Stewart looked pointedly at Lauren. She liked the way he was discreet and didn't just launch into an explanation of his presence.

She said, "Mr. Stewart is going to help us, Nanny, with Mr. Stratton. He came to speak to some of the children and to see Hope House."

Mr. Stewart looked around the sitting room. "It's so much nicer than I heard and that's taking into account the flattering reports. You have built a real home. These children are lucky to have all of you."

"Thank you. We are a good team. Terry, come here please." Lauren put her hand on Terry's shoulder. "This is Terry, he's the man of the house now. He wants to be an animal doctor and hopes to go to university next September. He was due to start this year but he stayed behind to help us."

Mr. Stewart stepped forward to shake Terry's hand. "Nice to meet you, Terry. Perhaps we could sit down, my mouth is watering with the delicious smell coming from those plates over there."

"Ian, you always had a sweet tooth," Nanny teased her friend.

*

The hours flew by but nobody seemed to notice. Ian was a charming man used to dealing with people from all backgrounds. He had them in tears, laughing at his antics from his childhood.

Terry stared at Mr. Stewart, focusing on every word he said. He spoke softly as if afraid to interrupt. "I can't believe you were a stowaway on a ship."

"Neither could the captain, he said he never saw such a scrawny slip of a boy. The Barnado's attendants said I had hollow legs. I was lucky, he took me under his wing. He protected me in ways

I didn't understand at the time. When we docked in America, he told his business partner to adopt me. Carlton sent me to school and then to Harvard. I graduated top of my class and this orphan from the wrong side of the blanket ended up in the diplomatic corp. I spent time in Europe where I had the privilege to meet men like Hans' father, Rudolf. A brave and remarkably intelligent man. Such a waste to lose him and others like him to a raving fanatic like Hitler. How the German people can tolerate him is beyond me. He isn't even German but Austrian."

Mr. Meyer clapped. "This is what I have been saying for a long time. The man is not German and is out to destroy our country. My countrymen behave like sheep. It is not good and it will not end well. I fear many millions will die before Hitler and his friends are stopped."

"Please don't talk about that," Lauren added. "I can't bear our children ending up fighting. If we go to war, how will people treat Hans and Rachel? They stayed here rather than with Edward's family. Edward's father gives us an allowance for the children's keep. He is very generous."

"He can afford to be." Mr. Stewart sighed. "I shouldn't speak like that. He is generous with his money but not his time or his feelings. It astonishes me Edward has turned out so well. His aunt Rae, she is very like Edward. A remarkable and courageous woman."

Lauren was curious about Rae but she'd be lying if she said she wanted the woman to return to the US purely for her own safety. If Rae was here, Edward would be too. "Do you think she will come back to America with him?"

Mr. Stewart looked around before shaking his head. "The Rae I know won't leave while there are people dependent on her."

That wasn't the answer Lauren wanted to hear. "You mean her husband's parents."

"Yes, but they aren't who I meant. Rae is involved in helping others." Mr. Stewart rubbed his chin before turning to Tim Egan and deliberately changing the subject. "Are you ready to get started with our fight?"

"Our fight?" Tim smiled. "I think you want to take on Stratton all by yourself, Ian."

Mr. Stewart's lip curled in disgust at the mention of Stratton. "I'll deal with that rattlesnake, but you will have to petition everyone else. We can start with the president and his good wife and work our way down. By the time December sixteenth comes around, the judge won't have any choice but to rule our way."

Lauren pinched herself, trying not to let her emotions overwhelm her. Becky's eyes, wide and shining, mirrored the hope Lauren felt. They weren't fighting alone any more, these men were going to do their best to help them. With their experience and connections, surely the odds of winning had risen in their favor?

CHAPTER FORTY-EIGHT

Tim Egan came back to Hope House a few days later with a photographer. They took a lot of photographs of the building and the grounds. The barn became a focus when Terry told them how it was burned down and how the community came together to do a barn raising.

To Lauren's amazement, Terry volunteered to stand in front of the barn for a photograph. One by one, the children all followed suit. Cal, Fred, Lottie, Clarissa, Sophie, and the rest of the orphans all stood staring at the camera. Shelley kneeled in front beside Joey. Even Carly, who never cared about her appearance so long as she was clean, asked Becky to style her hair before taking her place beside Terry, holding Maisie in her arms. Lauren's heart twisted when Ruthie took her place in the center, insisting Shadow be part of the photograph too. What if Ruthie's stepfather recognized her and came forward? Lauren pushed that thought from her mind.

Tim insisted on another photo, and this time the adults stood behind the children. Or at least Lauren and Becky did. Nanny was too small to be seen over the children's heads, so sat in a chair to the side. The Meyers chose not to take part.

The next day, he came back to show them the article about the fight for Hope House and the photographs. He had kept his promise and the children's backstories never made it into the story.

"I look older, don't I?" Cal asked, as Fred wanted to know why his eyes were shut.

Carly blushed when Tim pointed out how pretty she was.

Terry moved to her side, putting an arm on her shoulder. "You should have taken one just of Carly."

Lauren smiled at Terry showing the newspaperman Carly was his. She skimmed the article quickly before reading it out slowly for all the children. They listened in silence. Not all of them understood what was happening but they knew enough to know it was something serious.

Ruthie pulled at Lauren's arm. "What if nobody answers?"

"What do you mean, Ruthie?"

"The article asks people to write to us to show us their support. What if nobody writes? Will we have to leave Hope House?" Ruthie's eyes filled with tears. "Will I have to leave you?"

"Never," Lauren whispered, pulling the girl into a hug. With her arms around Ruthie, she faced the other children. "We are all in this together. This is our home and we will fight to win. But"— she glanced at Becky, who nodded—"if we lose, Becky, Nanny Kat, and I will do everything in our power to keep all of you children with us. We may have to leave Delgany but we will stay together."

The children crowded around closer, holding onto the nearest adult.

Tim shifted from one foot to the other when Lottie insisted on holding his hand and asked, "Mr. Egan, you is goin' to win, isn't you?"

He threw a helpless look at Lauren but she just stared back, waiting for him to answer the child. It was all very well insisting people needed to hear the story but this was a fight for these children's happiness. He had to be on board.

He bent down to pick up Lottie. "I promise you, sweetheart, I'll do my best."

Lottie put her arms around his neck, a smile lighting up her freckled face. "Nanny Kat says all we can do is our best."

*

A week passed by before Tim arrived back at the orphanage. Cal and Fred ran out to greet him, asking him loudly if he was going to take more photographs. They had cut the ones out of the paper and hung them on the wall of their bedroom.

Lauren and Becky exchanged a glance, Lauren wondering what had prompted the visit.

Lauren put down the dishcloth as Becky pushed her hair back from her face. Together they walked to the door to greet the newspaperman. Lauren wondered if Becky's heart was racing as much as hers.

"Lauren, Becky, I wanted to see your faces when you saw this." Tim waved some newspapers around as he came in. "The *New York Times* and *Washington Post* and many other national newspapers syndicated our article. I thought we did well when all the Virginia papers carried the story but this is even bigger. It made page two of the New York papers and page three of the Washington one."

Becky held out a shaking hand to take a newspaper, but Lauren couldn't move. She sensed there was more.

"I've had several phone calls. One from a Virginia county radio station, they want to interview you and the children. The editor says it would help their listeners understand if they heard from the youngsters themselves. How's that for publicity?"

Flustered, Lauren tried to find the right words. She didn't want the children subjected to the spotlight. What if they were asked awkward questions about their pasts? Too many people blamed the children for being illegitimate, as if it was their fault. Would it lead to bullying at school? She couldn't risk it even if it would help. She looked to Becky and her friend's facial expression was one of wariness, not joy.

"I don't think that's a good idea, Tim."

"Why don't we discuss it over coffee? Has Mrs. Meyer been baking?" Tim grinned at them with that schoolboy expression

Lauren was beginning to realize he used when trying to soften them up. You couldn't help smiling back at him and he knew it.

Lauren sent the children off to play after asking Cal to find Terry for her. Becky went ahead to boil the kettle, chatting to Tim as she did so. Lauren headed for Nanny's bedroom. To her relief the older woman was up and dressed, sitting in her window seat.

"Nanny, did you hear what Tim suggested?" Lauren said, as she helped Nanny up from her seat.

"Yes, Lauren, the windows are open and he always talks so loud."

"Will you come and discuss it with us in the kitchen?" Lauren asked.

Nanny's expression was serious. "Lauren, you need to make the call on this one. Trust your instincts, child. I won't always be around to guide you."

Lauren's breath caught. Nanny was tired but she wasn't ill. Was she?

"Don't look at me like that, Lauren, I'm not about to disappear just yet. I was just reminding you to trust yourself. You and Becky can make this decision. You don't need anyone else to help you." She folded her arms across her chest.

Lauren wasn't at all sure she believed Nanny. "Come and join us anyway. You like Tim and enjoy his company."

Nanny sighed but gave in. Lauren handed her her stick.

"Come on then, let's see what he has to say."

Tim argued that the radio show would give them exposure, with Becky arguing back that it was too risky. They couldn't control what the radio show host would ask.

Becky put her hands on the table, addressing Tim in her blunt fashion. "You know more than most that the gorier stories make for a higher ratin'. They won't care about the children, to them they aren't real people but *poor* orphans."

"Yes but—" Tim tried to argue, but Becky wouldn't let him speak.

"I don't want to do it. But it's Lauren's choice at the end of the day. She's in charge."

"No, Becky, it's our decision. Everyone here has an input. What do you think, Terry?"

Lauren saw Terry flush with pleasure at being asked. He straightened his shoulders and looked directly at Tim. "Will they come here to record or do we have to go to the station?"

"The station."

"Then I'll go," Terry said firmly. "They can ask me whatever questions they like. I ain't got nothin' to hide. This place used to be called a home for unloved orphans and it was horrible. Until Miss Lauren and Miss Becky arrived there is no way anyone would fight to keep it open. Hope House is a totally different place than what it used to be. Here we have a chance to be someone, to be a useful citizen of the United States. Here we aren't poor orphans"—he smiled at Becky as he mimicked her phrase—"but people, who want what every child needs. Somewhere they feel they can be anything they set their minds to be."

Becky reached out and clasped Lauren's hand as they both looked at Terry in awe.

Nanny clapped her hands. "There's your answer, Mr. Egan. Terry here can tell those radio people what they need to know. Becky and Lauren don't need to worry about the young 'uns getting upset."

*

Tim drove Terry to the station for the radio interview and dropped him home afterward. Terry didn't talk about the experience but headed straight for the barn. Lauren wanted to go check on him but Carly intervened. "Let me, Miss Lauren. I know him best."

There was no arguing with that. Carly came back about an hour later, her eyes bloodshot and puffy, her face streaked with dried tears. "He don't want to talk about it. He says it's done and over with and he'd be obliged if nobody mentioned it again."

The hairs on Lauren's neck rose as she stood up. Someone had hurt or upset Terry and she wasn't letting them get away with that.

But Becky stopped her, placing her hand on Lauren's arm. "We both know the world isn't always a kind place. Better they find it out now, while we are here to help them, than deal with it alone in the future. If Terry wants us to know what happened, he'll tell us."

Terry didn't breathe a word but Lauren badgered Tim until he arranged for them to listen to the interview. The reporter had started out asking polite questions and Terry answered them confidently. But then the mood changed, with the reporter asking about Terry's limp and whether Becky or Lauren had caused it to happen. He then grilled Terry about the other orphans and their backgrounds. Terry held his temper but it was clear the radio interviewer belonged to the group who thought orphanages should be kept secret, preferably located away from decent families.

Becky's temper flared as the interview drew to a close and she paced up and down the room calling the reporter all sorts of names, words she hadn't used since coming down from the mountain.

Lauren sat in silence, her nails digging into the palms of her hands. If this was how one reporter felt, what would the trial hold for them?

CHAPTER FORTY-NINE

"Afternoon, Lauren, was Delgany busy?" Becky asked as Lauren arrived back from town, shaking the snow from her clothes.

Big Will took her coat and pulled out a chair for her to sit on. She smiled her thanks.

"I don't know about the whole town but Miss Chaney says she is going to move the post office out here. She says we are getting more post than the rest of Delgany put together. Look at this, Becky."

Lauren upended a boxful of letters onto the table. They came from all over the States and this was only one of the three boxes she'd taken from the post office. "Some of these are from California and others from Washington. There's even one from Alaska!"

Fred looked at the piles in amazement. "Can I keep the stamps, Miss Lauren? Please."

"Yes. But give the duplicates you have to the others, will you please? Lottie likes to keep stamps in her book too."

Fred sulked. "She copies everythin' I do."

"Course she does, you are her hero big brother," Becky said, swiping him gently with the dishcloth. "Think you could sort these into states?"

Totally distracted, Fred was soon piling up the letters into different bundles.

"Did the Meyers not want to come up today?" Becky opened a few letters before moving the empty envelopes to a pile for Fred.

"No, they told me yesterday they have other plans today. They will be back next week. Maybe they are seeing family or something. I worry about them, Becky. I don't think they eat properly when they are alone in that house." Lauren frowned.

"Why do you think I keep sending them home with extras?" Becky asked.

Upset she had hurt her friend's feelings, Lauren explained, "I knew you were doing that but, even with our help, they seem to be really struggling."

"Lauren, I love you but we have enough issues at the moment. The Meyers have a family to look after them and we help where we can. We can't save everyone."

Nanny limped into the kitchen. "Who are we saving this week?"

Becky put her hands on her hips. "Nanny Kat! You should be restin'. The doc said he'd cut the legs from under you if you kept walking on that foot."

Nanny's lips thinned. "I'm old enough to know my own mind. What's all this?"

"Take a seat and start reading." Lauren handed her a bundle of letters.

Most of the letters offered support, some included cash, others said they had written to their senators and even the president on their behalf. There were also a few horrible ones suggesting children of immoral characters deserved to be on the streets.

Nanny pushed one of these to the side. "I wish I could write back enclosing a bible with relevant passages highlighted to these people. How dare they call children immoral. What part of not judging people did they miss?"

"Nanny, watch your blood pressure. They have sent us a blessin'," Becky said.

"How?"

"Paper helps start a good fire." Becky laughed, taking the letter from Nanny and depositing it in the wood box.

"People really do care, don't they?" Lauren whispered, wiping the tears from her eyes after reading a letter from a child who enclosed their pocket money of a dollar. "This child says he was saving the dollar to buy something but our children needed it more."

Nanny nodded. "He's right. We have court fees to pay. That's two hundred dollars right there."

"How much do we have now?"

Becky added the latest cash to their savings. "Two hundred and ten dollars."

Nanny patted the table. "It's the Christmas spirit. People still have it no matter what the papers say."

They hadn't finished opening the envelopes. The children helped, putting the coins and paper notes they found into the court jar, as they called it. Becky insisted on keeping the funds they raised separate to the household accounts. They had started the fund with the one hundred dollars Edward's father had donated for Hans and Rachel's keep.

Lauren picked up an envelope, recognizing the writing. "Nanny, Becky, this one is from John Thatcher. Listen…"

The two women sat down as Lauren read out the letter.

Dear ladies,

This time I'm writing with good news. You were right in suspecting the Dickensons, Lauren. A witness has turned up who says he saw Mr. Dickenson buying a large quantity of kerosene in a store. He thought it was suspicious but didn't think more about it until he saw an article in the paper. Please thank Edward for asking his man, Tim Egan, to write it. Our attorney went to the store and they had the receipt from the transaction. The attorney is going to call the store owner and this witness to the stand but he thinks it will be enough to clear

Lauren looked up to say, "He's crossed out Katie and written Cassie," before she continued to read.

The attorney thinks we will be here for another three to four weeks. He can't guarantee we will win but says our chances are good. They must be as the police allow us to keep our girl with us and not in the jail as before. We may not get back to Delgany for Christmas—if we do, Miss Chaney has kindly offered us a temporary home.

"That's wonderful news. Imagine it all being over for them by Christmas."

Becky's excitement made Lauren smile. She glanced at the paper again. "Alice added a bit too. She says, 'Please give my regards to everyone and keep praying for us. I hope things are going great back there. We miss you all.'"

Lauren handed the letter to Nanny and her eyes met Becky's. She saw the other girl was trying to be positive, to be excited for the Thatchers while at the same time worried for Hope House. She was conflicted. It was fantastic news and she was thrilled for the family but John had mentioned Edward. Where was he? And why hadn't he come back like he had said he would? He wouldn't leave her to face the court battle and possible end of Hope House alone. Would he?

Becky read her mind, spot on as usual. "Edward would be here if he could, Lauren. You know that."

"Of course he'd be here. He told me to stay with you every step of the way." Big Will moved to put his arm on Lauren's shoulder. "You hang in there, Miss Lauren, have faith."

Lauren looked away from their cheerful faces. She didn't want to be the damper on anyone's good mood, but *where was Edward?* He hadn't written back or sent a telegram. However hard she tried, her thoughts kept returning to him.

"Miss Lauren, you ready for the court case?" Big Will asked.

Lauren tried to look confident. "As ready as I can be."

"Don't mind her," Becky said. "Mr. Stewart has us primed and ready to go. We've had hundreds of letters wishing us well and telling us they've written to their senators and even the president. We're goin' to win, I just know it."

Instead of helping, Becky's words made Lauren feel worse. It was hard being responsible for the happiness of all these people, not to mention the children. How could she face them if they lost? Where would they live?

"You still with us, Miss Lauren?" Will teased her.

"Will, now you and Becky have come to an understanding, do you think you could call me Lauren?"

"I will, on my wedding day," he retorted, and ran before anyone could disagree with him.

Becky's eyes followed him as he left the room, an expression of love lighting up her face. Lauren was thrilled for her friend, but seeing her happiness made her miss Edward even more. "I think I'll have an early night, if you don't mind?" she asked, not expecting a reply.

Taking the steps one at a time, feeling she was climbing the mountain, she walked to her bedroom. Without undressing, she lay on the bed, her head swimming with problems. The overriding one being: what would happen to all the people she was responsible for if they lost in court?

CHAPTER FIFTY

Monday December 16th, the day of the court case, dawned. Lauren felt physically sick with nerves, her stomach churned and her legs felt weak. Becky wasn't feeling much better but she was better at hiding it. Nanny didn't show any sign of nerves at all.

"Nanny, where are you going?" Lauren asked. The older woman had spent the last week in bed, not even getting up for meals. Yet here she was, dressed in her best, right down to her favorite hat.

"I want to see that smirk being wiped off Stratton's face."

Lauren loved her spirit, but she was worried. Nanny wouldn't have stayed in bed last week if she had been feeling well. "But I thought you were going to stay here and rest."

"I can rest when I'm dead. I've been in bed this past week saving my energy to see Ian in action. Don't make me miss all the fun. Terry and Carly are here to look after the children. Terry said he would drive down for Mr. and Mrs. Meyer this afternoon. Earl Hillman will call in later."

"You have this all organized," Becky responded.

Lauren hugged her Nanny. "Thank you for coming. I don't think I can do this…"

"Yes, you can darling," Nanny said, looking her in the eyes and smiling.

Big Will drove the truck into Charlottesville with good wishes ringing in their ears from the children.

Again they parked the truck some distance from the court, but this time it was because of the crowds. They stared at all of the commotion, amazed.

"The last time I saw this many people was in New York at Macy's, Christmas 1930. Where are they going?" Lauren asked.

"Into the courthouse, by the looks of things. Look how many newspapermen there are. Where are Tim and Mr. Stewart?" Becky's voice quivered. Lauren didn't blame her for being nervous. Some of the press attention had been less than flattering, with hints made about Becky's suitability as an orphans' mentor given her family members had been in the colony for the feeble-minded.

Nanny spoke up. "Girls, you are both inspirational young ladies. Put your shoulders back, chest out, and show that crowd what you are made of. I am so proud of both of you."

"We don't know we've won yet, Nanny Kat."

"I'm still proud of you. Both of you." Nanny hugged Becky and then Lauren. "Let's get this over with."

There was no sign of a limp as Nanny marched toward that courthouse. Lauren and Becky took either side to protect the older woman from jostling, but when the crowd saw them coming, it was like the waves parting for Moses. People called them by name, trying to get them to turn for a picture or to give a comment, but the court officers and police provided a corridor to protect them.

Tim had suggested Big Will shouldn't accompany the ladies into the court, suggesting the judge might go easy on "frail, delicate" women.

Will's belly-laugh at this comment had them all in stitches. "Ain't nobody with one brain cell ever thought my woman be frail or delicate. Becky is a fiery warrior and Miss Lauren, she be as intelligent and powerful as any man."

Lauren thought of his words as she entered the imposing courtroom, not feeling either powerful or intelligent. Was she a fool to think they could take on the government and win?

They were escorted to their seats at the front of the courthouse sitting just behind Mr. Stewart. Tim came to sit behind them.

"If anyone asks, tell them I'm Ian's assistant," he whispered. "Press should be up in the press gallery."

"You're here as a friend, Tim," Becky said warmly.

Lauren couldn't help but look around the court. There'd been no word from Edward but she was still hoping for a miracle. He'd promised to be around for Christmas. It was only nine days away. She kept praying he'd just arrive at Hope House. She forced herself to concentrate.

"All rise."

The judge walked in sedately, followed by various members of the court. Lauren caught Stratton smirking at her. She itched to wipe that grin off his face but instead she smiled her sweetest smile. She relished the look of surprise on his face before she turned her attention to Mr. Stewart's back. He looked even more dignified, if that was possible. He shone from his shoes to the top of his head.

She swallowed as her mouth grew drier. The judge seemed to be reading the papers in front of him. Surely he had prepared himself before the court case? It wasn't as if he hadn't had plenty of time, having kept them waiting for almost four weeks.

"Ladies and gentlemen, we are here to rule in the matter of Virginia County versus Hope House owners, Miss Lauren Greenwood and Miss Rebecca Tennant."

"Excuse me, Your Honor." Mr. Stewart stood up.

The judge gave him a dirty look.

"We are here to present arguments," Mr. Stewart said. "It isn't possible to rule before hearing them."

The judge colored as if he knew the man was right. He banged his gavel before addressing him.

"Yes, of course. That is what I meant. I assume you have lots to say, Mr. Stewart."

"Just a few things, Your Honor." Mr. Stewart smiled politely.

"I thought you might. Do you want to get started?"

"I'd like to call my first witness."

Lauren tried not to smile at the dance of words between the two elderly gentlemen.

The man beside Stratton jumped to his feet. "You can't do that. You didn't mention any witnesses."

"Didn't I? I think you will find the list on the back of the last letter in the file we sent to your office," Mr. Stewart said.

"That's a list of the members of the government."

"It is," Mr. Stewart drawled.

"So, that doesn't count," the man protested, his face turning various shades of red and purple.

Ian looked down his nose, his mouth curling in disdain. "So, members of our government cannot be witnesses to a court case?"

Stratton's lawyer, as Lauren thought of him, turned almost purple. "Of course they can, but I fail to see why anyone would believe you would call the President of the USA to these proceedings. He has better things to do with his time."

"I wasn't aware the honorable gentleman was in charge of the president's diary."

The courthouse erupted in laughter. The judge banged his gavel and threatened to have everyone removed. "Just call your witness, Mr. Stewart."

Mr. Stewart called Stratton to the stand and by the time he was finished with him, Lauren almost felt sorry for Stratton. Mr. Stewart highlighted his tendency to lie, cut corners and—of immense interest to the judge—his collaboration with known thieves, the Bramley brothers. It was clear to everyone Stratton's future career was in jeopardy.

"Thank you for bringing the court's attention to the failings in how Mr. Stratton and his friends handled this issue, but the matter remains this is a compulsory purchase order. So we are only prolonging the inevitable. Don't you agree?"

"With respect, Your Honor, I don't."

"Why am I not surprised. Who are you going to call next, Roosevelt himself?"

"I wanted to, Your Honor, but our president was busy." Mr. Stewart smiled.

The spectators laughed once more.

"So who did he send in his place—Father Christmas?"

"Close, Your Honor. We'd like to call Mrs. Eleanor Roosevelt."

The court fell silent as the judge stared at Mr. Stewart as if he had sprouted wings and flown.

"You mean, the First Lady?"

"The one and same. Didn't you know we were acquainted? We share a love of flying. You should come with us sometime."

The judge was speechless. Lauren grabbed Becky's hand and held on fast as, to her amazement, the First Lady was escorted to the chair. You could hear a pin drop as she recited her oath.

The judge said, "Thank you, Mrs. Roosevelt, for honoring us with your presence today. You are of course welcome but I hope we haven't wasted your time."

Lauren watched the First Lady's reaction. The brown-haired woman was taller than many of the men in the room and sitting up straight, her hands folded on her knees, which were partially turned toward the judge, it was almost as if she was looking down on the courtroom.

Her blue eyes pierced the judge before she replied, "I don't believe my time is ever wasted if I can be of assistance to our most precious, our most vulnerable citizens. Our children are the best of America and they deserve the highest protection possible."

Her firm tone was set off by a smile. Lauren glanced at the judge who appeared flustered, his cheeks flushing, but with embarrassment or irritation it was hard to tell. He pushed his shoulders back before saying, "Well, of course but—"

The president's wife smiled before graciously interrupting. "I have no power to direct the judge. I'm aware of that. I am here on behalf of my husband, who wishes it known he has a personal interest in the welfare of the children at Hope House. One of the young charges, a girl called Shelley, wrote to me and asked me to tell my husband. Once he heard the contents of the letter, he sent me here on his behalf."

Lauren glanced at Becky, who was staring open-mouthed at the First Lady, as were most in the courtroom. The First Lady's voice drew her attention.

"Shelley wrote a charming letter. Perhaps I could read you a paragraph?"

Although posed as a question everyone in the courtroom knew it wasn't.

"'Dear Mrs. President. "'I'm writing to you as I know the president is a very busy man. I have a problem. The government are trying to take away our home and I know you mustn't have asked them to do it. You wouldn't be unkind to orphans like us. We need to live at Hope House, nobody beats us here. They don't lock us in no cellar or hold us upside down out a window.'" Mrs. Roosevelt took a breath. "'I am not worried about me but my boy, Joey. He is only four but I know he can grow into a man like the president as he has polio too. Joey doesn't know any other home. He calls me his ma but I is only thirteen. We don't know where his real ma and da are. He was left near a trash can, the sheriff found him. My parents left me home alone as they couldn't afford to feed me and my brother. I wasn't a nice girl so they left me behind. I am trying to be a nice person now.'"

The first lady swallowed before continuing.

"'We got a little baby girl here too, called Maisie. Her pa wants to keep her but he can't, so Miss Lauren and Miss Becky take care of her until he can come get her again. If Hope House closed, what would happen to Maisie? She could be left on a doorstep and taken away by wolves or other wild animals. Or dumped in garbage like Joey. Or taken somewhere where her name would be a number and not Maisie. She's a happy baby now, with big smiles for everyone. Please don't make her sad or let her die.

"'Please Mrs. President, can you ask your husband nicely to let us stay with Miss Lauren and Miss Becky and Nanny Kat? We loves them so much. There's lots of land hereabouts. You don't need our little piece for any park. Please listen to me. God bless you and Mr. President. P.S. Joey sends his love, he made his mark here.'"

Lauren wiped a tear from her eye as Nanny handed her a hanky. Becky coughed beside her. She wasn't the only one, given the number of sniffles and coughs in the courthouse.

The judge coughed. "That is a nice letter but—"

The First Lady spoke over him. "Please excuse me for interrupting, Judge. When I told my husband about this letter and the hundreds of other letters we got from all over the country, I said this was one time we couldn't look the other way. These people at Hope House have something special and it is in all our interests to let them continue. There are only a few people who have other interests at heart." She glared at Stratton and his lawyer. "My husband asked me to give you this paper. I think you will find it in order. He also asked me to give a letter to Miss Greenwood and Miss Tennant. Perhaps you would allow them to approach the bench?"

"This is highly unusual, Mrs. Roosevelt..." the judge spluttered.

"Isn't it? Much more fun than I have had in ages. I do love the southern hospitality and welcome offered by the people of Charlottesville." The First Lady smiled a winning smile.

The judge slid back in his chair, acknowledging defeat. There was only one ruler in the courtroom and it wasn't him.

Lauren and Becky stood up and looked at one another, eyes wide. Lauren would have fallen down again but for Becky grabbing her elbow. Together they walked slowly to the front of the courthouse, the sound of clapping echoing behind them.

"Congratulations, ladies, on your achievements. I've been reading of your exploits in the papers. The children look so cute and happy. I thank you on their behalf. This money is for you. I know you will spend it wisely."

Lauren and Becky both half-bowed, half-curtsied. "Thank you, ma'am."

The judge motioned for them to stand beside Mr. Stewart. He opened the letter the First Lady handed him.

By order of the President of the United States, the property known as Hope House and the surrounding lands are not part of the compulsory purchase order and shall remain untouched. Furthermore, the roads surrounding these buildings will be repaired and resurfaced. Trees will be sown along the boundary between the park and this land in order to afford privacy to Hope House and its occupants. Signed Roosevelt, December 14 1935.

Lauren threw her arms around Becky, and whispered into her ear, "*We won!*"

"Ladies…" Mr. Stewart said, quietly.

"Sorry." Lauren looked at the judge. "Beg your pardon, Your Honor. Thank you."

The judge smiled, his first real smile of the whole proceedings. "Your efforts on behalf of the children are to be admired. I salute you both."

Lauren and Becky exchanged a grin as they walked back to their seats, feeling as if they must be dreaming. Lauren became aware of someone watching her, and she looked up to see Edward.

She blinked to make sure it was him. He looked older, his hair showing grays for the first time, shorter than he usually wore it. His suit hung differently. She wanted to race to him but he just stood watching. She walked toward him, waiting for him to move, but he didn't. Becky came behind her and swept her along with the people following them.

Her stomach clenched as she reached him and came to a standstill, his eyes never having left hers the whole time. Did he not want her?

Edward began to speak, falteringly. "Lauren, I'm…"

"Where have you been? I've thought you were dead. You didn't write… not even a telegram."

"I'm…" He tried to answer but didn't get to finish as he collapsed at her feet.

"Edward!" She heard someone screaming his name, not realizing it was her. The court officers came forward, and Tim pulled her away, telling her Edward needed a doctor. Everything seemed to happen in slow motion around her. She saw tears on Becky's cheeks, Tim's mouth open and moving but she couldn't hear a word. She felt someone pulling her and, when she looked back, Edward was gone. Lost in a sea of men.

Becky's slap stung her cheek. Lauren stopped screaming, rubbing her face as she glared at her friend.

Becky hissed, "Lauren, get a hold of yourself. Edward's in the ambulance. Tim is drivin' us to the hospital. Anyone asks, you're Edward's fiancée." She used a softer tone. "Will has driven Nanny home, he'll stay with her until we get back. We need to go to the hospital now."

Becky half-pulled, half-dragged Lauren toward Tim's car. She saw his white face, the worry in his eyes, the fact he refused to look at her speaking volumes. She sat in the back of the car, her fingers making marks in her palms though she couldn't feel a thing. Edward couldn't be dead. Could he? Why would a young man collapse like that? Around and around the thoughts flooded through her head, not making any sense.

*

When they got to the hospital the nurse refused to tell them anything. Lauren couldn't work out what was happening.

"Mr. Belmont's next of kin are out of the country…" Tim tried to persuade the nurse to let them see Edward, but to no avail.

Becky tried too. "This is his fiancée, surely you will let her in or at least tell her what's happenin'."

The nurse's lips pursed tighter. There was no arguing with her. They sat in the waiting room—at least Becky and Tim did. Lauren paced, back and forth, until Becky forced her to sit down. "You're driving me insane, walkin' back and forward like that. The sound of your heels on that floor is makin' my head ring."

Lauren sat, clenching and unclenching her hands, refusing all offers of refreshments. He had to be all right, he couldn't die on her. She needed him. Why had she wasted all this time…?

The door opened and in walked a doctor wearing a white coat, beside him the familiar form of Ian Stewart.

"Miss Greenwood, please accept our apologies. Mr. Stewart has shown us a letter of wishes, clearly stating Mr. Belmont considers you his next of kin. Had we—"

Lauren interrupted. "How is he?" She didn't care about anything else.

The doctor scowled.

"Is he dead?"

"No, not at all. In fact, considering what he has been through, he is doing exceedingly well."

Lauren couldn't understand him. Edward well? But he'd collapsed.

Mr. Stewart moved forward and gently took her hands in his. "Lauren, be brave. Braver than you ever had to be before."

Lauren held his gaze but didn't speak.

Mr. Stewart spoke carefully, holding her hands as he spoke. "Edward has been tortured. He was caught, spying they said, and was imprisoned in Berlin before being released without charge. He has been through a rough time and should have never left the hospital, but he insisted on seeing you win the court case. He had every faith in you."

She couldn't hear him with the buzzing in her ears. "Tortured," she repeated. "How? Why? Can I see him?"

The doctor said, "He's sleeping now. You can come back at visiting time." With that he dismissed her and turned to leave.

"Wait. I want to see him now." The doctor's raised eyebrows suggested she try another tactic. "Please, let me just see he's alive. I haven't heard from him in weeks. I knew something bad had happened. I didn't imagine…" She couldn't say anything.

Becky spoke up. "Please, doctor. You may not know but the First Lady just helped Lauren save an orphanage. She deserves five minutes with her man—I mean, fiancé."

"One minute," the doctor conceded.

Lauren didn't argue. It was enough.

He led her through the doors past the officious nurse and into the private room. "The extent of his injuries is not immediately apparent but please take care when touching him."

Lauren walked toward the bed and stared at the man she loved, his face grayer than the hospital walls. He should have looked peaceful but she spotted a nerve pulsing at his jaw. She rushed to his side, but held her hands back, mindful of what the doctor had said. "Edward, darling, it's Lauren. Can you hear me?"

"He's sedated, miss."

She ignored the doctor. Bending to brush her lips against Edward's forehead she told him she loved him.

His eyes opened and he smiled. Then he closed his eyes once more.

"Sleep well, my darling." She kept her voice as steady as possible. She looked at his hands and almost gagged. They were covered in bruises.

The doctor indicated they should leave. With one last glance at the bed, Lauren followed him.

"What did those monsters do to him?" she asked.

The doctor refused to look at her but studied his notes. "He has signs of torture, broken bones, bruising, burns. The report from Germany suggested he was in an accident—run over." Only then did the doctor meet her gaze. "I've treated many victims of vehicle accidents but I've never seen injuries like this."

Lauren's heartbeat quickened at the doctor's words. She glanced at the doors separating her from Edward, before looking into the doctor's eyes. "Please help him. Make him better."

"We will keep him under sedation for several days to allow his injuries to heal. You have to trust us to do our best. Go home and get some rest. Your fiancé is going to have a long road to recovery."

"But he will get better?" Lauren whispered. Desperately willing the doctor to say Edward would be fine, she begged him with her eyes but he didn't meet her gaze.

"Miss Greenwood, for now, all I can promise is he will get the best possible care. Excuse me."

She stared at his back as he left the room. Becky moved forward, putting a coat around Lauren's shoulders. "Let's go home. The children will be frettin' as it's almost bedtime."

*

Nanny and Big Will must have heard the car as they were waiting on the porch as Becky and Lauren got out.

"You can stop lookin' so sad. Edward's alive and the doctors say they can help him get better." Becky's cheery words fell flat as Nanny and Big Will's expressions didn't brighten. Becky held out her hand to Lauren, but to comfort her or seek comfort, Lauren didn't know.

Becky's voice trembled. "What's wrong? The children?"

Nanny's eyes were watering. "The children are fine. Sit down, girls, we have had some bad news."

Lauren sat down but Becky went to stand by Big Will, who wrapped his arm around her. Lauren kept her eyes on Nanny's face.

The old woman faltered a few times, swallowing hard before she said, "Big Will drove me home from the courthouse. We were so happy with the win, we wanted to buy some candy for the children to celebrate. We'd also promised to tell Miss Chaney and Sheriff Dillon the outcome of the trial."

Lauren held her breath.

Nanny's eyes held Lauren's. "Miss Chaney had a telegram."

Lauren's pulse beat faster, causing her ears to buzz. She shook her head, whispering, "No, please God no."

"Norma?" Becky mouthed, her hand gripping Big Will's arm so tight Lauren could see her knuckles.

Out of the corner of her eye she saw Nanny nod and thought her heart would shatter.

"Norma died yesterday peacefully in her sleep. Bart was with her."

"Oh, the poor man. When is he comin' home? He needs to be here with his family."

Becky's words sunk into Lauren's brain but she couldn't speak. They'd been so happy, dancing around for joy at the ruling, then Edward collapsed and she'd thought that was more than she could bear. Norma, darling Norma who'd worked so hard to make Hope House the home it was. The one woman who'd have celebrated the win as much as Becky and Lauren was never coming home.

Lauren brushed a tear from her eye only for it to be followed by another. Becky was sobbing too. Lauren glanced at Nanny. Her expression suggested there was more.

"Bart?" She spoke so softly she wasn't sure Nanny had even heard her.

"Bart won't be coming home, Lauren. At least not for a while. He's sick."

Lauren put her biggest fear into words. "With TB?"

"Yes, but they think he has a good chance as it is in one lung and they caught it early. He's in isolation."

Lauren sank onto the swing as Big Will held Becky sobbing against his shoulder. "Do the girls know?"

Nanny nodded. "We told them about Norma. We weren't going to tell them about Bart but they were both demanding to see him."

Lauren pushed her feet to the floor. "I have to see them. To comfort them."

Becky looked up from Will's shoulder. "I don't think we should tell them about Edward just yet."

Lauren agreed. She couldn't speak about him at the moment. She stepped toward the house.

"Lauren…" At Nanny's voice she turned back. "Devastated as we are, Norma would have wanted the children to have a wonderful Christmas. Especially after all they've experienced over the last few weeks."

"What are you saying? We have to celebrate Christmas when our friend has just died?"

Nanny stood up, looking older than her years. "That's exactly what I mean. Norma would want it and those children deserve a little happiness. Nothing we do will change what happened. Let's honor Norma's memory by making this holiday as good as we can. The children are our priority, not our grief."

Nanny squeezed Lauren's arm as she walked past, pausing briefly at the front door before opening it. The children's shrieks of happiness engulfed them.

Becky blew her nose and, with an arm around Lauren's waist, she whispered, "This is what Norma would want."

Together they walked in.

*

Cal was the first to greet her. "Miss Lauren, you won the court case, why do you look so sad?" he asked her as soon she put her foot in the door.

Lauren tried to force a smile. "I'm just tired and upset about Norma, Cal. Where are her girls?"

"Upstairs in their room. They won't come down, not for no one." He spoke gruffly but she sensed he was hurting too.

She hugged him on her way past as she climbed the stairs to check the girls. She'd made Norma a promise to look after her daughters. She knocked and entered the room, seeing the two girls in bed together, holding hands and staring at the wall.

Lauren put her arms around Clarissa and Sophie. "Girls, your mother was one of the best, kindest women I ever knew. I'll miss her too. Very much."

"She's in heaven now. She didn't get to say goodbye," Clarissa sobbed.

That set Sophie off again. The girls cried and clung to Lauren who let the tears flow too.

"What will happen to us, Miss Lauren? Papa is sick too, will he die?"

"I hope not, Clarissa. If Bart has TB, they caught it early and that's a good thing. As for what you will do, you will stay here in Hope House. This is your home for as long as you want it to be. I promised your mama."

"Mama loved you, Miss Lauren."

"I loved her too, Sophie." After a while, Lauren eased herself away from the girls, who had fallen asleep. For a second she envied them. If only she could sleep and let the horror go away. But it was all too real.

Changed and dressed in fresh clothes, she came back downstairs to greet the Meyers and Nanny. She gazed around her in wonder.

"The place looks amazing. Look at all those decorations. You've been busy today," she complimented the children, wanting to put smiles on their faces.

"We wanted Christmas to be special." Ruthie pulled at Lauren's dress. "Do you think we are horrible for wantin' a real Christmas? Miss Norma used to love decoratin' the house."

"She did, Ruthie. I think it's very important for us to celebrate Christmas. I know we lost Norma and we are sad, but we have reasons to be happy too." Becky stepped closer to Lauren and put her arm around her. "Miss Lauren won the court case and we get to keep Hope House forever."

Shelley looked proud. "I helped. I wrote to the First Lady and she read my letter out. Becky told me."

Lauren smiled at Shelley, who was holding Joey's hand. "You certainly did, Shelley. Thank you."

"I love it here, this is our home," Shelley replied.

Big Will came in the back door, obviously having overhead the conversation. "I hope it will soon be my home too?"

Becky gave him a playful slap and rolled her eyes. "Will! I haven't had a chance to ask her yet."

He lifted her up and kissed her to the cheers of the children.

"Put me down," Becky protested.

He set her on her feet but didn't take his arm from her waist. "What you waitin' for?"

Becky blushed, her eyes darting around the room, as she appeared to lose her voice.

Lauren glanced from one to the other, before prompting, "Ask me what?"

When Becky stayed silent, Will answered, "I want to build a house for my woman and our beautiful babies."

Becky flushed and shouted, "Will!"

The children giggled. Will carried on regardless. "We don't want to move away so we wondered if you would let us buy a piece of land just by the orchard so we can stay at Hope House."

Lauren shook her head. "I won't sell you the land, Will."

Both her friends stood looking at her open-mouthed, too shocked to speak.

She smiled. "But I will give it to you as a wedding present." Lauren yelped as Will lifted her off her feet and swung her around. "Will, put me down right now!"

The children clapped at Will's antics. Even Nanny and the Meyers laughed.

"I can't take your land, Lauren." Becky had her hands on her hips ready to do battle.

Lauren shushed her. "Nobody asked you to take anything. You earned it. How long have you been working here without wages? If you spoke to Ian, I'm sure he'd tell you, you could file a court action."

Becky shuddered. "I never want to see the inside of a courtroom again."

Lottie—an innocent expression on her face—asked, "Is it time for our other surprise for Miss Lauren?"

"Lottie…" Fred growled at his younger sister.

Lottie looked confused. "What? You said she was going to find out when she came down from changing her clothes. Nobody told her about the telegram being delivered."

Lauren's knees buckled as she sank into the chair. Had Edward worsened since she left the hospital? It was only an hour away.

Nanny came forward and put a hand on her shoulder. "Lauren, it's good news. The telegram boy delivered it just as you were upstairs."

Shaking, Lauren begged, "Read it to me, please."

Nanny smiled. "I don't have to. I know what it says by heart. John, Alice, and Cassie are coming home. They'll be here for Christmas. Isn't that wonderful? Cassie is free."

Ruthie moved closer, climbing onto Lauren's lap. "Katie was pretendin' to be called Katie. Her real name is Cassie, which is much nicer, isn't it?"

Lauren cuddled Ruthie as tears ran down her face.

"Don't worry," Ruthie said, "Miss Lauren is cryin' happy tears."

EPILOGUE

Christmas Day dawned bright. Lauren lay in bed finishing reading the last of Edward's letters from his time in Germany, which had arrived belatedly over the previous two days. He had kept his promise to write after all, only somehow the letters had been left at the American Embassy in France rather than being forwarded on to her. Edward's plan to use the diplomatic pouch and bypass the censor had been a little too secure.

> *Darling Lauren, how I miss you. You have no idea how often I have wanted to take a train back to France and from there a ship to the USA. But I can't leave, not just yet. Things are happening here with Aunt Edith.*

Even reading it back the reference to the code they had devised made her smile. Hitler was Aunt Edith. The Nazis, her family, and so on.

> *I am reminded every day of your courage, bravery, and intelligence, and why it was so easy to fall in love with you, you share so many of Rae's best characteristics. Unfortunately you are equals in stubbornness. She refuses to go anywhere but Switzerland despite the letters I brought with me. She asked me to ask you to kiss her little hamsters and tell them she loves them. We talk a lot about you and she has insisted I get a ring on your finger as soon as I return. So,*

my darling, not the most romantic of proposals but will you marry me? As soon as I dock? As promised I will be home before the court date. We can be married and back from honeymoon before you show Stratton how wrong he was in thinking you were a delicate little flower.

A knock at the door brought Becky in with a cup of coffee. Lauren savored the rich aroma as she gratefully accepted the cup.

Becky said, "The children are awake but I've warned them that the first person downstairs will get wood for their present. Only Fred would be interested in that, but he's hoping he got a new thingy to hold his carvings while he is working."

Lauren grinned; she couldn't remember the name of Fred's requested item either but Will had taken care of it. "Funny how we have become dependent on the men, isn't it? You on Will and me on Edward. When we first met, neither of us would have admitted that time might come."

Becky couldn't disagree. She spotted the letter in Lauren's hands. "You reading it again? You must know every word."

Lauren sighed. "I do but it helps a little. I miss him so much but I couldn't leave the children or you and Nanny at Christmas."

"Good job you didn't. I can't hand out all the presents by myself." Becky walked over to the window and looked outside.

"Are you expecting someone?" Lauren asked.

Becky turned and gave a rueful smile. "I thought we might hear from Edward's mother. She was supposed to bring over gifts for Hans and Rachel. To make up for not taking them to live with her."

Lauren scowled. "They couldn't even come back from their annual Christmas vacation to visit Edward. I doubt they are thinking of the children."

"Don't go getting grumpy. It's their loss. I love having Rachel and Hans here and the Meyers are fast becoming part of the furniture. When I get married, you could ask them to move in. They could have my room."

Lauren grabbed Becky's hand. "Don't talk about that today. I know you and Will need your own space but I will miss you."

"What will you do? Have Edward move in here? It's a bit small, isn't it?"

Lauren looked around the room as if seeing it for the first time. "I guess but I'm not moving to Charlottesville."

"Good job Will has the sawmill back up and running at Hillmans'. You could build your own house too."

Lauren had thought about it. She loved living with the children but it would be nice for her and Edward to have some private space. "Who'd look after the children?"

"We would, and at night the Meyers would be here with Nanny. We won't be far away."

Lauren grinned. "You have it all planned out, don't you?"

Becky's answer was lost in the squeals of excitement from the other rooms.

"We best get downstairs before they do or chaos will reign," Lauren said, as she got up to get dressed.

*

After the children had unwrapped their first set of presents the door burst open and Katie, or Cassie as she was now known again, came through, Alice and John following behind with Ben, Earl, and Miss Chaney.

"Merry Christmas everyone," John's voice boomed, filling the house.

The children got overexcited welcoming everyone, and the noise level grew so intense, Terry whistled and told everyone to be quiet. "You're scarin' baby Maisie," he explained. But Maisie didn't look scared as she waddled around trying to climb up on anything that stayed still long enough.

Sometime later, another visitor arrived in the form of Tom Whitworth. He'd written since his last visit and Becky had replied, inviting him to come for Christmas. Big Will offered to collect him but today Big Will was nowhere to be seen. Lauren meant to ask Becky where he was but she seemed to be busy every time she looked.

"Can we open more presents now?" Shelley asked.

"Not yet, sweetheart, in a little bit," Becky answered, just as Lauren was about to say yes. What was Becky waiting for?

Chana put the turkeys in the oven while Carly saw to the vegetables and potatoes. Becky cooked too, but nobody let Lauren do anything but sit and chat.

When Lauren tried to set the table Nanny said, "You look exhausted after all those hours at the hospital. Enjoy your rest while you can."

They heard another vehicle pull up outside. To Lauren's surprise it was Sheriff Dillon and he wasn't alone.

"Edward!" she screamed, as Big Will helped him out of the car and almost carried Edward inside. He helped him to sit on the sofa before catching Ruthie as she tried to launch herself onto Edward's knee. "Not today, princess. Mr. Edward fell and is feeling a bit poorly."

Edward gave a weak smile and said, "Lauren, can you come here please? It's a bit hard for me to reach you over there."

The others laughed at his joke, as Lauren moved to his side.

"I shall hold Himmler personally responsible for this," Edward whispered. "This isn't what I'd planned."

She opened her mouth to speak, but he put his finger on her lips. "Lauren Greenwood, will you do me the honor of marrying me?" He held a box in his hand, open to reveal a perfect diamond ring glowing against a black velvet background.

"Yes! Oh, yes." Lauren leaned over and kissed him on the lips.

"Careful, Miss Lauren, you'll hurt him," Ruthie called.

Big Will laughed and said, "I don't think Mr. Edward minds, princess. Why don't you show me what Father Christmas got you."

"Yes, Mr. Will."

Lauren would have smiled but for Edward's lips still on hers.

A LETTER FROM RACHEL

Thank you so much for reading *A Baby on the Doorstep*. I hope you loved the story. If you did enjoy it, and want to keep up to date with all my latest releases, just sign up at the following link. Your email address will never be shared and you can unsubscribe at any time.

www.bookouture.com/Rachel-Wesson

Parts of the story are loosely based on real-life events. The true story of the mountain families moved off the Blue Ridge Mountains to make way for the Shenandoah Park are riveting and make for painful reading. Some families did fare better after they took the money they received from the park authorities to resettle. But most didn't and many, especially the elderly, spent the rest of their days grieving for the life they had enjoyed on the mountain.

The Shenandoah Park, like all the other national parks, are a source of major joy for many. Visitors come to seek escape from their busy town and city lives and to enjoy a piece of nature. The animals, insects, and fauna of the area have benefited from the parks as well. But with any good deed, there is often a human cost. The true stories of those families who left or were pushed off the mountain in order for the park to exist make for harrowing reading. I found the letters written by the people themselves, often full of mountain dialect and mis-spellings, were tear-jerking. If you would like to chat to relatives of those displaced, there are some Facebook groups you can join such as Children of the Shenandoah. Feelings run very high in parts of Virginia and some families refuse to discuss the subject with strangers. Some talk to newspapers such for the 'Trail of Tears' article in the *Washington Post* (February 28th, 1997).

If you would like to read more about the origins of the national parks, there are many books available online. The book *The Hollows* is no longer in print and I am not sure I could read it if it were. It is alleged to be extremely prejudicial and many people query the truth of the contents.

There are reports of families who were evicted from the mountain being subjected to prejudice, ridicule, and ill-treatment when they tried to settle in the lowlands. Others from families who lived on the mountain have spent their adult lives working for the national parks and believe they benefited from the move. I guess no element of history is ever black and white. There are always nuances only those who lived through the circumstances can completely understand.

As always, reading about the Great Depression inspired me as I learned about the courage and resilience of our grandparents and great-grandparents. Some people are comparing the Covid epidemic to the Great Depression and perhaps there are lessons we could learn from the 1930s on how to deal with the present health and financial crisis. People seemed to have come together more in the 1930s, with neighbors sharing what little they had, and that sense of community would be a welcome return.

I should note I am neither a Democrat nor a Republican. I don't believe in bringing political opinions into books. The idea of national parks were debated by parties of all political persuasions. The comments made by characters not trusting Roosevelt in relation to promises made by the authorities are true but they do not represent the political opinions of anyone, least of all Bookouture, my publishers, or myself.

The story of Hans and Rachel came from reading about the real-life horror of Hitler's rise to leadership in Germany. The atrocities inflicted on all those who opposed him—he held the families as responsible as the resistant individuals—make for gruesome reading. Some people believe the terror in Germany didn't start until the war began in Europe in 1939 but for some the terror started long before Hitler became leader and intensified from that moment on. I would like to say many Americans (and other nations) took pity on the Jewish children in Germany and rescued them in droves, but that was not the case. The sad reality is that while ordinary families and some exceptional individuals were willing to help, government and/or diplomatic officials all over the world had different ideas. Still, every life saved was a gift and a blessing.

One of the best parts of writing comes from reading the reactions from readers. Did the book make you question how far you would go to protect your family? Your children? Your land? Would you be able to hand your child to a stranger if it meant a better chance of saving their life?

If you enjoyed the story, I would absolutely love it if you could leave a short review. I enjoy interacting with readers so please do reach out to me. I am so grateful to everyone who buys and reads my books, allowing me to have the career I adore.

I hope you loved this book as much as the first, *A Home for Unloved Orphans*, as Lauren, Becky, and the children have many more adventures ahead of them.

Thank you for reading.
Love, Rachel x

@authorrachelwesson

@wessonwrites

rachelwesson.com

ACKNOWLEDGMENTS

This is the second book I have written for Bookouture and, as with the first, it wouldn't be the same book without the incredible insight and support of my editor team, Christina Demosthenous and Victoria Blunden. Individually each lady is incredible, together they are awesome.

I'd also like to thank all readers of my earlier books, who gave me the encouragement to pursue my dreams. Marlene, Meisje, Georgia, Tamara, the Janets, Robin, and so many more. I am so grateful for your help and support.

My daughter pointed out I didn't thank my family in my last book. I thought I had by dedicating the book to them! So thank you Remy, my ever patient husband, and our three gorgeous children for their support when Mom is writing.